Between Destiny and Fate

By:

Brian Bitton

MyBallyClare ♣ Music & Books
Portland, Oregon

$ 17.00 U.S.D.

This book is a work of fiction. Names, characters, places and incidents are products of the author's imagination or are used fictitiously. Any resemblance to actual events, or persons, living or dead, is entirely coincidental.

For information please contact, MyBallyClare Music and Books at:

MyBallyClare Music and Books
P.O. Box 83974
Portland, Oregon 97283
www.myballyclarebooks.com

ISBN: 978-0-9824036-1-7

Library of Congress Control Number: 2009911135

Published in Portland, Oregon 2010

Printed in the United States of America.

This book is dedicated to:

Aimee, Margot, Claire, Annette, Yvette, Jack, Franz, Emile, Simon, Jean, Pierre, Colin, Gerard, Jocelyn, Francois, and Chip.

The only order I used was to place the ladies first and the men second; however, they are all equal in my eyes.

ABOUT THE AUTHOR

Brian Bitton lives in Portland, Oregon where he enjoys telling stories through novels, screenplays, poetry, photography and music.

He is the author of, "A Few Days for a Lifetime."

If you would like to contact the author, or write a review, please contact, MyBallyClare Music and Books at:

MyBallyClare Music and Books
P.O. Box 83974
Portland, Oregon 97283

Or on the web at:
www.myballyclarebooks.com

PREFACE

*I*n February of the year 2000, I returned to Ireland. My journey was private. As was my destination. Some may believe I went to say, 'goodbye,' to people dear to my heart. People that some believe I wrote about in, "A Few Days for a Lifetime." As that story is a work of fiction, I'll leave the truth veiled in my memory.

About thirty days after I returned from Ireland, I felt it was time to write again. Thirty days later this story was finished. Since, I write my first drafts with pen and paper, I was halfway finished typing the draft into a word processor when I stopped. Due to the trouble I encountered when I tried to get, "A Few Days for a Lifetime," published, I simply stopped and pursued other interests until May of 2009 when I decided to take matters in my own hands. For I feel this story deserves to be read by the public.

My first novel, "A Few Days for a Lifetime," was a story I had to write. Therefore, I published, "A Few Days. . . ," first. This story; however, is a story I wanted to write. I wanted to touch the reader with a universal truth most fail to recognize; the power of choice. One of the underlying themes of this story is about the decisions we as human beings make; however simple or complex, and the outcome our decisions have upon our lives. As for other themes in this story, well, I'll let you as the reader come to your own conclusions.

A few people have asked what the Maquis looked like during WWII, so I decided to use a photo to answer their question. My initial thought was to have four people in a photograph on the back cover depicting Aimee, Dan, Emile, and Jack. (To put all of the Maquis in the photo would have been too excessive.)

Since, I've always been unlucky in my pursuit of finding people to show up for creative endeavors, even when they are paid, I chose to pose myself and use that photo as the author photo. Which, in reality, I believe was a wise choice due to the fact that I patterned, Dan Harrington after myself.

The cover photo is of a war scarred church in France. Although, this is not a religious story, a church in France plays a prominent role in the story.

To those who intend to criticize my choice of cover and author photos, this is all I have to say. There was never an option of having a painting depicting elements of this story on the cover as is found on most novels. For most novels a painting is a wise choice; however, I feel a painting could never convey the emotions within this book. Therefore, I stand by my choice. Whether I made the right choice, or not, I really don't care. I've never judged a book by its cover.

The dedication for this story evolved over time. My first thought was to dedicate this story to, "All those who have suffered from the destruction of war." Then, I decided to dedicate the story to a woman I loved. Her deceitful heart changed my mind. Therefore, I chose to dedicate this story to the only people I personally know who will stand up to tyranny. The only people I know who still believe in Life, Liberty, and the pursuit of happiness for ALL. People who are not afraid to place their lives on the altar of uncertainty and fight for the Divine idea my country was founded upon. Sadly, the only people I know who will take a stand against tyranny and fight for what is sacred is, Dan Harrington's friends. For they are more real to me than anyone I know.

The poem at the end of the story, Periwinkle Rose, looks deceptively simple and bored. It is not. In fact, the poem is highly esoteric. The meaning of the first two stanzas are known only to me, and will remain that way until the end of time. The third stanza deals with the story in this book, and the fourth stanza defines our existence.

I would like to thank, Paul Kisser for his help with the photography of the author photo. I would also like to thank, John MacClanathan for his insight and photography expertise.

And finally, I would like to personally thank, Darlene VanLuvanee for her expertise in graphic design. Without her help, the layout of this book would not have had the personal touch I greatly desired.

I hope you enjoy reading this story.

Sincerely,
Brian Bitton

1

*M*any years have passed since this story began. Many years have passed and I can still smell the polish on the black walnut desk where I sat. I can still smell the fragrant cleaning solution on the emerald green carpet. I can still hear the rain pounding on my office window overlooking School Street from three stories above.

Since the day of my birth, my whole life had been mapped out for me. I attended the best private boarding schools New England had to offer. My summers were spent at camps far from home. Only during two weeks for the Christmas holiday season, and four weeks during summer, was I able to spend time at my family's residence in the Back Bay area of Boston.

My mother, Mary, was kindhearted and caring. She hated sending me away, but my father insisted that I get the best education a young, wealthy child could get. Pressured by my father, she relented, although, I believe the decision sapped the life out of her. At the age of thirty-three she died. I was only ten.

The dean at school sent me home when I learned of my mother's death. At her funeral, I cried uncontrollably. Her passing affected me harder than I ever could have imagined. My loss etched a void deep within my heart. My only solace was knowing how much she loved me. For every time I came home to visit, her eyes would shine. A smile never left her face. Every time I left, her face grew long. Her eyes moistened, but no tears would fall. Weeping wasn't socially acceptable in wealthy society, at least not in public, and especially around my father.

A gentleman by most standards, my father, Robert Harrington, was hard on his family, especially toward me. Although he wasn't cruel or abusive, he was very strict and demanding in his pursuit of molding me into a respectful and dignified citizen of the upper class. I believe he was successful, to a point.

After private school, I did what was expected of me and followed in my father's footsteps. Like my father, I attended Harvard University, graduating alpha cum laud with a degree in philosophy. Afterward, I went to Harvard Law, graduating first in my class. My destiny was set in motion. I was to become one of the great lawyers of the wealthy crest. Though on the 16th of December 1942, after being a junior partner in my father's law firm for only a year and a half, fate stepped in. My destiny changed forever.

Around two in the afternoon, I was seated at my desk with my elbows resting on the edge, hands cupping my chin. Lost in thought as I stared at a client's affidavit laying on the desk when Patricia Hornbane, my personal secretary, knocked on my office door. "Mr. Harrington, there's a visitor here to see you," she said, breaking my trance. I was about to respond when my best childhood friend, Chip Taylor, stepped into the room.

"Hello, Danny boy," Chip sang.

"Chip," I said as I stood to greet him. We shook hands. Then, I offered him a chair before sitting down myself. Patricia Hornbane quickly left my office, shutting the door behind her.

As usual, Chip was dressed casually. He wore a light grey jacket over a white shirt, unbuttoned at the top, no tie. He had on tan khaki trousers with razor sharp creases running down the front and back of each pant leg. Polished brown oxfords adorned his feet. A dark grey fedora rested on the back of his head. Short blond hair sprouted from under the brim.

"Bet you didn't expect it'd be your old chum walking through your door?" He said with a sly grin that never seemed to leave his face.

"No, I didn't. Last I heard, you moved to New York to practice law."

"Well, Danny boy, I did. Had a job waiting for me on wall street, but I could've sworn I told you at Clancy's," Chip said, referring to a local pub a few blocks from Harvard University. After our graduation ceremonies from Harvard Law, most of our class met at Clancy's to celebrate. Of course, the life of the party, Chip Taylor was there.

"I didn't go," I admitted.

"Really? Could've sworn you were there. Then again, I got obliterated. Can't remember too much about that night really. Why didn't you go?"

I ran my fingers through my black hair. "My father thought it best that a dignified young lawyer not make an spectacle of himself."

"Oh, I should've known," Chip nodded. "Your old man's a stickler to the customs of wealth. How is he by the way?"

"He's well. Extremely well. Ever since Pearl Harbor the firm's been very busy. My case load alone has tripled in the past year."

"Good to hear business is booming during this tragic mess the world's gotten itself into."

"Yes, but hopefully it'll be over soon."

Chip shifted in his chair. "Hope you're right, but I think we've only just begun."

I stared at Chip for a moment before lowering my eyes to the desktop. "At least we're not involved," I said, repeating the words my father had said many times since the war began.

Chip folded his hands in his lap. The sly grin left his face. "You may not be, but I am."

I looked up. "Thought you were on Wall Street?"

"I was until Roosevelt asked my boss to head up a new organization to help win the war. He had to form it from scratch, so I went with him to help set up shop D.C.. Been a part of the organization ever since."

"You're in Washington D.C. now?" I clarified.

"Yep. That's why I've come to see you."

"Me?" I exclaimed. "Why?"

Chip leaned forward. "To offer you a job."

"I already have a job."

"I'm giving you a chance to serve your country."

I leaned forward, clasped my hands, and rested my forearms on the desk. "Chip, I'm a junior partner here and Sarah and I've rented an apartment while we look for a house. You remember Sarah don't you?"

Chip smiled. "How could I forget her? You two've only been together since you were fourteen."

"Well, we're married. Been married for about a year now. God sake, you were supposed to be my best man, but after law school you simply vanished. Haven't heard a word from you since. Even your parents didn't know where you were."

Chip's face grew long. "Oh, they knew, but life's more complicated now. More secretive."

"What's so secretive that you can't even contact your friends?" I asked. My voice rose an octave, but the tone remained even.

Chip stared at me for a moment. "Well, nothing, I guess. It's just that I've been traveling a lot trying to recruit new members. . . Sorry I wasn't there for you at the wedding."

"I wish you were, but that's neither here or there. Anyway, you're a recruiter? For the armed forces?"

"No. I really can't say unless you join us."

"Join you? You want me to join, but you can't tell me anything," I said dryly, and then leaned back in my chair.

"Do you believe in the tenants of freedom?" Chip asked as he leaned forward.

"Yes."

"Do you believe in the Constitution of the United States?"

"Of course, I do."

"Do you believe everyone should be free from oppression? That justice is universal? That injustice should be stamped out so all can enjoy the same freedoms we enjoy?"

"Absolutely, but I can see to that by sitting right here and doing what I'm doing right now. I don't need to go to D.C. to change the world."

"What if Germany or Japan wins the war?" Chip asked. "How will you feel if you did nothing to stop them?"

"The United States and its allies will win. I'm sure of that," I replied.

Chip slunk back into his chair. He remained quiet for a moment. A quizzical look crossed his face. Then, he sighed. "Aren't you bored?"

"Me? Of course not."

"Oh, come on. You've been bored since the first day we met. I know you despise following in your father's footsteps. That you've given up your dreams to follow his. I came here today to offer you the chance to break out of the mold. A chance at excitement. Adventure. A sense of self-worth you can't get working under the scrutiny of you father. Even foreign travel is possible if you wish. You might even get sent to Ireland where you'll have the opportunity to visit your relatives."

"I don't know them, or even where I'd find them."

"Why your father keeps them a secret beats the hell out of me," Chip sighed.

I stood and walked over to the window. Rain battered the glass, leaving it opaque. My thoughts raced from Chip's job offer, to my life, and then to my lovely wife, Sarah. Faster and faster my mind raced until my surroundings felt surreal. It was the first time in my life that I wondered who I really was and who I had become. At last, I turned from the window and stared at Chip. "Sarah's pregnant. She told me this morning. I'm going to be a father so I can't leave."

"Bring her with you," Chip softly pled.

"I can't."

"I'll find you a nice apartment in Georgetown. You can work one of the nine to five jobs and be home by six every night. You don't have to go abroad unless you want to."

I walked over to my desk, paused for a moment, and then slumped down into my chair. "I can't leave Boston. This is my home. I belong here."

"I understand," Chip said, and then the room fell silent.

After a while our conversation resumed. We reminisced about the past and the funny exploits we shared. Talked of the schools, teachers, and classes that shaped our lives. The athletic competitions we've won and lost. We talked about Sarah and the various girls Chip had known. Not once did we talk about the war or Chip's job, but the two subjects clung silently to our conversation as time slipped by.

Slightly past four, Chip stood to leave. He reached into the inside pocket of his jacket, pulled out a scrap piece of paper, and handed it to me. "Well, Danny boy," he smiled. "Here's an address if you ever change your mind. Just tell them I sent you."

"I don't think I'll be needing it," I said as I put the piece of paper in my pocket.

Chip winked. "Sure you won't." We shook hands by the door. "Take care Danny boy," he said before leaving my office and walking down the hallway.

"Take care, Chip," I muttered as I watched him stop at my father's office door and tip his hat to Carol, my father's personal secretary. Then, I heard him say, "Hello pops," as he darted into my father's office unannounced.

"Chip'll never change," I quietly chuckled as I returned to my desk.

2

On New Year's Eve, 1942, by special invitation handwritten by the governor of Massachusetts, Sarah, my father, and I attended the annual ball at the governors mansion. We arrived promptly at eight-thirty by a chauffeur driven Rolls Royce and led into the grand ballroom. Three lead crystal chandeliers hung from the ceiling. Exquisite paintings and tapestries decorated the walls. Highly lacquered and polished black walnut tables with matching chairs ran down both sides of the room. Wrought iron tables were covered with the finest food and hors d'oeuvres. A full bar offering the best liquor money could buy, crowded the doorway. At the far end of the room, a fifteen piece orchestra played soft melodies for the finest Boston society had to offer. Everyone in attendance either came from the wealthy elite, or gained fame and fortune from politics and finance. All of them belonged in the same class, the super rich, and my father's law firm represented them all.

Sarah was promptly whisked away to the parlor adjacent the ballroom. My father took a wine flute from a passing waiter and fled straight for the library to hobnob with the other men of importance. Without a word from either of them, I was left standing alone in a vast crowd of people filled with the self-righteousness of their own self-worth, and I knew most of them. They were the people I had grown up with, or met over the years solely because I was my father's son.

For the first time in my life, I felt alone. Like I didn't belong. That nothing in my life, either past or present, was real. That my life was a dream. A nightmare I was born into and would never end. I went over to the bar and ordered a cocktail. Then, I headed toward the parlor while people continually inquired about my wellbeing or told me how great I was. Everyone of them congratulated me on Sarah's pregnancy.

When I finally reached the parlor, I hovered by the door. My lovely wife was surrounded by a large group of women. The center of attention as the details of her pregnancy and the future of our unborn child were openly discussed amongst her peers. Not once did my eyes leave her. I was captivated by her beauty. Her sandy blond hair, shaped into a bob, cupped her rosy cheeks, accentuating her full red lips and dark blue eyes. The long, black sequined dress, cut low in the front and the back, showed off her dainty shoulders. A gold locket with our pictures inside nestled between the cleavage of her breasts.

From the first moment I saw her, I knew Sarah was the one for me. The lady I would spend the rest of my life with. We met one summer on the tennis court at camp. Chip and I had signed up for a session of mixed doubles. Sarah was chosen to be my partner. We lost horribly. Chip and his partner, whose name has long since withered from my memory, beat us in three consecutive games. After that, Sarah and I gave up. From that moment on, we were inseparable. She became my partner in all the activities I participated in, replacing Chip who didn't mind a bit. As usual, he was happily off chasing the other girls.

When Sarah and I were not engaged in an activity, or retired to our quarters for the night, we met under an elm tree by the lake and talked as the afternoon drifted by. It was there, under the old elm tree that I learned Sarah lived in Boston. That, like me, she spent most of her life at boarding schools far from home.

When summer came to an end, I went back to my all male boarding school in Vermont. Sarah went to her all female boarding school in Connecticut. We were miles apart, but managed to keep in touch by mail, sometimes by phone. Over time we both knew we were in love.

When I was sixteen, even though we barely saw each other, Sarah and I officially began our courtship. We managed to see each other more often during our college years, though, not very much.

Like my father, I attended Harvard. Sarah went to Simmons, her mother's alma mater. She graduated with a degree in English literature after my first year at Harvard Law. During the following summer, I proposed. Two years later, on June 26th, 1941, we were married in front of over 800 people. Our wedding was the social event of the season. Sarah was only 23. I was 24.

More women passed me as they went to join the group surrounding Sarah. Each of them congratulated me on her pregnancy as they went by. I thanked them all, but knew their pleasantries were superficial and only said to appease the customs of our social class.

A few minutes later, I left and went to the bar to order another cocktail. Then, I picked up a flute of wine as an excuse to seek out my father. Ever since Chip Taylor stopped by the office, I wanted to talk with my father about my intentions concerning the war. Now that I had alcohol running through my veins, I had the courage to face him.

I entered the ballroom and fled through the crowd toward the door at the other side of the room. Once again, it seemed everyone enquired about my health and Sarah's pregnancy that by the time I reached the library the ice in my cocktail had melted. A servant held the door open as I entered the library to the pungent stench of cigars. My nose burned. My eyes watered. Through the haze, I spied my father talking to a small group of men. All of them were smoking cigars and patting each other on the back for being the masters of the universe. Among them in attendance was the Governor, my father in-law, and Senator Taylor, Chip's father.

I handed the wine flute to my father and joined the group. A half hour slowly drifted by as I stood listening to their rants on world trade, city planning, and the corporate superstructure. Not once did they mention the war, so during a lull in the conversation, I took my chance and simply asked, "What about the war?" The men froze and snapped their attention to me. Never before had I been looked upon by so many men with trepidation beaming from their eyes as I was at that moment. The entire room fell silent.

"What about the war?" Henry Langston, Chairman of the First National Bank of Boston, asked. He was a short and pudgy, balding man in his early sixties with round spectacles too small for his face.

"What are we doing to help win the war?" I clarified.

"We're helping private enterprise find loop holes in the contracts they signed with the government. You know that," my father replied.

"And we're designing new machinery and transportation for the military," Bill Witherspoon, my father-in-law added.

"Lets not forget the charity fund raisers I host to raise money for the USO," the Governor beamed. "Our fine sailors, soldiers and airmen deserve a nice cold soda pop between battles."

I glared at the Governor. "Most of the money raised from your charity drives comes from the poor who don't have much money to spare while we donate nothing. So can we really feel good about ourselves when it's the poor who suffer the burdens of war and we're left unscathed?"

"The poor always suffer during war," my father roared, driving most of the men in the room not involved with our conversation to flee. "They suffer because that's all they're good for. To fight and die for us. And they'll continue to do so until the end of time. I told you that a year ago when you got that absurd idea to join the army after Pearl Harbor. Since you forgot, war is fought by the poor to protect the rich."

"Splendidly put, Robert," Bill Witherspoon chimed. "A man of our stature would be a fool to join the military. He could lose everything, including his life."

Anger grew inside, but I didn't let it show. My mind momentarily shut down as I looked around the room. Senator Taylor, who had not said a word since I steered the conversation to the war, took a step backward and stared at the floor.

"A man must stay home and protect his family's economic interests," my father was saying when I tuned back into the conversation. "Let the poor bastards do the fighting and dying. A hero's death is far more respectable than being poor."

"Hasn't anyone here ever been poor?" I asked, centering my attention on my father. "Haven't you father?"

The look on my father's face could have covered Florida with a sheet of ice. "I've never been poor, Dan Harrington. We've always had money."

"Mother said that back in Ireland. . ."

"Your mother is dead. Let her rest in peace!"

I saw the anger boiling under my father's skin, so I kept up the battle. "If we lost our fortunes. Forced into poverty. Forced to slave in a factory, then you're saying we too would have to fight in this war?"

"That's preposterous. We'll never lose our fortunes. Especially during times of war," Bill Witherspoon sneered.

"Very true. In times of war we prosper," Harry Langston proudly announced. The men in the circle raised their glasses and toasted his comment. Only Senator Taylor and I kept our glasses held low.

"So, we profit from the blood of others," I stated. Then, I excused myself from the circle and went to the veranda. A few minutes later, Senator Taylor approached and led me to a darkened corner away from the other guests milling about in the cool, clean air.

"I'm proud of you, Dan," Senator Taylor began when he felt confident we were out of earshot of the other guests. "I'm proud of the way you finally stood up for yourself and said what you believe."

"Then, Senator, why didn't you say something?" I asked. "I made a fool of myself in there."

"No, you didn't. Not one of those men regards you as a fool, and they never will. Not after tonight."

"How can you say that?"

"Because you frightened them. You've shown them you have confidence in yourself. That you'll stand up for what you believe in. That you won't break from your convictions, or be persuaded to change your beliefs to fit in. Those men envy you for it. . . Remember, they may be men of power and action when it comes to dealing with people who they feel are inferior, but they're cowards in the company of one another."

"If you know this, why don't you show your courage?" I asked.

"Because in the company of my peers, I'm a coward just like they are. I'm a coward because I need their support to retain my seat in Congress," Senator Taylor answered. Then, he sipped his wine as we both contemplated what he had said. When he spoke again, his tone was merely a whisper. "I know Chip tried to recruit you a few weeks ago, but you refused. I suspect your having second thoughts?"

"Yes. . . I am. For some reason, I feel I belong in the organization. I just can't figure out why. Chip never said what type of work it is. Do you know?"

"Yes." Senator Taylor paused to sip more wine. "I'm not at liberty to say exactly what he's doing though. What I can tell you is that it's of the utmost importance in winning the war. Without them, the future of the United States and the rest of the free world looks pretty grim."

I thought for a moment. There were many questions I had, but I only asked one. "If I joined, could I take Sarah with me?"

"Of course you can. The organization has nothing against families. It does like to put people where they're best suited though, but you can always choose to stay in D.C. if you wish."

Sarah called me from the doorway leading into the ballroom. "Excuse me, Senator."

"Think about what I said."

"I will, and thank you for the information," I said. We shook hands. Then, I turned and went to my lovely wife.

3

*I*n early February of 1943, Sarah and I went to a picture show. The news reel that played before the movie showed clips of the war in the Pacific and the staggered victories in North Africa. That night, after we went to bed, the footage played over and over in my mind. I couldn't sleep and got out of bed around two in the morning. I warmed up a stale pot of coffee, and then sat at the dining table with a stack of newspaper clippings I'd been saving.

Since the day Chip Taylor paid a visit, my thoughts seldom strayed from the war. I kept every news article, and I read and reread every one of them countless times. Once again, I found myself reading the stories as fast as my eyes would let me. Searching for an answer to quell my lust. To question my father's belief that wars were fought by the poor to protect the rich. When, I finished the last article, I found the answer I'd been looking for.

Dawn was breaking when Sarah joined me in the dining room, fatigue evident in her eyes. She had just come from the bathroom where she had experienced a bout of nausea. I offered to prepare a glass of warm milk to calm her stomach, but she refused. Knowing the warm liquid would have the opposite effect. She reached across the table and grasped my left hand with both of hers. Gently, she caressed my fingers. "Honey, what would I do without you?" She asked. "You're so good to me. Promise you'll never leave. I don't know what I'd do without you."

"I promise," I replied. "You're everything to me. We'll always be together. When the baby is born. When the war is over. We'll buy the house you've always dreamed of. We'll live there the rest of our lives with our children. When they're grown, we'll fill our house with grandchildren. Everyday will be filled with joy."

"I know we will. Together we're complete."

"When the war's over, we'll have everything our hearts desire."

"Why wait? Can't we have everything now?" She asked.

"No. Not while the war brings pain and suffering to the world. Many people have already lost their lives. Many more will die before it's over. Families have been torn apart, forced to flee their homes. Cities, towns, countryside's lay in ruin. How can we have everything when so many have lost everything? How can we turn a blind eye and continue building our empires without lifting a hand to help them?"

"Because it's not our war," Sarah replied.

"How can you say that? Whether you believe it or not, we're involved." I pulled my hand from Sarah's grasp and stood up. "We can't keep denying we're not affected. Fooling ourselves into believing we don't have an obligation to get involved. We're Americans. We have a duty to do our part." I began pacing back and forth. My voice rose, causing Sarah to slink back in her chair. "We may not be cowering under our beds as the walls crash around us. Running for a bomb shelter at the first hint of an air raid. Or searching through rubble for dead bodies after bombs have destroyed our city. Not once have we hidden in a culvert as enemy fighters flew over searching for refugees to strafe, but I can assure you, we're involved. As long as America is at war, we, as its citizens, are involved."

"America may be at war, but we're not and never will be," Sarah yelled as she pounded her fists on the table before running to the bathroom and locking the door.

It was the first time she ever raised her voice to me. I was ashamed for getting riled up and went to the bathroom door. From the other side, I could hear her sobs. I apologized many times, but she didn't answer or unlock the door. Then, the front door opened and closed. I went to investigate and found, Mrs. Gibbs, our housekeeper, entering the kitchen with two grocery bags. She was a short, obese woman in her early forties with graying hair and a pleasant smile.

"Morning, sir," she said as she set the grocery bags on the counter.

"Good morning," I replied.

"You look tired. Did you sleep well, sir?"

"I've had a rather rough morning," I said, and then excused myself. I went into the bedroom and got dressed. Then, I put on an overcoat and hat from the hall closet before returning to the kitchen. "I'll not be eating this morning, and I'd like you to call my office in an hour and tell them I won't be in today."

"Sure you're all right, sir?" Mrs. Gibbs asked.

"I'm fine," I replied. Then, I walked to the kitchen doorway and stopped. "Don't you have a son in the army?"

"No, sir. My son's a Marine," She proudly answered. "He's fighting the Japs. In his last letter he said he was awarded the Silver Star for bravery. Imagine that! My son the hero."

"They're all heroes," I solemnly replied. Then, I turned and left the kitchen, pausing for a moment to look at the closed bathroom door before leaving the apartment.

For most of the morning, I wandered the streets of Boston. I paid a visit to a couple of my former professors at Harvard and walked past the courthouse before turning toward the harbor. As I went, in every direction I looked I saw the American flag fluttering in the wind. Recruiting posters for the armed forces hung in the windows of the post office and most retail stores. War Bonds were advertised at every bank. Patriotic fervor was all around me, yet it was an emotion uncommon on the streets where I lived.

There was a long line of men standing outside of an enlistment center. Some of them wore threadbare clothes. Others wore the clothes of men who worked with their bodies. All of them stared at my Seville Row suit as I approached. A few of them had scorn in their eyes as I passed by. One of them spat on the sidewalk in front of me. Keeping my eyes forward, I went straight to the corner and turned. Boston harbor lay before me.

Merchant ships bound for Europe were laden with supplies. Crates and overfilled pallets covered in netting cluttered the docks. Hundreds of longshoremen scattered about trying to load the ships before the noon hour when the ships were due to rendezvous with convoys heading toward England. Two small fishing boats getting a late start drifted past a landing craft ferrying soldiers to a troop ship waiting at anchor five hundred yards from the shore. Everywhere I looked, men were busy at work. Men accustomed to long hours of manual labor. Men living in a world alien to the society in which I was raised. I didn't belong there, so I turned my back and left the harbor behind me.

The walk to my apartment building took thirty minutes. Usually it would have taken much longer, but I was anxious to get back, though when I finally arrived, I didn't enter. Instead, I hailed a cab to my office. Taking the elevator to the third floor, I walked into the firm and stopped at my father's office door. His secretary, Carol, looked up from her desk. "Mr. Harrington, we weren't expecting you today. Are you feeling better?"

"I feel great. Is my father in?" I asked.

"Yes, shall I let him know you're here?"

"Is he alone?"

"Yes, of course."

I entered my father's office and closed the door. My father was seated at his desk reading the morning newspaper, looking up only once to acknowledge my presence. "Sir, I have to talk to you," I said, and then sat down across from him. Suddenly, I felt like a small boy about to be reprimanded by the head schoolmaster.

My father read for another thirty seconds before folding the paper and laying it on his desk. Then, he glared at me. "You enter my office unannounced, and then have the gall to sit down without permission." I jumped to my feet and apologized. "Sit down," he roared, and then lowered his voice back to normal. "You burst in here claiming you have something to say, so say it. And it better be important."

"It is," I said. "I've been doing a lot of thinking these past few months. Mostly about my life, the war, and my future. This morning I've come to a conclusion." My father leaned forward in his chair. "Sir, I've decided to do my part in the war effort. So, I'm going to take a job that was offered me in Washington D. C."

"No, you're not." My father growled.

"It's only for the duration of the war. Once it's over, I'll be back."

"Haven't we already talked about your silly school boy dreams? Haven't we decided your place is here at the firm? No, I won't let you go. Your job is here. Your duty lies with your family. Haven't you taken into account what this would do to your family? What will Sarah do while you're traipsing all over D. C.?"

"She'll be with me. She'll go where I go. And when the war is over, we'll move back here," I replied matter-of-factly.

My father laughed. "Sarah's home is here. Her family and friends live here. You're a fool if you believe she's going with you."

"I'm not a fool. I'm her family and she's going with me."

"Don't be so sure, young, naive, Dan Harrington."

"I'm not naive. She's my wife and I know her better than anyone else."

"If you want to believe that, then that is what you'll believe, but I know you'll be going to D.C. alone," my father said with a sly grin. Content that he knew my own wife better than I did. Once again trying to retain his status as master of men. Though, at that moment, no matter how hard he tried, I wouldn't relent to his prowess. I was determined to stand my ground.

"If I arrive in Washington alone, then so be it. I've made up my mind. I'll go with or without her. I have to do my part. If I were to stay here and do nothing, I couldn't live with myself. I'd never be whole."

My father leaned back in his chair, tapping his right thumb on the arm rest. After a while he pulled a notebook and pen from a desk drawer, jotted a word down on a blank page, and then tore it from the notebook. He neatly folded the page, making sure each fold was sharply creased before stuffing it in his breast pocket. "You're determined to take this job in D.C. even if it means you'll lose your wife and position here at the firm?"

"Yes," I answered.

"You believe that if you were to change your mind, you'll feel incomplete? That you'd live the rest of your life with regret?"

"Yes. If I don't go, I'll never be able to face myself."

"What kind of job could tempt you to such an unfathomable degree that you'd lay your family and your livelihood on the altar of uncertainty?"

"I can't say for sure. I really don't know what I'll be doing. I only know that I have to go," I confessed

My father slowly rose to his feet. He walked over to the bookcases that lined the entire wall beside me and pulled an album from a shelf, staring at it for a minute before returning it to its proper place. Then, he walked over to the window, clasped his hands behind his back, and gazed out at the town he called home. Minutes ticked by. Neither of us said a word. I could hear Carol's typing in the other room. At length, he said, "I too know what it feels like to be drawn in a new direction. Destiny tugging at my sleeves. When the opportunity presented itself, I took my chance. Tested fate. I ended up here." He fell silent. I waited for him to continue.

"As you well know, your mother and I, God rest her soul, were born in Ireland," he went on. "We were happy there, even though the living conditions were deplorable. Poverty was rampant. Unemployment was astronomical. Both of us wanted more out of life than what Ireland had to offer. Almost a year before the 'Great War,' your mother and I emigrated to America. Settling right here in Boston. Being the only person in my family to have ever gone to college, I finished my degree in Philosophy at Harvard during the first year we arrived in this country. After that, I passed the entrance exam and began my first year of law school. I helped pay my tuition by working long hours at night in a factory. Your mother helped by slaving in a textile sweatshop. Her dowry hardly helped in the pursuit of my career. My only regret was your mother never finishing college. It was embarrassing at times."

My father returned to his desk and sat down before continuing.

"A year after you were born, I graduated law school and went to work for Tully and McNalley. At the time they had the best law firm in Boston. Representing clients from all walks of life, the stupid buggers. I stole their best clients when I opened this firm a couple of years later. Within a year I had the premiere law firm. I became a rich man over night."

My father leaned back in his chair and closed his eyes. I shifted closer in my chair, intent on learning my family history that remained a mystery up until then. Suddenly, my father stood and went to the bookcase. Once again, he pulled the album from the shelf. This time he opened it and gazed inside as I patiently waited. Curious to know what he was looking at. Then, with a snap, he closed the album and put it back on the shelf before sitting down behind his desk.

"I've always abhorred war," he said gruffly. "The history of Ireland is shrouded in bloodshed. Over 800 years we Irish have fought and died trying to expel foreign invaders. A feat we've never been able to accomplish. And I believe we never will."

"Did you fight?" I asked.

"No, but your grandfather did. He was involved with a group of reactionaries fighting the English. In 1903, he was shot and killed while on his way home from work." He paused for a moment, and then continued. "My brother John joined the British army at the outbreak of the 'Great War.' I received a letter from him a year later explaining how proud he was to be fighting for a noble cause. I wrote back and told him that he was a traitor. I never heard from him after that. . . Shortly after your birth, my mother sent a letter. Your uncle John died somewhere in France. Because he was a traitor, I haven't had any contact with my family since."

I stared at my father for a few moments before I had to look away. My jaw hung low as I pondered why my father would disown his family on account of the actions of his brother. Why he chose never to speak to his family again. Even his own mother who had given him life. Raised, fed and clothed him only to be forsaken by selfish principles that he tried unsuccessfully to pass on to me.

My anger grew. My teeth clenched. My arms instinctively folded across my chest. I was enraged. For I knew my father was holding back. There was more to the story than he let on, and I wanted to know the truth. Demanded to know the truth. "A pathetic reason to abandon your family," was all I could say.

"What do you mean pathetic?" My father roared.

"Then tell me," I yelled back. "Why haven't you told me about them before? I don't even know who my grandmother is, or if I have aunts and uncles. I do have aunts and uncles, don't I?" My father stayed silent. "Why must everything be a secret with you? Do you realize today is the first time you've talked about mother since she died?"

"Leave her out of this," my father ordered while pointing his index finger at me. He came to his feet. "Your mother is sacred, and I'll not let you use her as an excuse."

"Mother is sacred to me too," I said, and then lowered my head. A tear streaked down my cheek. "But I can't remember much about her. Spent most of my time away from home because you wanted me to be just like you. I never wanted to leave. I wanted to stay with mother. Then, she died. You closed yourself off from me and sent me back to school, but I was glad to leave."

"Who's pathetic now," My father chuckled with an evil grin.

I looked up. In an instant, my pain vanished. I was enraged again, though, I kept control of my emotions and didn't let them show. I wasn't about to give my father more ammunition to use against me. "I'll be leaving for Washington D.C. at the end of the month," I said calmly. "I'd like to come back to work here when the war is over, but that's up to you."

"If you leave, then you are not welcome here."

"Why won't you give me my job back?"

My father leaned forward and put his hands on the desk. "Oh, you must have misunderstood me," he said slowly with emphasis on each word. "Not only will you never get your job back, you'll never come back to Boston. You won't be welcome. Ostracized from the community. I'll see to it myself. When you leave, you're on your own."

"You'd do that to your only son?" I gasped. "You'd disown me like you did your own mother? Why? Is it your reputation you're worried about?"

"As I've said. I abhor war. If you run off to get involved with this one, I can no longer be your father. Still wish to leave?"

I didn't answer at first. My blood boiled and it took a moment to regain my composure. Then, I calmly said, "Yes. If you damn me for participating in a noble cause, then you lose a son. I won't lose a father. I never had one."

My father reached into his breast pocket, produced the piece of paper he had written on, and held it out for me. "Take it," he ordered. "The only family you have now live in this Irish town."

I grabbed the piece of paper and stuffed it into my pocket. Then,

I left his office without saying goodbye. I took the elevator to the first floor and quickly left the building. Once I reached the cool, fresh air, I pulled the paper from my pocket and read the name my father had written.

4

*A*fter leaving the office, I stood by the curb to hail a cab, but quickly changed my mind. By car, my apartment was only five minutes away, but I needed more time to think. The sky was overcast. Dark clouds rolled in from the east, yet, I was confident it wouldn't rain as I began walking toward home. I was wrong. The wind picked up. Rain poured from the sky, drenching me to the bone. A torrential ending for a turbulent day, though, I still had to face the evening.

A quarter past six, I walked through the front door of my apartment. I left my soaked leather shoes by the front door and walked with soggy socks into the living room to announce my arrival. Sarah was reclining in an easy chair and acknowledged by turning her head toward the window.

"What's wrong?" I asked. She didn't answer. I removed my coat and let it fall to my feet.

In an instant, Sarah turned to me. Tears fell lightly from her eyes. "Your father called," she snapped, and then turned away. "Is it true?" A lump grew in my throat. "Is it true?" She yelled while turning back to me. "Did you quit your job?" I stared at her in silence. "Well, did you?"

"Yes," I finally answered.

"How could you do this to me?"

"I have another job offer."

"In Washington D.C., right? Your father already told me."

"Then why are you asking?"

Sarah jumped to her feet. "Because I'm your wife," she yelled. "Your father told me that you really don't know what type of job it is. Is that true?" She took a step toward me. I took a step back.

"Yes. All I know is I'll be helping us win the war," I answered, feeling a tinge of fear enter my body. In the ten years Sarah and I had known each other, this was the second time she had raised her voice to me. The second time we argued.

"I can't believe my ears. You quit your job. A lucrative job to move to

Washington for a job you know nothing about? Call your father! Ask for your job back. Beg if you have to. I can't live like a pauper," Sarah wept. "How do you know the job even exists?"

"I have an address," I answered sheepishly.

"An address? All you have is a damn address? You're a fool, Dan Harrington," she screamed and left the room. I followed her and met a locked bedroom door. I begged forgiveness and pled for her to unlock the door. Muffled cries were her answer. An hour passed before I finally gave up. That night, for the first time in our marriage, I slept on the sofa. The next morning, I awoke from a fitful sleep by Mrs. Gibbs nudging my shoulder.

"Good morning, sir. Are you still feeling ill?"

I almost answered that I was, but knew sooner or later she would learn the truth. I couldn't lie. "Sarah and I are experiencing a bit of trouble at the moment."

"Is it the baby? Sometimes pregnancies can be troublesome on a young couple such as you and the misses. Especially during the first few months you know? A woman goes through a lot of changes, I can tell you that much for certain."

"No, it's not the baby. Sarah and I are moving at the end of the month. Sorry, I couldn't of told you sooner."

"Is it a house? Oh, mister Harrington you've found a house? I'm so happy for you and the misses."

"It's not a house. We're moving to Washington D.C."

"Oh, dear me," gasped Mrs. Gibbs. "What will I do, mister Harrington? I need this job to support my family. My husband can't support me and the little ones on his own."

"Don't worry, Mrs. Gibbs. By the time we move, I'll have found you a new job with another family."

Mrs. Gibbs kept the frown on her face as she asked, "Shall I prepare your breakfast now?"

"Could you check on Sarah first? Oh, and bring me a change of clothes?"

"I'll do that, sir," she replied, and then left the room.

For the next three days, Sarah remained holed up in the bedroom. Her only contact with the outside world was from the telephone beside the bed. Mrs. Gibbs was the only person she allowed to enter the bedroom. Even then, she wasn't allowed to stay very long. Mostly, she just brought Sarah food and water, and stood guard while she used the bathroom. Every time I inquired about my wife, Mrs. Gibbs responded with the same answer, that Sarah was ill and needed rest.

On the fourth day, around two in the afternoon, I answered the front door. To my surprise, Doctor Bernstein was waiting outside. "Dan, I've come as fast as I could," he said as he shook my limp hand. "Where is she?"

I ushered him down the hall and pounded on the bedroom door. "Open the door," I demanded. "Doctor Bernstein is here." When the latch turned, I would have burst through the door if Doctor Bernstein hadn't gently held me back.

Mrs. Gibbs cracked open the door and whispered into Doctor Bernstein's ear. "I'm afraid you'll have to wait out here," he said to me. I tried to look around his body as he entered the room, but the door closed before I could see anything. As the latch turned, I ran into the bathroom and vomited. Then, I went back to the bedroom door and pressed my ear against it. Not a sound came from the other side. I began pacing. An eternity passed in the next ten minutes when another knock sounded at the front door.

"Where's my daughter?" Jane Witherspoon demanded as I opened the door. I didn't have time to answer as she pushed past me. Usually her small frame wouldn't have been too much for me to handle, but I lost my balance and fell against the wall before falling heavily to the floor. By the time I regained my feet, Jane had vanished into the bedroom. So, I assumed my position outside the door and resumed pacing.

A few minutes later, Doctor Bernstein emerged from the bedroom. He put his hand on my shoulder and said he had some bad news. His face was grim as he nudged me into the living room. I was a nervous wreck as I sat down on the sofa.

"Dan," Doctor Bernstein said. "Sarah had a miscarriage."

Fear flowed through me. My body tensed. I wanted to scream. Tears welled up in my eyes and ran down my face. "How is she?"

"Not well, I'm afraid. Physically she'll recover in a couple of days. I've prescribed bed rest and plenty of fluids."

"And emotionally?"

"Emotionally the recovery process will take much longer. Miscarriages are tragic on a woman. Sometimes it can take months before they recover. Sometimes it takes years."

"Can I see her?"

"That wouldn't be a good idea right now," Doctor Bernstein advised. "She's blaming you. Down right adamant it's your fault. So is Jane. But I know better. These things happen for a reason."

My world crashed down around me, ripped apart by my own doing. I felt as though I had stepped from a precipice and was spiraling down into a dark abyss. Guilt ridden from the path I selfishly chose. For a brief moment, I didn't care about the world or its suffering. I didn't care about myself and wished Death would run toward me. Nothing mattered except my love for Sarah. I vowed to change my life back into what it was before Chip Taylor came back into my life. Then, something happened. Something that to this day I cannot explain. That afternoon, as I sat on the sofa, filled with grief, tears in my eyes, I felt a hand on my shoulder. Its weight comforting my trembling body. I heard explosions. The sound of bombs falling, people crying in agony, and then there was silence.

I looked at Doctor Bernstein. His hands were folded in his lap. The invisible hand remained on my shoulder. The tears ceased falling from my eyes, and I knew I was making the right choice by going to Washington D.C.

"I understand you and Sarah have been experiencing a bit of trouble," Doctor Bernstein stated. "Stress can trigger a miscarriage, but usually not this late in a pregnancy. Don't worry too much about it though. Often times it happens because of a deformity in the fetus. Nature's way of natural selection. A prenatal form of survival of the fittest, or by God's will if you believe in such a thing."

He kept talking, trying to console me with scientific logic as my mind drifted far away. My thoughts concerned the future and the presence I'd felt a moment earlier. At once, I knew the life I'd been born into, would be a life I would have to leave behind. I knew I was about to change forever. I accepted my fate. Fearless of the choice I made. Although, I knew great tragedy lay before me, I felt I had been reborn.

Doctor Bernstein was still talking when Jane Witherspoon entered the room and pointed her finger at me. "This is all your fault!" She yelled. Doctor Bernstein and I stared at her. Neither of us gave a response. "I'm taking her home," she said, and then stomped out of the room. Doctor Bernstein followed her.

A few minutes later, I heard all of then leaving. I went to the hallway and watched as Jane Witherspoon and Mrs. Gibbs carried Sarah through the front doorway. Doctor Bernstein was in tow with his medical bag in one hand and a suitcase in the other. None of them said goodbye. When the door slammed shut, I crumpled to the floor and wept until my eyes ran dry.

5

*L*ater that evening as I lay on the sofa with my eyes closed, furious pounding reverberated from the front door. The pounding remained steady as I walked toward it. The door shook as I unfastened the latch.

Immediately, the door flew open. I quickly stepped to the right as it went by, but I was pushed to the left as Bill Witherspoon rushed past and went into the living room. My father, with his hands clutched behind his back, slowly sauntered by with a sardonic grin. "Boy, you have really done it now," was all he said as he passed.

I followed the two men into the living room. My father-in-law was pacing by the window. My father was calmly seated on the sofa. I remained in the doorway.

"Get in here and sit down," Bill Witherspoon yelled while pointing at the sofa. Cautiously, I did as I was ordered, keeping my distance from my father as I sat down. Bill Witherspoon stopped pacing five feet in front of me. "What have you done to my daughter? And what's this nonsense about Washington D.C.?"

I looked at my father and didn't answer. My heart raced. My father smiled.

"Don't look at him. He's not going to help you. He's on my side." Bill Witherspoon sneered. His face was red. A vein protruded from his forehead.

"Answer the man," my father ordered.

I gulped hard, and then looked at Bill Witherspoon. "I've done nothing to Sarah. I would never do anything to her. . ."

"You're a liar, Dan Harrington." Bill Witherspoon yelled. His temper close to its breaking point. "How can you plead innocence when my daughter is home in bed. Weak from what you put her through? Don't try to deny your guilt. Your father already informed me of your intentions."

I looked at my father, and then back to Bill Witherspoon. "I am planning to leave, and Sarah is coming with me. When the war's over, we'll be back."

"What do you mean, we?" Bill Witherspoon snapped. "Your father said you intend to leave by yourself, and when you get there, you're going to divorce my daughter."

"That's a lie," I cried, and then stared at my father. A slight grin peeked at the edges of his mouth.

"Your father wouldn't lie to me," Bill Witherspoon shouted. "He's too well respected and dignified to lie. A man of integrity. Trusted by all. It's you, young Harrington, who is the liar."

The accusation sent fire through my veins. The effect it had on me wasn't something I would realize until many years later. At that moment, at the age of twenty-five, I was no longer a child in fear of his father. Never again would my peers attribute my success as a result of his stature, or scrutinize my failures as not living up to his standards. At that moment, I got to my feet and became a man.

"How dare you call me a liar," I growled. "How dare you come into my house and insult me? Not once have I ever lied to either of you." Bill Witherspoon's face turned white. "You've taken the word of my father and believed it without asking me if it was true or not."

I turned to my father. "And you," I thundered, pointing my finger at him. Watching as he pressed further against the sofa. "How dare you tell lies. How dare you cause a rift in my marriage."

"He's gone completely mad," Bill Witherspoon said.

I spun around and faced him. "I'm not mad. What I've told you is the truth. If you don't believe me, then ask Sarah. I love her. I've always loved her, and I would never, ever do anything to hurt her."

I went to the window. Bill Witherspoon lowered his head as I went by. "Today, Sarah lost a child. Our child. Not once have either of you offered condolences."

"Why should we? The miscarriage is your fault," my father snarled.

"Maybe it was," I replied. "Doctor Bernstein doesn't think so, but I accept full responsibility."

Bill Witherspoon looked up. "That Jew doesn't know what the hell he's talking about."

"And you do? Now you've both worn out your welcome. Get out!" My father was about to reply, but decided it wasn't wise and fled to the front door with Bill Witherspoon hot on his tail as I walked toward them. In a flash, they exited. Bill Witherspoon warned me to stay away from Sarah as I slammed the door closed.

The rest of the evening and through the weekend, I stayed in the apartment. Mrs. Gibbs never came back and I resorted to cooking on my own. Admittedly, I wasn't the best cook. The only culinary training I ever received was at summer camp, and if I hadn't taken the courses while I was there, I would have starved. Although, after choking down some of the meals I prepared, starvation seemed a better choice. That weekend, I must have lost ten pounds.

I telephoned Sarah many times over the next week, but the Witherspoon's housekeeper kept answering. Following Bill Witherspoon's instructions, she wouldn't let me talk to my wife. Nor did she inform me of her condition.

When Thursday came around, I was awaken from a fitful sleep to find strange men and Jane Witherspoon in my apartment. The men began packing Sarah's belongings into boxes while Jane supervised. She said nothing to me. Even after I said good morning, she refused to show common decency. All I received from her was a scowl.

I got dressed and left the apartment while they finished packing Sarah's belongings. All morning I walked the streets of Boston. All afternoon, I sat alone in a park. When I returned to the apartment after dark, everything was gone except for my personal belongings. My clothes and two suitcases were still in the closet. A blanket, three of my favorite novels, and my personal papers were piled in the corner of the bedroom. A bar of soap, my razor and toothbrush, and one roll of toilet paper were in the bathroom. The kitchen cabinets were wide open, revealing their emptiness. That night, I slept on the floor.

The next morning, I went to the bank to withdraw money to buy a new bed. The teller said my account was frozen. When I talked to the manager, he said there was a problem with my account and that I couldn't withdraw any money until it was fixed.

"How long will it take?" I asked.

"Shouldn't be more than a couple of days, mister Harrington," the bank manager replied, but I saw right through him. I knew my account would be frozen until long after I'd left for Washington D. C..

With only ninety-three dollars in my pocket, I left the bank and wandered the streets until nightfall. Then, I returned to the barren place I called home. For the remainder of the month, I subsisted on dry bagels and water. At night, I slept on the floor.

Many times, I tried to call Sarah from the telephone booth on the corner. Every time the maid said she wasn't home. Then, on the 27th of February,

I called her one last time. Bill Witherspoon answered. When he realized it was me on the other end, he told me never to call his house again. I told him that I would be leaving at 10 a.m. the next day. "Good riddance," was all he said, and then hung up the phone. I was upset and made one last call to my father's office.

"Hello, you've reached Harrington Law. How may I help you?"

"Hello, Carol, it's Dan. I'm leaving in the morning, and I wish to have a word with my father."

"Just a moment," she said, and then put the phone down. I could hear her knocking on my father's office door. Moments later, she came back on the phone. "I'm sorry, mister Harrington, but your father instructed me to hang up." I was about to reply when the phone went dead.

The next morning, I went to the train station around eight in the morning and waited on the loading platform with my two stuffed suitcases until the last minute before boarding the train. At ten sharp, the train pulled out of the station. I was alone, heading to a place I'd never been, and never got the chance to say goodbye.

6

*A*fter long delays in Hartford, New York, Philadelphia, and Baltimore, I arrived in Washington D. C., a little past eleven the next evening. That night, I slept on a bench in the train station and woke early the next morning with a stiff back. I ate breakfast and read the newspaper before hailing a cab, giving the driver the address of my destination as I shut the door.

Once we were on our way, he began asking questions. Personal questions which I didn't care to answer. Trying to remain aloof, I asked him questions of my own. Superficial questions concerning the weather, the best places to eat, and which tourist attractions I should visit. Every question I asked, he answered with pride and gave a brief history. In fact, the cab driver talked so much that when we finally arrived at an unmarked building close to the Capitol, I was more than happy to pay my fare and say goodbye to the man forever.

I lugged my two suitcases up the stairs and through the entrance of the building. Two men stood guard at the back of the foyer and followed me with their suspicious eyes as I walked toward the reception desk. "Can I help you, sir?" A blond lady in her early forties asked as I set my suitcases on the floor.

"I hope so. A friend of mine offered me a job a few months back. Gave me this address." I held out the piece of paper Chip gave me. The woman took the paper and read the address before she put it in her desk drawer. "Have I come to the right place?"

"Yes, sir," she replied. "What's your friends name?"

"Chip Taylor."

"Just one moment please," she said while picking up the telephone. She dialed a three digit number, covering the phone with her hand as she asked the person on the other end if Chip was in the building. Then, she quickly hung up and said, "I'm sorry, sir. Mister Taylor is not in today. If you'd like to have a seat, someone will be with you shortly."

I sat in a chair by the front door. For the next thirty minutes, I watched a constant flow of people enter and exit the building. They all had security passes which the guards scrutinized while staring at me out of the corner of their eyes. I was intimidated and nearly got up and left. Thankfully, a dark haired man with tan skin and soft features approached from behind the reception desk. He wore a light tan uniform that was void of any markings, and a pair of highly polished black oxfords. "I believe you're the friend of mister Taylor?" He asked.

"Yes, sir," I answered as I got to my feet. "I'm Dan Harrington."

"Nice to meet you mister Harrington. I'm Gibson." We shook hands. "Follow me, please."

Gibson led me over to one of the guards who immediately pat searched my body and rummaged through my suitcases. Satisfied that I wasn't armed, the guard let me go. Then, I followed Gibson to a small room with one table and two chairs.

For the next half hour, Gibson conducted an informal interview and gleaned more information out of me than I thought possible in such a short time. Afterward, I was given an indoctrination form, which was the basic run of the mill Civil Service application, and a Personal History Statement. I promptly filled out both of them, and then I was taken by car to a nearby medical clinic where an ancient doctor gave me a complete physical examination.

Afterward, I was driven back to the unmarked building and led back to the same small room with one table and two chairs. "I understand you're fluent in German, French, and Dutch," Gibson said as we sat down.

"And some Latin," I added. "Though not as fluent as my German and French."

Gibson excused himself and left the room. A few minutes later he returned with a large file containing all of the information the organization had gathered on me since Chip Taylor recommended me for employment. For the next hour or so, I was asked more questions as Gibson flipped through the file. Again, I was surprised how much he knew about my life, including the scores of every major test I took in school and the personal backgrounds of every teacher I had.

Once Gibson was satisfied I had answered all of his questions correctly, he closed the file and laid it on the table. Then, he leaned back in his chair and rubbed his eyes. "We're currently seeking individuals with your linguistic abilities," he said, and then smiled as he leaned forward and rested his forearms on the edge of the table. "I can't guarantee employment with us until you're tested, but it looks promising. I'll emphasize that employment in this organization is strictly voluntary, and you may quit at any time. If you do decide to quit, you'll have to sign a release form stating that any and all information you've acquired while employed with us will remain confidential. Furthermore, you're not allowed to speak to anyone about what we do here. And that includes your wife. We deal with a lot of sensitive information vital to the war effort and its disclosure could cause grave harm to the United States and its allies if any of it were leaked to the public. As for pay, every job has its own pay rate, and the rate will most likely remain the same throughout your employment with us. If you're looking to get rich, then we're not for you. Do you understand?"

"Yes, but I have a few questions," I said.

"And they are?"

"First of all, I'd like to know who I'll be working for, and second, what type of job I'll be doing?"

Gibson leaned back in his chair and rested his hands, fingers entwined, in his lap. "I can't tell you very much at this point. We need to assess your strengths and weaknesses before anyone can answer your questions. All I can tell you right now is you'll be working as a civil servant for the United States Government, and with your linguistic abilities, you'll most likely be considered for a job overseas. Do you have any more questions?"

"Not at the moment," I lied. There were many questions floating around in my head, but I knew Gibson was being as tight-lipped as Chip Taylor had been a few months before.

"Very well then. If you'll grab your suitcases and follow me, there's a car waiting to take you to the testing center."

I followed Gibson out of the back of the building to a black car with its engine running. A driver and a plainclothes security guard sat in the front seat. An unidentified man sat in the back with me. None of us spoke as we drove through Washington D.C. and out to the Virginia countryside. Around five in the evening the driver pulled up to a large two story country house in Fairfax, Virginia.

For the next three and a half days, I was tested and assessed on a variety of subjects designed to test my intellectual abilities. How well I worked under pressure. My ability to withstand frustration, and how well I worked alone. At the end of the third day, I gave an oral speech in front of a large crowd to assess how I acted under the scrutiny of an audience. After the many cases I fought in court, the final test was by far the easiest. It was also the test I scored the lowest on due to being, '*overly confident.*'

On the last day, I underwent three psychological evaluations by three separate staff officers. Each of them were skilled psychologists who ran their own psychiatric clinics before the war. More importantly, they all had their own peculiar way of asking the same questions. A quirkiness only a fellow psychologist could understand.

Each evaluation lasted for about an hour and centered mostly on my childhood, the relationships I had with my father and wife, and how I felt my life was shaped by their influence. I was also asked why I wanted to serve my country, and how I felt about unconventional warfare which was viewed as underhanded and sometimes outright illegal by the majority of civilized society. I answered that under the present circumstance, the United States and its allies should utilize any and all means necessary to win the war. Once again, I was reminded that employment in the organization was on a voluntary basis, and asked if I wished to continue. I answered that I did and was immediately released as fit for duty.

The next day, I was taken by car to a place called, "Area F," a temporary base on the grounds of the Congressional Country Club on the outskirts of Washington D.C., and put with a group of thirty men living in a cluster of tents next to club house. Our time was split between physical conditioning and more testing. My muscles ached the entire two weeks I was there, but by the end, I was in the best physical condition I had ever been in my life.

After our training at, "Area F," we were given weekend leave. My two days were spent holed up in a hotel room overlooking the Potomac river. I kept the curtains drawn and passed the time by ordering room service, drinking wine, and writing letters to Sarah. Ever since, I left Boston, she was constantly on my mind. Twice, I telephoned her parents house from the hotel lobby. Both times her mother answered and reminded me not to call their house anymore. On Sunday, I returned to, "Area F" with a blinding headache and queasy stomach. Some of the men I went through the training with told me that I looked as bad as I felt.

The next morning my group went to a place called, "Area B-2" for six more weeks of training. Located on the grounds of a private hunting lodge in the Catoctin Mountains of northern Maryland, we were housed in one story cabins furnished with bunk beds and a wood stove. It was here that our specialized training began, and it was here we learned that we were all members of the Office of Strategic Services (OSS). An organization none of us had ever heard of before.

The training was extraordinary. We were all motivated and learned a lot.

In only six weeks, all of us were proficient in dismantling, reassembling, and firing a vast array of small arms from around the world. We also became proficient in Morse Code, map and compass reading, first-aid, and basic survival skills.

Language classes were taught in the evenings. Refugees from occupied Europe and the Pacific gave fascinating lectures on the present living conditions in their home countries, with the strengths and weaknesses of the occupying armies being the main focal points of their lectures.

More importantly, we were given our first lessons in hand-to-hand combat. Our instructor, John Keenan, a thirty-eight-year-old army major with an illustrious history, had a small frame and seemed too frail to stand up to our hardened bodies. In the beginning of his first lesson, I almost laughed when he asked for a volunteer to demonstrate a knife fighting technique. I quickly raised my hand before any of the others in the group and smiled when I was chosen. I wanted to be the man to prove we were hardened warriors.

Major Keenan told me to step forward. As I did, he struck me in the groin without warning. His small fist felt like a freight train. I doubled over and fell to the ground. All of the men laughed as I fought for air. "Let this be a lesson to all of you," Major Keenan said while standing over me. "In a fight, you do everything you can to win because your enemy is trying to kill you." Needless to say, I learned the lesson well.

At the end of training, Colonel Baxter, the commander of, "Area B-2," pulled me away from the group and escorted me to a small cabin adjacent to the mess hall. Three men in dark suits were seated at the far end of a long rectangular table. I was ordered to sit across from them, and told only to speak when I was directly asked a question. Then, for the next fifteen minutes the room remained silent. The three men seldom blinked their eyes as they stared at me. I remained fixed like a statue firmly planted in my chair, wondering why they were here and what they wanted from me. The sharpest knife couldn't have cut through the tension.

"Why did you leave Boston?" The man seated to my left began the questioning in French.

"To join the OSS," I instinctively answered in French.

"What did you do before joining the OSS?" The man seated on my right asked in German.

"I was a lawyer," I replied in German.

"How many people lived with you before you left Boston?" The man seated directly across from me who looked to be in his late fifties asked in

Dutch.

"Only my wife," I replied in Dutch, instinctively using the language spoken to me, and so it went. The three men asked many questions in French, German, and Dutch, and I answered them in the language they used.

An hour passed, and I still sat in that room answering questions. Sometimes I'd answer with one word. Other times, I answered with a lengthy explanation. The whole time not one word in English was uttered. Finally, as abruptly as it began, the questioning ended. The three men got up from the table and huddled together in the far corner of the room, whispering to each other before returning to their seats. "He'll do, Colonel Baxter," The man seated on my left said in flawless English, causing my jaw to drop at his annunciation.

"Please excuse us, Colonel Baxter," the man seated across from me said. He also spoke flawless English, and from the way the other two men acted, I surmised that he was their leader.

"We've chosen you for a very important job," the man seated across from me said after Colonel Baxter had left the room. "Your linguistic skills are impeccable, but you need more practice with your Dutch. Nothing a little coaching can't overcome."

"The job we're offering you is vital to our success in Europe," the man on my right said. "I understand you're married?"

"Yes, I am," I replied.

"The job we have in mind could put you in grave danger of losing your life or limb," the man seated across from me stated.

"It's strictly voluntary of course," the man on my right added.

I thought for a moment about my marriage and how I haven't seen or heard from Sarah since the day she had the miscarriage. I thought about my father and how he no longer thought of me as his son, so knowing the bridges I had burned, I accepted.

"A wise choice, sir," The man on my left said with a sly grin.

"Welcome to SI," The man across from me said, referring to the Secret Intelligence branch of the OSS whose primary function was to infiltrate enemy occupied territory and gather intelligence, recruit sub-agents, form resistance groups, and conduct sabotage and subversion on enemy targets.

Immediately after the interview, I was driven in an unmarked staff car to a place on the north shore of Lake Ontario in Oshawa, Canada called, "Camp X." The next training session didn't start for another two weeks, so I spent my days filing reports. In the evenings, I went jogging. At night, I wrote letters to Sarah. She was on my mind every moment of every day, and I missed her so much that my heart ached.

When training commenced, I was put with a group of nine other OSS Secret Intelligence recruits. Up until that time, my training had been very exciting, but at, "Camp X," I underwent the most intensive and amazing training a person could wish undergo. To this day I'm still filled with awe when I reminisce about what I learned.

In the first few weeks, hand-to-hand combat was a main fixture on the training schedule. I learned how to silently dispatch a sentry, how to defeat multiple attackers, and how to kill an attacking guard dog with my bare hands. Furthermore, the Sykes-Fairbain knife fighting technique was heavily emphasized from an instructor who was once a pupil of Fairbain himself.

Firearms training was more in-depth than what I had received at, "Camp B-2." The double-tap philosophy where every target was shot twice was ingrained in our brains. We mastered firing a pistol from the hip, shooting at moving targets, and engaging multiple targets. On moonless nights, we learned how to shoot and hit targets that were practically invisible to the naked eye.

Instruction on sabotage was everyone's favorite course. We learned how to blow up bridges, demolish buildings, set land mines, and even how to use a wrench to derail a train. Not only did we learn how to disarm the explosive charges and mines we set, but also those of our enemy.

Other areas of training consisted of courses on survival, the use of wireless radios, including more instruction on Morse Code. We were taught how to use codes and ciphers, given advice on how to recruit sub-agents, and how to write and distribute propaganda. There was also a course on surreptitious entry taught by a retired professional burglar.

The last few weeks consisted of a two week long exercise in which the members of my group were split up and sent on our own. Our objective was to live off the land while gathering intelligence from clues scattered around the two hundred and fifty acre parcel of land. The last objective was to return back to one of the three rally points located in the heart of the main camp. The tricky part was that we had to do it without being seen or captured by field officers posing as the enemy.

Out of the ten members of our group, only two of us made it safely back to a rally point without being caught. One of the men was a short actor from Hollywood who ended up gaining more fame as a secret agent than from any of his movies. The other man to make it back without being detected was myself. I chalked up my accomplishment as pure luck, but my peers treated me like a hero.

Our training, among other things, set us apart from the other branches of the OSS. All of the branches had their own vital tasks to accomplish, but once we were posted behind the lines in occupied Europe or the Pacific, we would be the eyes and ears of the entire organization. We were the elite, and we knew it. After four months of intensive training, we were all eager to join the fight against evil. Every one of us would get our chance, but some of us would pay the ultimate price.

7

*A*fter, "Camp X," I was taken to New York harbor where I boarded a troop ship bound for Europe. Newly commissioned with the rank of lieutenant, I was billeted next to, 'Officer Country' with other men dressed in plain, army green uniforms. Out of all of them, I had only seen one of them before. For he was also at, "Camp X," although, we had orders not to speak to each other.

The trip over to Britain was an extremely long seven days. The stabilizers on the Queen Mary's hull had been removed so the ship could move faster through the water. Along with the constant zigzagging to avoid enemy U-boats and the increased speed, most of the men on board lined the deck rails and took turns hanging their heads over the side. Pale green faces dry heaved or let loose their last meal into the dark water lapping along hull. Over 15,000 men were in a constant state of sea sickness, including some of the sailors.

Enemy U-boats were a constant concern. At least twice daily General Quarters sounded. Men scurried from the deck to berthing areas deep within the iron coffin while sailors manned the guns and depth charge racks. Fortunately, every alarm was false and the men below gradually returned to their perch along the railing.

Another danger threatening our passage, and easily visualized by all on deck, were icebergs. Rising majestically on the horizon, their eerie shapes grew in size as the ship neared. We all sighed as the ship passed well out of their path.

Besides the ships crew, some of the passengers were assigned duties while aboard. My group was put in charge of guarding the officers quarters. We rotated six hour shifts with one man on duty at all times. Because of the motion sickness, a small aluminum trash can was provided. At the end of our shift, we would take the full trash can to the officer's lavatory and flush the contents down the toilet, and we were lucky. Unlike the rest of the ship where men stood in line, sometimes up to an hour just to use the toilet, the officer's lavatory was almost always vacant.

Up until the voyage, I had remained aloof, keeping my distance from the other men in training. For my background was drastically different from most of them. At, "Area B-2," almost all of the men were prior military. Most of them were radio operators culled from the army and navy, and all of them were middle-class Americans accustomed to manual labor. I was amazed how freely profanity spouted from their lips. I learned many uses for the F-word. Not only was it never used as originally intended, I learned that it could be a noun, verb, adjective, adverb, and also as a conjunction. My social upbringing was forever scarred.

In contrast, at, "Camp X" every man in my group was an ivy leaguer and held professional jobs before joining the OSS. Some were stock brokers. Others were company managers, or held positions in the entertainment field. One was a dentist. Still, they came from lowest rungs of the upper class, and the language they used was frowned upon within the society I'd been raised. Although, they possessed a much more civilized tongue than the men at, "Area B-2."

The second reason I kept to myself was because from the moment I left Boston, part of me had stayed behind. An inner struggle blazed within my soul, pulling me back and forth from my duties and Sarah's love. During rest periods, I often found my thoughts drifting back to her warm embrace, only to snap back to reality at the commencement of the next training course. I knew I hadn't allowed myself to be fully immersed in the training, and part of my learning suffered from it. Although, I may have been one of the top two in the group, I didn't feel ready to undertake the duties which lay ahead. Now, while on the Queen Mary full of miserable men, I made the decision to invest one hundred percent of my energy and ability into my wartime career. Furthermore, on the rolling seas of the North Atlantic, I met my first true friend since leaving Boston.

It was during the second day of the voyage. I was in the mess deck, attempting to choke down a slab of ham, mashed potatoes, and creamed corn as cups and food trays slid around the crowded table in motion with the ship. The low hum of the engines and the loud roar of men talking, trays clanging, combined with the constant rocking of the ship, made my stomach churn. I rose quickly and went to put away my dinner tray, but after ten paces, I bolted to the nearest trash can and relieved myself of the food I'd just eaten. A young man standing guard came over to where I had my head stuffed in the trash can. "There, there, my friend," he said in French. Then, he added in English, "Let me get you topside." He was five foot eight inches tall with a muscular body and a full head of black hair. His face was set in stone when he wasn't talking and he gave a slight grin when he laughed.

"Thank you very much," I replied in French as he half carried me to a vacant spot at the railing on the deck. Then, he disappeared.

A few hours later, he found me in exactly the same spot he had left me. We began a conversation in French. A practice we would carry on throughout the rest of the trip when we weren't on duty or sleeping. His name was, Jacques Marceau, but he preferred to be called Jack. His parents emigrated to America after the, 'Great War' and settled in Holly Beach, Louisiana where he was born. Growing up with French parents, he spoke French at home and English everywhere else. His father, Stephan, was a fisherman and taught him how to catch fish in the Gulf of Mexico. The main reason he never got sick on the voyage over to Britain.

Jack had a younger sister, Anne, who helped his mother, Audrey run a small French restaurant located just off the beach. During the summer months when he wasn't fishing with his father, Jack helped his mother and sister at the restaurant. He became quite an accomplished chef under the tutelage of his mother and planned to study the culinary arts in Paris before the war started. In the summer of 1942, he joined the navy and became a radio operator. Unlike my father, his father was proud of his son.

Around nine p.m. on October the 8th, 1943, the Queen Mary arrived through a dense fog at the Firth-of-Clyde in Scotland. I was on duty and remained posted in Officer Country for an hour after the ship docked. I was probably the last passenger to disembark.

It was raining slightly when I left the ship. In the dim light, I saw men and machines everywhere I looked. Regiments formed into columns and marched away. Jeeps, trucks, and tanks left in a steady convoy away from the wharf while longshoremen lifted tons of cargo from the ships tied to the dock. Out at sea a lone fog horn pierced the thick fog, announcing more ships waiting their turn.

As I inched my way toward a group of men forming a column, a cockney voice called out from the darkness on my left. "Are you lost, leftenant?"

I didn't respond. Even though everyone on the operational side of Secret Intelligence was a commissioned lieutenant at completion of training at, "Camp X," I wasn't used to being addressed by my rank.

"Leftenant," the voice thundered, causing me to jump. "Are you lost?" A captain of the Royal British army asked, and I instantly saluted.

The captain hobbled up to me with the aid of a cane. He looked to be around forty and had definitely seen his better days. He walked with a slight limp in his left leg. His left arm was amputated above the elbow, and his sleeve was bobby-pinned to his chest. Over his right eye was a leather patch. A jagged scar ran down from his left eye to his upper lip, creating a small gap in his neatly trimmed moustache. He could scare any young man with his appearance, but it was his eyes that frightened me the most. For they stared at me with purpose, filled with intensity. Eyes that had witnessed the depths of Hell, and returned without life.

"Sir, I have orders to report to the Motor Pool, and I've no idea how to get there."

"Well, old boy, if I wasn't here directing traffic, you'd be in a fine pickle, wouldn't you?" The captain smirked.

I would've replied harshly had I not noticed the Victoria Cross pinned to his chest. The medal demanded respect, no matter who wore it. "Yes sir," I replied.

The captain smiled wickedly. Then, he gave me directions to the Motor Pool, pointing his cane in the direction I needed to go. I thanked him, and then saluted. He returned the salute with his cane, and then he did an about-face and hobbled away, barking orders at other men as he went.

I followed the captain's directions through the warehouse area. Open doors showed the insides of buildings overstuffed with food, ammunition, equipment, firearms, and many more items needed to fight a war. Past the warehouses sat row upon row of Jeeps, trucks, half tracked vehicles, and tanks waiting to be driven to a safe place out of sight of German bombers. As I looked around, I began to understand the vast scale in which the war in Europe was being fought, and I hoped I would play a vital role in its outcome.

I finally found a small building marked, "Motor Transport" and joined the rest of my group. We were escorted to a nearby train station and left immediately, arriving a little after dawn at Hently-on-Thames, a small town about forty miles west of London. Our base was Fawley Court, a manor taken over by the military and surrounded by Nissen huts. There we underwent more physical conditioning, fine tuned our radio skills, and worked intensively with codes and ciphers. During the second week, I heard French speaking radio operators were in high demand, so, I approached Major Thorne, our commanding officer, and pled my case to get Jack transferred to my SI group. Major Thorne relented and said he would see what he could do.

I didn't know it at the time, but Jack Marceau was already a member of the OSS and attached to the Operational Groups (OG) currently undergoing training for the Jedbourough teams. Major Thorne put up a tough fight to get him. The OG's commanding officer didn't want to let him go, but SI branch had a higher priority. A week later, Jack arrived and became a member of Secret Intelligence. Over the next few months our friendship grew. At night, when we weren't on an exercise, we played cards. I introduced him to Sherlock Holmes mysteries. The only vice I had as a kid. Jack reintroduced me to Shakespeare. I say reintroduced because I didn't care too much for his plays when I was younger. Although, "A Midsummer Night's Dream," caught my fancy.

On December 2nd, 1943, we went to Beaulieu in southern England for more in-depth training of the same courses I went through at, "Camp X." Ran by Britain's Special Operations Executive (SOE), these courses were mostly refresher training for all of us except Jack. Since he was originally slated for the Jedbourough teams, he never went through, "Camp X." Still, even though every course at Beaulieu was new to him, at the end of the four week training period, he was as proficient as the rest of us.

It was during our time at Beaulieu that I received my first letter from Sarah. With great care, I opened the envelope and sniffed the inside for any trace of her scent before carefully removing the letter. A few tears fell from my eyes as I read.

> My Dearest Dan,
>
> I'm sorry I haven't written earlier. Mother ordered the butler to bring her the mail before anyone else had a chance to look through it. She kept telling me that you haven't written. I was so heartbroken until today when I got the mail from the postman. Four of your letters were waiting for me. Now, I know you have been writing since you left. Please forgive me for doubting your love.
>
> I want to apologize for how I acted after we lost the baby. I wasn't myself. If I acted differently, showed how much you mean to me, maybe you would have stayed in Boston. I miss you very much.
>
> Your letters are very vague. I wish I knew where you are, and what you are doing. We shouldn't keep secrets from each other. Please be safe.
>
> Father is expanding the business. In early January, I'll be traveling with him to New York to help him set up the

new office. Your father will be traveling with us to take care of the legalities, but I think he is really going for a vacation and won't stay very long. He has really changed since you left. I know he can be harsh, but someday, I hope the two of you can work out your differences.

Please take care of yourself, my dear. Come home safe.

Yours Always,
Sarah

P.S. If by the chance you happen to get to Paris, please buy me something nice to wear.

I read the letter a few more times before returning it to the envelope. Then, I put the envelope in my left breast pocket where it would remain for the rest of my training.

At the conclusion of training at Beaulieu, my group was given a three day pass for the Christmas holiday. We all went to London. A bad choice if you ask me. Allied soldiers mobbed the streets. The cinemas were sold out. Every pub and tavern was standing room only, and filled with drunk soldiers and prostitutes. Jack somehow managed to get us tickets to, "Taming of the Shrew." I didn't want to go, but after seeing the play performed, I finally understood Jack's fascination with Shakespeare. After the play, we had a hell of a time getting back to our billets at the Red Cross Club. With the blackout being strictly enforced, it was almost impossible to avoid the drunk soldiers stumbling through the streets. At the entrance to the Red Cross Club, I accidentally bumped into a group of them. A fight ensued. Jack and I quickly dispatched the drunk men by using techniques we learned in hand-to-hand combat training. Luckily, their hangover the next morning would be far worse than the beating we gave them.

At the end of our three days, I was glad to leave London. Our next destination was an old mansion on a large English estate in Peterborough called, 'Milton Hall.' By now everyone was itching for action. We wanted to get the training over with as soon as possible, but it was here that our training proved invaluable.

Milton Hall was the main training area for the men who would later make up the Jedbourough teams. They would be assembled into three man teams and parachuted into occupied Europe to conduct guerrilla warfare against the Axis armies. Our job was to use the skills we learned at Beaulieu to conduct surveillance on the Jedbouroughs during their exercises and report their movements back to headquarters at the mansion. Jack and I had a lot of fun. More importantly, we learned how to work better as a team.

We were at Milton Hall for a month before being trucked to Ringway Field in Manchester for an accelerated jump training class. Most paratroop units received a month of training, but we were called, "specials," and our training only lasted five days. Furthermore, we so called, "specials" were not allowed to mingle with the regular troops, so our billets were in safe houses lining the edge of airfield.

The first two days were divided between classroom lectures on parachuting techniques and simulated jumps which took place on a static apparatus set up in one of the safe houses. The third day we made two jumps from a balloon 700 feet above the ground. On the fourth day, we made our first actual jump from a British Whitley bomber. On the fifth day, we waited until sundown and jumped at night. The pitch black ground came up so fast, I almost didn't have time to brace for the landing.

Immediately after jump training, we were whisked away to an operational holding area to wait for assignment. Within hours of arrival, John Stockton, a former stock broker from upstate New York, was the first to receive orders. He and a French army captain on loan from the SOE parachuted into Brittany and were instantly captured. Stockton was arrested as a spy. The French officer was arrested as a traitor and a spy. Their charges carried a stiff penalty. After an intensive week long interrogation, both of them were executed by the Gestapo. Their deaths deeply impacted the rest of us, bringing the harsh realities of war to the forefront. From that moment on, we all knew the price of failure.

Three weeks passed before the next assignment came up. Jack and I were chosen because we were as 'thick as thieves,' and only given thirty-six hours to prepare. Plenty of time for two eager and qualified men who had spent almost a year in training.

The morning of the day we were set to leave, Jack and I were each issued a STEN Mark II silenced submachine gun, and a HiStandard model B twenty-two caliber pistol which came with a detachable silencer. Then, we each received a Sykes-Fairbain commando knife, a pair of binoculars, and a few peculiar items essential for our mission. Jack was issued two SSTR-1 radio sets, complete with extra batteries and crystals, and three books filled with codes and ciphers. After a successful landing in France, he was ordered to cache the extra radio where no one else would know of its hiding place, not even me.

Two female agents from the 'Cover and Documentation' section of the OSS provided us with new clothes and identities. First, they had Jack and I put all of our personal belongings in our duffel bags. Sarah's letter was the last item I put into mine before giving it to the operations officer for safe storage. Then, they dressed us in clothes taken from French refugees. We were posing as farmers so the women gave us patched blue denim work clothes, hand-knitted socks, heavy dark brown coats with a compass hidden in one of the buttons, black leather shoes, and black berets. For the first time in my life, I looked like a peasant.

The two women gave us our cover names for the assignment, and the documents to go with them. My cover name was, Marcel Le Bon, a French farmer from Parthenay. Jack's cover was, Stephan Le Perrier, my longtime friend also from Parthenay. Then, the female agents quizzed us on our new identities until supper time.

After supper, we had a three hour briefing. Our assignment was to drop into Normandy after midnight, rendezvous with the Maquis at our drop zone, and find a safe haven to conduct our intelligence operation. We were to report on enemy strength, troop movements, and local attitudes toward the occupying forces. If possible, we were to train the resistance forces into an effective fighting unit, and assist them in carrying out sabotage against the enemy.

At the end of the briefing, we were given the start of a phrase the Maquis would use as their identification. Jack and I were to say the ending of the phrase which would identify us to the Maquis leader. Then, we were given another phrase to give only to the Maquis leader that neither Jack nor I knew what it meant.

Once the briefing was over, Jack and I were isolated in a small room. I sat down in an easy chair to relax. Jack began pacing back and forth in front of me. After a while, his pacing grated on my nerves, so I asked him to stop as a wall clock slowly ticked off the time.

"I can't," Jack snapped. "I always pace when I'm nervous."

"Just sit down and relax. There's nothing to worry about." Jack sat down for a moment, and then got up and resumed pacing. "For Christ's sake, Jack, you're making me nervous."

"Sorry, Dan. I can't help it. The last time I was this nervous was at my Senior Prom. I've always been nervous around girls, and I almost didn't go."

"Why did you?"

"My friends dared me to ask, Mabel Cross. The ugliest girl in school. I never passed on a dare, so I asked her. It was the worst time of my life. It wasn't her fault. She's really nice, but I couldn't stop fidgeting. Nearly passed out, I was so nervous."

"Jack, there aren't any girls in here."

"I know, but I can't stop thinking about John Stockton and that French fellow. I don't want to die."

"I don't want to die either."

"But what if something goes wrong? What if we're captured?"

"We won't be," I said.

"But what if we are? I don't want to be tortured by a God damn sadist."

"Don't worry, Jack. Everything'll go as planned. Before you know it, we'll be walking the streets of Paris, drunk with wine, as the bells of liberty ring across Europe."

"I don't know Dan. Hope you're right."

"I am. You'd think I was crazy if I told you how I know."

"I already know you're nuts. We're both are, so just tell me."

I stalled for a moment, and then said, "I had a dream. . ."

"What? A dream? You're crazier than I thought," Jack cried.

"Jack," I shouted, and then lowered my voice. "You asked."

He stopped pacing. "Sorry, Dan. . . What about your dream?"

"Well, it's a dream I've had many times since I was a child. A dream that always brought me discomfort. Every time it begins, I'm laying in mud. It's dark. Foggy. There's a shattered post with barbed wire attached to it. Bright flashes illuminate the horizon. The ground shakes. Men are crying. I can see a couple of them. I want to help, but my body won't move. That's when I see a figure. Cloaked in black. Moving slowly like a shadow across the bleak landscape. It stops at each man. Their cries cease until silence invades the landscape. I'm the only one left alive. Then, the figure comes toward me. Sort of kneels down a foot from my face. It stares into my eyes, but I can't see its face. I know I should be scared, but I'm not. I just lie there as serenity invades my body. Almost as if the world has come to a halt. Then, I wake up. . . Strange isn't it?"

Jack slumped into a chair and lowered his head. "You dreamed about death."

"Yeah. Up to a few weeks ago, I believed I did. Now, I know I dreamed of life."

"Life?"

"Yeah, life. The night after we learned of John Stockton's execution, I had the same dream. It went as it always had, except this time. After the figure kneeled in front of me, I didn't wake up. Instead, I laid there in the mud and watched the figure drift away. . . I was still alive."

Jack leaned back in his chair and sighed. "Your dream doesn't include me."

"Don't worry. You'll be with me, and therefore, you'll be safe too."

Jack didn't respond. He sat quietly, and I was glad he wasn't pacing anymore.

At 11 p.m. sharp, a young RAF lieutenant came into the room. "Make ready your gear and stand by," he ordered, and then left. We put on our jumpsuits over our French civilian clothes. Then, we checked and double checked our gear. Everything was in order. A half hour later, the RAF lieutenant escorted us to a Whitley bomber that had its engines running. Seven large cylinders filled with extra weapons and supplies were already loaded on the plane and strapped down. We were seated by the bombay doors. Then, at two minutes to midnight, the plane surged forward, picking up speed before lifting into the black sky. A little over an hour later, the bombay doors opened. The pilot circled a few times to find our drop zone. Then, without warning, the green light flashed. The seven cylinders were quickly pushed out of the plane. Then, I jumped. Two seconds later, Jack followed. Neither of us knew what danger lurked below.

8

*T*urbulence gripped my body. I nearly cracked my head on the edge of the bomb bay as I passed through. A second went by. Then, I jerked sideways. The harness tightened around my body as the chute mushroomed, instantly slowing my fall into the black abyss. A light rain pelted my face.

'*Where are the signal fires marking the drop zone? Is this the right place? Has our welcoming party been captured? Are German soldiers waiting for us?*' I wondered in the few seconds I fell through the sky. Then, I braced just in time for a landing that threw me hard on my left side. The parachute fell over me, entangling me in its cords. I panicked as I fought my way out of its binds. At any second I expected to hear a German voice ordering me to surrender. Yet, all I heard was a soft yelp as Jack landed on top of a hedgerow.

Within seconds, I was free from underneath my parachute and out of its harness. I laid down on the wet grass with the HiStandard pistol in my right hand. The Normandy countryside remained still. The sound of approaching soldiers never came. All I heard was Jack quietly wrestling to free himself from the hedgerow. We had arrived undetected in occupied France, and we were all alone. Our welcoming party was no where near.

A few moments went by until my eyes adjusted to the dim light of the stars poking through thin patches of cloudy sky. I was in the middle of a small field surrounded on all four sides by hedgerows. Jack was somewhere to the east. So, I gathered up my parachute, crouched over, and ran as silently as I could toward the hedgerow where he landed. When I was within a few yards of it, I softly announced myself. I wasn't about to come this far and get shot by my own partner. Luckily, he heard me in time and lowered his pistol. The silencer was already attached to his weapon, and I followed suit. My hands shook as I threaded the silencer onto the barrel.

"Where's the Maquis?" Jack whispered.

"Beats me," I whispered while my heart pounded out of my chest.

"Damn French. Always late for their own party," Jack joked.

"Maybe we're early?"

"We're probably late and they've gone home to bed," Jack said as he held his wristwatch close to his eyes to see the dial. "No, we're right on time, so where the hell are they?"

"Where are the signal fires? Why did the pilot give us the green light when the drop zone isn't even marked?"

"Good point," Jack conferred as he looked around.

Thanks to the genius of Q-Branch, the research and development branch of the SOE, the camouflaged jumpsuits came with a built-in shoulder holster, a waterproof canister to conceal an agents fake identity papers, and a pocket on the left pant leg which contained a small folding shovel. The purpose of the shovel was to bury the jumpsuit and parachute after landing, but Jack and I implemented ours only to bury our parachutes under the hedgerow. We still had to find and bury the seven cylinders of supplies and weapons that were dropped with us, so we kept our jumpsuits on to keep our French civilian clothes from getting dirty.

Once our parachutes were buried, we spread vegetation over the area to camouflage the disturbed dirt. Then, we headed west. Knowing dawn would break in a few hours, we searched for the cylinders as fast as we could. Fortunately, the first two were just on the other side of the western hedgerow. The next five were laying in a straight row in an open field on the other side of another hedgerow further to the west. Their parachutes fluttered in the breeze, making it easy for us to spot. Also making it easy for the Germans if they had spotted them first. Thus, ending our mission before it began.

Weighing close to 150 pounds apiece, Jack and I lugged the cylinders, one at a time, to a central spot we found in a dense grove of trees to the south. Then, after we removed the food and gear we needed, we dug a large hole and put the seven cylinders and their parachutes in it before filling the hole with dirt. I spread some vegetation over the disturbed ground to conceal our cache. Meanwhile, Jack hid his extra radio in an undisclosed location. Dawn broke by the time we were finished. The light rain raged into a downpour, soaking us clear to the bone.

"What now?" Jack asked while he picked up his suitcase with the other SSTR-1 radio inside.

"Let's get as far away from here as possible," I replied as I put on my pack.

Staying well hidden amongst the trees, we snuck southward. Putting as much distance as we could away from our cache. Our route gradually ascended up a small hill until the trees stopped at a thick hedgerow at the top. It was too tall to see over and too dense to see through, so we crept along its base until we came upon a small hole with an animal trail passing through it. Somehow, Jack managed to tear and claw his way inside. Five minutes later, he returned feet first. I had to pull on his ankles to help him the last few feet.

"Give me the map," he gasped.

I produced the waterproof map from my pack and gave it to him. Although, each of us had our own individual maps, they were a part of our escape and evasion kits that were sewn into the lining of our coats in the event of capture.

When Jack finally caught his breath, I asked him where we were. He didn't answer and kept turning the map around, trying to orientate it to the geographical features he saw on the other side of the hedgerow. After a few minutes, he used his compass to orientate the map to magnetic north. Then, he ran his index finger down a road drawn on the map, tapped a spot on the map twice, and then laid the map and compass in his lap. "We're a long way from home," was his only reply.

"What?" I asked while stealing the map from him. "Where are we?"

Jack pointed to a spot on the map where our drop zone was. Then, he moved his finger a short distance to where we actually landed. Finishing by tapping on a spot where we were at that moment.

"You sure?" I asked.

"Yeah."

"Can't be?" I used my finger as a ruler, checking the distance between our drop zone and our current position against the scale. "We're over twenty miles from where we're supposed to be."

"Just a stroll through the park," Jack stated dryly.

"Don't forget where we are," I barked in a low whisper. "We haven't rendezvoused with the Maquis? We haven't any idea where the Germans are. For all we know, they could be listening to us right now. . . "

"Easy boy," Jack interrupted. "Nobody knows we're here. The Germans aren't looking for us, and we're still alive. That's a pretty good outlook from my point of view. Remember back in jolly old England when I was nervous? Remember your dream?" Jack raised his arms over his head and looked up as the rain fell through the trees and pelted his face. "No need to get anxious on a lovely day like this."

I stared at him for a moment as the rain landed on his face and dripped off his chin. Then, I laughed. "You're right. We sure have lovely weather."

"And all day to enjoy it," Jack grinned.

Since, Jack still held the rank of Petty Officer Third Class due to a mix-up in his promotion, OSS Headquarters in London assigned me to lead the mission. Being in charge, I took the first six hour watch while he slept. Then, he took the next six hours, but four-and-a-half hours into my sleep, he nudged me awake while holding his hand over my mouth. For a few seconds all I could hear was the rain falling through the trees. Then, a dog growled from the other side of the hedgerow. I pulled my commando knife slowly from its sheath and waited for the fierce beast to come charging through the small hole. Jack held his HiStandard pistol with both hands and pointed its muzzle at the opening, poised for an attack as five long seconds slipped by. Then, to my relief and Jack's terror, a German soldier said, "Come on, Fritz. No time to chase foxes," as he pulled his reluctant guard dog away from the other side of the hedgerow only eight feet away.

Ten minutes passed before I finally relaxed and put my knife back in its sheath. In the dim light, I motioned for Jack to grab his gear, and then we crept toward the west. A few minutes later, I stopped under a low hanging branch of a fir tree and listened for the sound of approaching feet. Jack kneeled by my side. His ears tuned to the sounds of falling rain while his eyes scrutinized every nook and cranny. When I was confident we were alone, I put my mouth close to his ear and whispered, "What did you see on the other side of the hedgerow?"

Jack put his mouth up to my ear and answered, "Just a field with a road running through it about three hundred meters down the hill. There was a small cottage on the other side of the road, but it didn't look habitable."

"Could the Germans be using it as an outpost?"

"Definitely not. The roof's missing and one of the walls has been knocked down. If they're in there, then they're as miserable as we are."

"Could they be hiding somewhere close by?"

"No, everything was clear. Just fields and hedgerows."

I thought for a moment to put our situation in perspective. We were in a grove of trees on the eastern side of the small town of Mortain. As a crow flies, we had over twenty miles to travel to get to our rendezvous point with the Maquis. To get there we would have to cross fields and pastures, bypass a few small towns, and go over the Hills of Normandy. All the while trying to avoid the German patrols and local population. Until we met up with our contacts in the Maquis, we couldn't trust anyone.

"Should I radio London and give them a situation report?" Jack asked.

"No. Not until we know our exactly where we are and it's safe to transmit."

"All right, but the poor buggers are going to think we've been captured."

"I know, but I don't want to get their hopes up when we're still in danger."

Setting a course due north, we walked quietly through the silent countryside while keeping the town of Mortain to our left and the field we landed in the night before on our right. We skirted rolling pastures while the thought of stepping on a land mine kept our feet light and our minds focused. The Germans marked their mine fields with small signs warning people of the hidden danger, but in the dark of night, we were lucky if we could make out each others facial features from only a few feet away.

Livestock dotted the pastures. Every so often, we came to an abrupt halt when we spotted a sheep laying on the wet grass. It's funny how the woolly animals looked like kneeling German soldiers in the dim light. Once, I almost mistook a flock of sheep for a German patrol waiting to ambush us. Luckily, a lamb cried out and I relaxed the pressure I had on the trigger of my Stengun. I admit. I was scared, but I was under control. Those long months of training fashioned me into a confident soldier and spy. The perfect weapon for clandestine warfare, and I was beginning to enjoy my role.

An hour later, we reached the Hills of Normandy and stopped to rest at by a small, gentle flowing stream. The sound of the water reminded me of rain trickling down a drainpipe after a Boston storm, and for a few seconds, I wished I was back home with my wife.

"Should I radio London now?" Jack asked.

I looked at my watch. Although, it wasn't our scheduled transmission time, in our predicament, I didn't feel London would mind. "Make it quick," I said. Then, while Jack removed the radio and crystals from his suitcase, I opened two tin cans of mystery meat and gave one to Jack. At one time the meat might have been ham, but with its benign taste, I really couldn't tell. What ever it was, I really didn't care. Neither did Jack. For we were starving and ate the slimy substance with smiles on our faces.

In no time flat, Jack set up the radio. Using a predetermined code system, he added letters to some words and omitted some letters from other words. The theory behind the code was to inform London we were safe, and not captured. Jacks message was simple, *"Arrived safely. Wrong drop zone. Proceeding to rendezvous point.*"

London replied, "*Understand. Informing reception. Party waiting.*"

"Seems we're late for a party," Jack grinned as he removed the headset.

"Fashionably late," I replied.

Jack stowed the radio in his suitcase while I buried the empty tin cans. Then, we began our trek over the Hills of Normandy as rain fell heavily from the sky. Pelting our faces as we clawed our way up the slippery hillside while boulders and patches of dense vegetation hindered our ascent. We were miserable and all I could think about was curling up in a nice, dry, warm bed.

When the summit came into view, I sighed. At the same moment a man coughed. Jack and I froze. The man coughed again, and we quickly laid on the soggy ground with our weapons at the ready. Then, a dull glow from an oil lamp flashed across the hilltop as the coughing man entered a bunker only one hundred meters in front of us. In the brief moment of light, I saw the distinctive shape of two German helmets peeking over the top of a row of sandbags. My stomach tied itself into knots. Seconds ticked by. Minutes passed and we waited for the tiny muzzle flashes from German rifles. The volley of steel that would bring our lives to an end.

'*Did they see us? Are they waiting for us to move so they'll know our position,*' I wondered as I peered in the direction of our enemy. A part of me wanted to fire upon the bunker. Another part was gripped in fear. Goose bumps rose on my arms, and when Jack put his hand on my leg, I almost jumped out of my skin.

I stared at him. His face was taut. Fear beamed from his eyes. He glanced down the hill and I understood his wish. Silently, we slunk back, leaving our enemy to their own fate.

It was 5 a.m. when we finally made it to the northern base of the hill. Fog blanketed the valley. Dawn nipped at the horizon. We needed a hiding place to pass the day, so we spread out and searched. Jack found a small culvert running away from a dirt road with dense vegetation growing on both sides and two inches of water flooding the bottom. We sloshed our way seventy-five feet down the culvert until Jack stopped at a one foot by one foot hole in the vegetation on our left. He grinned, and then darted through the small opening. Seconds later, he poked his head out. "Come on in," he beckoned, and then disappeared back into the bushes. Reluctantly,

I followed, covering our tracks as I went.

Jack was sitting on his suitcase, grinning as I clawed my way into our hideout. "Well, what do you think?" He asked. "Sort of reminds me of a duck blind."

My eyes drifted around the three-by-four-foot natural opening in the vegetation. Thick, dark, green leaves and knotty roots surrounded us. The muddy ground squished beneath our feet. I stood and looked over the bushes. At full height, I could barely see over the top of them. The culvert ran north to south. We were on the west side of it and I could see a hedgerow a hundred meters in front of us to the north that ran east to west and then south from the eastern corner. Three large fir trees grew at the northwestern corner and grass filled in the empty spaces. The scene was one of tranquility in this war ravaged country that I was reluctant to call my new home. "Remind me never to go duck hunting," I replied as I sat down.

"What'd you expect? The Hilton?"

"No, but room service sounds good right about now."

Jack studied my face for a moment. "What's wrong, Dan? You've been edgy since we left England."

"I just miss my wife," I sighed. "I know I made the right choice to join the OSS. It's just when I think of my wife, I want to be back in Boston. Back in my old life, representing clients, eating fancy dinners, and loving my lovely Sarah."

"Don't worry, buddy, you're gonna make it through this."

"Oh, I know. With Sarah's love in my heart, I'll make it. I just miss her."

"I know what you mean. Mabel may have been the ugliest girl in school, but she was the nicest. Maybe I'll write her a letter when this is all over."

"You should do that. Nice girls are hard to find."

"Yeah. . . I'll write her. It'll be the first thing I do when I get back to England."

"Until then, we best keep our minds on the mission."

We ate more of our rations. Then, I took the first watch as Jack slept. In the cramped space he had to curl his legs up to his chest and rest his head on his suitcase. I kneeled next to him. My Stengun rested across his body, pointing toward the small opening. My ears tuned to the sounds around us.

When dawn broke, the rain stopped. The bushes kept us shadowed from the sun, so our clothes didn't have a chance to dry out. I was miserable and looked at Jack. He was smiling in his sleep.

Around 9 a.m. a low hum came out of the west, gradually growing to a rumble as it grew near. A crescendo of diesel engines, intermixed with the clamor of squeaking metal tracks, pierced the serene countryside. The ground began to shake, waking Jack from a deep sleep. Terror flashed from his eyes. Concern drawn upon his face.

"What is it?" Jack asked.

"Tanks," I replied. "Wait here."

"Where you going?"

"To take a peek," I stated and didn't wait for a response as I crawled through the small hole leading to the culvert. I kept myself hidden in the confines of the hole and looked toward the road. A German officer, sitting proudly in the turret of his Panzer, crept by, then another, and another. Trucks, some filled with infantry, others with supplies, and one marked with a Red Cross followed closely behind. Then finally, almost a half hour later, the last vehicle passed, and I crawled back into the hideout.

"Write this down," I ordered while I consulted our map.

Jack produced a piece of paper and a French fountain pen from his suitcase. "Ready when you are."

"Twenty-one tanks, thirty-six trucks carrying infantry, fourteen supply trucks, and one ambulance heading southeast from Vire to Flers at ten-miles-per-hour."

Jack snatched the map from my hand. "God damn it," Jack fumed while shaking his head from side to side.

"What?"

"We're still twenty miles from our rendezvous point."

"Radio London and give'em the convoy's make up and direction of travel."

Jack's eyes lit up. In no time he had the radio set up and the message sent. Then, a grin cut across his face. "Air Corps is diverting part of a bomber group from a mission over Germany. We should see them in a few minutes."

For the first time in our wartime careers, Jack and I witnessed actual combat. Seven minutes after Jack sent the message, five B-17 Bombers with an escort of eight P-48 Thunderbirds flew over our heads. Shortly after, the B-17s drop their payloads while the Thunderbirds warded off the attacking Me-109 Messerschmitts. From where we sat, we saw a spectacular display of aerial combat. I personally saw two Messerschmitts burst into flames. One of them exploded in mid-air. The other one landed well out of sight. Its pilot bailing out long before it crashed.

"Now there's a job for me," Jack said in awe.

"Not me. Too dangerous," I replied.

Jack lifted his eyebrows. "Too dangerous? Christ, Dan, forget where you are?"

"I feel safer down here. Get some sleep."

"I can't."

"I can't either," I confessed while both of us grinned like school boys peeking into the girls locker room.

9

Shortly after night fall, we left our hiding place. I took a compass reading and picked a prominent landmark in the direction we needed to travel. Then, we resumed our journey toward the rendezvous point. There were more pastures to skirt, more hedgerows to go over, through, or around, and more towns to stay clear of in our trek toward our destination. Once in a while a German armored transport or staff car with blackout lights slithered down a lone country road. With the increased daylight bombing raids they felt safer traveling at night. Very seldom did they dare muster into convoys and travel in the brightness of day. Our bombing raid earlier was a testament as to why.

Two miles due west of Le Beny Bocage, Jack and I crept down a culvert toward a road a hundred meters ahead when the sound of an engine hummed from the south. We laid down in the soggy mud to wait until the car went by. A minute later when the car came abreast of the culvert, the earth crumpled. The car burst into flames. Exploding with a force that blew the front end up in the air, toppling it backward until the car lay upside down, killing all of its occupants upon impact.

Since, I was staring at the car when it exploded, the sudden, intense light temporarily blinded me. Fortunately, Jack had closed his eyes. For he still had his night vision to see the two dark silhouettes approaching rapidly from the road.

"Halt," Jack yelled in French. The two men froze and raised their hands.

"Don't shoot. They could be friendly," I said in French while blinking the sight back into my eyes.

"Drop your weapons," A deep French voice calmly ordered from behind us.

My body tensed as the Stengun fell from my fingers. Then, I raised my hands and slowly turned around. The dark silhouette of a third man was crouched ten paces from me. He had a rifle in his hands with its muzzle pointing at my chest. Somehow, Jack and I had missed him on our way toward the road.

The two men who blew up the car kept their hands up. Jack nervously covered them with the muzzle of his Stengun. Imminent death hung in the air. At any second, I expected my life to abruptly slip away as time came to a halt.

All five of us were allies. Joined together in the fight against Nazi Germany, but trust didn't come easy in this part of the world. For all the Frenchmen knew, Jack and I could be German agents posing as British airmen shot down during a recent air raid. As for myself, under the present circumstances, I knew convincing the three Frenchmen of our allegiance wouldn't be easy. My mind raced to find a solution. Then, it occurred to me. We were all speaking French.

"We're definitely not in London, my dear Watson," I said in English.

"Indeed, we're not mister Holmes," Jack replied in English, following my lead.

"English?" The man with the rifle asked. He was middle-aged with a medium build, shoulder length black hair, and a full mustache that he kept neatly cropped at the edges of his mouth.

"American," I quickly replied.

The man relaxed his grip on the rifle. "Drop your weapons and follow me," he ordered.

Jack let his Stengun fall to his feet. Then, he raised his hands and slowly turned around. We still had our HiStandard pistols and commando knives concealed in our jumpsuits, and neither of us was about to give them up. A small consolation when fate sways in the wind of uncertainty.

Keeping our hands in the air, Jack and I followed the man armed with the rifle further away from the road. The two saboteurs picked up our Stenguns and Jack's suitcase, and followed close behind. Cold perspiration dripped from my chin.

We got fifty meters deeper into the countryside when a German armored transport barreled down the road toward the burning staff car. "Run," one of the men behind us yelled.

Never before or after have I ran as fast as I did on that night. All five of us raced down a culvert that abruptly stopped at a hedgerow. In full stride the man with the rifle dove over the top, disappearing in an instant. Jack and I followed suit and landed hard on the other side. I quickly rolled to my right as Jack's suitcase appeared in mid-air, landing where my head had been a second earlier. Then, the last two men tumbled over.

Shots erupted from the road. Bullets sliced through the hedgerow and whizzed by my body. Some of them struck the ground around me. "This way," the man with the rifle cried. The rest of us quickly got to our hands and knees and crawled after him. Thirty meters later we fell into the bottom of a deeper culvert. At that instant a German MG42 machine gun began raking back and forth along the hedgerow. The fierce volley of steel flew over our heads as we hugged the sludge at the bottom of the culvert.

It was a standard German tactic to shoot into a hedgerow to flush out the Maquis. Most of the time they were successful as the fleeing Maquisards got to their feet only to be ripped to shreds. Lucky for us, the Maquis group we stumbled upon knew the tactic and stayed frozen in place. Jack and I stayed solely because it was our only option.

When the machine gun fire swept away from us, the man with the rifle ordered us to run. I didn't need any coaxing and ran hunched over with the group. In a flash the Germans trained their fire on us. Bullets popped into the dirt on all sides of me, and I remember thinking how they sounded like a hoard of bees, yet, I knew their sting was much more deadly.

Near the end of the pasture the man with the rifle ran up the side of the culvert and disappeared through a small opening in the hedgerow on our right. Everyone else quickly followed as the din of the machine gun grew dim and dimmer.

We ran in a northeasterly direction, skirting pastures, running beside hedgerows, and through fields until we stopped deep in the countryside at a small cottage with a slate roof and chipped whitewashed walls. All of us panted for air as our hearts raced with adrenaline.

"Who are you?" The man with the rifle asked us again.

"Americans," I replied.

"Pilots?"

"Yes," Jack lied.

The two men who had blown up the German staff car eased their trigger fingers. I couldn't make out their faces in the coal black night. All I could tell was that one man was taller than the other by a full foot.

The man with the rifle ordered his two saboteurs to search us. The shorter man had Jack and I face the cottage with our hands on our heads. It was apparent that he had other talents than just blowing up cars. For in a few seconds he found our hidden pistols, extra ammunition, and commando knives. He also found the hidden compasses in the buttons of our coats. After that, the man with the rifle disappeared into the cottage while Jack and I nervously waited in front of the muzzles of our own Stenguns.

A few minutes later the man with the rifle returned with an old woman in her early sixties. She was short with graying hair and hunched over shoulders. Her face was set firm. Years of hard labor in the fields and the German occupation had taken their toll on her body. However; she still possessed the vitality of a young girl. "Bring them inside," she ordered.

I was prodded in the back with the barrel of my own Stengun as I went into the cottage. Consisting of two small bedrooms on one side and a kitchen spanning the entire other half, it came as no surprise that the cottage was sparsely furnished and immaculately clean. The kitchen had a few pots and pans, and cooking utensils hanging on the wall over a wood stove. Lining the inside wall was a small porcelain wash basin, food preparation table, and a hutch with its doors missing revealing two plates and three cups. A dining table with two chairs sat in a far corner of the room. An oil painting of a bowl of fruit hung above it. Two windows, one by the wood stove and the other next to the painting, were blacked out with heavy blankets.

The bedrooms themselves were also sparsely furnished. One of them had only a bed frame without a mattress. A broom stood in the corner. The other room had a small bed piled high with quilts, and a small wardrobe. A worn rug covered the entire floor except where it was pulled back in the corner, revealing a trap door.

The taller of the two saboteurs dropped through the trap door first. Jack and I were forced to go next, followed by the shorter saboteur, our backpacks, and Jack's suitcase. Then, the trap door closed. The rug was pushed over our only exit, and then the wardrobe, completely sealing us off from the outside world. We were being held captive by the people we were sent to help, and I knew this ordeal would have been avoided if we had only landed at our drop zone.

The secret room, constructed around the turn-of-the-century, was once utilized by the old woman's deceased husband as a repository for the spoils of his illicit trade. Now it was a makeshift hideout for downed allied flyers. A charade that Jack and I were desperately trying to sell.

The room itself was the size of the bedroom above, and barely tall enough for an average sized man to stand at full height. There were two buckets, one filled with drinking water and the other used for excrement, on the wood planked floor close to the trap door. A goose down mattress with a slight musty smell lay in the far corner of the room. On top of it was a ratty old blanket that looked like a dead animal in the pale yellow light flickering from an oil lamp.

Jack and I were ordered to sit on the mattress while the two men sat against the wall across from us. They rested the Stenguns across their laps and kept the muzzles trained in our direction. Neither of them spoke. In the dim light, I could finally make out their faces. The shorter man had black hair, neatly cropped above the shoulders, and bushy eyebrows. He was middle-aged with a stare that cut like ice and boredom written on his face. In contrast, the taller man wore a constant, crooked smile. He was much younger, about seventeen, and stood over six feet tall. His lanky body and long neck moved with an assured clumsiness that I've never witnessed before. Almost as if he suffered from a slight retardation of his motor skills.

Within minutes, Jack fell fast asleep. I tried to fight my fatigue, but soon after, I too closed my eyes as my mind drifted far away. I dreamed I was at my wedding, but it wasn't Sarah who stood next to me at the altar. She sat in the first pew with tears streaming down her cheeks as I said, "I do," to a woman from somewhere in my past, but from where I could not remember.

The lanky man shook me awake. For a few seconds, I thought I was still dreaming. That, I had fallen asleep after the wedding and was now engulfed in a nightmare. Then, I realized that I'd returned to reality and sat up and rubbed my eyes.

"Good morning my friend," Jack said in English.

"Quiet!" A woman's voice ordered in French.

I looked to the other side of the room. Four sets of eyes stared back at me. Two sets belonged to the two saboteurs. Their faces alight with excitement. The third set came from the man with the rifle who seemed bored. The fourth set of eyes beamed from a tall, middle-aged woman with a Luger pistol held steadily in her right hand. She was clad in black clothing and leather boots. An olive drab satchel hung lazily from a brown leather strap slung across her chest. Short, strawberry blond hair peeked from beneath her black beret, highlighting her rosy cheeks and pale skinned face. A stark contrast to her steel blue eyes that sent a chill through my bones.

"Who are you?" She asked in English.

"American pilots," Jack lied again. "We were shot down four days ago."

"I don't believe you. If that were true, you wouldn't be wearing French boots and carrying a radio," She snapped.

I swallowed the lump in my throat. The cover story Jack and I hastily constructed was doomed from the start. For our combined knowledge of aviation was slightly more than a school boy's fantasy. Furthermore, the state of our appearance, and our confiscated equipment rightfully identified who we really were. There wasn't a soul in the room who didn't know we were spies, but which side we were spying for remained a mystery to our captors. No one spoke. Tension hovered in the still air like fog on a moonlit beach. Perspiration formed on my forehead. Then, after what felt like an eternity, the woman said, "Paris is warm in the winter."

Jack and I stared at each other. The biggest grin filled Jack's face as our eyes lit up. "And wet in the summer," we both replied simultaneously, finishing the woman's sentence. Everyone in the room exhaled. The woman had given the correct beginning of the password phrase, and we correctly finished it. Somehow, either by chance or by fate, we were finally with the very same Maquis we were sent to rendezvous with.

The Maquisards lowered their weapons. "I'm Aimee," the woman said as she shook our hands. "That's Francois and Yves," she added while pointing at the two saboteurs. Francois was the tall, lanky fellow with the crooked smile. Yves had the bushy eyebrows.

"This is Stephan Le Perrier, and I'm Marcel Le Bon," I said, introducing Jack and I under our cover names.

The man armed with the rifle leaned it against the wall, and then approached us. "Welcome my friends. I'm Simon," he said, and then gave me a kiss on each cheek before repeating the customary French greeting with Jack.

From the moment, I met him, I could tell Simon had a colorful past. Later on, I learned he was born of unwed parents. His father he never knew. His mother committed suicide when he was five, so he was sent kicking and screaming to an orphanage in the heart of Lyon's slums. Ridiculed by his fellow orphans, scorned by the clergy, corporal punishment fell easily on his young body.

Although, he suffered many years under the hand of religion, Simon's tarnished soul never broke. His spirit never waned. At the age of fifteen he fled his life and lied about his age to get into the French army during the last year of the, 'Great War.' Because of his youthful appearance, he was assigned kitchen duties and spent the rest of the war spooning slop into the dirty cups of battle weary veterans. It was a job he hated, but anything was better than his life at the orphanage.

When the war ended, Simon deserted, changed his name, and joined the French Foreign Legion where he stayed until the German Blitzkrieg of

1940 crushed his battalion. He found himself stranded behind enemy lines as the Allied armies collapsed and hastily retreated toward Dunkirk. A month later, he joined the Maquis, who gave him another name and identity papers forged from copying existing documents. Shortly thereafter, the Germans forced him into conscripted labor and sent him to Germany to work in a steel factory. He purposely performed poorly in every duty the Germans assigned. Six months later they were more than glad to return him to France. A very unwise decision, for Simon was highly trained in demolitions and a perfectionist in the art of sabotage. His hatred for the German race ran deep, and I could tell out of all of them, he enjoyed killing them the most.

After the introductions, our weapons and gear were returned to us. Aimee apologized for the treatment we received up until then, making it clear that they had to be very cautious to protect the secrecy of their group. Jack and I understood and accepted her apology. Then, she told us to remove our jumpsuits which we were more than glad to get rid of. Yves took the jumpsuits and left the hideout to bury them in a safe place far away from the cottage.

A little while later, the old woman served a hearty meal. The kind of meal I couldn't find in Boston. For the portions were much larger and the pretentiousness found in American French restaurants was nonexistent. Needless to say, I felt like a happy, contented, stuffed pig, and all I wanted to do was lay back down on that musty mattress and take a nap, but it was time to get down to business. It was time to begin the job Jack and I were sent to do.

"We have to get to Saint Lo," I said.

"Impossible! The Boche are searching the entire city," Simon said, referring to the Germans by the derogatory French term. "All Maquis have been warned to stay away."

"We'll take our chance," Jack stated.

"It's suicide?" Aimee snapped.

"We have to find a man named, Blossom," I said.

"Impossible!" Simon reiterated. "The Boche arrested him the day after you were supposed to arrive. They already have him in Paris."

"Stop," Aimee growled. "There'll be no more talking of Blossom. His fate is now in the hands of God."

"Will he talk?" Jack asked.

"No," Simon replied.

"Are you sure?" I asked.

Aimee cut through me with her steel blue eyes. "He won't talk. The Boche murdered his wife and son, my husband," she said through clenched teeth.

The room fell silent. My mind took a step back. A part of me aged a thousand years as the sorrow, the agony, the never ending pain I've carried since my mother died fell over me like an iron blanket. The other part of me remained a boy.

"Who's taken over Blossom's command?" Jack asked, long after the silence became too unbearable for all in the room.

"I have, although our numbers have diminished," Aimee answered. "Most men won't serve under a woman, so they've joined other groups. These men and twelve others are all that remain."

"Why not give the command over to a man?" I asked.

"Blossom's orders," Aimee replied.

"She was his adjutant before he was arrested," Yves said. How he returned to the small room unnoticed, I'll never know.

"Aimee's strong. A fierce fighter. Very capable of leading us to victory," Simon added and I could tell his praise hinted at more than mere admiration.

Even though, Jack and I grew up in male dominated societies, he was more willing to accept the fact that we would be working with a Maquis group led by a woman. Most likely, his acceptance stemmed from growing up with a mother who ran her own business. I, on the other hand, had never been exposed to a female leader. As such, I was reluctant until I witnessed her ability to lead. My only solace was knowing Jack and I took our orders directly from London, at least for now.

"I'll have to radio London and inform them of Blossom's arrest," Jack said, and then he looked at his watch. "Is it day or night?"

"Night," Francois answered. Somehow he never stopped smiling. Even while he spoke.

"Good. That gives us a little over three hours until I have to make contact," Jack announced. Then, he plopped down on the mattress.

Our scheduled transmission time was 11:10 p.m. With all the radio traffic filling the airwaves, each radio operator was designated a set time to contact Bletchley Park, the secret communication center ran by British Intelligence. Home to all European theater allied intelligence communications networks, Bletchley Park was the medium used to send and receive most of the radio traffic to and from Nazi occupied Europe. Since we dealt with OSS headquarters in London, we were honored to have their expertise in relaying our transmissions.

For the next few hours, I passed the time by cleaning my weapons and quizzing Aimee on the enemy strength in the area, their defenses, and the local attitude toward the German army and the occupation. Jack passed the time by cleaning his weapons and the radio. Since, Yves and Francois didn't have firearms, he taught them how to dismantle, reassemble, load and fire the MkII Stengun. Without actually firing a live round, at the end of his short training session, I believe they grasped the basics.

At 10 p.m. sharp, we left the cottage. I was glad to be in the fresh air again. Something about living under a house just wasn't that appealing.

Yves led us a mile deep into the countryside to a wooded area about five hundred feet from a dirt road where the rest of Aimee's group were assembled. Only seven of them were armed with either a rifle or a hand gun. The rest carried a various assortment of farming equipment and axes. One woman carried a butcher knife. Since Jack had given Yves and Francois basic instruction in the use of the Stengun, we let them borrow ours, keeping the HiStandard pistols for ourselves.

Aimee did an impressive job in splitting up her small unit into groups of two's and strategically placing them in a circle around our perimeter for security. In the center of the circle Jack set up his radio in total darkness as Aimee, Simon and I hovered close by. If we were attacked by a German patrol, we could help Jack pick up the pieces of his radio and escape.

According to Simon, half of the German occupation forces in France were old and worn out. The rest were either recuperating from wounds received on the eastern front, or members of elite units. Almost all of them were seasoned veterans filled with pride. Having sharpened their deadly skills in the deserts of North Africa, the green fields of Italy, or the snowy plains of the Russian frontier, they were experts in the art of killing. Professionals at attacking their prey, beating it into submission, and then stomping over it as they searched out their next victim. However, being a large force relying on conventional tactics and armor, the mighty Nazi war machine proved inept at countering the unconventional warfare of the Maquis. Outnumbered and under equipped, the Maquis effectively utilized all means available to wreck havoc on the German occupiers, causing great strain on the German high command. It was a classic example of the Samson and Goliath tale, and as I sat next to Aimee in the complete darkness of night while Jack tapped out a message to London, I was glad to be on the winning side.

"Madam, there are two trucks coming this way," a female voice whispered out of the darkness. I nearly jumped out of my skin at the sound of her voice.

"From which direction?" Aimee asked.

"Northwest," the woman replied.

"Show me," Simon ordered.

"I'm going too," I stated as Simon stood to follow the woman.

"Wait," Aimee whispered. She paused for a second to consider her options for the group. In the meantime, Jack was quickly dismantling the radio and stuffing it into his suitcase. "If there's trouble, rendezvous back at the cottage," Aimee said, and then she put her hand on Simon's forearm. "Be careful!"

"I will, mon Cheri," Simon said. Then, he and I quickly followed the woman back to the place where she spotted the two trucks. They were parked in a field about two hundred meters to our left. In front of them, German soldiers slowly advanced toward us.

Simon ordered the woman and her cohort to warn the others. Then, he released the safety on his rifle and laid down under a thick hedge. I laid down by his right side and cocked my pistol. Adrenaline raced through my body. I was both intensely excited and scared at the same time.

"Don't fire. They'll see your muzzle flash," Simon warned. What he didn't know was that the HiStandard pistol didn't produce a muzzle flash when the silencer was attached, even in complete darkness.

When the soldiers had advanced to within one hundred meters of the tree line, Simon tapped me on the shoulder. "Look there," he whispered. I turned my head and saw two more trucks sitting in the field far to our right. For a brief moment, I thought they had just arrived. Then, two rifle shots rang out from the trees on our left and I said a quick prayer to Sarah.

10

*T*he tree line erupted with Stengun and sporadic rifle fire. The Germans shot back like fireflies dancing on a hot summers night as they leap-frogged closer to our position while a machine gun raked hot lead over their heads.

Taking careful aim, Simon squeezed the trigger. The sound of his rifle was deafening. The machine gun fell silent. A group of four German soldiers turned their advance toward Simon's muzzle flash. Bullets sliced through the bushes and slammed into the ground around us as two soldiers fired while the other two advanced.

Simon fired again, sending an advancing soldier crumpling to the ground. "Get back," he ordered over the din. Instantly, he left my side and disappeared deeper into the trees. A split-second later, I was hot on his heels, racing blindly down a trail through the darkness, hunched over as bullets whizzed by my head.

On our right a Schmeiser submachine gun barked. I dove for cover behind a tree. Simon kept running. In an instant, I was alone with German soldiers closing in from my rear and from my right. I leaned against a tree trunk and fired two consecutive shots at a German helmet only ten feet away. The soldier yelped as he fell backward. Dead before his body hit the ground. Then, I turned to the approaching rifle fire coming from behind. Emptying my pistol magazine as I displaced to a clump of small bushes to reload. Two more soldiers appeared. Again, I emptied my magazine and they fell to the earth. My world was in chaos.

Having spent my last bullet on the two soldiers, I tucked the pistol into my waistband and pulled the commando knife from its sheath. I planned to recover a rifle and ammunition from one of the dead soldiers, and then flee. Though, as I poised to move, a figure ran down the trail and tripped over one of the corpses. Hurling myself over the top of the small bushes, I fell on top of him. My knife pierced his chest as he fought to escape. Even with my knife buried deep in his chest, he screamed and fought like a rabid animal.

I stabbed him a few more times until his form remained still. Air and blood bubbled from his wounds and gurgled from his lips. I covered his mouth with my free hand. His warn blood flowed through my fingers as his last breath escaped his lungs. Then, he began to twitch as his nerves fought one last gallant battle for life. I held on until his body shook itself still. Then, I withdrew my knife from the dead man's chest and cut a shoulder strap from his tunic before rolling away and vomiting as the battle raged around me.

It's sobering to kill another man. To know you tore the life from another human being. A man, like myself, who had a family and friends. People who loved him, and who he loved. To this day, I've often wondered who he was and what he was like. Sometimes, I wonder if he and I would've been friends under different circumstances. Yet, I know it's futile to have such thoughts. I have no regrets for killing him. We were enemies. Engaged in the art of war where some men die, and the survivors carry their deaths forever etched upon their hearts.

The gunfire died down. Now only single rifle shots cried through the night, followed by long pauses of silence before other shots rang out. I was still lying by my victim when I heard footsteps cautiously coming my way. The Germans were making one final sweep through the trees and I had no intention of sticking around. I cut the cartridge belt from my victims waist before returning my knife to its sheath. Then, I picked up two rifles from the dead soldiers I had killed and quietly made my way toward the tree line.

When I came to the edge of a field, I stayed just inside the trees and fled south. A few hours later, having traveled a little over two kilometers, I came to a small ravine with a stream flowing down the middle. Heavy vegetation and trees covered the sides and formed a natural canopy. '*A good place to rest,*' I thought as I slid down the gentle slope into the ravine.

"Nice to see you again, my friend," a voice said from the bushes on my right.

I froze. Suddenly, I realized it was Simon who spoke to me. He was with a woman named Margot. The same woman armed with the butcher knife and it was stained with blood. Proof that her hatred for the German race ran deep.

A scar ran from Margot's right cheek bone down to the edge of her mouth. In the dim light it looked like she had an evil grin. Standing five-foot-four-inches tall, her thirty-year-old body was as thin as a waif, making it hard to fathom her engaged in hand-to-hand combat with a man twice her size.

"Traitor," Margot spat.

"Traitor?" I wondered.

"No, he's not, Margot. He's our friend. Come to help kill the Boche," Simon said.

"How else would the Boche know where we were? Since this man and his friend arrived, Blossom's been captured. The Maquis has split up, and now this. We can't trust him."

"Impossible. He doesn't know who Blossom is," Simon pled.

Margot pointed her butcher knife at me. "He's a spy. His friend called the Boche on the radio and told them where to find us. Jean-Luc is dead because of them."

"They've been heavily guarded since we found them. Tonight, Stephan was not on the radio long enough to alert the Boche. He didn't know where we were if he had. They can't be traitors." Simon motioned for me to step forward. I did, though, I kept my distance from Margot. "Look at his clothes," Simon continued. "They're stained with blood. Boche blood."

"Margot. Simon's telling the truth," I said. "The ambush was just as much of a surprise to me as it was to you. I swear to it."

"I don't believe you," Margot growled.

"Please, Margot," Simon pled.

I held one of the German rifles in front of me with the muzzle pointed at my chest. "Take it. If you believe I'm a spy, then shoot me."

Simon's eyes opened wide as he stared from Margot to me, and then back to Margot. My heart pounded as she grasped the rifle.

"Don't shoot him," Simon begged.

I was petrified and said a prayer to Sarah. My life passed before my eyes in the few seconds Margot kept the rifle pointed at my chest. I waited for the sound of the muzzle blast. The pain as a bullet tore through my chest. The split-second that would take me from the living and deliver me to the dead. Then, suddenly, Margot threw the rifle at my feet. "I still believe you're a traitor, but I won't shoot you until I know for sure."

"Thank you, Margot. Thank you," Simon's voice cracked.

I let out a sigh of relief as I held out the other rifle. "Take this. It's better than your knife." Margot glared at me as she freed the rifle from my shaking hands.

"Good. Now we go. By morning the Boche will be searching the whole countryside for us," Simon said. Then, he walked deeper into the ravine. I divvied up the rifle ammunition and gave half to Margot. Then, I followed Simon. Margot kept her distance. Her cold stare raised the hair on the back of my neck.

Needing to put as much distance as possible between us and the place of the attack, we left the ravine and skirted its edge for two kilometers before reentering the ravine and stopping for a rest. I washed the blood from my hands and drank a gallon of water before we continued. No one spoke. About a half mile northeast of the small town of Vassy, Margot led us through a tall hedgerow into a small field dotted with hay stacks. She stashed her rifle and ammunition into one of them, and then stared at Simon and I. We stared at her blood stained butcher knife tucked into her belt. "Well, hide your weapons," she snapped.

Simon looked at me. I could tell by the look on his face that he was thinking the same thought I was. Neither of us liked the idea of being unarmed in unknown territory. Defenseless to fight our enemy scouring the countryside in search of us and all those who remained alive after last nights battle. Yet, I needed Margot to trust me, so, I shrugged my shoulders and pushed my weapons deep into the damp hay. Simon reluctantly did the same as Margot stomped away.

She was halfway across the field, heading toward a white farmhouse with a slate roof by the time we finished hiding our weapons. We ran to catch up to her. The scowl on her face clearly showed I was an unwelcome companion.

We went through a wooden gate that opened to the backyard of the house. An elderly woman dressed in a smoke grey skirt and purple sweater turned in our direction as we approached. Her eyes squinted, and then lit up when she saw Margot.

"Grandma," Margot sang. Simon and I looked at each other, and then to Margot and Annette, Margot's grandmother.

"Margot, my dear, I'm surprised. . . " Annette said, stopping in mid-sentence when she noticed the stains on our clothes were from dried blood. Her smile dissipated. Her shoulders shrugged. "Are you hurt?"

"No, Grandma, this is Boche blood," Margot triumphantly replied.

Annette scanned our faces for a moment. Then, she grabbed Margot's arm and began to pull. "You must come inside. All of you. Quickly before someone sees you."

We followed Annette into the house. The kitchen was on our right with an L-shaped counter running down the north and east walls. Two windows, one on the north wall next to the wood stove and the other on the east wall over a large porcelain sink, were both covered with white chiffon curtains. Two heavy, black wool blankets utilized to cover the windows at night were neatly folded on the kitchen counter next to the sink. The pantry was in the northwest corner of the kitchen. To the left of it was a stairway leading upstairs to four small bedrooms. Directly in front of us was a harvest table with six ladder-back chairs hindering a straight passage to a cramped hallway that led to two more bedrooms on the ground floor.

On our left was the living room. In the near corner was a small desk. A bronze Victorian lamp with a light blue lamp shade stood next to it. A bay window in the south wall had its white chiffon curtains pulled back, revealing a two foot high stone wall separating the small front yard from a dirt road.

A small fire glowed from a whitewashed brick fireplace imbedded in the west wall of the living room where, Pierre, an elderly man with ash white hair and strong shoulders stirred the contents of a cast iron pot suspended above the yellow flame. He turned and stared. Then, his eyes opened wide when he caught sight of his granddaughter. "Margot," he announced, loud enough for all of France to hear, causing another man, Margot's father, Jean to rise from one of the two easy chairs facing the fireplace.

Jean steadied himself with the aid of a cane. His left arm was missing above the elbow. Small, quarter inch scars peppered the left side of his cheek and neck. A wreck of a man, or so I would have thought if it hadn't been for his deep blue eyes. For they danced with life and were void of defeat. A brightness I had never seen before, nor since.

"Bon jour, Papa," Margot said as she embraced her father and kissed both of his cheeks.

"Bon jour, my dear. It's good of you to come, but why are you here?" Jean asked.

"The Boche. They burned down the school," Margot replied.

"All the Boche know how to do is destroy," Pierre growled. Then, he looked in my direction. "Who are your friends?"

Simon and I were introduced with the customary embrace and a kiss on both cheeks. Relief washed over me as I realized Margot's family quickly warmed up to Simon and I. Yet, I remained cautious in Margot's presence.

"Father, we need a change of clothes and a place to rest," Margot said.

Jean looked us up and down. He frowned for a moment, and then his smile returned brighter than before. "You're Maquis," He proudly announced.

"Oh, dear," Annette sighed.

"Hush woman," Pierre jowled. "Bring them food and some clean clothes to wear."

Annette quickly left the room.

"I'm afraid for you, but I'm also proud," Jean said, brushing Margot's hair from her face.

"You should be, monsieur," Simon said. "She's a fierce fighter."

"And trustworthy," I chimed. The contemptuous look on Margot's face closed my mouth.

"Of course she's trustworthy," Pierre snapped.

"After the pain she's suffered at the hands of the Boche, you would be too," Jean added. "Did she tell you how she got the scar?"

"Papa don't," Margot screamed. Then, she ran out of the house as Annette returned with an arm full of clothes and dropped them in the chair Jean had been sitting in.

"You know better than to bring up her past in the company of strangers," Annette snarled.

"Sorry gentlemen," Jean said as Annette left the house. "It was wrong of me to bring it up."

"No apology necessary," I replied.

"Jean tell them how she got the scar," Pierre said from where he stood by the fireplace.

"It's none of our business," Simon replied for the both of us.

Pierre stared at Jean. "I don't want her to fight any more than you do, but if we want her to be whole again, these men must know her past. They'll fight harder. With more passion. They'll keep our little girl safe."

"Very well," Jean sighed. He hobbled between Simon and I, and sat at the dining table. "Please, sit down gentlemen. I trust neither of you will speak to Margot about what I'm going to tell you."

Simon agreed for the both of us as we sat at the table on both sides of Jean while Pierre hovered by the fireplace. Tension grew in the room, and I confess, I didn't want to hear about Margot's past without her permission. I was dropped into France to garner information and conduct sabotage and subversion operations against the Germans. For my job to be successful, I had to stay objective. However, what Jean told us forever changed my view of Hitler and his army of death.

"In 1937, Margot met Paul Wiesse in Paris," Jean began. "She was young. Barely twenty-three. Paul was a few years older. Very good people,

Paul and his parents. . .They were Jews. . .In 1938, Margot and Paul married. Uncommon, I assure you. A Catholic and Jew getting married, but I gave them my blessing. God's love covers all religions, and as I said, Paul was a good man."

"Tell them what they need to know," Pierre said softly from the fireplace.

Jean glanced at Pierre, and then lowered his eyes to his right hand fidgeting on the table. "In spring of 1940, Margot got pregnant. A month later, the Boche came. Within weeks France fell. The Jews were ordered to board trains bound for Germany. Some fled to other countries. Others were abducted."

Jean paused for a moment to steady the anger rising within his soul before he continued. "Margot came home late the day Paul was taken. She found the word '*Juden*' scribbled on the kitchen wall. There were blood stains on the floor. She panicked and went to the police station to find out what happened to her husband. The police told her they would check and return him when he was found. That night she was arrested by the Gestapo. . ."

"They took her to a pasture outside of Paris," Pierre cut in. "Paul was there along with five other Jews. They were handcuffed together. A Nazi bastard ordered Paul and the other Jews to stand side by side."

"One by one, the officer shot all of them," Jean said, lifting his eyes off the table. "They murdered Paul and the others as Margot was forced to watch. Then, the Boche raped her. Repeatedly. The bastards sliced her face open when they were finished. She was beaten to within moments of her life. . ."

"They threw her on the pile of dead Jews," Pierre growled.

Jean lowered his eyes. "The next morning a farmer found the bodies. Margot was barely alive." Jean looked up. "It's a miracle she survived."

"The farmer took her to a doctor. It took her over two months to recover," Pierre said.

"She lost her child and will never be able to conceive another. . . Since then, my daughter hasn't been the same. Her hatred for the Boche is too great. Now that she is Maquis, I hope she'll lose the hatred that eats at her soul. Maybe if she kills enough Nazis, she'll become my loving daughter again. That's why I tell you her story. So you can look after her and bring her home safely after the war is over."

"Father, that's not the only reason I fight," Margot said from the front doorway. "I fight, like you did, to rid France of the Boche."

"One question," Simon said. "How did you join the Maquis?"

"Blossom," Margot said. Then, she stomped over to the table and sat down. "His men smuggled me out of Paris and brought me to Saint Lo. I taught at Saint Michelle's as a cover since the Boche seldom suspect women of being Maquis. The fools. Stupid, stupid fools. We're just as good at killing them as any man."

"Why aren't you still in Saint Lo?" I asked.

Margot glared at me. "Ten days ago that monster who murdered my husband came to Saint Lo. Because of the scar he gave me, Blossom feared for my safety and hid me until he could get me out of the city. I was still hiding when the bastard heard I taught at Saint Michelle's and came looking for me. When he couldn't find me, his men burned down the school the night before you and your friend came to France, only you didn't land where you were supposed to."

All eyes in the room turned in my direction, so I told them everything that happened up until the time Jack and I ran into Simon and his sabotage party. In the end, everyone was satisfied with my story, except for Margot. She still didn't trust me, but the pendulum was about to swing in my favor.

"So, are you French?" Annette asked.

"No."

"English then?" Pierre asked.

"Actually, I'm American," I replied. The room let out a sigh.

"Then you can help us?" Pierre asked.

"That's why I'm here," I answered.

"My father means you can help us right now," Jean said while leaning back in his chair.

"I don't understand."

"We need you to talk to someone for us," Annette said as she sat at the table. "Will you help us?"

"I'd be honored, but I need to know who it is first," I said with a hint of irritation seeping from the sides of my mouth.

Jean leaned toward Margot. "Get your niece. She's asleep upstairs."

"No, I'm not, Grandpapa," a young girl said as she raced down the stairs and stopped next to Jean. "Shall, I go fetch him?"

My eyes focused on the girl. She was about ten years old with aqua blue eyes and long auburn hair tied in a ponytail that fell over her left shoulder and danced upon her chest. For a dainty thing, she was full of awe and energy. Every new experience was an adventure she embarked upon with the determination only a child could possess.

"Yes, Claire, bring the gentleman," Jean said while petting the young girls head.

Claire dashed across the room and out the front door. Annette and Pierre followed her while the rest of us waited for the man they would bring. I secretly hoped it was Jack, but knew it couldn't be. For who ever it was, I knew he didn't speak a word of French.

11

*T*wo minutes went by. Margot grew impatient and fidgeted in her chair. At length, she got up and went to the kitchen counter and stared out the window. Her right hand clenched the butcher knife tucked in her belt. Her knuckles turned white from the grip she had on its handle.

Two figures, one shorter than the other, darted past the window. Margot's chest heaved as adrenaline flooded her body. A second later the front door swung open, and I was relieved she didn't instinctively pounce on the two people entering the room.

"Here he is. Here he is," Claire chimed as she came through the door, literally pulling this poor fellow in an American flight suit behind her. He had jet black hair and a tightly clipped moustache. Fear beamed from his gray eyes when he noticed Simon and I staring at him from where we sat at the table. Margot holding the handle of the butcher knife added to his distress.

"Claire, where's your manners? Show the gentleman to a seat," Jean said. His one good arm pointing to the vacant chair opposite of me. Claire did as she was ordered. Then, she hovered behind the man, giddy with excitement that made me smile.

"It's clear. No one saw us," Pierre said as he and Annette entered the house. Pierre quickly shut the door and bolted the lock. Annette went to Margot and laid her hand lightly on Margot's shoulder. Margot sighed and set the butcher knife in the sink. Then, she folded her arms in defiance while her gaze burned a hole through me. '*She'll never trust me,*' I thought as I diverted my eyes from her.

"Claire, go upstairs and watch for the Boche," Jean ordered.

"Oh, Grandpapa, can't I stay this time?" Claire begged.

"You know we must be careful. Now go upstairs as you were told," Annette purred. After fifty-four years of marriage with stubborn old Pierre, her tone of voice was so persuasive that I almost went with Claire.

With Margot stationed at the kitchen windows facing north and east,

Annette at the opposite end of the room looking out the south bay window, and Claire upstairs at the west window, all angles were covered. Anyone approaching the house would surely be seen by any one of them.

"Claire, is it clear?" Pierre yelled up the stairs. I faintly heard her answer that it was. Then, Margot announced her end was clear. Annette nodded in agreement. Once that was done, I began the informal interrogation by first announcing my questions in French, and then asking the man in English. After the man answered, I translated his answer into French, except his profanity.

"Are you an American?" I began.

"Bloody hell, you speak English? About bloody time someone speaks my language," the man said. He leaned into the table as a grin spread on his face. From his accent, I knew he was British, yet, I repeated the question to retain control of the interrogation. "Not a Yank, lad. I'm British," was his reply.

"What is your name?" I demanded.

"Colin Forsythe," he answered with a tinge of rebellion.

"Your real name?" I growled, using one of the interrogation tactics I learned at, "Camp X." The goal was to see how the respondent reacted under pressure by listening to his voice inflection and reading his body language.

"That is my bloody name. You'd know that if you looked at my identification papers that bloke took them from me," he hotly replied while pointing his finger at Jean.

I asked Jean if I could see Colin's identification. Jean nodded at Pierre who in turn left the room. A moment later Pierre returned and dropped a small, yellow card the size of a passport on the table. Colin's picture was pasted on the front, along with his name, title, the company he worked for, and a peculiar statement written at the top in bold letters in English, French, and German which simply read, **The Bearer of this Card IS NOT a Spy**.

I'd never seen anything like it before and stared at Colin for a moment. The American flight suit he wore was completely contradictory to everything about him, so I asked if he was a pilot.

Colin slumped back in his chair and pointed at his identification card in my hand. "No, I'm not a bloody pilot. I'm a journalist. You'd know that if you could bloody well read," he sneered.

He was getting hot under the collar, and I smiled knowing I had him just where I wanted him. Conducting an interrogation can be a tricky business when one is searching for the truth. Even trickier if the respondent is being perfectly honest with the interrogator. Therefore, I chose to play the good cop, bad cop routine. Since, I was the only person who could speak English, I played both roles, a tedious affair to pull off by myself. The trick to it is starting out in an accusatory manner, and then gradually become friendlier as the interrogation progressed, all the while keeping pressure on the respondent.

"Who do you work for?" I asked.

"The Times," Colin replied. "That too is on my identification."

"Who's your boss?"

"Jack Keating."

"Why are you wearing an American flight suit?"

"I was shot down," Colin yawned.

"You said you weren't a pilot."

"I wasn't flying the damn plane. I was just in the bloody thing when the Jerry's filled it full of holes."

"What kind of plane was it?"

"A B-17 bomber."

I paused to look around the room. Everyone, except Colin Forsythe, looked perplexed. "What were you, a civilian journalist, doing on a military bomber?" I asked nicely.

"Reporting the war, of course. What the bloody hell do you think I was doing?" Colin snapped. I didn't say anything. Moments passed. The room stayed silent. All eyes were on Colin and his eyes danced between ours. Skepticism drifted between us until Colin finally continued. "You see, old boy, I wanted to join the RAF and fly the Spitfire, but I got rejected. Bad knees, you see. . . Since, I couldn't fight, I got a job with the Times. Practically begged to get a military posting. Then, I bloody well begged some more to be a combat correspondent. Drove my editor barmy, I did. Finally, the old bastard caved and sent me to Chelveston field where the 305th American bomber group is based. I weaseled my way onto the, *Peggy Sue*. A rickety old plane the Yanks were flying. Luckily, I was with a veteran crew. . . Poor buggars. . . Well, laddie, we set off four days ago for a morning jaunt over Dresden. . ."

"Dresden's a long way from here," I snarled.

"God damn laddie. We didn't get shot down over Dresden. A little ack-ack couldn't hurt us. Captain Fuller and his mates were too damn good for that. No, we got it from a whole mess of fighters as soon as we crossed into France. The buggers were every where. One of the bastards shot part of our bloody wing off. Luckily, the navigator, poor chap, shoved me out of the bleedin' plane."

"And the others?"

Colin's shoulders fell limp. "I don't believe any of them made it, old boy. . . I didn't see any parachutes."

"Where did you land?" I asked.

Colin pointed at Pierre. "Right on that chap's hay cart. And, I tell you, there wasn't a lick of hay on it. Damn near broke me arse."

Margot giggled before I translated Colin's answer to the rest of the group. Then, they all joined her in laughter, though, I couldn't laugh. I could only stare at Margot and wonder why her laughter began before I translated what Colin had said. She read my thoughts, for they were clearly written on my face. A smile spread upon hers. "I teach English," she stated bluntly in English, catching Colin and I completely off guard by her perfect annunciation of our native language.

"Nazis," Claire yelled while running down the stairs. Instantly, the laughter died. "The Nazis are coming."

"How close are they?" Jean demanded.

"A kilometer," the innocent young girl answered.

"Claire, take your friend back to his hiding place," Annette shouted. Claire grasped Colin's arm and pulled him outside. "Pierre, go to the wood pile. Act like you're getting wood. Jean, go upstairs and make the beds look slept in. The rest of you get undressed."

In that part of France underclothing wasn't worn, but there wasn't any time for modesty. Margot, Simon, and I quickly shed our dirty clothes and dressed in the fresh clothes that were in the chair. At the same time, Annette gathered our old clothes and left the house. A minute later, she returned.

Luck shined upon us that morning. For only three minutes had passed since Claire sounded the alarm before a German truck rolled into the courtyard. Soldiers scrambled from the back of the vehicle while a German officer barked orders. My pulse quickened as I fought my body to remain calm.

The moment heavy footsteps stopped at the front door, a burst from a Schmeiser submachine gun pierced the early morning air. My heart sank. Time stopped. I said a quick prayer and bid farewell to my lovely wife who was safe thousands of miles across the sea.

Annette screamed when the gun fired. She ran toward the front door, but was knocked to the floor when the door swung open. Two soldiers barged in. Jean, Simon, and I instinctively stood up from the table. Margot left her position by the kitchen sink to help Annette, but one of the soldiers kicked her to the floor. She didn't scream. She didn't moan. Her only response beamed from her eyes as she laid on the floor and tightly held her rib cage.

Pierre came into the house with his hands up, followed by a mean looking SS lieutenant who had a Luger pistol pressed into Pierre's back. Two more soldiers entered behind them and searched us before searching the rest of the house.

Margot and Annette were pulled to their feet and pushed in our direction. We were all ordered to put our hands up and stand in front of the fireplace. Outside, Claire screamed. I could hear her muffled pleas between sobs as she neared the house. Then, a moment later, a sergeant pulled her into the room. Annette took a step in Claire's direction, but stopped when the lieutenant pointed his Luger at her head.

"There'll be no heroics, or you will all be shot," the lieutenant snapped. Then, he took Claire by her hair and taunted her with his Luger by rubbing the barrel on her soft cheeks. She became docile, though I could see her jaw clamped shut and defiance in her eyes. "Now where have you been, little girl?" The lieutenant asked.

"I found her at the chicken coup, sir," the sergeant replied.

"Gathering eggs for breakfast, little girl?" The lieutenant asked. At that moment an egg broke in Claire's hand. The yoke oozed through her small, tightly clenched fist. "Now, now, what have you done? Am I frightening you?"

"That will be all, lieutenant," an SS colonel said as he came into the house. "Put her with the others and wait for me outside."

"Yes, colonel," the lieutenant said, letting go of Claire's hair as he shoved her in our direction. Then, he slowly slid his Luger into its holster before abruptly turning and marching out of the house.

"Give my your papers," the colonel ordered.

For the next twenty minutes the colonel sat at the table and scrutinized our identification. Sometimes he used a magnifying glass to closely look at the stamps on our identity and ration cards. Sometimes he held our cards up to the light. Particular attention was paid to mine and Simon's army demobilization certificates, and Simon's driver's license. After that, the colonel ordered Margot over to the table and held her identification card next to her face. He asked how she got the scar, and she replied that it was from an accident while harvesting hay. Satisfied, the colonel ordered her back to our group. Then, Claire was ordered over to the table.

"I understand you were gathering eggs." The colonel said softly.

"Yes, monsieur, I was."

"Are all of your eggs broken?"

"Yes, monsieur."

"Sergeant," the colonel barked. The sergeant snapped to attention. "Take the girl and the two women to get more eggs."

Once the sergeant left the house with Claire, Margot and Annette, the colonel approached us. "I'm Colonel Buchart, Deputy Intelligence Officer for OB West," he said, referring to the German headquarters of occupied France, Belgium, and the Netherlands. "Who are these two men?" He asked Jean while pointing at Simon and myself.

"They're hired workers to help me with the farm," Jean replied.

"I see. How long have they been here?"

"Two months," Pierre replied.

The colonel backhanded Pierre across the mouth. "Only speak when spoken to," he screamed. Then, he stared at Simon and I. "I'm looking for two spies. Have any of you seen them?"

"No, monsieur," we all answered in unison.

"Need, I remind you the penalty for harboring the enemy?" Colonel Buchart asked, and then he began pacing behind the two soldiers who kept the muzzles of their submachine guns aimed our way. Even though, I knew one false move, one small discrepancy could get us all killed, I wasn't afraid anymore. These Germans, the self appointed masters of the human race, were nothing more than brutes in uniform. Without their weapons, their pitiful Reich and childish pride, they were cowards, sent to spread the evil of the lunatic they called, Fuhrer.

Colonel Buchart approached until he stood face to face with me. "I know who you are," he said in English. "Give yourself up and I will spare their lives."

I didn't respond, or gave any inclination that I knew what he was saying. It was a tactic the Germans employed to ferret out suspected spies. Thanks to the in-depth counter-interrogation training I underwent at Beaulieu, I didn't give in to his ploy. He moved over to Simon and said the same thing to him. Simon didn't flinch. Instead, Simon's eyes cut through Colonel Buchart as if our hated enemy wasn't even there.

Colonel Buchart resumed pacing.

The lieutenant reentered the house and snapped to attention. "We found nothing, herr colonel."

Colonel Buchart quickly dismissed his junior officer. Then, he turned to us. "When I find you've lied to me, You'll all be shot. . . Including the child." Abruptly, he turned and left the house, ordering the two soldiers with the submachine guns to follow him. A few moments later, I heard the lieutenant order his soldiers onto the truck, and then they were gone.

Margot returned to the house after the soldiers left. Annette and Claire came shortly after. The women resumed their lookout positions. Again, Claire protested at having to go upstairs. Then, the house turned deathly silent. Each of us drowning in our own thoughts as we contemplated our brush with fate. After fifteen excruciating minutes, Jean called Claire down from upstairs.

"Claire, how's our guest?" Jean inquired.

Claire smiled. "Oh, I hid him under the chickens," she laughed.

Simon and Margot snickered. Jean failed to see the humor in the situation and growled, "We have to get him out of here before the Boche come back."

At the time, I believed the surprised visit by the Germans had shaken Jean up a bit. Later, I learned his demeanor came from his experience during the, 'Great War.' As a young man, he honorably served France. Rising to the rank of sergeant before being captured and forced to clear land mines for the Germans. When one of his fellow prisoners accidentally tripped a mine, the explosion killed four of his comrades, and stole half of his left arm and forced him to walk with the aid of a cane for the rest of his life. After the war, his wife walked out on him. Leaving him to raise Margot and her younger sister, Audrey alone. In 1933, Audrey died giving birth to Claire. Since then, he's blamed the German race for setting in motion the events that took the life of his daughter, and thanked God for giving him Claire.

"How do we get the Englishman back to England?" Pierre asked.

"We'll take him to Mortain," Margot replied. "Francois' parents will know what to do with him."

"What about, Aimee?" Simon asked. "We're supposed to rendezvous with her at the cottage. She'll know what to do with him."

"Too risky," I said. "The Germans are crawling all over the countryside. Since, Colin can't speak French, he'd be a dead giveaway. . . We should take him to Mortain. Besides, I have the rest of my supplies buried near there, and we'll need the arms and ammunition."

"Marcel's right," Margot said, referring to me by my cover name. "It'll be safer in Mortain, and we need the weapons to kill the Boche."

"Okay, but one of us needs to return to the cottage and inform Aimee of our plans," Simon said. Everyone agreed.

"Where did you put our old clothes?" I asked.

Annette stared at me. "Why?"

"Last night I took a shoulder strap from a dead soldier and I want to know who we're up against."

"I'll get it for you, but only the strap. Your old clothes will be burned," Annette said before stomping out of the house. When she returned, I held the shoulder strap for only a few seconds before tossing it in the fireplace. A grave look crossed Simon's face as he watched the grass green colored strap burn.

"Who were they?" Margot asked.

"Panzer grenadiers," I answered.

"Who?" Jean asked.

"Blitzkrieg," Simon responded, causing Margot's face to turn white. She had a reason to be afraid. We all did. For where ever there are Panzer grenadiers, tanks lurk near by.

After breakfast, Claire went to school. Annette tended to the house while Margot was lucky enough to take a nap. Simon and I toiled the day away in the fields with Pierre and Jean, making sure we all stayed away from the haystack that concealed our weapons. I was dead tired. The farm work sapped more energy from my reserves, so to keep my mind off the strenuous work, I thought of Sarah. I wondered what she was doing. If she and her parents forgave me for leaving. If I would ever be allowed in their lives again. I knew my father never would. I was dead to him, but maybe in time, we would form the father and son relationship that we never had.

When Margot woke up, she spent the rest of the day at the chicken coop. I didn't know it at the time, but found out later that she and Colin spent the day engulfed in conversation.

Late that afternoon, Claire returned from school with news that lightened my heart. Seated at the dining room table, we listened as she said the Germans had searched the entire town of Vassy and surrounding areas. A clear sign the Germans were still searching for the allied spies. Which meant Jack was still alive, at least for the time being.

As the sun set, Margot and Annette served dinner. Margot chose not to eat with us and took her dinner and an extra helping to the chicken coop. It seemed no one could keep her away from Colin. Her determination to remain by his side perplexed all who knew her.

After dinner, we sat around the table debating who should rendezvous with Aimee. "Margot should go. She won't attract attention from the Boche patrols," Simon insisted.

"No, you go," Margot replied. "It'll be safer for the Englishman if I went with Marcel to Mortain. If we run into trouble, we can hide the Englishman and act as lovers. If you men are seen together the Boche will know you're Maquis."

"I agree," I said. "Simon, you know Aimee far better than the rest of us, and Margot knows who we need to contact in Mortain, so it'll be safer if she takes us."

Jean had remained silent during the debate, contemplating the situation. Slowly, he left the table and walked to the fireplace. Then, he offered everyone a cigarette. Simon, Pierre, and Margot took one. I declined. "Margot's right," Jean finally said through a cloud of smoke. "It's better she goes with Marcel and the Englishman. Simon you'll go to the cottage and inform the others."

Simon reluctantly agreed. A half an hour later, after being loaded down with food, the three of us took our leave. I promised I would return after the war was over. Pierre, Jean, and Annette said they hoped it would be soon.

Margot fetched Colin from under the chicken coop and had him change into French civilian clothes. His old clothes were immediately taken to the house and put in the fireplace where Pierre turned Colin's flight suit into ashes. Any remnants of burned clothing would have warranted a death sentence if the Germans paid another unexpected visit.

Meanwhile, Simon and I retrieved the weapons from the haystack. He hugged me and wished us luck. I returned the gesture. Then, he vanished into the night. "Be well my friend," I muttered as Margot and Colin approached.

Margot took one of the rifles and I carried the other one and my pistol. Colin was unarmed, so Margot gave him the butcher knife. Then, we set off on a new adventure in a new chapter of my life.

12

*T*he Normandy countryside is quite gloomy in early spring. Mist clings to the fields and drifts through hedgerows like evil spirits searching for mortal souls. The eerie fog sends chills down your spine. The damp air grips your body with cold hands. It seems at any moment the Devil himself will rise from the Earth and take you to his lair.

Margot knew the countryside well. She led us southwest between Vassy and Vire, and then cut due west on our first leg over the Hills of Normandy. By then the rising sun cast a sliver of light on the horizon, so we settled in a briar patch to wait out the day. Many hours passed. Dull hours in which we sat in quiet contemplation until the sky turned black. Then, we resumed our journey. Heading due south, we went over another hill and arrived outside of the town of Cherence. From there we skirted between Cherence and Sour Deval by way of fields boxed in by hedgerows until we came to the outskirts of Mortain. Dawn peeked over the horizon as we snuck into town, scurrying like church mice through the foggy streets and down an alley to a heavy wooden door.

Margot tapped lightly. No one answered, so she knocked harder. The door opened slightly. A short, obese woman asked what we wanted.

"We're beggars in need of food," Margot replied, giving the woman a prearranged code Francois had told her. The woman opened the door and looked up and down the alley before ushering us inside. When the door was shut and bolted, a match was lit and set to an oil lamp's wick. Gradually, the room filled with light.

"My God, you're alive," a voice said behind me. I turned just in time to receive a bear hug from Francois. My Stengun was clutched in his left hand. He then gave Margot a bear hug and asked who Colin was. Margot told him. At that moment, I noticed Gerard, a short, wiry man about my age and a member of Aimee's group standing to the rear of Francois.

"Only three of you?" Gerard asked.

"Yes, where are the others?" Margot replied.

"They're retrieving supplies with Stephan," Francois answered. I was glad to hear Jack was still alive. "Yves and Simon are missing. Jean-Luc is dead, I'm afraid."

"Simon was with you," Gerard said as he stared at me eye to eye.

"He's dead," I said before Margot could reply. After she had accused me of being a German spy, I mulled over the possibility of a traitor within our midst. I should have voiced my thoughts to her earlier, but I didn't expect us to run into any of Aimee's group in Mortain. Now that we had, I decided it was best to keep tight lipped until we met up with Aimee.

"Sure he's dead?" Gerard asked.

"Yes, a Boche shot him in front of me," Margot replied, going along with my lie.

"Are you positive Jean-Luc is dead?" I asked, only to taunt Gerard.

"Yes, I tripped over his dead body during the shooting," Gerard sneered. "He was shot in the back."

Having barely slept in the last three days, I was dead on my feet and asked for a place to rest. Francois showed us to a small room hidden behind a panel in the upstairs bedroom. It was only big enough for two adults, but somehow Margot and I found enough room to lie down while Colin and Gerard sat cramped in the corner. A few hours later, I changed places with Colin. Margot offered to change places with Gerard, but he said that he wasn't tired. After that, he didn't say a word, which was fine with me. We sat in silence as he read the bible while my mind drifted back to my lovely Sarah.

Around seven in the evening, Francois opened the door and asked me to go with him. Margot came along. Gerard protested for not being invited, but finally relented after Margot begged him to stay with Colin.

We followed Francois downstairs. A short, obese man with greasy hair stood waiting for us. He was François' father, and I wondered how two short, fat people could be the parents of such a tall, lanky fellow.

"Good evening," I said as I held out my hand.

"Ah, no time for pleasantries," Francois' father said. "This pilot, was anyone else with him?"

I looked at Margot. She shrugged her shoulders. Francois just smiled. "No, why?" I replied.

"Good, I'll take him out tonight," Francois' father grumbled. "The rest of you'll need to rendezvous with your Maquis,"

"I'm going with him," Margot stated.

"I can only take the pilot."

I looked at Margot for a moment. "She goes where the pilot goes," I insisted.

"It'll be dangerous," Francois' father cried.

"I don't care," Margot said.

Francois' father looked at his son, and then back to Margot. "All right, you'll need to watch the streets for us. Alert us if anyone comes."

"I'm going with you," Gerard said as he slipped into the room. "Francois, take Marcel to where Aimee's hiding. Margot and I'll meet you there after we get the pilot to a safer place. Just let me know where you'll be."

"We'll come back and get you," Francois said.

"No need to take the chance of getting caught. Just let me know where to meet you," Gerard insisted.

"I can't, Gerard. Aimee said not to tell anyone where she was," Francois said, standing his ground.

"God damn it," Gerard cried, and then stormed back up the stairs.

I pulled Margot out of earshot of the others and whispered, "Watch your back. I've a weird feeling about him."

"So do I," Margot admitted.

"At the first sign of trouble, get back to Vassy. Aimee and the rest of us will meet you there. And be careful."

Margot hugged me. "I will. Sorry for not trusting you."

"No need to apologize. I would've thought the same."

It was close to midnight when Francois and I left for the rendezvous point. Heavy fog shrouded the town. Light rain fell from heaven and dampened our clothes. The temperature hovered a few degrees above freezing, but I was sweating. My heart was pounding. For I knew that in the dense fog we could literally bump into a German patrol and have to fight our way out of town.

Francois led the way to the end of the alley. Visibility was practically nonexistent so we listened for the distinctive sound of hobnailed boots. A futile decision, for we could barely hear the rain landing on the cobblestone street and trickling down the ceramic drain pipes.

Francois said he would cross the street first. Then, I would follow thirty seconds later. Although, I couldn't see the features on his face, I knew he was smiling. He tapped me on the shoulder, and then he was gone. I couldn't even hear his footsteps in the silent town.

I counted to thirty, and then crossed the street. As I entered the next alley, I ran into Francois. His body heaved lightly and I knew he was laughing at my blindness. Clearly enjoying the comedy one can only experience in a dire situation. When at any moment the breath you take could be your last.

We followed the alley to the next street. Again, we used the thirty second delay between crossings. This time I stopped within inches of him. Either my night vision was getting better, or the fog was thinning.

We repeated our process until we arrived at the edge of town. A German guard post was nearby, though, we couldn't see where it was. We only knew it was there due to the whispering of the soldiers. Clearly not the highly disciplined soldiers my superiors warned me about, and if I had ammunition for my pistol, I would've killed them for their carelessness.

In a low crouch, I tip-toed across the street and down a small grassy embankment to a hedgerow while Francois covered me. Fifteen seconds later he was at my side. From there we went across a field to a tall hedgerow. Then, we turned east and went through five more fields before we came to a large clearing. The fog continually thinned as we left the town, and in the darkness I saw the silhouette of a house. A road separated the house from another field that sloped upward to a tall hedgerow with trees on the other side. I had never been there before, but for some reason, I felt like I had.

"Aimee's grandparents house," Francois whispered. "The Boche drove a tank through the wall after killing them."

"Were they Maquis?" I asked.

"No," he replied solemnly. "Come."

We crept up to the back of the house and leaned against the wall below a window. "Glad you fellas could make it," a familiar voice startled us from inside the house. We turned as Jack's hand reached down from the window and patted Francois on the head.

"Jack!" I exclaimed softly. "Fancy meeting you here."

Footsteps rapidly approached from where Francois and I had just come from. We aimed our weapons in their direction. "Don't shoot," Aimee ordered from inside the house. "It's Jocelyn and Emile."

"Who?" I asked.

"The Prince and the Pauper," Jack replied.

"Shakespeare?" I asked.

"Mark Twain," Jack snickered.

"I know Mark Twain," Francois smiled.

"Quiet!" Aimee whispered. "Everyone inside."

Aimee and Jack loaded us down with twice the gear any normal man could carry. Then, we set off across the road and up the grassy slope. I could already feel the burden on my back as we reached the hedgerow. One hundred and twenty pounds of ammunition, extra magazines, and supplies were crammed in my backpack. Along with the rifle I took from the dead German soldier, I also carried five Stenguns slung over my shoulder. To keep them from clanging against each other, I had lashed them together with a short length of paracord. My only comfort came from knowing I wasn't the only one loaded down with the tools of war. All of us, man and woman alike, carried their fair share.

We went through a small opening in the hedgerow. The young woman who had warned us of the German attack popped up from behind a bush. "All clear," she announced. Her name was, Yvette, and she was around twenty-two years old with shoulder length jet black hair, pudgy cheeks, and a curvy body with ample breasts. When she saw Francois, her brown eyes opened wide. "Monsieur, is Gerard with you?"

"No," Francois answered. "He's with Margot and my father."

"Are they going to meet us at the cottage?" Yvette asked.

"No, I told them I'd go back for them," Francois answered.

"And the others?" Jocelyn asked. I immediately understood why Jack called him the Pauper, for he had straight blond hair that fell down around his pale white face covered in freckles. He wore the customary dark blue denim trousers and matching jacket local farmers wore, and the clunky sabots that looked too uncomfortable for anyone's feet.

"Yves is missing," Francois stated.

"And Jean-Luc is dead," I added.

"What about Simon? Have you seen him?" Aimee asked.

"Sorry, Aimee," Francois replied.

I watched Aimee fight back her tears. "We've lost three good friends," she said, choking on her words. "Remember them when you fight."

"Two men," Emile interjected. "Yves in only missing. Knowing my good friend, he's probably with a farmer's wife."

Emile was lean and stout, and dressed smartly in creased black wool pants, a heavy knit black turtleneck sweater, black leather jacket, and a black wool beret. He had dark hair and a tightly trimmed moustache under a pointed nose and cunning eyes. At twenty-eight years old, he could have easily passed as a Hollywood actor, and I surmised that is why Jack called him the Prince. Although, I soon found out I was wrong. For, Emile never ceased complaining about his aching joints.

Aimee sent Francois and Yvette back to Mortain to retrieve Gerard and Margot. They were to backtrack the route Margot, Colin, and I used to get to Mortain. Other members of Aimee's group had set off two hours before

Francois and I met up with Aimee. They took a route closely resembling the same course Jack and I used on our trek toward Saint Lo after we missed our drop zone. For our group, Aimee chose the longest route, much to Emile's chagrin.

On our jaunt back to the cottage, I kept thinking how different my present situation was compared to how I thought it would be. Back in London, I thought I was going to be a spy attired in a long trench coat and stealing secrets from locked safes. I thought I'd be immersed in the French population, gleaning information from unsuspecting Germans and supporters of the Third Reich. I didn't think I'd be traipsing around the French countryside, overloaded with arms and ammunition, hiding from German patrols while trying to conduct subversive warfare with a band of French nationals crying out for the death of Germany. Although, I must admit. I was having the time of my life, and I knew Jack was too.

Aimee led us northeast to the outskirts of Flers. We spent the day hiding in a small oak grove. That night we cut north and went directly between Vassy and Conde until we were three miles due west of Rommel's headquarters before bedding down for the day in a sympathetic farmers barn. At sundown, we trekked northwest until we dropped down into the same ravine I ventured upon after the attack. Only this time, Simon and Margot weren't there to greet us.

Over the past three nights, Jack kept up his radio schedule with London. Meanwhile, I got the opportunity to learn more of Jocelyn and Emile's history. Jocelyn was a farmer from Mortain, and a distant cousin of Margot. Emile on the other hand was an orphan who grew up in a Catholic orphanage on the outskirts of Paris. At the age of seventeen, he left and tried to join the army, although, he was denied due to his chronic aching joints. So, he enrolled in the Sorbonne and completed a degree in Literature. Afterwards, he joined the French Communist Party and fled Paris when the German army entered the city. Having met Blossom at the onset of the occupation, Emile joined the Maquis and quickly became one of Blossom's most trusted men. He was also one of the men who rescued Margot after the Germans failed to murder her.

Aimee didn't say much to anyone on our journey. The others thought nothing of it, but her vacant eyes told me all I needed to know. I felt ashamed for keeping the truth from her for so long that I was weary when I sat down next to her in the ravine. "Simon's not dead," I said quietly.

Aimee's eyes lit up. "He's not? How do you know?"

"He was with Margot and I after the attack, and left us to meet you at the cottage."

"Why didn't you tell me this earlier?"

"I believe there's a traitor amongst us."

"I've thought the same thing, but who?"

"Margot and I believe it's, Gerard."

"Gerard?" Aimee asked, feeling the weight of the accusation. Saddened at the thought of what it would do to Yvette when she found out.

"Yes," I sighed. "He was very aloof when I saw him in Mortain. Tried pressuring Francois into telling him your location."

Aimee's face grew taut. "He was unaccounted for after the Boche attack. We must find him before he kills all of us," she barked and immediately gave the order to move out. With Gerard's blood in her eyes, she drove us at lightening speed toward the cottage.

13

*F*or the next two hours we zigzagged nonstop with the natural layout of the ravine. The cool spring mist, combined with our perspiration made our clothes stick to our bodies. I was miserable. Emile's constant complaints about his aching joints made it even worse. Jack and Jocelyn, considering the heavy loads they already carried, surprised me when they offered to help Emile carry his load, but he proudly refused. It's a miracle Emile kept up with us as Aimee's anger pulled her down the ravine twenty paces in front of us.

We stopped to rest five hundred meters past the spot where I entered the ravine after the attack. I sat down next to Aimee. Emile and Jocelyn crumpled at her feet. Jack remained standing. If I didn't know him better, I would have thought he was ready to go another six miles.

"Want me to carry the radio?" I asked.

"No thanks. I had to sign for her in London, and I'm not going to let her out of my sight."

"Why the urgency, mademoiselle?" Emile asked while lying flat on his back.

Aimee looked at Jack and I before she answered. "Gerard's a traitor." The ice in her tone sent shivers down my spine.

"He can't be. He's Yvette's fiancé. A man of honor," Jocelyn stated.

"If Gerard's a traitor, then Yvette is also a traitor," Emile observed.

"Not necessarily. She could be in the dark just as much as we were," Jack chimed.

Emile raised his head. "This is France, monsieur Stephan. Where love has no secrets."

"Humph! This is occupied France where the Boche spread their poison," Aimee spat. "Let's go!"

My body cried fatigue. For a moment, I empathized with Emile. When I stood my back ached. My shoulders were worn raw. My feet lit on fire inside my wet boots, and I could only imagine what Jocelyn's feet felt like in his wooden shoes.

We entered the forest directly above where we had stopped to rest. Our weapons were cocked with the safety levers engaged. If the Germans were waiting to ambush us, we were ready to fight.

The silence of the forest peaked my adrenaline. Not a single bird chirped or small animal scurried out of our way. All I heard was the wind gently blowing through the trees.

About three hundred meters from the western edge of the forest, a lone rifle shot echoed toward us. Then, the whole world exploded on our left. Ten seconds later, the silence returned. I heard footsteps running in our direction and had just enough time to duck below a bush.

"Don't shoot," Emile yelled as I raised up to fire. The figure swept past me. I turned just in time to see the man get tackled by Jack.

"It's, Yves," Aimee bellowed. "Let him go!"

Jack continued to wrestle with Yves who was clearly frightened and fighting for his freedom. For a split second, I wondered why Jack wouldn't let him go, but then I heard another set of footsteps rapidly approach. Swinging my rifle around with my finger tight on the trigger, Gerard ran into view with a Schmeiser submachine gun in his right hand.

"Stop!" I ordered. Gerard stopped dead in his tracks. "Drop your weapon."

Gerard hesitated. "Now," Aimee and Jocelyn demanded in unison. Emile was torn between keeping his rifle pointed at Gerard and helping Yves who was still wrestling with Jack.

Reluctantly, Gerard dropped the gun as Margot emerged from the bushes behind him. "Don't shoot," she screamed while running past Gerard. The next moment she was by me, casting her rifle aside as her butcher knife flashed into view. In an instant she was on top of Yves and Jack. The butcher knife poised above her head. Everyone's eyes filled with terror as the knife began its downward stroke.

Emile leapt onto the pile, grabbing Margot's wrist as he rolled her away from Jack and Yves. "Kill him!" Margot pled.

"Don't move, or I'll shoot," Jocelyn growled at Gerard who had crept a few feet forward while everyone's attention was centered on the melee.

Gerard froze and slowly raised his hands. "Yves is a traitor," he said.

"Gerard's right," Margot emphasized. "I saw him cavorting with the Boche. He was helping them torture Simon."

"Drop the knife," Aimee ordered, and then she turned to Gerard. "Is she telling the truth?"

"Yes," Gerard replied.

"Damn right she is," Jack spat as he managed to land a punch squarely on Yves' right cheek, knocking him cold. "This bastard smells like sauerkraut and cheep beer."

Emile loosened his grip on Margot. "This can't be. He's a good friend."

Margot freed herself from Emile. "It's true," she said. Then, she kicked Yves in the head.

"Enough!" Aimee growled. "We need him alive."

I lowered my rifle. "Where's Simon?"

"Francois, Yvette, and the Englishman are taking care of him," Gerard answered.

"And the others?" Aimee asked.

"Dead. The Boche murdered them," Margot growled.

"All of them?" I asked.

"Yes, all of them," Gerard replied. "The Boche hung them in the trees with a sign warning of reprisals if they're disturbed."

"What about the old woman?" Jack asked.

"She's hanging with the others. They destroyed her cottage," Gerard replied.

"There's more. Yves informed on Francois' parents. They've been murdered," Margot added.

"Impossible," Emile said angrily. "Yves doesn't know who his parents are."

"He knows Francois' from Mortain and that his last name is Devereaux. That's all he needed to know to get Francois' parents killed," Gerard stated.

"But my parents also live in Mortain," Jocelyn wailed.

Margot wrapped her arm around Jocelyn's shoulder. "I'm sorry."

"No," Jocelyn cried as he tore himself from Margot and ran a few feet away.

"What about your parents?" I asked Margot.

"They're safe. Fortunately, I have a different last name than my father. You and Simon are the only one's who know where they live."

"Could Simon have told the Germans while they were torturing him?" Jack asked while in the process of tying Yves' hands behind his back with a short length of paracord.

"Never," Aimee spat. "He'd never talk. He'd die before he'd bow down to the Nazis. . . Where is he?"

"Just a moment," I said as I stared at the submachine gun lying at

Gerard's feet. "If you're not a traitor, why do you have a German gun? And how did Yves get away?"

"That's easy, monsieur. Yves and the Boche officer were away from the other soldiers. I only had one bullet, so I shot the Boche officer first. When Yves ran, I took the machine gun and chased him," Gerard smiled.

"Why didn't you shoot Yves first?" Jocelyn asked as he slowly turned around with eyes filled with angry tears.

"The officer was armed, Yves wasn't. Besides, now that we know he's a traitor, he can't hide," Gerard replied.

"I'm innocent," Yves moaned.

"We'll see about that," Jack said while giving a tug on the paracord to make sure Yves' hands were tightly bound behind his back.

Emile crawled over to Yves and turned him face up. "Tell me my friend, is what they're saying true?" Emile asked. Yves didn't respond. He only stared into Emile's eyes. Emile pushed Yves further into the ground as he stood and looked from me to Aimee. "It's true. He's a traitor." Then, Emile spit on Yves' face before strapping on his pack and picking up his rifle. "Kill the Boche lover."

Aimee asked Gerard to take her to Simon. Emile and Jocelyn followed them. I introduced Margot to Jack, and then we too set off to find where Simon and the others were. As we went, Margot prodded Yves with her butcher knife.

We stopped at the tree line bordering a sloping valley with the remains of the old woman's cottage far on the other side. From the distance, I could see only one wall left standing and it was black from a fire the Panzer grenadiers started after the house was demolished with their anti-tank rockets.

I found Simon cradled in Aimee's arms in a small trench the German squad dug for a defensive position. She spoke softly between kisses on his forehead while Yvette bandaged the last wound on his legs. The Germans had cut most of his pant legs off, revealing where they had extinguished their cigarettes on his legs and sliced small chunks of flesh from his upper thighs. To most it would've been a ghastly sight, but I had to turn away to hide my laughter. For Simon had absolutely the whitest legs I'd ever seen, and if that weren't bad enough, they were as skinny as a chicken. Then, I saw something swaying in the breeze. A sight that to this day, I've never been able to shake from my memory. The old woman, along with two of the six men Aimee sent out as the advance party, hung from the trees. They were stripped naked and soaked in their own blood. Later, Simon told me the Panzer grenadiers caught four of the six Maquisards alive after a brief fight. Then, after hanging them by the neck, the soldiers used them for bayonet practice. Some of the men were still alive when the sadists rammed their bayonets into our comrades twitching bodies.

Francois and Colin were in the process of cutting down the last two men and the old woman while Gerard and Jocelyn dug graves for our fallen heroes. Emile stoically kicked each of the twelve dead German soldiers in the head before heaving the corpses onto a pile.

"We have to leave as soon as our friends are buried," Simon said. I finally tore my eyes away from the ghastly sight and looked at Simon. "The Boche will be back in the afternoon." Then, when Simon saw Yves, he tried to get up, but Aimee and Yvette held him down. All Simon could do was spit toward Yves and vow revenge.

"He'll be dealt with shortly," Aimee said without emotion.

About that time, a man screamed as he ran toward us. I turned at the moment Francois barreled past me. In an instant, he was off his feet, diving into Yves, knocking Jack and Yves to the ground as he landed on top of them. The momentum broke Yves from Jack's grasp, but he couldn't get away as Francois got on top of him. Then, Francois screamed as he brought his hunting knife down into Yves' chest as Aimee yelled, "No!"

In a grisly display of unbridled rage, Francois' knife fell upon Yves. The rest of us stared, horrified as Francois continued to pound his knife into Yves' flesh while tears streamed from his eyes and vile expletives spewed from his mouth. Five minutes later, it was over. Francois stopped with his knife poised above his victim. Blood covered his right arm and dripped from the blade. No one spoke. Francois looked at us. His smile was gone. He stood and spit on Yves' corpse before walking back to the old woman swaying from the trees. Once again, silence pervaded the countryside. Jack wiped away the blood that splattered on his face during the onslaught. Margot sat on the ground in shock. Colin, Gerard, Jocelyn, and Emile came over to where Yves lay. All of them, except Colin spit on the corpse. Colin just stared. Then, he looked at me, and then to the rest of the group before looking back at the corpse. Then, he took a few steps backward and vomited.

To my surprise, the Maquisards were not finished with Yves' body. Everyone within sight of the corpse silently watched as Emile produced a Hitler Youth knife he took from one of the dead Panzer grenadiers. Then, Jocelyn held Yves' head as Emile proceeded to remove it from the rest of the body. After a little effort, Emile cut through the spinal cord. Then,

Jocelyn took a bayonet and mounted the severed head on top of the dead Nazis. Yves paid the price for his treachery in blood, and I felt no remorse. My only solace was knowing my lovely Sarah would never have to witness the barbarity of war.

"Better than a guillotine, no?" Emile commented while wiping the blade of his Nazi souvenir on the ground, turning the green grass red. Jack and Gerard carried the rest of Yves' corpse to the pile of dead Germans and heaved the lifeless form on top, making the pile four feet high.

"We have to go before the Boche return," Simon advised.

"First, we bury our friends. Then we'll go," Aimee said.

"But they'll be here soon," Simon pled.

"How do you know?" I asked.

"They return every two days to relieve the bastards. Today is the second day," Simon replied.

"How many Boche?" Yvette asked. Her eyes gave away her anxiety.

"Twelve. Maybe more," Simon replied, and I could tell he too was filled with anxiety.

"How will they arrive? On foot?" Aimee asked.

"We must post sentries," Margot commented as she grabbed her rifle and went to the edge of the tree line only ten feet away.

"They come by truck. Sometimes two, but the last time there was only one," Simon answered, and then quickly added, "They're Panzer grenadiers. We must leave now!"

"Which way do they come?" I asked.

"By the road in front of the cottage. Why?"

I looked across the meadow to the road by the cottage. It came toward us for about five hundred feet before it veered off to the north and disappeared behind a stand of trees. "They'll have to leave the road to get here," I observed.

"Yes, they turn off the road and drive along the trees before cutting over here. The Boche radio the trucks to tell them it's safe." Simon confirmed as he pointed to a large, black field radio with a five foot antenna disguised with a tree branch.

"Margot?" I called.

"Yes?"

"Go get Stephan," I ordered.

"Bring the others," Aimee said as Margot sprinted away. "Yvette, take Margot's spot."

Yvette sat down at the edge of the tree line. Two minutes later, the rest of the group sat down in a semi-circle around Aimee, Simon, and I. "We're running out of time. The Germans will return before we can bury our dead and get out of here," I said.

"How many?" Jocelyn asked.

"Twelve, maybe more," Simon answered while Margot translated for Colin.

"They'll be here soon," I added. "If we left now, they'd catch us. So, we must fight. Jack?"

"Yes."

"Can you fix that radio so it can still receive, but will only transmit static?" I asked while pointing to the German field radio.

"I'll try."

"Colin, you and Emile finish burying our friends. Francois, Jocelyn, I need you to strip the clothes off the German soldiers and hang seven of them naked in the trees where our friends were," I ordered, bringing a grin to Francois' face. It was the last time, except when he was killing Germans, that I saw his face turn into anything resembling a smile. "Simon, can you walk?"

"I think so."

I gave him my rifle and extra ammunition. "Take Yvette's place."

"What will you be doing?" Aimee asked.

"You'll see. Gerard show me where you killed the officer?" Gerard nodded. "Aimee, take Margot and Yvette with you and gather all the weapons and ammunition. We don't have much time, so let's get to work."

After the tragic morning events, our small band of makeshift soldiers had a new fervor for revenge. Everyone quickly set off the accomplish their tasks. Gerard led me to the dead German officer's body and proudly pointed to the hole in the man's forehead. Except where the bullet exited the back of the man's skull, splitting the headband of his cap, the rest of the uniform was unblemished and intact.

Gerard helped me undress the dead officer and carry the body over to the pile of dead Germans. A sadistic smile crossed his face as he announced that the dead officer would swing in the same spot the Germans had hung the old woman.

An hour later all of my comrades gathered in the trench to find a pile of German uniforms at my feet. Since, I spoke German, I was already dressed in the officer's uniform which brought a low murmur from the crowd. Then, when I ordered everyone to don a German uniform, they all groaned. "We have to fool the Boche so they'll get close enough for us to kill them," Aimee said which quickly quelled their displeasure.

The stockpile of German weapons was more than we could use. There were two MG42 machine guns, five anti-tank rocket launchers, three Luger pistols, and ten Kar 98 bolt action rifles. Jack gave a quick course on how to use each type of weapon before Aimee divvied them out. It was only fitting that Simon, Francois, and Jocelyn each received one of the Luger pistols. They earned it. Margot was adamant about using one of the MG42's, but gladly yielded when Aimee told her to be Colin's assistant machine gunner. Jack and Yvette were elected as the other machine gun crew. Everyone else received rifles. All of us carried a Stengun as a backup weapon. Since, I was impersonating a German officer, I had to borrow Simon's Luger.

Although, I devised the plan, Aimee set up the ambush. Her first hand knowledge of small unit tactics far outweighed mine. As such, with over four years of proven combat strategy, she was the master tactician.

The radio marked the center of our ambush. I manned the radio, and Simon was placed with me to act as security. Aimee positioned Emile ten meters on my left overlooking the meadow, with Colin and Margot's machine gun fifteen meters left of him. Jocelyn, our left flank, was placed only five meters left of Colin and Margot. On my right, Aimee situated herself ten meters away with Jack and Yvette's machine gun fifteen meters to her right. Francois was our right flank. Gerard, due to his sharp shooting abilities, was placed in a stand of trees across the road to be our sniper. His job was to kill any German soldier hiding behind a truck when the shooting started. Now all we had to do was wait for them to come.

14

Since the beginning of time the most virulent characteristic of warfare has been waiting for your enemy to arrive. A time when anticipation fills your veins, uncertainty knocks at the door of your psyche, and survival is your only prayer. You try to pass the time by letting your mind wander in search of peaceful thoughts, only to find yourself in a constant struggle to ward off your deepest fear, that at any moment your enemy will arrive and kill you.

Although, most will fight when the battle call sounds, because of this inner struggle, many brave souls have froze at the sight of the enemy. Their failure to fight inevitably hastens their death. Then, there is the small minority who flee the battlefield at the first sign of hostility. Most of them die by the hands of their own comrades after being marked as cowards.

Despite the presence of fear hovering over us, fleeing never invaded our minds, and never would. We were eager to fight. After witnessing the atrocities committed by Hitler's pawns, we prayed for their arrival. Only their blood could quench our insatiable thirst for revenge.

I sat by the German field radio with its handset held to my right ear. Three feet in front of me, Simon laid on his side. A camouflaged shelter-half covered part of his body. A German cigarette dangled from his mouth. His rifle, along with five other rifles and two Stenguns lay next to him. When the fighting started, he didn't want to stop to reload and miss the opportunity to kill as many Germans as he could. "Do you want a cigarette?" He asked.

"I don't smoke," I replied.

"It'll calm your nerves."

"No thanks," I said, and then a few seconds later, I reached over and pulled the cigarette from his lips and took a long drag. A coughing fit followed.

"Quiet!" Aimee whispered. I leaned back against the radio and put the handset back to my ear. My eyes watered. I felt dizzy. My lungs felt like they were about to explode as Simon chuckled quietly.

"What are you thinking about?" Simon asked after his laughter died.

"My wife," I answered.

"You're married? Ahhh, to be in love. There's nothing sweeter."

"And you?" I asked.

Simon pointed in Aimee's direction. "Mon Cheri. Someday we'll be as one."

"Boche!" Emile whispered from our left. Simon put out his cigarette and turned to face the meadow. I passed the alert to Aimee on our right.

"I see them," she whispered after a moment.

I kept the handset pressed to my ear as I peered over the side of the trench. Two German trucks stopped in front of the cottage ruins. Then, a German voice sounded in my ear. I squeezed the lever on the handset, and then released it.

"Wolfs Den One, are you there?" The German voice repeated.

I crossed my fingers, hoping Jack had been successful in Jerry-rigging the radio to only transmit garbled messages. "This is Wolfs Den One. Repeat your message," I responded in German.

"Lieutenant Meier, are you there?" The German voice cried through the handset.

"This is Wolfs Den One. Your message is jumbled. Please repeat," I said. The radio remained silent. A lump grew in my throat. "This is Wolfs Den One, repeat your message." Still, the radio remained silent. "Damn," I said out loud.

"What's wrong?" Simon asked.

"They're not responding."

"You must do something. They'll send for reinforcements," Simon pled.

I looked around as an idea popped in my head. Grabbing the binoculars, I crawled out of the trench. "Cover me," I said as I walked out of the tree line. Panzer grenadiers were formed in a skirmish line in front of the trucks. I put the binoculars up to my eyes and saw a German officer standing in the back of the lead truck looking at me through binoculars. I waved. The officer waved back. I hunched my shoulders and raised my hands, giving the officer a visual signal that I didn't understand. It worked. The two trucks began slowly moving toward us while the soldiers walked in front of them. The truck on the right had a driver, radioman, the officer and the machine gunner and an assistant. The truck on the left had only a driver, a machine gunner and his assistant. With thirty-nine dismounted soldiers and eight riding in the trucks, we were outnumbered four to one.

"No one fires until Simon fires," I ordered. Simon passed the order up and down the line. "Simon, when I turn toward you, shoot the Boche radio operator. He's sitting in the passenger seat in the truck on the right."

"What are you going to do?" Simon asked.

"I'm gonna get back in that trench as fast as I can, that's what I'm gonna do," I replied while keeping my back to Simon.

Since my hair was longer than a German soldiers, I had it tucked up under the officer's cap. In spite of the temperature holding steady just above forty degrees Fahrenheit, sweat ran profusely down my cheeks. My jaw clamped shut. The excessive pressure caused my head to throb. Now, even though I didn't smoke, I wished Simon would offer me a cigarette.

The Germans advanced to within fifty meters of our position when I turned and ran to the tree line. Simon's bullet whizzed past as I dove over a small bush. Instantaneously, the German soldiers returned fire. Since, I was their only target, all of their bullets flew in my direction. An MG42 machine gun from one of the trucks ripped a long burst, and then fell silent as Emile and Aimee hit their mutual target. Then, the rest of our group returned fire. The Germans dove on the open ground and continued to pepper the tree line with rifle and machine gun fire. My heart pounded as I got on all fours and crawled toward the safety of the trench.

The truck on our right tried to back away. Jack's machine gun tore through the engine compartment, causing the engine to burst into flames, setting off a chain reaction which ignited the fuel line. A deafening roar followed as the truck exploded, sending shrapnel to the four corners of Earth.

I leapt over another small bush at the edge of the trench. As I flew through the air, I felt a tug on my left side just below my rib cage which sent me spinning sideways. My left shoulder landed on the binoculars hanging from around my neck as I fell into the bottom of the trench. Instantly, my left arm went numb.

"They're coming," Aimee yelled from the right. Margot screamed on my left.

"Bloody bastards," Colin yelled as his machine gun went silent. Two seconds later, he resumed firing. Only this time he fired nonstop while vile expletives spewed from his mouth almost as fast as the rate of fire of his machine gun.

I poked my head over the top of the trench while pulling the Luger out of my holster, only to duck back down again as more bullets slammed into the dirt around me. Then, I jumped up and emptied the Luger, killing a soldier bearing down on Simon as he switched rifles. A hand holding a grenade swung up from the meadow fifteen feet in front of me. Simon placed a lucky shot square in its wrist, though it was too late. The grenade landed five feet in front of Simon as I dove to the bottom of the trench and covered my head as it exploded. Simon yelped as two fragments tore into his left forearm.

Meanwhile, Jack swept his fire across the windshield of the second truck, instantly killing the driver and shattering the windows as two German soldiers broke through the tree line in front of Aimee. Gerard killed one of them with a miraculous shot to the neck. The other soldier knocked Aimee to the ground and was bringing his knife down when Yvette peppered him with her Stengun.

On my left, Jocelyn carefully fired at any German helmet rising above the one foot grass. Emile fired more wildly to keep the Germans pinned down as Colin reloaded the machine gun. Over the din of battle, I heard him signing, "God Save the Queen."

My left arm was still numb, so I reloaded the Luger with my right hand and fired blindly into the meadow as I crawled over to Simon. His forearm was bleeding profusely, but he picked up a Stengun and resumed firing.

A bloodcurdling scream approached from my right. I turned and saw Francois running in my direction. His Stengun blazing at the German soldiers trying to run away. He literally scared them into a retreat. The fleeing soldiers that Francois didn't kill were quickly cut down by Aimee, Jack and Yvette.

Gerard ran from his sniper's nest and assaulted the German left flank. At that moment, Jocelyn, Colin and Emile burst from the tree line and rushed the last few remaining soldiers. Aimee and I quickly joined them. Our firing ceased only when we were satisfied every soldier was dead. Then, Gerard and Francois walked through the decimated German ranks and fired a bullet into each soldier's head. Less than three minutes had passed since the first shot was fired.

"Aimee, Simon's hurt," I said, even though she was already in a dead sprint by the time I uttered her name. "Emile, count the dead Germans. Stephan?"

"Yes," Jack answered.

"You, Gerard, and Francois gather the weapons," I ordered, referring to the weapons strewn about the meadow.

"Bloody bastard," Colin yelled, and continued to repeat himself as he pummeled a dead German's head with the butt of a rifle. It took all of mine and Jocelyn's strength to pull him away. "Bloody bastards killed Margot."

"Where is she?" Yvette asked. The rest of us turned in the direction of Colin's machine gun nest. Margot slowly walked toward us. Blood oozed from her right shoulder where a bullet entered and exited the fleshly part of her muscle. Colin forced her to sit down and cradled her in his arms while Yvette went to work with a surgical needle and thread from a German first-aid kit. There was nothing I could do to help, so I turned and walked back to the trench.

"Hello, my friend," Simon said as I approached. Aimee had bandaged his arm and was now whisking the hair away from his face.

"How are you?" I asked.

"He's hurt," Aimee murmured to no one except herself. "Can't stop getting hurt."

"Ah, ha, but the Boche can't kill me. I'm invincible," Simon boasted.

"Can you walk?" I asked.

"Of course, I can. With the help of mon Cheri, I can do anything," Simon replied, and then kissed Aimee on the cheek. The display of affection made me think of Sarah and how much I missed her. There was no doubt in my mind that my love for her got me through the battle that day.

"Are you shot, Marcel?" Aimee asked while pointing to my left side. I looked down to a bullet hole the size of a dime in the tunic three inches above my belt. There was no blood, so I removed the tunic and checked my body with shaky hands. God was with me that day. For a layer of skin was missing where a bullet grazed my side just inches below my ribs.

"Marcel, Aimee?" Gerard said as he ran to us. "The truck's not broken."

"Of course it is," Aimee said. "Stephan blew it to bits and filled the other with holes."

"But it will work. Come. . . "

"We can't drive that damn truck," I stated rather harshly.

"But we can use it to take our supplies deeper into the forest. . . We can cache the extra rifles and ammunition, and hide the truck somewhere else."

Simon smiled. "It's a good idea, no?" He asked Aimee, and then added, "load the truck, Gerard," before Aimee could respond.

Except for Margot and Simon, the rest of us loaded the truck in less than ten minutes. Jack insisted we take along the German field radio, so

I helped him carry the monstrosity to the truck. Then, everyone got in the truck. Margot sat in the passenger seat due to the seriousness of her wound while Simon had to ride in the back with the rest of the passengers. Gerard was in the driver's seat. Jack sat next to him and held onto Margot. We were all set to go; however, as with all good plans, something had to go wrong. After a few unsuccessful attempts to start the motor, the truck coughed to life. "Now what do I do?" Gerard asked.

"What? Don't you know how to drive?" Jack snapped.

"Ahhh, no. It looked easy," Gerard replied.

"What's wrong?" Simon asked through the shattered back window.

"Gerard doesn't know how to drive," Jack answered.

"Then you drive," Aimee and I said simultaneously.

"Well, I don't know how to," Jack admitted.

"Simon can drive," Aimee said as she turned to Simon. He replied that he was too weak to drive, but would give instructions.

"Can anyone drive?" I asked the rest of the group. Everyone said they couldn't, except for Colin. For he couldn't understand a word of French and didn't answer.

"What the Devil is going on?" Colin asked. Everyone looked at him.

"Gerard doesn't know how to drive," I answered in English.

"Then you drive!" Colin said.

"I don't know how to either," I confessed.

"Blimey, thought all you Yanks had a motorcar."

Simon ended up giving Gerard his first driving lesson. After explaining how to use the clutch and shift lever, Gerard ground the transmission into gear. Francois and Jocelyn who were all the way in the back fell out as the truck lurched forward. Jocelyn quickly got back in, but Francois decided to walk. At a snail's pace, the truck crept toward the tree line. Gerard, with Jack's help, cranked the steering wheel to the left. Then, Gerard gave the engine a little more gas as the truck crawled across the meadow toward the dirt road. A couple of times the truck bounced up and down when the tires drove over a German corpse, and I do believe that had Gerard been a better driver, he would have meant to run over the dead bodies.

We turned right onto the road and followed it for three kilometers. Gerard didn't miss a single rut. Simon winced every time we hit one, and I personally felt like a kernel of corn in a hot pan.

The sun dipped below the horizon as the road broke from the forest. Meadows divided by tall hedgerows stretched as far as the eye could see. I understood why the French called this part of Normandy the, *'Bocage.'*

For thick hedgerows grew up to fifteen feet high on both sides of the single lane road, and there was no where to turn around if we encountered a German patrol. We were locked in with no where to run.

A half kilometer deeper into the Bocage, a road intersected the one we were on. Gerard turned right, taking us in the direction of Conde, a small town ten kilometers east of Vassy. By now night had arrived. We didn't dare turn on the headlights, so, I sat on the hood of the truck and gave directions to keep the truck heading straight down the road, but it was useless. Gerard bounced us back and forth between the hedgerows on both sides of the road while I fought to keep the shrubbery from knocking me off the truck. Then, after a kilometer of abuse, the truck sputtered and rolled to a halt. We were happily out of gas. Francois had walked the entire way.

Simon kept a mental note of the number of captured weapons as we unloaded the truck. Margot was propped up against a tree trunk and blissfully nodded off to dreamland. Jack sat next to her and transmitted our situation to London. Bletchley Park asked if we needed the assistance of a Jedbourough Team. I told Jack to answer, no. The last thing we needed was a group of commandos to look after. We had enough trouble of our own to worry about.

With all the weapons, gear, and extra supplies we recovered from the forest outside of Mortain, along with the fifty-two rifles, two MG42 machine guns, five anti-tank rockets, four Schmeiser submachine guns, and enough grenades and ammunition to outfit half a light infantry company, it was without a doubt, too much for our small band to carry, but that didn't stop Aimee. She split us up into a Conde and Vassy group. Then, she subdivided those groups into teams of two or three people. Emile and Margot, being part of the Vassy group, left first. Margot insisted on carrying a firearm. Aimee relented but only allowed her to carry a Stengun and one extra magazine due to her wound. Emile had to carry his full pack, personal weapon and three Kar98 rifles. On top of that, since Margot was in a weakened state, Emile had to help her walk.

Simon and Yvette, being part of the Conde group, left shortly after Margot and Emile. Yvette, loaded down with a backpack totaling her body weight, also carried a personal weapon and two extra rifles. Simon, though he could barely walk, insisted on carrying a pack and extra weapons. Aimee conceded and let him carry a pack with only fifty pounds of gear and five Stenguns. Aimee and Francois made up the second Conde group while Jocelyn and Gerard made up the third. Between them, they carried all of their personal gear plus an MG42, all of the anti-tank rockets, and four rifles apiece. Gerard also carried a Schmeiser submachine gun. After killing the officer, he took the weapon as a trophy. Jack, Colin, and I, making up the rest of the Vassy group, carried the remaining arms and ammunition, including that damn German field radio.

Loaded down with more gear than a pack mule could carry, I hated life. So did my two companions. When we stopped to rest, they begged to get rid of some of the weight we carried. They didn't have to beg very long. We cached the extra weapons and ammunition deep inside a briar patch, and then continued on our journey. Colin refused to cache the MG42 with the other weapons, lucky him. I was stuck carrying the German field radio with Jack. As its weight got heavier the longer we carried it, I suggested many times that we just get rid of it, but Jack refused. He insisted that in the future the radio would prove its weight in gold. He was right. In the coming months the German monstrosity proved to be an invaluable asset in conducting our mission. However; until we reached Margot's parents house, I hated that damn thing. Fortunately, by the dawn of the third day, my face broke into a smile. Jean and Pierre were herding sheep from one pasture to another and neither of them noticed us.

15

*T*here are times when your friends are happy to see you. Then, there are times when you know your friends dread the sight of you. When Jean and Pierre saw me without Margot, the latter was the case.

I was unarmed. My clothes were dirty. My face and hands were covered in grime. Exhaustion radiated from my body. I could barely walk as I crossed the field while Jack and Colin hid in a culvert behind me. Their rifles clenched tightly in their hands just in case a German patrol was in the area. It was widely known that the Germans set up observation posts in the countryside to watch the French farmers go about their business, and I wasn't about to compromise our safety until I consulted with Jean and Pierre first.

"What happened?" Pierre asked as I approached the two men.

"Where's Margot?" Jean inquired as he hobbled up to me with the aid of his cane.

"She's not here?" I asked.

"No," Jean replied.

My brow furrowed. Panic settled in my bones. "She should've gotten here by now."

"Where've you been? What happened?" Jean asked rapidly. His concern for his daughter was more genuine than my father had ever shown to me.

"We had a little trouble with the Boche. . ."

"What kind of trouble?" Pierre snapped.

I lowered my head for a moment, and then looked at the two men. "We fought them. . . Margot was wounded."

Jean's face turned white. "My God, how bad?"

"Shoulder, but it's not bad," I replied.

"Which way are they traveling?" Pierre asked.

"My friends and I'll go look for them," I replied.

"I'm going," Pierre insisted while stomping his foot.

"Who are these friends of yours?" Jean inquired. I led the two men over to where Jack and Colin were hiding. Again, Jean's face turned pale white when he saw Colin sitting in the muck at the bottom of the culvert. "What's he doing here?"

"Enough," Pierre commanded. "We have to find Margot."

Jack stepped forward and announced he would be Pierre's guide. Colin demanded to go with them, but Jack refused. Tempers rose. I tried to calm them down when Jean stepped into the fray. "The Englishman goes with Pierre. It's too dangerous for him to stay and I need more time to find a hiding place until we can get him out of Normandy," Jean said, and that was the end of the argument. Not another word was said as we all nodded our farewells. Then, as Jack, Colin and Pierre walked away, a smile spread across my face. At that moment, a weight I hadn't noticed before, lifted off my shoulders.

After Jean and I stashed the extra weapons and that damn field radio in a haystack, we went into the house to wait. Jean paced nonstop in front of the fire place. Annette stayed glued to the kitchen counter, washing the same dishes as she stared out the window. Claire was sent to the Quinnec's house a quarter kilometer up the road to ask for their assistance in hiding Colin while I sat at the dining table. My head in my hands as I prayed.

A half hour after the search party left, Claire walked into the house with news the Quinnec's would help. They were a couple in their early fifties and all four of their sons were conscripted to Germany. In January of 1945, the Quinnec's would lose their sons forever when allied bombers blew up a munitions plant outside of Hamburg. Only one son was returned to Normandy for proper burial. The other three were never found.

"My God, they're coming," Annette announced. Over two hours had passed since the search party left.

"Claire, watch for the Boche," Jean ordered as he rushed outside. Annette and I were right behind him. This time Claire didn't put up a fuss and ran up the stairs.

Pierre led the way with Margot's Stengun slung over his shoulder. His face was grim. Jack and Colin carried Margot on top of two German camouflaged shelter halves stretched between two German rifles. She was barely conscious. Colin talked to her to keep her awake, rousing my admiration for the small, foul-mouthed Englishman. Emile brought up the rear and passed out when we reached them. After having no sleep in over three days, he was sapped of energy.

Sometimes in life, when nothing seems to be going the right way and everything around you looks grim, things have a way of working themselves out. Some people call it, 'Fate.' Others believe it's natural law where the pendulum swings between right and wrong, morality and immorality, or good and evil. I call it God's will. For, I have no doubt after the evils I've witnessed and the power of moral justice that crushed the darkness of Hitler's evil, that a God exists. Whether, God is Judah, Allah, Buddha, or any of the other names he's commonly known by, I don't know. In truth, I don't believe he's any one of those. I only know he has left an indelible mark upon this Earth that only a fool would deny. I also know without God's love and Margot's unrelenting faith in him, she would have died on her journey back home.

Margot was taken into the house and laid on Jean's bed. She had a fever and slipped in and out of consciousness. Her bandage was removed. Colin held a damp cloth to her forehead and held her down while Annette cleaned her festering wound.

When Emile collapsed in the field, I removed his backpack and carried him upstairs to Margot's bedroom. He was still fast asleep when I laid him down on the bed. Then, after Jack and I hid the rest of the weapons and equipment in a haystack, Jack laid down on Claire's bed and joined Emile in never-never land. I couldn't sleep and sat with Jean and Pierre at the dining room table.

"We have to get the Englishman out of here. If the Boche come, he'll give us away," Pierre said.

"What about my daughter? He won't leave her side," Jean stated.

"Then she must go with him," Pierre said.

"The Quinnec's don't have room for both of them," Jean observed.

I leaned forward and whispered, "If the Boche come and find Margot has a bullet wound, they'll kill all of us. So, if the Quinnec's have enough room for Colin, they'll have enough room for Margot as well. It's our only choice."

Jean ran his only hand through his hair. "Marcel's right. Her wound would give us away."

"Then it's settled?" Pierre asked.

"Yes," Jean answered, concern drawn across his face. "We'll send her with the Englishman."

After Colin and Margot were safely stashed in a small room hidden in the Quinnec's cellar, I helped Jean and Pierre herd the rest of their sheep into a field adjacent to the one I found them in earlier. Although, I was exhausted, I helped them with their chores well into the late afternoon. It was my way of saying thanks for their hospitality.

Supper was ready when we returned from the fields. Jack and Claire were seated at the table finishing a card game when we sat down. Emile was still asleep in Margot's bed.

"What are your plans?" Jean asked between bites of food.

"We're to lay low for two weeks. Then join up with the others," I said.

"Where do you intend to stay?" Pierre asked.

"They'll stay here, of course," Annette interjected.

Jack wiped his mouth. "We'd be much obliged, but we don't want to add to your burden."

"Nonsense," Jean snorted. "Our only burden is the Boche. Our friends are always welcome in our home. . . Besides, we could use your help around the farm."

"Thank you," I said.

Claire kissed Jack on the cheek, and then giggled, causing Jack's face to turn beet red. "Now we can play cards, yes?"

"Yes," Jack replied sheepishly. It was evident how easily Claire's adoration changed from Colin to Jack. For she had a keen eye when it came to spotting an easily embarrassed young man. An innate trait she fully exploited in the coming months to glean information from young, unsuspecting German soldiers. Looking back, because of her young age, I would've preferred her to be more on the shy side, but it was her young age that fooled many soldiers into believing she wasn't a member of the Maquis. A grave mistake they often made while openly talking about military affairs as she wandered through their ranks. Troop movements, training exercises, morale, and even what the Germans had for dinner proved valuable to the success of our mission. More importantly, Claire's information allowed us to keep one step ahead of the roving patrols. Without her help, our mission would have failed.

Later that evening, Jack and I recovered his radio from its hiding place in the haystack and hiked a kilometer deep into the countryside. Pierre and Jean came along to provide security, although, I believe they tagged along only because they relished the excitement. Earlier, Jack had enciphered a prearranged message on a one-time pad. Now, as he sat in the dark tapping out the message, Pierre and Jean hovered over him, completely in awe of Jack's radio abilities. As I've stated before, Jack was twice as fast at Morse code than I was.

The content of the message was simple and was relayed to London in less than two minutes. Once again, we informed London of our ambush of the Panzer grenadiers and our intention of laying low for a while. At my insistence, Jack asked for a nighttime supply drop of much needed medical supplies, a biscuit-tin radio and more explosives. He finished the transmission by informing London of our captured German field radio before signing off.

"The drop is scheduled for tomorrow night at 2330 hundred hours," Jack said as he removed the headset from his ears. "We're to light only one small fire as a marker."

"Where?" I asked. Jack gave me the coordinates which was a half kilometer north of our current position.

"The medicine?" Jean asked.

"It's coming," Jack smiled. "Margot should be on her feet in no time."

Pierre patted Jack on the back. "And the Englishman?" He asked.

"I'm afraid he's with us for now," Jack answered.

"Hmmm, at least, she'll be happy he's staying. This war can't drive their love apart," Jean smiled, causing my brow to furrow.

How foolish I had been. How foolish and blind I was at not spotting the budding love between Margot and Colin. The signs were there all along, but I failed to recognize their existence. Maybe it was their age difference, or the scar on Margot's face that kept me from seeing their love. Deep down, I knew that neither was the case. The truth is that it was my blindness from growing up in a society where outward signs of affection were seldom displayed, and when it was, everyone turned a blind eye. Therefore, on our hike back to the house, I questioned the love Sarah and I shared. In the end, I knew in my heart that my love for her, and her love for me, was as deep as the first time our lips met.

The next morning, Emile joined us for breakfast. He was well rested and surprised to learn how long he slept. After breakfast, he went with Jack and Pierre to Vassy. Claire rode her bicycle ahead of them to be their lookout until she turned down the road to her school. I stayed behind to help Jean and Annette with their chores. In the early afternoon, I took a nap. Annette ventured over to the Quinnec's to check on Margot and Colin, and was still gone when I awoke to Claire's laughing down stairs. From where I lay, I heard her making fun of the Germans as she reenacted an encounter she had with five soldiers. She ended her skit by saying she overheard the soldiers talking about two American spies. I immediately got dressed.

"Claire, do the Boche know we're in Vassy?" I asked while running downstairs.

"No, Marcel," Claire giggled. "The idiots think you've gone to Caen."
The whole room exhaled, and then laughed along with Claire.

That night, we went to the supply drop as planned. Everyone, except
Claire, was in attendance. Jack radioed London who immediately radioed
back. Confirming our supply drop was on schedule. At 11:25, we heard the
drone of an airplane. Pierre lit a small campfire. On the black landscape,
the pilot had no trouble dropping two supply cylinders on target. One
landed only ten feet from our fire. Then, Jack and Emile quickly doused
the flames with water. Once again pulling a dark veil over the peaceful
countryside.

After gathering the supplies and burying the cylinders and parachutes,
Annette took the medical supplies over to the Quinnec's while we carried
the rest of the gear back to the house. London sent us five thousand 9mm
rounds for the Stenguns, a hundred pounds of medical supplies, an extra
SSTR-1 radio, eight biscuit-tin radios, five thousand francs, and a three
page leaflet on German army radio procedures.

Once we hid the supplies, I took the extra radio a half kilometer from
the house and buried it under a hedgerow where only I knew of its location.
Since, Jack already had a radio, I needed one in case something happened
to him. When I returned to the house, Jack was throwing the three page
leaflet into the fire.

"Won't you need that?" I asked.

Jack pointed to his head. "It's all in here. Now I can talk to the Germans
when I want to."

"But you can't speak German," I pointed out.

Jack smiled. "You can."

Annette was still over at the Quinnec's when I finally went to bed.
Pierre paced by the fire until she returned around 3 a.m.. In the morning,
I learned that Margot's fever broke. Signaling the start of a fast recovery,
and the beginning of the game Jack and I were sent to play.

16

*F*or the next two days, Jack, Emile, and I helped out on the farm. As usual, Emile complained about the hard work, although, after he found out what I did before the war, he kept his mouth shut. Still, I can't deny he was a hard worker. No matter how much his muscles ached, he was always right beside us pulling his own weight.

It was Emile's distaste for farm life and his urbanite upbringing that led me to make a fruitful decision. Using the five thousand Francs London sent, Emile rented a vacant store with a small apartment above it in Vassy. To my surprise, he bought a printing press a local farmer had rusting away in his barn. Two days later, after a deep cleaning and a little bit of motor oil stolen from the German motor pool, Emile had a fully functional printing press. Paper was hard to come by, but with a little help from London, he started a local gazette. Everyday after the local German Cultural Attaché Officer looked over the gazette and stamped its approval, Claire and a couple of her friends delivered the gazette to the inhabitants of Vassy and surrounding areas. Any information the children gathered was passed on to Emile, or Jack, his apprentice. Then, the vital information was passed to London during our nightly radio transmissions.

By night, when Emile wasn't cavorting in the local tavern, he wrote propaganda leaflets which were secretly disseminated amongst the local population. Sometimes, when a farmer or businessman traveled to other parts of France, Emile's leaflets traveled with them. I know of one account where one of Emile's leaflets traveled as far as Marseille. I also heard a rumor that one of his leaflets made its way as far as the United States, but I can't be certain if that were true or not.

Once in a while, Colin collaborated with Emile. As an actual journalist, Colin's prose that could just about persuade anyone into believing anything he wrote. Furthermore, with Margot's help, Colin was learning French at lightening speed. Because of his quick comprehension of the language, Emile forged a few identity documents for him. Subsequently, making Colin an honorary French citizen. By the way, the first French phrases Colin learned contained profanity.

With the medicine London sent and a week of bed rest, Margot stood on her own without feeling dizzy. Four days after that, she was helping Annette in the kitchen, although, she still retired for the night at the Quinnec's. The love she and Colin shared was too great to keep them apart. Every time, I saw them together, I longed to have Sarah back in my arms. I missed her more than ever with each passing day.

Two weeks after we abandoned the German truck, we were returning to the house after a nightly transmission with London when Jack brought us to a halt. Two bicycles were propped against the house by the front door. Neither, Jean nor Pierre knew whose they belonged to, and since the countrywide blackout was in effect, we couldn't see past the thick blankets covering the windows of our home. Jack hid behind the well in the courtyard and covered us with his pistol. Jean crouched on one side of the front door while I stood on the other side with my pistol drawn. Pierre knocked three times and waited thirty seconds so Annette could douse the inside light before he entered the house. "The sky is bright tonight," he said, and then Annette replied, "only because of the stars." Announcing it was safe to enter the house.

I lowered my pistol and beckoned Jack to follow us. Once inside, the front door was bolted shut. An oil lamp was lit, illuminating Aimee and Simon sitting at the table, greeting us with warm smiles.

"Simon," Pierre sang.

"Fancy meeting you here," I said as Jack hid our pistols under a loose floorboard.

"How've you been my friends?" Simon asked.

"Oh, the usual," Jack replied as he sat down at the table.

"Any news of the others?" I asked.

Simon laughed. "We've been getting fat laying around waiting to fight. Francois is taking it the hardest. His need to shed Boche blood grows angrier every day."

"Gerard's been in contact with other Maquis," Aimee interrupted. "They need arms and ammunition. We've given them our extra rifles, but we need more. . . Will England help?"

"We can ask," I replied as Annette poured everyone a glass of wine.

"How many are you talking about?" Jack asked. Simon pulled a piece of paper from his pocket and slid it across the table. Jack's brow furrowed. "This is a grocery list."

"What?" Jean cried.

I snatched the list from Jack. On it was listed forty grams of butter, a hundred eggs, 123 grams of beef, and eight pounds of bacon. "What's this?" I asked.

"A list of the supplies we need," Aimee answered.

"It's in code in case the Boche stopped us. The imbeciles would never think we're trying to get weapons to kill them," Simon laughed.

"He's clever, yes?" Aimee asked.

"Yes, he is," Annette replied.

The list Simon made was easily decipherable after I knew what each item meant. The eggs stood for grenades, and he was asking for a hundred of them. The beef meant rifles. Bacon meant light machine guns, and the butter was code for explosives.

"Why do they need forty kilograms of explosives?" Jean asked.

"It's not for them," Aimee grinned.

"I'm going to blow up the Boche trains in Vire," Simon chuckled.

"I'd love to see that," Pierre said while tenderly slapping Simon on the back.

"Oh, dear, you're too old to be playing soldier," Annette groaned.

By now the wine was having its way with us. "How's Emile?" Aimee asked.

"Good," Jack replied.

I told Aimee and Simon about Emile's gazette and the propaganda leaflets he produced. Simon proposed a toast.

"Has he found a girlfriend?" Aimee asked.

"Knowing Emile, he's found many," Simon laughed while raising his glass in honor of Emile's philandering ways.

"Actually, he's become quite friendly with the local prostitute," Jack smiled.

"What? Only one?" Simon laughed louder while everyone else in the room, except Annette, joined him.

"There's only one whore in Vassy, thank God," Annette snapped. "Though, she's quite beautiful."

"He could always find the pretty one's," Aimee smiled.

"And the Englishman?" Simon inquired.

"He's with Margot not far from here," Jean replied.

"You have to get him back to England. He could jeopardize all of us," Aimee cried.

"No need to worry," Jack said.

"Margot's teaching him French," I interjected.

"He's learning fast," Annette added. Then, she poured more wine while Pierre stoked the fire and lit a cigarette. The room filled with smoke as Jack and Simon joined him by the fire. It was the first time I saw Jack smoke a cigarette and for some reason, I craved one myself.

"But he doesn't have any papers," Aimee was saying about Colin as my mind drifted back into the conversation.

"Emile's forged him a few documents. Now, he's known as, Henri Cotillard from Monaco," I replied.

"A Frenchman, eh?" Simon blurted from the fireplace.

"Yes. Besides, he'd never leave Margot now they are in love," Jean stated.

"Then they are both invited to our wedding," Simon announced.

Aimee held up her hand and showed us a plain, silver ring. "We're getting married after we drive the Boche from France," she said with the biggest smile I'd ever seen.

Annette held Aimee's hand and rubbed the ring with her fingers. "Ah, we must celebrate," she whispered with wild, searching eyes.

"We're celebrating now," Jack slurred as he slapped Simon on the back, causing Simon to lose his balance. Instinctively, Simon latched onto Jack's arm and pulled him down on top of him. As they fell into the easy chair the contents of their wine glasses spilled down Simon's shirt, erupting the room in laughter at their folly, and so it went. For the next few hours our impromptu party raged like no party I've ever attended. The next morning, with blinding headaches, Jack went with Aimee to Conde. I worried about their safety since Jack took his radio concealed in a suitcase and Aimee had five of the biscuit-tin radios hidden in the bread basket on her bicycle. The last three biscuit tin radios were divvied out to Emile, the Quinnec's and Pierre. From then on, every night from nine to midnight, the radios were tuned to the BBC as instructions for the resistance groups throughout Europe were sent out in simple phrases. Each resistance group had certain phrases to listen for, and none of the groups knew what the other groups phrases meant.

Simon stayed behind to help Colin and I gather up the cached weapons from our ambush of the Panzer grenadiers. It took us thirty-six hours to locate the briar patch and begin our trek back to Vassy. Then, just as dusk closed in, we witnessed the force of our allied air corps. From overhead, just barely visible through the clouds, a formation of B-17 bombers with P-51 Mustang escorts dropped their payload three hundred meters on the other side of a knoll we were traversing. The ground shook and crumpled as we cowered on the ground with our hands over our ears. Then, almost as fast as it began, the bombing stopped. We crept up to the top of the knoll and surveyed the damage. In only seven seconds, the bombers destroyed an entire German convoy heading toward Saint Lo. Then, a bullet struck the ground beneath our feet. With the barrel of the MG42 blazing, Colin laid down covering fire as Simon and I maneuvered into position to kill the survivors. Moments later, when Colin's gun fell silent while he reloaded, a couple of soldiers returned fire. Colin cursed as their bullets slammed into the dirt around him. Simon fired three consecutive shots into one of the soldiers. As the dead man fell the soldier next to him twisted in our direction. Firing once, I placed a lucky shot between his eyes. Colin resumed firing. Sweeping his weapon from right to left while Simon and I chased his bullets to finish off the rest of the survivors. Once the enemy was defeated, we surveyed the damage.

Craters ten feet deep and just as wide pocked the road and field surrounding the demolished convoy. Trucks, some broken in two, others turned on their side, burned brightly in the approaching darkness. A hundred feet in front of us a fuel tanker erupted. Munitions caught in the intense heat exploded, sending more shrapnel into the bodies littering the ground as Simon and I dove into a bomb crater. Colin cursed the piece of shrapnel that imbedded in the stock of his machine gun.

"He has spirit, no?" Simon said as we crawled out of the crater and dusted ourselves off.

"Damn right, I do," Colin grinned as he walked up to us. Then, he stopped and looked around. "Bloody hell. Would you look at that?"

Bodies, some missing arms, or legs, or both, covered the ground. The sweet taste of blood and charred flesh filled the air. Burning diesel and cordite drifted on the breeze. The light of the fires flickered on our faces. It was strange. Surreal how the vibrant colors of France, the carnage of the convoy and the warmth upon my face filled my heart with peace, calmed my soul. Paradise.

Then, a shudder rippled through my body. We gathered our weapons and some of the weapons strewn around the burning convoy, and left in a hurry. It was as if the Grim Reaper himself had covered the area with his black cloak, and we feared if we stayed too long, we would become his bounty.

Shortly before three in the morning, we arrived at the outskirts of Vassy. Somehow, we miscalculated and found ourselves over a kilometer west of the sleeping town. Fog rolled across the serene pastures. Silence invaded our senses. A slight drizzle fell upon us as we turned south. A half hour later, after taking the long way around the town, we trudged along a hedgerow a mile from Margot's house. About two hundred meters on our right a diesel engine idled. Through the light of the fading moon, I saw a large house, barely visible behind a patch of trees. An Opel truck was parked in front.

"Don't move," a voice whispered from the hedgerow. Then, a lone pistol fired. Its report echoed from the house.

Never before, nor since, have I been more afraid for my life than when I heard those two words. In that half second the world ceased to exist. My body froze. My heart stopped. My breath vanished from my lips. I was dead, and yet, I was more alive than I had ever been as the purest thoughts filled my mind. As serenity flushed through my veins. I was at peace. The world was at peace with me. It was Heaven. Then, a half second later, reality gripped my body. I trembled. My hair stood on end. My lungs burned for oxygen while I rapidly gulped down air as darkness fell upon me.

17

*T*wo seconds passed. From the moment I heard the words, "Don't move," to the time I woke up lying on the ground, only two seconds had passed. To me it was a lifetime.

In an instant, seven muzzle flashes danced around the house, followed by one flash and its report from the back of the truck. Then, five more muzzle flashes converged on the truck. "Get over here you fools," the same voice whispered. This time I recognized the voice belonged to Jean.

We rolled toward the hedgerow. Jean poked his head out of the bushes only a foot away. "What's going on?" I asked.

Margot crawled out of the hedgerow and kissed Colin on the cheek. "I'm glad you're safe, my love," she said.

"What's going on?" I repeated.

"The Renaulds. . . They were hiding Jews. Emile's friend, the prostitute, told him the Boche were going to search the house while they were asleep," Jean replied.

"We came as fast as we could," Margot cut in.

"Who's *we*?" Simon asked.

"Aimee and the others," Margot replied.

The truck pulled away from the house. Jean peeked over the hedgerow and immediately dropped down. "Come on, hurry!" He said, already on his feet. We followed him through the fields back to his house. Aimee and the others were already there.

"Hurry we must go before the Boche come looking for us," Aimee said excitedly.

"Wait!" Jean exclaimed. "What about the Jews?"

Jack stepped forward. "Monsieur Renauld was shot. Gerard is driving the others toward Saint Malo. He'll ditch the truck on the road to Granville and escort them the rest of the way on foot."

"He has friends in Saint Malo who'll help him," Yvette added. "Now we really must go."

"Margot, Simon and Marcel will stay here. If the Boche come snooping around, I don't want them getting suspicious. The rest of you take the extra weapons and go," Jean ordered.

We loaded down Aimee's party with all the weapons they could carry. Then, after a quick goodbye, they slipped out the doorway into the night. As expected, the German Abwehr officer and his men flooded Vassy and the surrounding countryside. They searched Margot's house in the same manner as before; however, their search was quicker than the last time. By late afternoon, we knew Gerard's plan worked when Claire reported that most of the German forces were sent to the Granville area. I prayed for all of us that Gerard had managed to flee undetected. Two days later, Aimee and the rest of the group returned. "Any sign of the Boche?" She asked.

"Yes, that bastard brought his men and turned the place upside down again, but the imbeciles didn't find a thing," Jean smiled.

"The Nazis went to Granville," Claire laughed.

"They'll be back soon enough," I stated. I wasn't in a laughing mood. After the Renaulds and the Jews were saved, the Waffen SS rounded up twenty civilians from Vassy and hung them in the town square. Reprisals for killing the German officer and his men at the Renaulds house. It was supposed to be a warning. A scare tactic meant to subdue all subversive activities and pit the French populous against members of the Maquis. It had the opposite effect. More and more men and women who had remained stoic toward the German occupation now picked up arms, and it was Jack's radio that played the vital role in arming the countryside. By mid-April the entire town and countryside around Vassy was a hot bed of resistance activities. Putting aside their political and economic beliefs for the time being, the French in the area united against their common enemy and suffered very few casualties.

Raids were conducted nightly against the German supply depots. Explosives, specially designed to look like coal was parceled amongst the coal supplies for German locomotives. Many trains never reached their destinations after unsuspecting German engineers loaded the tainted coal into the locomotive's furnace. A special grease was used on the bearings of the locomotives axles. Once the grease reached a certain temperature it overheated and seized the wheel bearings. If the train didn't derail, countless hours were wasted in repair. Sometimes with the same type of grease which caused the demise in the first place.

The German communication system was a favorite target. At night, we cut telephone lines. The next day soldiers repaired the lines. By the morning after, the lines were cut again. One section of line was cut and repaired so often that by the time we left that section alone, the line had over twenty splices holding it together. Sometimes, we rigged an explosive device for a careless repairman. Their bodies disintegrated when they tried to remove the device. The soldiers countered our tactic by shooting the device until it exploded. Simon countered by setting an explosive charge and taking down the entire pole. Guard posts were installed as a deterrence, but I would have loved to see the look on the guards faces when in the morning the telephone line hung dangling in the breeze.

The German field radio came in handy just as Jack said it would. Claire's friend from school, Joseph, an eight-year-old boy with black bushy hair and thick glasses, spent most of his free time listening to the German communications and translating it for our group. Since the Germans required all school age children in Vassy to learn their language, most of them rebelled. That all changed after Jack persuaded them otherwise. The end result was the intelligence we sent back to London grew threefold. In addition, by listening to the field radio, we knew where the German patrols were and where they were headed. We could avoid them. We could harass them, and we could kill them. The choice was ours. The radio was our ace in the hole.

In conjunction with the increased daylight bombing raids, our group attacked at night. Many nights we dug into the hard packed roads to place an explosive booby trap, or waited with Simon in the rain until a vehicle passed directly over his surprise. He would turn the lever on the manual generator, thus, sending electrical current to his charges. After the vehicle lifted into the air and burst into flames, Simon always said, "Viva la France," as he casually stuffed the generator in his bag. Then, we fled as fast as we could.

Emile kept up his daily gazette and propaganda leaflet operation. Through Brigette, the local prostitute, he was introduced to the local German commander. As an amateur poet, the commander loved sharing his poetry with Emile. Using alcohol and their mutual love of words, Emile exploited the relationship. After a few empty bottles of cheap Bordeaux and an appalling stanza or two, vital information concerning defenses, troop movements, and visiting generals easily fell from the commander's lips.

When, Emile got word an enemy patrol would be prowling the countryside, he helped set up booby traps or an ambush without so much as a complaint. Saying it was the best way to rid his memory of the commander's horrid prose. Although, he never smiled, as Francois did, after doing the deeds necessary to kill the enemy.

Then, on May 2nd, 1944, London ordered us to cease all sabotage activities until further notice. We resumed our daily farm chores and kept up our nightly contacts with London. It was during our lull in activities that one night, after Jack signed off his radio and removed his headset, he gleefully whispered, "I've been promoted to lieutenant." The rest of the night and into the wee hours of morning, we celebrated with wine and Annette's fine cooking. The very next day, Jack went into Vassy in a drunken stupor. While there, Emile introduced him to Brigette, and for the next few days Jack floated on air. That is until I heard him scream while trying to urinate. A few nights later during a supply drop, he raced to open the two dropped canisters. His eyes lit up when he found what he was waiting for. Five days later, his smile returned. "Even lieutenants can get the clap," he remarked.

On May 21st, London gave us a green light to resume our sabotage activities. Bletchley Park also sent, Jack and I, a secret phrase to listen for on the nightly BBC broadcast. Since, Pierre monitored the biscuit-tin radio, I told him to listen for, "Peter is in the garden." Pierre replied in silence with a warm smile. At the time, I didn't tell him what the phrase meant; however, when I think back, I believe he already knew.

Two days after we resumed our operations against the Germans, a knock came at the front door while we were preparing for a raid. Pierre turned the Biscuit-tin radio off. The inside of the house fell silent as we waited for the front door to come crashing in. Then, we heard Jocelyn and Francois talking to someone outside as the knocking returned to the door.

Annette stashed the biscuit-tin radio in a bag of flour. Jean doused the lamp, and then Margot peered past the heavy blankets over the windows. "It's Gerard," she announced.

Yvette ran to the door, flung it open as she sped into his arms, knocking him to the ground. Gerard yelped. "He's hurt," Jocelyn announced as he and Francois carried Gerard into the house and laid him on the dining table. The front door slammed shut. The lamp was relit, revealing Gerard's face twisted in pain.

"Did I do that?" Yvette cried.

"It's his foot," Francois stated.

Everyone looked down. Gerard's right foot was wrapped in a blood stained cloth. "I stepped on a mine," he gasped. "One of those little wooden ones."

Annette rushed to his side and began removing the bandage. "Margot boil some water. Jean bring me a clean bed sheet," she shouted.

"I'll get the medical kit," Colin said as he ran out of the house.

"The rest of you hold him down," Annette ordered. With all his might, Gerard fought us while Annette removed his bandage. I'm amazed we held him down. "Quick, Margot, bring some brandy," Annette yelled even though Margot was only five feet away. In a flash, Margot produced a carafe at Gerard's feet. "Not here. Have him drink it. And hurry up with the water."

The front door flew open, and then slammed shut. "I've got it," Colin sang as he placed the medical kit at Gerard's feet. Yvette sobbed. Her hands shook as she poured brandy past Gerard's clenched teeth while Claire held his right hand.

"Francois, take Yvette outside," Annette ordered.

"No," Yvette protested as Francois tore her away from the table. With Colin's help, he managed to pull her outside. Then, Colin assumed Yvette's duty with the carafe.

My eyes scanned the ghastly sight. Everyone's countenance was locked in somber doom as if Death himself had entered the room. Time ground to a halt. Gerard groaned and writhed in slow motion while Jack and Pierre put all of their weight on his right leg to keep his foot steady. The rest of us held him down with all of our might. How, I do not know, for I felt as light as a feather slowly falling from the sky. I gazed at Margot stirring water in the black kettle over the fire. Deep within, I knew her strokes were frantic, but in my eyes her hand moved slowly like the hands of a clock being wound backwards in time. Then, I heard Yvette's wailing through the thick walls of our makeshift hospital. My heart pounded in my throat, bringing life back to its frantic pace as my eyes focused on Aimee. "Go outside and clam her down," I growled. Aimee paused for a moment, and then went outside.

Gerard screamed as Annette cut away the infected flesh from his wound. "Margot, put the poker in the fire. . . And hurry up with the water," Annette barked.

"The water's ready, Grandmama," Margot replied.

"Bring it here," Annette ordered.

Claire ran her free hand through Gerard's hair. "Don't be afraid my friend. God is with you," she said softly, bringing tears to my eyes. Jocelyn stuffed his leather knife sheath between Gerard's clenched teeth. Then, my stomach turned as Annette cauterized the wound. The smell of burning flesh filled the room. Although, Gerard had passed out when the red hot poker was put to his wound, his body didn't stop twitching.

After a thirty minute fight, Gerard's wound was closed and bandaged. He had lost three toes and part of his right foot, yet in time he would undergo another surgery to have the rest of his foot removed by a physician.

Yvette was allowed back inside and remained by Gerard's side as we carried him on a homemade stretcher to the Quinnec's secret hiding place in their cellar. A room Colin thereafter called the, '*Saint Maquis Hospital.*'

Over the next few weeks, the only time Yvette left Gerard's side was when we needed her help. Her devotion to her fiancé was more than I ever could have wished from Sarah.

Later on, I learned that after Gerard safely escorted the Renaulds and the Jewish family to Saint Malo, he stepped on a wooden shoe-mine in a field outside of Avranches. After wrapping his foot, he walked over forty kilometers back to Vassy. An insurmountable feat for most people, but not for Gerard. If you knew him, you'd know it was his love for Yvette that saved his life.

Our sabotage and subversion activities continued throughout the rest of May and into the first few days of June. Allied air raids steadily increased with each passing day. Convoys, airfields, and army installations took the brunt of the beating. Then, Emile learned the German commander in Vassy was leaving to participate in a war game, so Simon, Emile, and I buried explosives in a drainpipe under the road the commander would take. At exactly 10:49 p.m., the commander's car crept down the road with its blacked out lights peering into the darkness. Once it passed over the drainpipe, Emile had the honor of detonating the bomb. The car blew fifteen feet in the air before crashing to the ground. Its gas tank exploded on impact, reducing the car to a molten fireball. In the bright, illuminating flames, Emile stared at us. "It was necessary. The bastard's prose was too horrible to bear," he said stone faced as Simon and I chuckled.

A few days later, after we returned in the early hours of June fifth from a scheduled radio transmission, Jack pulled me aside. "What did London say?" I asked.

Jack furrowed his brow. "London said to tell Zelda that, 'the water is under the bridge,'" Jack replied, using the code name London used for Aimee.

"The water is under the bridge?" I repeated. "Isn't that the same phrase we were told to give to Blossom?"

"Yeah. Know what it means?"

"No."

"There's one more thing I don't understand."

"What's that?" I asked.

"Well, London said you and two other members of the group are to go with her. I'm supposed to stay here and take over command. . . What's so important we have to break up the group?"

"I don't know, but I'm sure she does," I said. Then, I left Jack standing alone to find her. A few minutes later, I pulled Aimee away from Simon. "London said, 'The water is under the bridge.' Know what it means?" I asked. Aimee didn't respond. "Me and two other people are to accompany you. Jack's taking over command, so what does it mean?"

Aimee sighed deeply. "It means I have to return to Saint Lo."

"What for?" I asked.

Aimee paused for a moment, and then sighed. "I have to set charges under the buildings the Boche are occupying."

"When do we leave?" I asked

"Tonight."

"I'll tell Simon."

"No," Aimee said while stomping her foot. "He's not going with us. I'll take Margot and Emile instead."

"Colin and Margot aren't going to like that."

Aimee's eyes cut through me. "Doesn't matter what they like. The only reason I'm taking you is because London ordered me to. . . It'll be very dangerous for one person and almost impossible for the four of us."

"We'll succeed," I said.

"We better. If we don't, we'll be. . ." Aimee words drifted away. I saw the concern in her eyes, but her courage never waned.

After sleeping most of the day, I awoke to the sound of people arguing. I quickly got dressed and went downstairs. Simon was pleading his case as to why he should go with us to Saint Lo. Emile begged Aimee to pick someone else.

"Damn the both of you," Aimee roared while banging her fists on the table. "Simon, you're staying." Aimee turned to Emile. "As for you. I've never known you to run from a fight. I need your talent at acquiring things. So, you're coming." She turned back to Simon. "You're staying and that's final." Then, she rose from the table and stomped out of the house. Simon gingerly followed her. Despite the fierce downpour bellowing outside, they stayed in the pouring rain for over an hour before returning to the house. Both of them were drenched to the bone. Their somber faces hid the secrets they shared.

That evening, shortly after sunset, Aimee, Margot, Emile and I made our final preparations before setting off on our journey. Pierre had the biscuit-tin radio tuned to the nightly BBC broadcast. The announcer was reading off his usual list of peculiar phrases when he brought everyone in the house to a standstill. Everyone took a moment to let what he said sink in. At exactly 9:52 p.m., the phrase, '*Peter is in the Garden,*' cracked through the static on the radio. The allied invasion of France had begun.

Within minutes, our entire group gathered in the courtyard. My small group heading to Saint Lo said our farewells. I patted Claire on her head and whispered into her hear, "Take care of Stephan."

Claire pinched my cheeks and kissed me on the forehead. "I will, Marcel," she replied. Then, my group left for Saint Lo while Jack's group left to disrupt the German communications and transportation routes. Only Claire and Annette remained behind.

18

As a crow flies, Saint Lo lies over 43 kilometers north of Vassy. With the rolling countryside, foul weather, impenetrable hedgerows and the ever present German army, our journey was much longer.

The first night we hiked due west and covered eleven kilometers before stopping at six in the morning. We hid in a small grove of trees. All the while, expecting to see the German army on the move to stop the allied invasion; however, the countryside remained peaceful. Besides, the light rain dampening my clothes, I enjoyed the sixth of June, 1944. Had I known the extent of the bloodshed occurring on the Normandy coast, my view of that day would be one of the darkest days in my memory.

When nightfall came, we plotted a course between the towns of Percy and Tessy. Since allied aircraft continually bombed the railroads and strafed targets of opportunity during the day, the German army was forced to move at night. The constant sound of their half tracks and trucks kept our attention focused, our footsteps light, and our silhouettes in the shadows. We felt like hunted animals, although, the hunter didn't know we existed. By the morning of June the seventh, we had only traveled sixteen of the 43 kilometers. After that, our movement toward Saint Lo slowed to a crawl.

Time was critical, but caution overruled urgency. The best way for us to cover the amount of distance we had to travel in the shortest amount of time would be to travel by day. It would also be the most foolish. With the enemy in hardened defensive positions during the day, we would be ducks in a shooting gallery. We had no other choice and continued traveling at night, yet, as the days passed, the burden took its toll. Not only were we cold, wet and hungry, each of us carried over a hundred pounds of gear, weapons, and ammunition. I, myself also carried the radio London sent. Still, no matter how miserable we got, our spirits remained incredibly high. Our sense of duty drove us forward. All the while, our enemy lurked in the darkness.

During the night of June 24th we found ourselves in a quandary. We were within 500 meters of the western edge of Saint Lo, and completely surrounded by German soldiers. Somehow, we entered their perimeter undetected. In less than two hours the sun would break the horizon, leaving us nowhere to hide. Then, as if on cue by Satan himself, artillery shells began exploding all around us. Our liberators were hurling death at our enemy and we were like ants in a fire storm.

"We're going to die," Emile cried.

"Someday, yes, but not tonight," Aimee said with a hint of indifference. Then, she led us back the way we had come. Luckily, the allied barrage kept our enemy's heads down. Twice we came upon enemy positions as we retreated. In the dark and confusion, we easily slipped past them and backtracked two kilometers to a briar patch surrounded by hedgerows, trees, lush green fields, and a dirt road as the artillery duel continued in the distance.

A light mist dampened our clothes as dawn broke. The fog thinned as morning wore on. We huddled together and shivered to keep warm. At least we were hidden from our enemy as their trucks bringing fresh troops to Saint Lo drove past only twenty meters to the west. "I wish I was on one of those going the other way," Emile whispered.

"If you were, it'd mean your death," Margot snapped with a tone coated in ice, a reminder of her late husband's fate. A reminder of the consequence of failure, sealing Emile's mouth shut for the rest of the day.

Although, we were very tired, only Aimee managed to get any sleep. The rest of us kept our eyes glued to the dirt road. I counted over forty trucks loaded with fresh troops and ammunition heading toward Saint Lo. When the trucks returned they were overloaded with dead and dying men. Most of them were only boys in uniform, or old men with gray hair.

A little after noon three P-51D Mustangs swept out of the sky and strafed the convoy in front of our hiding place. Steel and tracers spewed from the wings of the metal birds and destroyed three trucks and ripped apart countless soldiers who had been wounded in previous battles. Sliced and diced in their search for a safe place to mend their broken bodies, only to find death. Their moans, their screams, their sobs raked my nerves. Aimee barely stirred from her sleep.

After the first strafing, the enemy convoy broke apart. Soldiers disembarked and scattered to the four winds as the P-51's swooped in for a second pass. One soldier hobbled toward us on crutches as bullets walked down the road. He dove into the briar patch only ten feet away from me, and through the thick, entangled branches, I dispatched him to Hell. He looked to be only fifteen.

Later that afternoon, a few refugees from Saint Lo waded through the carnage. With the battle raging around the town, I was surprised any civilians would have wanted to stay as long as they had.

"Think I'll see Colin again?" Margot asked as we stared at the somber procession.

"We all will," I replied, hoping I was right.

For the next five hours, my mind drifted back to Boston. I wondered how much money my father and his cronies were making from the bloodshed. I wondered how they would feel if this battle was taking place outside of Boston instead of thousands of miles across the sea. What I knew was that if they had to go through what the French population was going through, they would have perished long ago. Those who didn't die amongst their useless wealth, would surely be traitors, serving new masters for their insatiable greed. Either way, their trip to Hell would be sealed. For war makes a person's emotions grow stronger, their view of life more vivid, their convictions permanent.

Thoughts of Sarah entered my mind. In my head, I began a conversation with her, yet, the topics we discussed were not the topics we would discuss in person. That's when I realized, I was no longer the same person she once knew. A pain struck my heart. At that moment, I realized that the woman I talked to in my head, was not my lovely wife. I couldn't remember what she looked like. All I could see was the woman who I dreamed was standing next to me at the alter, and for some reason, she reminded me of Aimee.

When darkness fell, the Germans resumed their convoy. The endless sound of diesel engines and the squeaking tracks of Tiger tanks rolling toward Saint Lo kept us on edge. We knew where ever tanks went, infantry went with them. So we displaced further into the countryside to avoid detection.

I set up the radio in a culvert alongside a tall hedgerow. Mud sucked at my ankles as I set the crystals in place. With the rain pelting my face, mud sticking to my clothes, and the soft wind coming from the north, I shivered uncontrollably. Yet, somehow, my fingers managed to tap out a message on the Morse code key.

London wanted a detailed report on the forces surrounding Saint Lo. I gave them what I could, which wasn't much. Under the circumstances they should have been satisfied, but they never were. I radioed back that I would give a full report the next night, and asked if they had heard from Jack. London failed to answer. Instead, they signed off. I prayed Jack and the others were all right.

"What did they say?" Aimee asked through chattering teeth as I stowed the radio in my pack.

"They want a full report by tomorrow night. That means we've got to get inside the city," I replied with my teeth also chattering from the cold.

"Impossible. The Boche are everywhere," Margot growled.

"No, not everywhere," Emile whispered while keeping his eyes glued to Saint Lo. "We have to get into the sewers, no?" He asked. For some reason he was unaffected by the cold.

"Yes. Why?" Aimee asked. Emile remained in silent contemplation. "Why?" Aimee begged.

"The sewers empty into the Vire river, no?" Emile finally said.

"Yes, but the Boche are concentrated in that area," Margot stated.

"So?" Emile barked. "We'll float down the river, sneak past the Boche, and enter the sewers."

"You can't swim," Aimee pointed out.

"You can't either," Emile replied.

"This is ridiculous," I said. Then, I stood, put on my pack, and walked out of the culvert.

"Where you going?" Margot asked.

"Saint Lo. You can all stay here and argue if you want, but I have my orders," I snapped, sending a burst of fire through my body and striking the cold from my bones.

Reluctantly, they filed in behind me. After a hundred meters, Emile took the lead. "If we must go, then I'll lead the way," he said flatly as he trudged ahead. Which was exactly what I wanted. He was the craftiest person I've ever known, and if there was any chance of getting past the Germans, Emile was the only person who could manage it.

The rain came down in buckets. The continual artillery barrage was lighter than the previous night, and I surmised the weather caused the slight reprieve. I didn't care if my guess was right or wrong. I only cared about getting into the town without being detected.

German forces carpeted the fields surrounding the town. Most of the time we crawled through the cold mud and snaked around our enemy. Sometimes we had to sprint short distances across open areas, or jump over trenches. Twice, as artillery shells fell, we laid down and let careless soldiers run past. One time a soldier ran by so close that he splashed muddy water in my face when his hobnailed boot landed directly in the center of a large mud puddle. A mud puddle I occupied at the time. Why he never saw me is a mystery which I've contemplated all of my life.

When we finally reached the medieval stone wall on the south side of town, every bone in my body ached. My empty stomach was tied in knots. My kidneys felt like stones. My teeth clenched like a vise. I was physically and emotionally spent. Adrenaline had taken its toll on my body, but my will never wavered. My spirit carried me forward.

Emile knew the town well. Once we were over the wall, he led us two blocks to the west and then a half block north to a small doorway. We cautiously followed him inside and up a flight of stairs to a small windowless room on our right. There was a broken chair in the far corner and plaster from the ceiling scattered about the floor. "Wait here," Emile whispered, and then slipped out of the room. A few minutes later, he returned with two bottles of wine and three tins of caviar.

"Where'd you find this?" Margot asked as she took the caviar from him.

"That's a secret," Emile replied. Later, I learned the windowless room we were in was Emile's apartment up until nine months ago when he had to flee Saint Lo after getting caught in bed with another man's wife.

The apartment building stood three stories high with five apartments and a communal toilet per floor. The building itself was sandwiched between another apartment building on the south side, and a building on the north side that had a small cafe on the first floor and small boutiques on the second and third floors.

After, I ate my portion of the caviar and drank a few sips of wine, I passed out. Later the next day, Margot nudged me awake. "Marcel, who's Rosalie?" She asked as I blinked the sleep from my eyes.

"Who?"

"Rosalie. You kept saying her name."

"I don't know," I replied. Rosalie was a name I hadn't heard before. What I did know is that it was the 26th of June. The day of my wedding anniversary and Sarah was thousands of miles away. While I looked around the small room, I wondered what she was doing right at that moment. I wondered if she missed me.

"You all right?" Margot asked.

"Yes. . . Where's Aimee and Emile?"

"They're searching for food," Margot answered, distress beamed from her eyes. A weary smile etched upon her face. I couldn't take my eyes off of her. Since the moment I saw her, I couldn't see past the hideous scar on her face. Now, as I lay on the floor of Emile's apartment, I saw her for the first time. I saw her natural beauty that had been there all along. Now, I understood what drew her to Colin's heart.

A few minutes later, Aimee and Emile returned empty-handed. "The bastards looted the place," Emile remarked.

"See any Boche?" I asked.

"No, we used the back alley to enter the cafe," Aimee said.

Emile hung his head low. "The whole place is destroyed. We must leave at once."

"No one is going anywhere until it gets dark," I said.

"But we must. My Brigette, she could be killed," Emile pled.

Aimee put her hand on Emile's shoulder. "Who's Brigette?"

"She's the whore in Vassy," Margot replied.

"She's my lover," Emile corrected. I detected a slight wetness filling his eyes.

When darkness fell, we crossed the street to another apartment building and entered the sewers through a manhole in the foyer. Up until that moment, I've never experienced such a horrid place. The death, the maiming, the blood of war, I could handle. Human excrement oozing through the bowls of the town, I could not. As we walked through the sewer, the vile substance clawed at my nostrils, filled my boots, and crept up my pants leg. I pinched my nose, but even then, the stench found its way past my vise-like fingers. Then, we came to a dead end. An errant artillery shell had completely blocked the tunnel. "We'll have to find another way," Aimee gasped while choking the smell from her lungs. I was relieved. At the same time, I was distressed. For I knew our mission wasn't over. We would have to find another sewer that would take us to our destination.

"We should go to Saint Michaels," Margot proposed, referring to the school she taught at when she was brought to Saint Lo after her husband was murdered. "The building's gutted from the fire, but the structure's intact."

"Impossible! Saint Michaels is on the other side of town," Emile stated.

"Then where do we go?" Margot asked.

"I'll have to radio London soon. They'll want to know what's going on," I said, sounding like a sick duck because I was pinching my nose. The others pinched their noses in playful mockery; although, I noticed they didn't remove their hands after their laugh.

"We need to get out of town before we're killed," Margot said.

I looked at Margot. "If I don't radio London and let them know the enemy strength, then we may never get out of here. . . We'll need the air support to sneak back through the Boche lines."

In the dim glow of her flash light, Aimee stared at the muck sticking to her legs and sucking at her feet. Then, she looked at the rest of us. "Marcel's right. He needs to radio England. We'll kill the Boche tomorrow night."

"But Aimee, we're out of food and wine," Emile pled.

Aimee turned to Emile. "We'll look for food and another way into the sewers while Marcel is using the radio."

"I'll need someone to provide security while I'm transmitting," I said.

"Then, Emile, Margot, you two search for food and try to find a way into the sewers. I'll stay with Marcel. Meet us back at Emile's apartment before sunrise," Aimee ordered. Then, we gladly sloshed our way out of the sewer.

The ground shook beneath our feet as artillery threatened to level the town. After a visual search of the vacant street, Aimee and I raced to Emile's apartment building and crept up the stairs to the third floor. Artillery shells had blown holes in the ceiling of the hallway, leaving piles of debris, almost three feet high in some places, on the tiled floor. In some of the vacant apartments the entire ceilings and walls were caved in, leaving broken tiles and wood beams smoldering on the floor.

We went into the communal toilet to set up the radio. All that was left of the room was a crushed bathtub, a broken toilet, and a sink dangling from the wall by its rusty pipes. Amazingly enough, with debris covering the floor, large holes in the ceiling, and chunks of concrete missing from the walls, the porcelain sink was still intact. If it weren't for the mineral deposits where water had dripped from the chipped chrome faucet, the sink would have looked brand new.

A slight drizzle began falling through the holes in the ceiling. Then, when I had the radio completely set up, the sky opened up with a furious downpour. Aimee helped me cover the radio with my backpack to keep its circuits dry. Then, a few seconds later, the rain vanished. Aimee remarked how strange the weather had been acting the last few months. I joked that it was because of my presence in France. "It must be," she replied, and I do believe she meant it.

As usual, London wanted more information than I could give. After informing them of the artillery gun emplacements on the east and west side of Saint Lo, and the replacement infantry battalions moving in from the south, they still wanted more. So, I sent them my opinion on the state of Saint Lo. Still, London wasn't satisfied and asked for more information than I could give. Furthermore, their manner was curt and vague, and left me wondering if I was doing a good job.

Then without warning, London gave us a new assignment before they cut the transmission. I looked at my watch and got sick to my stomach. Over twenty minutes had passed. Five times longer than standard operating procedure allowed. My hands moved like lightning to disassemble the radio and put it back in my backpack. All the while my ears strained to hear footsteps coming down the hallway, yet, none came. German radio detection teams were notorious for catching allied spies. The most feared servants of the evil empire by any man or woman listening through an earpiece. Thankfully, the allied bombing gave the Nazis other things to worry about.

After packing up the radio, Aimee and I crept down to Emile's apartment. Since there weren't any windows in the room, Aimee lit a candle. "We have another assignment," I said as we hovered over the flame for warmth.

Aimee looked at me. "We do?"

"London wants us to scout the town and report on the Boche strength and defensive positions."

"What about the sewers?"

"They didn't say. I'll ask tomorrow night, but until we hear different, everything's still a go."

Aimee leaned against the wall. "Where's Margot and Emile?"

"I don't know," I said, reading the concern on her face. "They still have a few hours before daylight. . . Why don't you get some sleep? I'll keep watch and wake you when they return."

Aimee relented and laid down on the cold, cement floor, and I wondered why there wasn't a bed in Emile's small apartment. "I wish Simon was here," Aimee mumbled before falling asleep. I blew out the candle and leaned against the wall next to the doorway. My Stengun rested in my lap as thoughts of Sarah drifted through my mind.

I don't know how many hours passed after Aimee fell asleep before I noticed the dim light glowing in the hallway outside the apartment door. Over the constant din of artillery, I listened for footsteps as my index finger found the trigger of the Stengun. Then, I realized. The light came from the sun. Dawn had broke across the battered town and Margot and

Emile hadn't returned. I wondered where they were and prayed for their safety. I didn't want to alarm Aimee, so I let her sleep. She would learn of their absence soon enough.

19

*A*rtillery has a way of numbing the soul. Every shell fired, every explosion, chisels away one's nerves. In the beginning, a person is awed by the destructive force. They revel in the chaos. Life flows through their body as Death sails through the air and lands around them, sometimes at their feet. Trees shatter, dirt and rock are strewn to the four winds, and civilization crumbles. Then, reality sets in. As the earth trembles, our souls realize the scythe is meant for us. That we are its intended victims. A demise brought on by our own selfish greed. For we are the one's who have raised our swords and beckoned Death from his lair hidden deep within the depths of Hell.

After a while, our emotions corrode until all that remains is fear. Our mortality is no longer questioned. The strong accept their fate, and rise against it, while the weak cower and perish. Although, the scythe will one day find each and every one of us, for those who fight its strength, most will be victorious. For courage is virtue over fear.

The artillery barrage intensified around Emile's apartment building. The shells screamed seconds before impact. It seemed they landed in the streets and on the buildings around us, even right outside Emile's apartment door. Aimee woke the moment the first shell exploded on the floor above us. Small chunks of plaster fell from the ceiling as we ran into the hallway and down the stairs to the first floor.

"Don't they know we're in here?" Aimee yelled over the noise, terror burning in her eyes. "They're gonna kill us."

"Follow me," I ordered while pulling on her arm. I yanked her outside as more shells landed on the apartment building. We ran down the deserted cobblestone street toward the corner as more shells nipped at our feet. Aimee slapped me on the left shoulder. I turned and saw her run toward a doorway. It took me a moment to change direction that by the time I burst through the doorway, the barrel of her Stengun was already smoking. Three German soldiers lay under a thick oak table where only a moment before they were filled with life. Over the din, I never heard the shots when Aimee dispatched them to Hell.

"Bastards," Aimee yelled as she repeatedly kicked one of the corpses. Although, the artillery barrage continued to shake the ground beneath our feet and fill the room with dust, I let her continue, knowing her anger would stave her fear.

"Let's go," I yelled when a shell exploded outside the door.

"Where?"

"We can't stay here."

"I'm not going out there," Aimee said while pointing toward the door leading to the mayhem on the street.

I looked at the German corpses underneath the table. "Help me move this into the hallway," I said as I grabbed one end of the table. Aimee cast a puzzled stare as she picked up the other end. Together we moved it into the hallway directly below a support beam. In grammar school, I learned that during an earthquake the safest place to be was either outside, in a doorway, or under a table. Having never been in an earthquake, I surmised the barrage possessed some of the same characteristics, though, I wasn't about to stand outside and wait for the barrage to end.

"Just a moment," Aimee said as I scurried under the table. Her pack was then thrown under the table and knocked me flat on the floor. Once I righted myself, Aimee dove under the table with three German canteens, a bread bag, and a smile. Then, while chunks of the ceiling and stone wall fell on the floor around us. While the room filled with dust, we ate black bread, Limburger cheese, and drank cold water.

An hour went by before the barrage lifted. The room was piled four feet high with stone, concrete, wood beams, and plaster. Burying the corpses until some unlucky soul uncovered them. The support beam above the table was broken in two and had crashed down upon the table with such a force, I was surprised the table held its weight. Daylight shined through large holes gouged in the walls and parts of the ceiling in the hallway behind us. Dust covered our bodies a half inch thick.

"Where the hell is Margot and Emile?" Aimee sighed once we had clawed our way out from under the table and dusted ourselves off.

"I hope they're all right," I stated.

Aimee smiled. "Don't worry. They're resourceful."

We checked our gear and picked up our packs. I had two small holes from flying rock in mine. One passed clean through my pack and the other one imbedded itself in the radio's receiver.

"Listen!" Aimee said. "Hear that?"

"No." Then, the ground began to shake. A moment later, I heard the screeching, metallic sound of a tracked vehicle. "Tanks," I sighed as our eyes opened wide.

"Hurry," Aimee cried as she climbed over the table toward the back of the building. I followed her into a small room on the left side of the hallway. The outer wall was completely demolished.

"This way," I said as I pulled her from the room. We clawed our way up the debris filled staircase to the second floor and hid behind a pile of debris. Destruction was everywhere. Besides, a few small sections of wall, the entire upper half of the building was destroyed. The building immediately to the north was one large pile of cement, glass, and wood. The building adjacent to it, the same building where we had entered the sewer, was gutted. Every window was blown out. Large holes pocked the outer walls, and the bone dry timbers used to support the roof lay burning on the ground floor.

The entire block due east was one large pile of rubble. I could barely make out the remnants of stone and brick walls that only hours before supported two, and three story buildings. What had taken many men and countless months to build, was destroyed in minutes by the hands of war. Amazingly enough, all of the buildings on the block where Emile's apartment was, were still standing. However; they too were heavily pocked and the street below was filled with rubble.

Although, it would be like throwing spit-wads at a raging bull, I kept my Stengun pointed toward the sound of the approaching tanks from the southeastern edge of Saint Lo. Moments later, two Tiger tanks crept into view. Twenty-one soldiers sat on top of the beasts. Then, the tanks turned left onto the street running in front of Emile's apartment. Aimee and I laid as flat as we could amongst the rubble. Even though, we were on the second floor, a soldier could have easily seen us if he stood up and looked in our direction.

When the tanks faded in the distance, I sat up and looked around. Through the trees to the south, I saw the Germans refortifying their defenses. Beyond them was the plush green fields and the tangled bocage of Normandy. The northern and eastern sides of the town were obscured by the rubble and skeletons of once lively buildings. To the west, I could only see the vacant buildings that were once filled with painters, sculptors, writers, and musicians of Saint Lo's cultural district.

"See anyone?" Aimee asked as she sat up.

"No," I replied.

"Good. Lets go!"

"Where?"

"Vassy."

I stared at Aimee for a moment. "I'm not leaving. Our orders are to stay here and report on the situation. Besides, we can't leave without Margot and Emile."

"We'll give them until morning. If they're not back by then, you can stay if you want, but I'm not staying here a minute longer than I have to."

"But we've got a job to do."

"To hell with the damn job." Aimee looked at the rubble around us. "There's nothing here. Only Boche. Death walks the streets of my town and if we stay, he'll find us."

I leaned back against my pack. A gentle breeze blew against my face. "When Margot and Emile show up, you can all leave if you want to, but I'm staying. Our allies are bound to break through any day now." Aimee stared at me for a moment before rising to her feet and lifting me to mine. We strapped on our packs, and then worked our way down to the first floor. In a small room at the back of the hallway, we exited the building through a large hole in an outer wall and cautiously made our way across the debris toward the street. Once there, Aimee crossed first. At full speed she darted and jumped over debris piles until she stopped just inside of Emile's apartment building. Then, she covered me while I crossed.

We went up the stairs and entered Emile's apartment. More cement and plaster coated the floor. I knew Aimee secretly hoped Margot and Emile were there, but when we didn't find them, the look of disappointment that crossed her face was too unbearable to see. Out of respect, I turned my head and cleared a spot on the floor. Within seconds after sitting down, I drifted into a deep sleep. I can't remember the dreams I dreamt, but I felt Aimee's hand nudging me from my rest. Hours had passed. Darkness had settled over the town. The artillery batteries were still silent.

"They're not back," Aimee said.

"Who?" I yawned.

"Margot and Emile."

"How long has it been since sundown?"

"A half hour, or so," she replied.

"Give'em time. They've got all night to get back. In the meantime, I'm going to radio London." Then, I went upstairs to the toilet on the third floor while Aimee remained in the apartment in case Margot and Emile returned while I was gone. After informing London that I couldn't receive messages due to the shattered receiver, I transmitted the previous days events before I returned to the apartment. Shortly after, the artillery barrage resumed. Although, this time the allies sent their shells to a different part of the city.

For the next two days, our routine stayed the same. We took turns sleeping during the day while the other provided security. At night, once I had radioed London, Aimee set off in search of food and water. Every time she left, I thought she wouldn't return, yet, every time she did, and I wondered why. For I knew it wasn't just the enemy and artillery that wrecked havoc on her mind. Something filled her heart with fear, but she never told me what it was. Nor did I ask. I was only glad she stayed.

On the 30th of June, the waiting finally got to me. I went stir-crazy and threw a fit from the constant shelling, lack of food, and extreme boredom. That night, after sending a message to London, we left the apartment for the last time. I offered to help her sneak through the German defenses, but when finally given the chance, she said, "I'm not leaving until every Nazi bastard is stripped from my streets."

Before my radio receiver was broken, London requested information on the German defenses. Aimee thought it would be best to move clockwise just inside the perimeter of the town and gather information while we looked for another entrance into the sewer system. She still intended to blow the sewer line below the German headquarters. Since, I had been carrying over forty pounds of explosives for over three weeks, the idea of lightening my load was very appealing.

From Emile's apartment, the western edge of Saint Lo was only a half kilometer away. Under peaceful conditions, I could have jogged there in less than five minutes. But under the cover of darkness in a battered town filled with our enemy, our one way journey took over six hours. There were just too many factors against us to move any faster.

First of all, our footwear was too noisy on the cobblestone streets and brick sidewalks. Even with the din of artillery, an enemy soldier hidden in a camouflaged position could hear us long before we saw him. Therefore, we crept at a snail's pace.

Second, there were too many obstacles to overcome. Abandoned horse drawn carts, furniture, razor sharp barbed wire, and the ever present piles of rubble made a clamor when we touched them. Once, Aimee stepped on a broken piece of tile as she skirted an antique sofa. It sounded like glass breaking into a million tiny pieces, and my heart skipped a beat. We froze like statues and stayed that way for twenty minutes or more before taking another step. All the while my heart raced.

Now, I understand that most people reading this will feel twenty minutes is too excessive to be frozen like a statue, so I'll take a moment to explain why it's not. Imagine you are standing in a room with fifty people. Everyone is talking and after a while the noise in the room raises to a level where you are almost shouting at the person standing next to you. Now imagine a wine glass breaking on the tiled floor at your feet. Some of the people in the room may continue talking, but most of them will fall silent and look in your direction. This situation is very similar to when Aimee stepped on the tile, except for one major difference. If an enemy soldier lurked near by when Aimee broke the tile, their attention would immediately tune to the sound, and they would remain focused to it for a very long time. So, we froze like statues to wait out the attention span of any soldier who heard the tile break. After all, when people are trying to kill you, twenty minutes is not very long if you want to live a long and fruitful life.

Another factor hampering our progress was the illumination from the German artillery batteries firing on the west side of Saint Lo and the incoming shells pounding the German defenses. In split-second flashes of light, the horizon lit up, casting our shadows against the sides of buildings. Therefore, we moved through the interior of the battered buildings to stay hidden as much as possible. Sometimes even that wasn't enough when all that remained were a couple of crumbling walls and piles of concrete, brick, wood and stone.

Furthermore, there was the Devils' ordinance that failed to explode on impact. They lurked beneath the rubble waiting to send an unsuspecting soul to Hell. Luckily, Aimee and I were spared Satan's trap. But I wonder if it was more than luck that led us safely to our destination that night. For when we stopped at the edge of a cobblestone street, one building filled my sight. "There's my church. The *Eglise Notre Damn*," Aimee whispered, and then stared at me. "Look familiar?"

"No. . . Why?" I asked quietly. She responded with a blank stare. I looked at the church. We were about five hundred feet from its courtyard and the grounds looked deserted. "If we can get to the top of the steeple, we'll be able to survey the German defenses," I whispered.

"We can hide in the chambers below the altar during the day. The priest should still be there," Aimee said. In the dark, I could tell she was smiling.

"You lead the way."

Aimee led me to within two hundred feet of the church grounds when she suddenly stopped. Instinctively, we both kneeled and peered into the darkness. Aimee had her Stengun pointed toward the front entrance of the church and I immediately spied what she was staring at. A German soldier was urinating just outside the front door. When he moved to go back inside, I saw the distinctive shape of an MG42 machine gun barrel protruding out of a sandbagged emplacement in front of the doorway. Then, a roving guard walked from the back of the building. As soon as he disappeared around the front, Aimee and I backtracked a half block to a set of row houses. Most of them were surprisingly still intact.

We entered the third house and went upstairs to a small room where we could see the church through a double window. The right window pane, although it had many holes in it, was still in the window sill. The left window pane was completely intact and partially covered by a dusty curtain hanging from a bent curtain rod. There was an overturned chair by the window and a mildewed mattress on a 19th century bed frame along the right side wall. A maple armoire with a broken door laid on its side in the center of the room.

"There's no place like home," I said. We dropped our packs and weapons in the doorway and pulled the mattress from the bed frame and put it on the floor next to the window. Then, we gathered our weapons and packs and sat down on the rotting fabric, welcoming the comfort the mattress gave.

"What do we do now?" Aimee asked.

"Well, since the Germans are using the church as an observation post, I'm going to radio London and see if we can't get them to bomb it," I replied. Aimee's eyes filled with tears. "Sorry, the church has to be destroyed."

Aimee lowered her eyes to the floor. A moment later, she wiped her eyes and whispered, "I understand."

After, I radioed London, I spent the next few hours contemplating religion. As a young boy, I was forced to attend services at Sacred Heart Methodist church with my mother. She grew up Catholic, but my father forced her to become a Methodist after they emigrated to the United States. He told her the Methodist faith was more respectable. He also said that to show our faith in God, we had to attend church every Sunday. So, when I was home from boarding school, I went with my mother every Sunday. Thinking back, I can't recall my father being with us, but I remember the excuse he gave. Every Sunday morning he told us that he had a lot of work to do on a case. Yet, somehow he always found time to play a round of golf every Sunday afternoon.

After my mother died, my father stopped sending me to church. He never gave an explanation, and I never asked why. Since then, I've only been inside a church five times. Once only because it was my wedding day.

By the time night faded into day, Aimee was softly snoring on the mattress. I used my pack as a backrest and peeked out the window through a small hole in the curtain. '*How long will I have to wait?*' I wondered. Hours passed and still the church remained intact. Allied shells fell no where near it. No aircraft flew overhead to bomb it, and I wondered if London received my request.

The artillery barrage slowed by midmorning. By noon the guns fell silent in our part of the town. "What's wrong?" Aimee yawned.

"The shelling stopped," I replied.

Aimee sat up with wide open eyes. "It's over?"

"No."

Aimee frowned as she crawled next to me. "Is my church still there?"

"Yep," I answered, and then paused for a moment. "I don't like the silence."

After transmitting another message to London, I spent the next three hours trying to fix the radio's receiver. I was under trained and didn't have the necessary equipment, so I gave up and fell asleep while Aimee kept her eyes glued to the church.

By nightfall, the church was still standing. Since, the artillery stopped, I awoke feeling completely refreshed. Aimee was still staring out the window; however, I don't think she paid too much attention to what she was staring at. "What's happening?" I asked.

"Nothing. The Boche guard keeps walking around the church, but other than that, nothing. . . My town has died."

"It'll be reborn."

A few minutes later, I sent another message to London while Aimee searched for food. She came back with our canteens filled with water and one rotting apple. After cutting the apple in half, we devoured our portions, core and all. The only part we discarded was the stem.

Aimee fell asleep before dawn. I kept watch until noon before she relieved me. Then, once again, I asked London for the destruction of the church before I fell asleep. When I awoke after dusk, the church was still standing. "Well, it's up to us," I said.

"What do you have in mind?" Aimee asked as a tear fell from her eye.

"When the barrage resumes, we'll take out the machine gun nest and the roving sentries. Then, we'll enter the church and kill the remaining soldiers. Once the place is clear, we'll set our charges to make it look like artillery shells hit the place to cover our tracks."

"What do we do in the meantime? We can't stay here and starve."

"We'll move north to check out the German defenses and find food," I said. Then, I put my hand on her shoulder. "When the artillery resumes, we'll destroy the church and leave this town once and for all."

Aimee stared at me for a moment, and then lowered her head.

An hour later we left our dry abode for the pouring rain. In no time, we were soaked to the bone and freezing. For the next eleven days, we lived off the land. Rotting fruit and vegetables were our main source of nourishment. Once in a while, I shot a stray cat or sewer rat with my silenced pistol. Then, we would hide in a cellar and cook the meat with a candle.

In the eleven days we journeyed north, we had barely traveled a half kilometer from the vacant house by the church. Most of the time, we hid in cellars while the enemy lurked above. Our nerves frayed. Our patience wore thin. Our minds wavered on the edge of insanity, and we prayed for a reprieve.

Then, in the twilight hours of the thirteenth of July, our prayers were answered. The artillery resumed in our part of the town. The Germans rushed north to stop our allies, while Aimee and I made our break to the south. We arrived at our cozy row house just before dawn. The church still loomed through the window.

20

The thirteenth of July, 1944, was one of the longest days of my life. Knowing our allies had begun their assault on Saint Lo, neither Aimee, nor I could sleep. We spent the whole day taking turns watching the church and planning our attack. By nightfall, we left the house and inched our way to within fifty meters of the church. There we removed our packs and crawled across the street, stopping behind the two foot stone wall separating us from the back of the church. The roving sentry was leaning against the wall only fifteen feet away. The red glow of his cigarette was a beacon in the dark. I could tell he was nervous because every five seconds the ash on his cigarette turned bright red as he inhaled. I took a deep breath and held it as I aimed the HiStandard pistol on the glow. Slowly, I pressed the trigger to the rear. In an instant the pistol jumped. Red streaks sparkled around the soldier's face as my bullet hit him in the mouth and stopped in the back of his brain. Then, his head slumped forward as he crumpled to the ground. I crept up to him and put another bullet between his eyes. He had a face of a teenager and a Hitler Youth knife on his belt. I removed a letter from his pocket as Aimee crawled up to look at my handy work. Then, we snuck around to the front corner of the building.

Three soldiers were crouched behind a sandbagged machine gun nest at the entrance of the church. I aimed and pressed the trigger of my Stengun, spewing bullets into the man-made shelter as Aimee ran in front and emptied her magazine into our prey. Their steel helmets clamored as they struck the stone steps, muted only by the din of the artillery pounding the German defenses across the Vier river.

We quickly changed magazines, and then quietly entered the church. Once inside the sound level dropped to a low murmur. A candle burned in the stairwell leading to the steeple. Another candle burned in the center of the sanctuary floor where three sleeping forms lay on top of makeshift beds. My pistol made sure they slept forever.

The pews had been removed and stacked in a heap by the altar. In their place was two cases of ammunition, a few crates of food, and the sleeping quarters of the men I just killed. Next to them was the holy water basin. Socks hung from a string over the baptismal. Every religious item was stripped from the church. Even the icons that were bolted to the walls were ripped from their frames, and I wondered what became of them. Then, I had an eerie feeling that I had once stood in the church before, but knew it was impossible.

"There's no one else here," Aimee whispered in my ear.

I pointed at the stairway leading to the steeple. "They're up there," I said quietly.

We each put on a pair of socks over our shoes to muffle our footsteps. Then, Aimee kneeled down by the candle glowing in the stairwell and gently blew on it until the flame extinguished. After our vision adjusted to the dark, we crawled up the spiral staircase and stopped just below the bell in the steeple. A German lieutenant peered through binoculars to the north. He had a walkie-talkie in his right hand and was talking to a soldier on his left while another soldier who was looking through binoculars toward the west reported the damage caused by the allied shells when I squeezed the trigger. In less than two seconds, Aimee and I sapped the life blood out of the three bastards and sent their souls to Hell.

"Quick, get our packs," I ordered as I turned and ran down the stairs with Aimee hot on my tail. We stopped at the front door, removed the socks over our shoes, and then quietly ventured outside. I carried the young corpse from the back of the church to the machine gun nest, and then went back inside the church. A minute later, Aimee returned with our packs. I grabbed mine and raced back up the stairs and set five small charges. Then, I grabbed the walkie-talkie, pinched the pencil fuses on the charges, and raced back down the stairs.

"Set up more explosives outside," Aimee said as she reached into a food crate. "I'll fill our packs."

I left my pack with Aimee, and then lugged the two cases of ammunition outside. In three minutes, I had a charge underneath the four corpses, and one under the two cases of ammunition. I also put two charges, thirty feet apart, along the stone wall in front of the church before racing back inside. Aimee was on her knees reciting the Rosary. Though I had never been a Catholic and was never taught the Rosary, I somehow knew the words and kneeled beside her.

"Simon and I were to be married here," Aimee lamented when we finished.

"Don't worry. The charges won't destroy the church," I said. Then, we strapped on our packs, picked up our weapons and ran out of the church. We got a block away when the charges in the steeple blew. A few minutes later the rest of the charges exploded. By then, we were about ten feet from an intersection when the drone of a diesel engine reverberated from our left. The sound of hobnailed boots on the cobblestone road came from our right. Thankfully, Aimee pulled me into a gutted building seconds before a platoon of grenadiers ran past and faded down the street.

"You must go," a tired voice said behind us. Instinctively, we spun around and put two bullets each into an old woman sitting on the floor.

"My God," Aimee cried as she rushed to the woman's side.

The old woman coughed up blood as life drained from her wounds. Tears flooded Aimee's eyes and landed on the woman's face.

"Help me," the old woman gasped. Aimee began to shake. I pulled her away and checked the woman's wounds. Dark red blood oozed from her kidney and pooled on the floor. I pressed my hand against the wound in her chest to stop the blood from squirting out with her heart beat. "You've returned. Your search is finished," the old woman wheezed as she gazed into my eyes.

"What?" I asked.

The woman gasped. Her head fell forward. Her body went limp. I closed her eyes and laid her on the floor. When, I stood, Aimee stared at me with her mouth hanging open. Her tears had ceased falling. The fear in her eyes gradually withdrew. "I knew I was right about you," she said in a trance.

"Me?" I stammered. "You shot her too."

"Don't you know?"

"Know what?"

Aimee cast her eyes to the floor. Then, she looked me straight in the eye. "Doesn't matter. Lets go."

I looked at the old woman. "Shouldn't we cover her up?"

"Leave her," Aimee ordered, and then she went to the doorway. "I know where I must take you."

"Where?" I asked as I followed her outside. Something didn't feel right about leaving the old woman's body laying in her own blood.

We crossed the street heading east and got thirty feet down the block before a tank rambled our way. We darted into a vacant building on our right and barely made it to the back room before a Panther tank crept by. More soldiers ran through the streets. Officers barked orders. The Germans were consolidating their defenses as the dim glow of dawn broke the horizon. Ten minutes later the town was flooded with sunlight. We were trapped, listening to what seemed like the entire German army passing by just outside the door. At least we had food.

Thanks to the German army, Aimee and I stuffed ourselves with sausages, carrots, apples, oranges, apricots, and rock hard black bread she took from the church. We even shared a half bottle of red wine, which was a mistake. I could barely keep my eyes open while Aimee slept. If it weren't for the presence of the Germans outside, I would've passed out. Time crawled. Countless hours later, Aimee woke up and I fell asleep within seconds. Soon after, I woke to the sound of a German officer yelling at a tank commander over the roar of an engine. It was pitch-black in the room, but I could feel Aimee's nervous presence only two feet away. I ran my hand down my chest to make sure my Stengun was still there. Then, I kneeled and put my hand on Aimee's shoulder. She was trembling. "Don't worry. They don't know we're here," I whispered softly in her ear. Suddenly, the tank's engine shut off. Aimee gripped my arm. I rubbed her shoulder until her fingers relaxed. Then, I crawled into the front room and peered out the bottom of a window. The tank was parked in an intersection forty feet away. Fifteen soldiers with camouflaged smocks and small branches strapped to their helmets surrounded the tank. 'Specialized troops,' I thought, and then I crawled back to Aimee. An hour later, I fell asleep, waking just before dawn. The tank remained in its position all night. To our relief, around ten in the morning the tank rumbled off to the north and took the soldiers with it.

Aimee stared at me, and then sighed. "I've got something to show you when it gets dark."

"What is it?" I asked.

"My cafe," Aimee replied.

"Your cafe?"

"Well, it was until the Boche stole it. Then, my Husband and daughter," Aimee stopped abruptly.

My thoughts flashed to Simon. "You're married?"

"I was until the Boche shot my husband with twenty-seven other men. Now, I fight for his revenge. . . I fight for mine."

"And your daughter?"

Aimee shook her head. "She's in Spain. Blossom got her out. I didn't want her to live under the Nazis. I didn't want her poisoned with hate."

I didn't say anything for awhile. On a personal level, I didn't know

Aimee very well, although, I could see in her eyes and feel in her voice the great suffering she had endured. I could tell under her thick, battle-worn facade, she was soft and gentle. A woman who only wanted to raise a family and drift pleasantly into old age. At that moment, I thought of the old woman we shot and asked Aimee if she knew her.

"Not very well, why?" Aimee asked.

"I don't know. It's just. . . What she said to me. I don't understand it."

"When I show you my cafe, if you still don't know, then you can forget what she said. . . Get some sleep," Aimee whispered.

"It's your turn."

"I'm not tired."

I stared at her for a moment, and then laid down on the floor, wondering what her cafe had to do with what the old woman said. The correlation between the two didn't make any sense and I spent the rest of the day wondering why.

Artillery shells fell on the buildings across the street, snapping me from my thoughts. Night had fallen. In the pitch-black, we strapped on our packs and were out of the building within ten seconds. We turned right and ran full speed to the end of the block as the buildings crumbled behind us.

We scanned the area, then I crossed the street while Aimee covered me. Then, I waved her across. We ran another twenty feet before entering the first house of a row housing complex. The outer walls were either completely demolished, or had holes large enough to drive a bus through. The interior was one large heap of rubble. Small fires burned in a few spots. Smoke filled our lungs.

The artillery blasts grew louder. Shells walked toward us in the street outside. Rifle and machine gun fire echoed through the town. There was no time to think as I followed Aimee over and around the rubble. Quite a few times, I slipped on the loose debris and caught myself with my left hand or landed on my knees. All the while men ran and died in the street just on the other side of the crumbling wall. Their screams synchronized with the flashes of light. Fear was everywhere. The Reaper's scythe was collecting its bounty.

"See it?" Aimee asked when we reached a window on the east side of the row houses.

"See what?"

She pointed at a building across the street. Its northern side facing the town square was demolished. Its western wall remained mostly intact and there was a small stairwell leading to a cellar. "My cafe," she replied. Her white teeth illuminated her smile. "Come. . . We'll hide in the cellar." Then, she crawled over the window sill and ran into the street. Half way across a single rifle shot rang out. Aimee fell forward and crumpled to the ground.

I leaned out the window and fired at two soldiers, emptying my magazine as the last one fell. Then, I changed magazines, slid over the window sill and ran toward Aimee. Three more bullets echoed down the street. One of them struck my pack. I spun around and fired at three soldiers running toward me. They fell to the ground. Their steel helmets clanked as they slid across the cobblestone street. Then, another bullet landed by my feet. The muzzle flash came from a second story window a block away and I emptied a full magazine into it.

Aimee screamed as another bullet hit her in the arm. I grabbed her by her pack and dragged her across the street and down the stairwell. With all my weight, I kicked the cellar door open. Then, I pulled her inside and down another short staircase and across the room. "Where you hit?"

"The stomach," Aimee winced, "and my arm."

The cellar door flew open as two soldiers rushed in. My Stengun barked, sending them sprawling down the stairs. I changed magazines and waited until I was confident no more soldiers were coming. Then, I slowly left Aimee's side and crept up the short staircase. The only sounds I heard were the constant sounds of war. I peeked outside. We were alone. I closed the door and stacked the corpses against it. One of the dead men had a flashlight attached to his harness so I used it to check Aimee's wounds.

"Tell Simon, I love him," Aimee gasped as I knelt down beside her and carefully removed her pack and put it under her head.

"You can tell him yourself," I replied as I ripped open her shirt. Blood trickled from a bullet hole the size of a dime four inches below her rib cage. I felt her other side and checked her back. There wasn't an exit wound which meant the bullet was lodged somewhere in her abdomen, most likely her spine.

Aimee grabbed my arm. "I'm dying Marcel. Please, tell Simon, I love him."

I brushed the hair from her face. "Don't give up."

"Can't feel my legs. I'm dying," Aimee said, and then let out a long moan. "Promise me, you'll tell him. Promise."

I choked back my tears. "I promise. . . I'll tell him, but you have to fight. . . Stay alive for Simon."

"And my daughter," she cried.

"Yes, and your daughter," I said as she passed out.

Using the supplies we had and the first-aid kits off of the dead soldiers, I managed to stop her stomach wound from bleeding. Since the second bullet passed clean through her right triceps, I wrapped a piece of cloth around her arm and tied the ends together. Her breathing was faint but steady. I covered her with my coat and prayed.

Outside the fighting drew near. Its tempo gained momentum. Dust fell from the ceiling. The ground shook. The noise was unbearable. Sometimes there was silence, a reprieve lasting only a few moments before the roar of battle resumed.

Many hours passed while I watched Aimee's chest rise and fall. Over time, her breathing grew shallow. Her pulse grew faint. "Hang in there my friend," I said ever so softly in her ear.

After a while, I turned on the walkie-talkie I took from the church. Radio traffic was constant. Frantic German officers shouted orders at beleaguered troops and desperate tank crews. Reports of the allied advance never ceased. Officers ordered redeployment while their troops begged to retreat. "We fight to the last man! No retreat!" An officer barked through the headset, and I was loving every minute of it. Then, an idea popped in my head.

"We're going to die. We must surrender," I cried into the walkie-talkie in German to add further despair to the German defenders.

"Who said that?" An officer asked.

"We're defeated. All is lost," I stammered.

"What're you saying?" Aimee weakly asked.

I smiled. "How do you feel?"

"I can't feel my legs," she groaned. "What're you saying?"

"I'm telling Boche to surrender," I laughed.

Aimee laughed, and then cringed. "Make it stop! Make it stop! The pain is. . . " she groaned before passing out again.

I checked her pulse. It was very weak. Her forehead was hot, so I poured water on a piece of cloth and wiped her face to cool her down. Her rosy cheeks turned a pale white. Death was close and I prayed our allies would arrive soon. My pounding heart brought sweat to my brow, sending a chill through my body as I sat on the cold, dusty floor of the cellar next to my dying friend.

Seconds felt like hours. Hours felt like days. It seemed the fighting was right above us. I could hear frantic German voices, the sound of rifle fire, and the rattle of machine guns. Then, artillery shells began falling in the town square, on the streets surrounding it, and directly on the cafe above.

I ran to the two German corpses and removed their steel helmets. I put one on, raced back to Aimee's side, and put the other helmet over her face. Then, I used my body to shield her from the small chunks of cement falling from the ceiling. The room filled with dust so I stuffed my nose in the cradle of my arm.

The bombardment began walking its way south. Small arms fire grew intense, and then it too slowly drifted south. Tanks pushed their way through the town and I hoped they were our liberators. Then, the sounds of war drifted away.

I searched through the small chunks rubble and found the flashlight covered in a half inch of dust. The light was out, so I slapped it a few times to get it to work. Then, I found the walkie-talkie. A large chunk of cement had crushed the receiver, so I threw the useless thing across the room.

"Simon?" Aimee mumbled. I removed the steel helmet from her face. "Simon, is that you?" She asked. Her eyes were blank as she stared at the ceiling.

"It's Marcel," I quietly answered.

"Where are we? Where's Simon?" Aimee moaned. "I'm so thirsty." She turned her head to look at me. "Marcel, please give me some water."

"I can't, Aimee," I said as I moistened a piece of cloth and stuck it in her mouth so she could suck on it.

Aimee spit the cloth from her mouth. "Please, Marcel, find Simon. Tell him, I love him."

"Hang on, Aimee," I pled.

Aimee winced, and then groaned. "Marcel," she screamed. Then, she gasped for air as she wailed sharply. Her chest heaved, fighting to fill her lungs with life. A few seconds later, her breathing grew faint. Her hand gripped my arm like a vice. She raised her head slightly. Then, all strength fled her body.

"Don't give up, Aimee," I stammered. Tears began washing the dust from my face. "You can't die," I cried.

"Marcel. . . Marcel, promise," she choked. "Promise you'll find my daughter. Take care of her. Please Marcel. . ." Her voice trailed off. Her eyes closed. Her grip on my arm loosened.

My chest tightened. My breathing grew quick and shallow. My hands shook. I took the helmet off my head and threw it across the room. "No," I yelled. Then, I lowered my head. "Why?" I asked, and then stared toward heaven. "God, why?" I lowered my head and embraced Aimee as I wept.

I wept until my heart ached. I wept until my tears ceased to fall. Until my head was on fire and my body was weak. Until my trembling body ceased to move. It was then, I realized Aimee was more than just a friend. She was like a sister. A sister I never had and now she was gone.

In time my courage, my strength returned. I laid Aimee's body down and stood up. Although, the building above was reduced to rubble during the last bombardment, the cellar remained almost completely intact. On the floor there were a few piles of cement and wood from the ceiling. Dust covered everything. The empty wine rack had fallen on its side, and the two German corpses still kept the door shut. When I moved them out of the way, the cellar door sprung open as a few jagged pieces of stone tumbled into the room. But that was all. A wall of broken stone and cement filled the stairwell. At the very top sunlight poured through a one foot opening. American voices drifted from the street above as a jeep rattled by.

"Help me. Help me," I yelled in French. A few seconds later two American rifle barrels poked through the opening. "Don't shoot," I cried in French.

"What?" One of the soldiers yelled in English.

"No shoot. No shoot," I yelled in broken English, trying to give them the impression that I was a French national. I wasn't about to give away my cover until I knew it was safe to do so.

One of the soldiers pulled his rifle from the opening and poked his head in. "I'll be damned," he said to me face to face. Then, he pulled his head away. "Hey Sarge, we've got civilians over here."

The sound of many boots ran up to the hole. Then, a dirty face peeked at me before disappearing. "Jones, get Anderson over here. The rest of you dig that lucky son-of-a-bitch out of there," the sergeant ordered.

I began pulling chunks of rubble into the cellar as the American soldiers dug the rubble out of the stairwell. In five minutes there was an opening big enough for the sergeant and private Anderson to crawl through. At that moment, the sergeant saw the two dead Germans and ordered private Anderson to have me put my hands up. I waited until private Anderson told me in French before I raised my hands. Then, the sergeant patted me down and found the HiStandard pistol in my belt.

"Ask him why he has this," the sergeant ordered.

Again, I waited until private Anderson translated the sergeant's order before I answered in French that I was in the resistance.

The sergeant then searched the cellar, hovering over Aimee's body for a while before returning to my side. "Tell him he's coming with us," the sergeant ordered. After private Anderson translated, I replied that I wouldn't leave without Aimee's body. Private Anderson translated and the sergeant looked at me and sighed. "Very well, tell the Frenchy he can bring the woman."

Private Anderson helped me carry Aimee's body up the stairs. The soldiers outside pulled her through the opening and I followed after. Five American soldiers eyed me and Aimee's dead body with a mixture of suspicion, indifference, and awe.

When the sergeant and private Anderson crawled out of the cellar, I asked that my weapons and gear be brought with us. The sergeant quickly denied my request until I stated there was important information about the German army in my gear.

"Ah, hell," the sergeant roared. Then, he turned to two of his soldiers. "Jones, Blake, get down there and bring the Frenchy's gear back to the CP (Command Post)."

I cradled Aimee's body in my arms and followed the sergeant. Private Anderson and another soldier followed behind us. My eyes wandered as I walked through the town square. It looked like a fleet of bull dozers had rolled through the town. Only a few crumbling walls, a couple of light posts, and a statue were left standing. American tanks and infantry waded through the rubble in the opposite direction and all I could think about was wanting to know what day it was. I wanted to know how long it took to reduce the entire town of Saint Lo into a rock quarry.

The sergeant led us across the town square to a battered wall. We crossed to the other side through a large hole, and then followed it southeast to where another battered wall intersected it. This walled intersection of crumbling civilization shielded nine soldiers from a sniper lurking in the area.

Two of the nine soldiers monitored large field radios, while the other seven huddled over a map lying on wood planks held up by a pile of broken red brick. "Sir," the sergeant said.

A captain with a bandaged left hand and a frown on his face looked up. "Get those civilians out of here!"

"They're resistance, sir. He had this on him," the sergeant said as he handed the captain my HiStandard pistol.

"Does he know anything?" The captain asked.

"Says he does," the sergeant replied.

"Then, ask him what the hell he knows, damn it!"

"Yes, sir," the sergeant said, and then he ordered private Anderson to ask me what I knew about the German forces. Private Anderson translated, and I asked him if it was safe to talk.

"Sir, the Frenchy wants to know if it's safe to talk?" Private Anderson said.

"Damn French," the captain groaned. "It's not safe anywhere in this God damn country. . . Tell him it's safe anyway."

After private Anderson translated the captain's message, I gently laid Aimee's body down and brushed her hair from her face before I stood up. "I'm an American," I announced in English. Every soldier within earshot stared at me with their mouths agape. "I'm a lieutenant in the OSS. The receiver on my radio is broken, and I don't know if London received any of my messages. So, I'll need your assistance in getting a message to them."

"I'll be damned," private Anderson chuckled.

"I've heard about you folks, but never thought I'd find one of you out here. I'm Captain Marble of the 2nd Infantry Division, and you are?" He asked with an outstretched hand.

"Sir, right now I'm, *Nobody*," I replied as we shook hands.

"*Nobody*? That's a fine name. Now what can you tell me about the Germans?"

I gave Captain Marble every bit of information I knew about the German movements, mobility, strength, and the surrounding terrain from Vassy to Saint Lo. As I talked, Captain Marble hovered over his map and marked every spot I pointed at with symbols that were unknown to me. Meanwhile, his intelligence officer scribbled notes as a radio operator sent a message to the 2nd Infantry Division headquarters, informing them of my presence. In turn, the message was forwarded to SHAEF (Supreme Headquarters, Allied Expeditionary Forces) who passed the message onto OSS headquarters in London. Then, my gear was returned to me and I gave the sergeant the rest of the explosives that were in the packs.

When the briefing was over, I asked for a shovel. Private Anderson and another soldier whose name I've long since forgotten, carried Aimee's body on a stretcher to the northern edge of Saint Lo. It was there, under a large, ancient elm tree where I laid my friend to rest. On a broken plank from an ammo crate, I scrawled, *Here lies a daughter of France. A gallant warrior and a good friend. Died in Battle on July 18th, 1944. May Heaven embrace her soul. May her spirit rest in peace.* At the bottom, I wrote, *Aimee.* Then, I hammered her tombstone in the ground and wiped my eyes. "How will I find your daughter when I don't know her name?" I asked softly.

When I returned to the command post, the intelligence officer said London ordered my immediate return to England. The next day, I hitched a ride on an ambulance to Mulberry harbor. From there, I was ferried out to a troop ship taking wounded men back to England. Thirteen hours later, I arrived in Southampton. Rain fell heavily as I walked down the gangplank. My heart sank as my feet touched solid ground. I felt as if I had left something behind. I felt as if I had left my family, my home, and I realized that I had.

21

*T*he Southampton docks buzzed activity. Trucks, cranes, and men danced against time to load equipment, men and supplies bound for Normandy. Orders barked from smartly dressed officers drifted through the foggy night to men covered in grime. I was awestruck by the perfection carried out by so many in such an impossible amount of time.

"Lieutenant Harrington?" A short, obese, middle-aged man with round spectacles and a tired smile inquired as I stepped from the gangplank. He was accompanied by a tall, slender fellow whose face was devoid of emotion. They both wore long, black overcoats, and fedoras on their heads. "Lieutenant Harrington?" The short man asked again.

I stared at the two men. After many months spent in France under a pseudonym, I paused until I realized the short man was talking to me. "Yes, sir," I answered.

"Ah," the short man smiled warmly, showing off crooked pearl white teeth. "I'm Fellsworth, and this is MacAnally. We've to escort you to London." Since we were in a secure area, I didn't bother to ask them for identification.

MacAnally carried my pack as I followed the two men across the dock to a black sedan parked in the shadows between a row of warehouses. My pack was stowed in the trunk while I was ushered into the back seat. MacAnally sat next to me while Fellsworth and an unnamed driver rode in the front. Even though it was damp, they kept their windows rolled halfway down. After what I'd been through the last month and a half, I didn't blame them. The poor souls were stuck with my body odor, the smells of a French sewer, and death. I didn't think anything of it until I got out of the car and a lovely, young, female yeoman stepped away and pinched her nose.

After a long, hot shower, I dressed in a fresh army green uniform. Then, a guard escorted me to a small room in the basement with one table and two chairs. A single light bulb dangled by a frayed cord from the ceiling.

MacAnally sat across from me as I ate bacon, eggs, and toast. The meal quenched my hunger, but I longed for French cuisine.

When I finished eating, MacAnally led me to an adjacent room. Fellsworth, along with four other men sat at a long conference table. The walls were bare. Like the previous room, a solitary light bulb hung from the ceiling, humming softly as the men stared at me.

A Royal Marine sergeant entered and whispered into Fellsworth's ear before leaving the room. The door was shut and locked from the outside. Then, the debriefing began. For the next five hours I was stuck in an uncomfortable wooden chair telling the men every minute detail of my mission, the Maquis members I worked with, and the German strength and armament in my area of operation. Every question they asked, I answered, and I asked a few questions of my own. Though, I seldom received an answer. Fellsworth and I did most of the talking while the other men interjected sporadically. To this day, their identities remain a mystery. Due to their accents, I believe two were British, one was French, and the last one was an American. MacAnally remained mute throughout the debriefing process.

During the debriefing, there was one line of questioning I'll never forget. When a short man with a large nose and thick British accent asked if I knew Brigette, I promptly replied, "No, but Jack had contact with her on quite a few occasions."

"Did you at anytime know she was working for British Intelligence?"

"No, sir. As far as I know, she's just a common prostitute. Why?"

"She's gone missing. We believe the locals murdered her, but won't know for sure until somebody speaks or her body turns up."

"We understand Emile's her lover," a fat man with black slicked back hair and a ruddy complexion said in a thick British accent.

"I wouldn't say he's her lover. More like an acquaintance," I clarified. "But he's been missing for quite awhile now, so, I don't know how you can blame him."

"They're not blaming him," Fellsworth said. "They're merely trying to pose the question that it's possible he and Brigette could be hiding out somewhere."

"She has information we need," the fat man added.

"Well, gentlemen, anything's possible in France right now. Though, the last time I saw Emile, Saint Lo was crawling with Germans and I fear he's dead," I stated.

"I see," the short man said, and then looked at Fellsworth.

Fellsworth nodded, and then turned to me. "We've just learned of a plot to assassinate Hitler. Fortunately, the attempt failed. Brigette's assignment was to glean information from the German High Command and pass the information on to Bletchley Park. If she's still alive, we need to locate her and find out if any more attempts will be made on Hitler's life."

"Why would you want to keep that bastard alive?" I asked.

"He's losing the war," the fat man replied. "If he were to be assassinated the war could go on for many years."

I thought about the statement for a moment. My conscience told me that under no circumstances should Hitler be allowed to live. But in the end, I had to agree. Hitler was Germany's quickest downfall. "Have you gentlemen contacted Jack? He might know where Brigette is. If not, at least he can inform the locals of her ties to the allies."

"Jack hasn't contacted us in over a week. We think he might have been compromised. Normandy's literally turned upside down since the invasion and many of our agents have ceased transmitting," Fellsworth said, and then he smiled. "We've sent in a Jedbourough team to search for him though."

"When was the Jed team sent in?" I asked.

"Last night," the fat man replied.

"Then, you have nothing to worry about, gentlemen. When Jack and the others find the Jeds, he'll ensure their safety. Should expect him to be back on the air within a few days," I smiled.

"The Jedbourough team was sent to find Jack," the American said dryly.

"I understand that, sir, but I know Jack. He'll find the Jeds before they find him."

After the debriefing, I was given a short rest and relaxation period. Three days into it, I got bored and asked for another assignment. That evening, I got my wish, but it wasn't what I had in mind. They were sending me to Beaulieu to be an instructor. I requested to be sent back to France instead, but was denied.

That same night MacAnally escorted me to a car waiting in front of the building. Another car pulled up beside us. The back window rolled down and Fellsworth stuck his head out. "Jack radioed this morning. He and the Maquis are knocking the hell out of the Nazis," Fellsworth laughed. "And you were right. He found the Jed team first." Fellsworth and I shook hands. Then, he wished me luck as his car drove away. I could only smile as I watched him leave.

Beaulieu was exactly the same as when I left it. The same instructors were there. The same courses were taught. The only difference was the warmer weather.

The first week I got a crash course on how to be an instructor. At night, I spent my free time writing to Sarah. I couldn't sleep. She was constantly on my mind. I longed to hear her voice, to hold her in my arms and kiss her sweet lips. Three weeks later, my letters trickled back. All of them were unopened. All of them had, "Return to Sender," on the front. I felt my life was over, but I didn't give up hope and kept writing her everyday. On a daily basis, I received each and every one of them back. All were unopened. Then, in the middle of September, I received a large, brown envelope. The return address was my father's law firm. Inside was a thick packet with, "Dissolution of Marriage" written in large bold lettering on the front page. A short letter from Sarah was attached.

> My Dearest Dan,
>
> I pray you don't hate me for wanting a divorce. I was very lonely after you left and heartbroken for losing my child. I want a man in my life who will take care of me. I want a man who will love me and give me everything my heart desires. Please don't hate me when I tell you that I've met such a man. He's very kind, loving, and wealthy. We're very happy together. I hope you will understand. I beg of you to sign the divorce papers, for we plan to be married next spring.
>
> I know this must be hard on you. After not hearing from you for so long, I thought you were dead. I know it would be easier on both of us if you were. I know you probably wish you were now, but I hope you can find the strength to get over this. I hope when you're finished playing soldier you can find a suitable woman to settle down with.
>
> Cordially,
> Sarah

Tears cascaded down my cheeks. My heart felt as if it had been ripped from my chest. I felt there was nothing more to live for. As Sarah wished in her letter, I too wished I was dead. I wished I had never been born. The only thing that kept me going day after day was my instructor duties. Only then, while I instructed my students, was my mind able to break away from my life.

By the time I received Sarah's letter, France was celebrating its third week of liberation. I wondered where Jack and the rest of my friends were. I longed to be with them. They were my only family now. There was a bond between us that was thicker than blood and I needed them to help me through my grief. The long sorrow filled nights were too much for me to handle alone. Then, in the middle of November, I got a reprieve from the pain constricting my deadened heart. I got a new chance at life. Or death. I didn't care which. In the middle of the night, Fellsworth whisked me away to a secret location deep in the Welsh countryside. I arrived early in the morning at a seventeen bedroom manor surrounded by acres of cultivated fields and meadows. Three men greeted me as I got out of the car. They were all OSS officers who kept their true identities from me. I only knew them by fictitious names common throughout the English speaking world.

Mike was a sixty-year-old, thin haired, skinny scientist with bifocals. He was from the R and A Branch and accredited with inventing some of the famous gadgets used by agents in the field. John, another scientist from the R and A Branch, was middle-aged with black bushy hair and had the demeanor of a German officer. Chris, on the other hand, a twenty-eight-year-old from SI Branch who had straight black hair and a trimmed moustache, enjoyed creating fictitious stories about his career in the OSS. He once claimed to have shot down an Me 109 Messerschmitt with a Colt 45 pistol. I didn't believe him, but that story actually turned out to be true.

For the next three days, I was told only to speak German. Mike gave me instruction on a new radio he invented. It was the size of a shoebox and had a mouthpiece microphone and earphones that could be set to amplify the quietest sound. With its compact size and range of over five hundred miles, the radio was considered state-of-the-art for its time and classified, Top Secret.

John gave me instruction on the newest gadgets used for making dead-drops. They were nothing fancy. Some were just hollowed out stakes that I learned to lower down to the ground from the inside of my pants. Then, I would nonchalantly raise my foot six inches and step on the stake to push it into the ground. My favorite gadget, the one I got the most amusement from, was a hollowed out nail with a screw top. All I had to do was insert a small message, screw on the top, and hammer the nail into a wooden fence post or tree. A great idea, but a hammer wasn't provided and the nail easily bent when it was struck.

Chris had me pour over geographical maps for western Germany, Holland, and Belgium. Every inch, every coordinate is forever etched in my brain. Chris also taught me every aspect of the German, Dutch, and Belgian cultures that by the end of those three days, I was more of a German, Dutchman, or Belgian than the actual people who lived there.

On the morning of the fourth day, I was woken before sunrise. Chris led me to the front door of the manor as an ambulance pulled up in front. I was ushered outside and into the back of the vehicle. A wooden box was crammed in behind me. Then, the ambulance pulled away from the manor. I had no idea what was happening or where I was going. All I knew was that I wasn't alone.

Moments later, a dim overhead green light came on. An armed guard in uniform sat next to me. Across from me sat a man and woman. Another armed guard sat in the front passenger seat, and I assumed the driver was armed.

The woman was one of the women from Cover and Documentation who had dressed Jack and I before we dropped into France. She had me change into a three piece black wool suit and white shirt, topping off my ensemble with a black fedora. Then, she gave me Dutch identity documents and ration cards. The name on them was, Benoit Parlett.

When the woman was finished, she sat down next to the man who had remained silent. He was in his fifties and fit as a bull-terrier. His short grey hair and blue eyes hid his stress very well. When he spoke, his voice was deep and friendly. "Lieutenant Harrington," he began. "I've chosen you for an assignment that is of the gravest importance to the safety of our allies and all mankind. As you can tell, we've taken great precaution in preparing you for this mission. It's of the utmost secrecy. Even our allies don't know of it, and it will remain that way. You are never to speak of it to anyone ever. Is that clear?"

"Yes, sir," I answered.

"I understand you're going through a divorce. Will it affect you in any way with your assignment?" The man asked.

"No, sir," I quickly answered, and wondered how he knew I was getting a divorce since, I hadn't told anyone.

"Good. Now, I can't tell you very much right now. Truth is, we don't know much ourselves. So you're going to have to use a lot of ingenuity to pull it off. All I can say is one of our agents has gone missing. His last transmission was six days ago from a small farmhouse two miles east of Eschweiler."

"Germany?" I asked rhetorically.

"Yes."

I choked hard. Infiltrating France was one thing. Infiltrating the heartland of the Nazi empire was another. "Sir, if I may ask? Why am I posing as a Dutch national?"

"You're cover is Dutch because you're only escape routes are through either Belgium or Holland. Our allied forces should be breaking into Germany in a matter of weeks. Some units already have, so it'll be a lot easier to pass through our lines as a Dutchman than a German."

"I understand," I stated.

"Now all you've got to do is get to the farmhouse and see if our agent is still there. If he's not, let us know, and then get the hell out of there."

The assignment sounded simple enough and that's what concerned me the most. In the murky world of espionage, the simplest way is often the deadliest. However, with my pending divorce, I didn't care.

It was past midnight when the ambulance pulled up to the security gates at the airfield in Aldbourne. Our driver spoke to one of the guards, and then to another man before turning his attention to us in the back. "Sir, it's Richards. He wants to talk with you," the driver said.

The man who briefed me on the assignment got out of the back of the ambulance. A few minutes later, he got back inside and told the driver to take us to Beautomes, a safe house located five minutes from the airfield. "Well, lieutenant, seems you've missed your flight. We'll try again tomorrow night," the man said.

At Beautomes, I ate an early breakfast, and then went to bed. The woman from Cover and Documentation woke me at seven sharp and led me downstairs after I got dressed. The rest of the morning I poured over maps of Belgium, Holland, and Germany until lunch time. After lunch, I checked and rechecked my gear. Then, I made a quick transmission to Bletchley Park to check my radio before I test fired my HiStandard pistol out of a back window of Beautomes.

Included in my gear was an assortment of dead-drop canisters in various sizes. The longest was a five inch spike with a one inch hollowed out core. A compass was hidden behind the third button down on my coat. A silk map was sewn inside the liner. I objected to the map since I already had the map committed to memory, but I was overruled. They claimed it was a precaution in case I got lost. I knew it was a death sentence if I was captured.

Other items in my arsenal consisted of a small lock-pick set, two thumb knives hidden in the soles of my shoes, and one in my lapel. A seven inch throwing knife and three pen-guns were concealed in the lining of my suitcase. I also received a pair of leather gloves which had a single shot pistol sewn onto the top of the right hand. The pistol was fired by making a fist and striking an opponent, thus, depressing a plunger that fired a single twenty-two caliber round at blank range. That evening, just after I put on a jumpsuit over my civilian clothes, I was given one last item. A small vial filled with cyanide which I discreetly threw in a trash can when no one was looking.

Ten minutes after sundown, an ambulance drove me to the airfield. It pulled alongside the, Northern Lights, the name of a Whitley Bomber with its engines running. The back door of the ambulance opened and a guard ushered me into the bomber. The copilot smiled as I climbed aboard. A few minutes later, the plane taxied onto the runway. Then we were off, climbing into the black sky to take our place in formation of a bomber group heading to destroy a munitions factory on the outskirts of Düsseldorf, Germany.

22

The bomber leveled off at 12,000 feet. Cold air blew through the gun ports on the side of the plane, bringing the cabin temperature to twenty degrees Fahrenheit below freezing. I wrapped myself in two wool blankets the navigator gave me. The thick gloves I wore kept my hands just warm enough to keep my fingers from frostbite. Everyone wore oxygen masks. How the flight crews kept their jovial outlook in these extreme conditions, I'll never know.

The crew of my taxi were all young men between the ages of nineteen and twenty-two-years-old. The pilot and copilot were the oldest of the bunch, but I wouldn't put their ages much older than twenty-four. At the time, I was only 27, but I felt like an old man amongst children.

I don't know the exact time we entered German air space. I wasn't about to bare my arm and look at my watch. Bundled tightly in a ball, the cold permeated every inch of my body. I shivered. I cursed under my breath. I was bored. Sarah haunted me. How I wished for some excitement to take my tormented mind off my life.

The bomber group glided down to five thousand feet. The air got warmer. I could finally remove the oxygen mask, but I dared not cast the wool blankets away. When the bomber leveled off, the bombay doors opened, blasting me with cold, fresh air. Almost immediately, anti-aircraft batteries opened up. Flak filled the sky like an upward wind. The plane jolted and bounced from side to side. Pieces of shrapnel ripped through the fuselage. Through the headset, I heard the calm orders from a tense pilot and the frantic gibberish from the crew relaying damage assessments throughout the plane. No matter how many bombing missions a person had been on, they never got used to the flak. I was no exception. I feared at any moment a jagged piece of metal would rip its way into the aircraft and tear deep into my body. Yet, my main concern was the open bombay doors and the bombs dangling unprotected from the death coming from below.

The navigator took control of the plane. From deep inside the belly of the aircraft, he kept his eyes glued to the bombsight. His hands skillfully on the flight controls. Somehow, he kept the plane on target as it shook and jittered. Outside, the flak grew thicker. The tail-gunner screamed as a piece of shrapnel tore through his leg. The machine gunner across from me raced to his aid. Then, the navigator depressed the bomb release. The sky filled with an eerie, high pitched drone that gradually faded away. Leaving only the sound of the planes engines, the wind coming through the bombay door, and the ever present flak. Soon after, I heard the faint rumble of bombs as they found their targets in the frightened town below.

How many lives were lost? How many buildings crumbled? How much of the German will to fight remained after our bombs pounded their heartland? I didn't care. I only knew I was alive.

The pilot resumed control of the aircraft as soon as the last bomb dropped from the plane. Once we were out of Düsseldorf's airspace, the plane banked to the right and broke away from the bomber group. Five minutes later, I was poised at the open bombay as the copilot approached. "Well, laddie, hope you've enjoyed your flight. Can't say I wish I was in your shoes, but good luck," the copilot yelled over the drone of the engines.

We shook hands. "Thank you, lieutenant. You men are very brave," I sincerely replied.

"No, sir. You're the one who's brave. We're not jumping into Germany in the middle of the bleedin' night. You are," the copilot laughed. Later, I learned the Northern Lights never made it back to jolly old England. I was the last person to see any of them alive.

"Make ready," the navigator yelled. I looked through the bombay doors at the black carpet of nothingness below. My heart pounded. I began to sweat in the cold, crisp air. "Go," the navigator thundered.

"Good luck, sir," the copilot yelled as I jumped through the bombay doors. Turbulence sent me tumbling end over end. I stretched out my arms and legs to even out. Then, I counted to three before pulling the ripcord. My body jerked upward as the chute blossomed, slowing my descent into Hell. I released the straps holding the suitcase to my chest and let it fall down only to dangle on a cord twelve feet below my feet. Eighteen seconds later, my feet unexpectedly landed on a branch that gave way. The quiet countryside filled with the sound of breaking branches and rustling leaves as I fell through the thick canopy. My body jerked straight as I came to a halt, dangling from my parachute. My suitcase was stuck on a branch somewhere above me. The cord attached to it was tangled around my right leg which quickly went numb. My sight slowly adjusted to the dark night, yet I couldn't see the ground below. All I knew was a stream was close by from the sound of water trickling over rocks.

Minutes ticked by before I knew I was alone. Using the knife that came with the jumpsuit, I cut the cord attached to the suitcase. The cord quickly unraveled from my leg as the suitcase whizzed by my head. When it hit the ground, I heard a faint pop and wondered what it was. I looked down and still couldn't see the ground below. I spit twice and listened for it to fall, but over the sound of the water I didn't hear a thing.

"Well, here goes," I whispered as I cut the parachute lines holding me up. Expecting a long drop, I was caught off guard as I fell only five feet. My knees buckled, throwing me flat on my face into a patch of wet moss. I cursed, and continued to curse for the next hour as I fought to cut the parachute from the trees. Once I was finished, I buried the parachute and jumpsuit in the exact spot I had landed.

By now the dim glow of the rising sun painted the horizon. I had a vague idea of where I was, but didn't know for sure. Nazi Germany was the last place on earth I wanted to be lost. Luckily, I was only one kilometer north of Eschweiler, which meant I only had to climb over the ridge to the east to get to the farmhouse where our agent made his last transmission.

It took a half hour to claw my way through the thick forest to reach the ridge line. The overcast sky blocked most of the sunlight, but the valley below was still a beautiful sight. The yellow, brown, deep purple and light green colors of autumn never looked more refreshing. I felt like I was in a painting by Monet, and for a moment, I forgot about the war. I forgot about my mission and my divorce as I devoured the scenery and breathed its fragrant aroma. I was at peace with the world. I was at peace with myself. Then, a vision of the woman in my dreams clouded my view. Again, I stood next to her at the altar. We were about to be married, only this time, tears fell from her eyes.

Gradually, the scene faded into the memory of Aimee dying next to me. Then, of Francois killing Yves, the old woman hanging from the trees, and my mothers funeral. Then, I saw my father engulfed in flames as money burned at his feet.

I snapped back to reality panting for air. Perspiration beaded on my forehead. I removed my fedora and wiped the sweat on my sleeve. Yet, the picture of my father remained. There was only one thing I could do to stop the vision. I opened the suitcase and removed the HiStandard pistol and stuffed it into my waistband before fleeing into the valley below.

Three farmhouses were nestled on the valley floor. All of them were whitewashed stone structures with dark wood trim and pointed roofs. One of them stood two stories high and had a matching barn. The other two were one story structures with the smaller of the two only five hundred meters to the southeast of where I stood. It looked habitable but abandoned. A shutter hanging by a single hinge thumped lightly against the side of the house. The painted walls were chipped. Vegetation grew wildly along the foundation, and the gate to the chicken coop stood agape. There wasn't a single indication of life. Which was exactly the place I would choose to hide if the entire German population was looking for me, so I crept toward it. Ten minutes later, I cautiously knocked at the front door. Silence. I drew the pistol from my waistband and opened the door. Immediately, I dropped my suitcase and buried my nose in my sleeve. My eyes watered. The putrid smell of death lurked within and I believed I was too late.

I felt like fleeing, but fought the impulse and stepped inside. Light dust covered the floor. There were no footprints. I was the first person to enter the crypt since Death paid a visit. His mark was everywhere. A half eaten apple rotted on the dining table. A butter knife lay beside it. A dead carnation hung over the side of its vase. Its wilted petals curled and brown. A symbolic reminder that mortality finds all who live.

A picture of Hitler hung over the fireplace. I stared at it. Captivated by evil before I broke away and searched the rest of the house. In a back bedroom an old man lay on a bed under a layer of quilts. The taut skin on his face was dry as leather. Dark kidney spots were visible on his skin. His eyes, black from decay, bulged from their sockets. His mouth hung open. '*Was he frightened when he took his last breath?*' I wondered. Beside the bed, and elderly woman sat in a chair. Her eyes stared vacantly at her husband. Her mouth was closed. Gray hair rested on her shoulders. I poked her with the muzzle of the pistol. She fell slowly to the floor. Her death was more recent than her husband's, though only by a day.

A cold chill rippled through my body as I realized that even in wartime people still died from natural causes. At length, I slowly turned from the grisly sight and left the house. On the porch, my body shook, trying to rid the stench of death from my clothes. I knew then I didn't want to die of old age. For Sarah was no longer with me, and I didn't want to die alone.

When I stopped shaking, I looked around. A gentle breeze rustled the trees and swayed the tall grass. Birds sang peaceful songs. Then, a rush of exhilaration passed over my body. I casually stuffed the pistol back in my waistband and picked up the suitcase. My steps landed softly as I walked toward the next farmhouse. A four foot high stone wall surrounded its perimeter. I hopped over it and kneeled down behind a small bush. The lawn was neatly clipped. The shrubbery was trimmed. Four chickens ambled down the gravel walkway, poking their beaks between the pebbles in search for food while a large, fluffy, grey Himalayan cat watched them from the open front door. A woman's singing drifted delicately from inside. I couldn't hear her words, though, in my mind, I thought I knew. Anger boiled in my veins. My hatred for the German race peaked as I walked toward the front door. With every step, her voice grew louder, the song more sweet, my anger more intense.

The cat hissed, and then ran inside the house. I followed it and quietly shut the door behind me. The woman kept singing. Her voice came from the first room on the right. The aroma of eggs sizzling in a skillet told me that she was in the kitchen, and for a moment I was reminded of Boston. A place I no longer called home.

The suitcase fell from my fingers as I darted into the kitchen. A large, blond haired, middle-aged woman spun around. She dropped the spatula from her right hand as she brought both hands up to her mouth and screamed. I slapped her hard across the face, knocking her to the floor. Then, I kicked her in the chest and pounced on top of her, pulling her arms behind her back.

She was German. She was my enemy, and I wanted to kill her. I wanted revenge for Aimee's death. I wanted to ease the pain of my divorce. Tears welled up in my eyes, but refused to fall.

"Who are you?" The woman cried while struggling to get away. "What do you want?"

I slapped her across the face. "Shut up!" I yelled. "I'll ask the questions. If you don't answer, then I'll kill you. Understand?" The fear in her eyes told me that she did. "Where's the American spy?"

"Who?" The woman cried.

"The American spy. Where is he?"

The woman stopped struggling. "I don't know what you're talking about. Who are you? Gestapo?" She asked.

I slapped her again. "Answer me! Where's the American?"

"There are no Americans here," the woman sputtered, panting for air from under the weight of my body.

"You're lying," I growled. Then, I pulled the pistol from my waistband and pressed the muzzle against her neck, fighting the urge to pull the trigger. "Tell me where he is, or I'll kill you." She didn't reply and I pressed the muzzle further into her neck. "I won't ask you again."

The woman sobbed heavily. Her body shook. She knew she was seconds away from death. "A man came here two weeks ago. He was wounded and I sent him away. But he was German, not American."

"Sent him away? Where?"

"I don't know."

"Don't lie to me," I said slowly as I pressed the muzzle deeper into her neck. "Which way did he go?" The woman didn't answer, so I pressed the muzzle further into her neck.

"East," the woman sobbed. "He went east."

"East?"

"Yes. I swear to you, he went east," the woman moaned. Her body relaxed. Tears streamed from her eyes.

"I don't believe you."

"I'm telling the truth. I swear. Please, don't kill me."

"You're lying," I thundered. "Why would he flee deeper into the Fatherland?"

"I don't know. I really don't, sir."

"Who've you told?" I asked.

"No one. I thought he was a wounded soldier. Thought he was German. I didn't know he was a spy. Please sir, don't kill me," the woman pled. Her strength was spent. Her weeping quieted. She gasped under the weight of my body.

I kept the pressure of the muzzle on her neck. I hated her. I hated her and felt sorry for her at the same time. She was my enemy. A member of a race of people who terrorized and murdered countless people. She was as guilty as the rest for following a man they all called, 'Fuhrer.' A man spawned in the depths of Hell, sent forth to quash all that is good. Yes, I believed she was as guilty as Hitler himself, and yet, I felt pity. I felt sorry her soul that had been led astray. I felt contempt that she had embraced the ideology of hate, and I was ashamed I had unleashed mine.

I realized that given the right circumstances, we can all succumb to hate. I realized that as human beings a constant struggle between good and evil rages inside each and every one of us. That wars fought within our souls are much more devastating than any war fought at any time throughout history. Only we can decide which side is victorious. Which side ends in defeat. Our own salvation lies with our own choice, and when that choice is based on prejudice and hate. When we feel superior over our fellow man, our choice is reared from Hell.

I pulled the muzzle an inch from her neck, though, I kept pressure on her body. She was still my enemy. I would kill her instantly if she tried to resist. I knew I would have to kill her eventually to keep her from alerting the Gestapo, but I had more questions to ask. There was a concentrated German military presence in the area, and I needed to know their strength and location. I needed to know about the local Gestapo. Had they already questioned her about the missing American agent? How many times had they come by her house? I didn't believe for a second she told me the truth about the wounded man, and knew she told someone about him.

For a brief moment, my thoughts centered on the eggs sizzling in the pan. I smelled them burning. Then, a faint thud come from the back of the house. The corpulent cat jumping off a bed onto the hardwood floor was my first guess. Then, I heard it again. This time I knew it was a human footstep. "Who else is here?" I whispered in the woman's ear.

"No one. I live alone," she replied.

"Don't lie to me," I softly growled as I jammed the muzzle back into her neck. Then, I looked to the doorway.

"I'm not lying. I live alone," she cried. Then, a crash came from the living room. "Run, Gustav, run! He'll kill you," the woman yelled as she struggled beneath me. My finger steadily tightened on the trigger. I was about to fire when a shaky hand grasped the doorjamb. Then, the barrel of a Luger pistol appeared.

I pulled my pistol from the woman's neck and pointed it toward the doorway as a man came into view. He wore wool pajama bottoms. His feet were bare, as was his chest. A large bandage covered his eyes. His whole body shook. "Don't shoot her," the man cried.

I knew the voice. The blond hair was a dead giveaway as to the man's identity. "Chip Taylor, lower your weapon," I yelled in English.

"Who?" Chip asked in German.

"Damn it, Chip, it's me, Dan Harrington. Now lower your weapon," I said in English.

A faint smile crept across Chip's face. "Danny boy? What're you doing here?" Chip asked, and then fainted.

I jumped off the woman and ran to Chip's side. The woman pushed past me and cradled him in her arms. She begged him not to die as she tenderly kissed his forehead. My jaw dropped. I couldn't believe my eyes. Chip, embraced in the arms of our enemy, and she offered him love, not hate. I removed the Luger from his limp hand and stuffed it in my waistband while the burning eggs filled the room with smoke.

23

There were times over the next two days that I thought Chip would die. His wounds were slowly healing, but he needed nourishment. I fed him all of the extra rations I could spare. The German woman, Veronica, fed him what she could. In those two days, she starved herself so Chip could live. I admired her for that, but I kept a close eye on her. She was still my enemy and I couldn't find the strength to trust her.

Every second, I worried the Gestapo would break down the door and shoot all of us. Chip was a wanted man. The Nazis knew he had been in the area two weeks before, but it seemed they moved their search elsewhere. Not a single vehicle came down the road in front of the house. The only traffic I saw was a lone horse drawn cart and rider.

I barely slept. When I did, I bound Veronica's hands and feet, and then tied her to the bedpost. I would've hated the person who did that to me, but I think she understood why. Once she told me that she didn't care what I did as long as I didn't harm Chip, or Gustav Prost as he was known to her.

Radio communication with London was completely out of the equation. When my suitcase fell from the tree on the night I parachuted into the lions den, one of the pen-guns fired as the suitcase struck the ground. Its bullet bored into the radio. Now the radio was a useless piece of scrap metal with diodes and wires. The radio Chip had was a British model with dead batteries, so I buried both of them under a bush along the stone wall surrounding Veronica's front yard. Chip and I were on our own unless London sent another agent to find us, and I didn't care to wait around and see if they would.

On the third day, I was in the kitchen with Veronica. My pistol followed every move she made as she scrambled three eggs. Except for the sound of the sizzling eggs, the house remained quiet. Then, I heard a groan.

"Veronica," Chip yelled from the bedroom. "Veronica, give me a hand."

Veronica removed the skillet from the burner and turned to me. "Shoot me if you want, but I'm going to help Gustav."

I waved her past with my pistol, and then followed her into the bedroom. Chip sat up in bed. A jovial smile spread across his face. "Veronica, my dear," Chip sang as she sat next to him on the bed. Chip moved his hands across the bedspread until he found her body. They embraced.

"How are you, my love?" Veronica asked.

"Hungry," Chip replied. "Is there anything to eat?"

"Chip," I said from the doorway.

Chip loosened his embrace and turned his head in my direction. "Who's there?"

"It's Dan."

"My God, I thought you were a dream," Chip smiled. "Where am I?"

"Germany," I replied.

"What're you doing here?"

"I've come to get you back to England. From now on speak to me in English when the woman's around," I ordered in English. I didn't want Veronica listening to our conversations.

Chip furrowed his brow. "All right, Dan, but you can trust her. She saved my life."

"We can't trust anyone," I snapped. Then, I ordered Veronica to sit in the chair in the far corner of the room. Reluctantly, she pulled herself away from Chip's embrace. Dejection written across her face as she did as she was told. Knowing her fate was set in motion. Knowing she didn't have long to live. She knew it all along.

"How'd you lose your sight?" I asked.

Chip sighed as he lowered his head. His hands fidgeted with the blankets. "Well, Danny boy," Chip began, and then paused for a moment. "It was dark. I was walking just outside Stolberg when a car came from behind. I tried to remain calm. Hoping the car would pass, but it stopped behind me. It was the Gestapo, so I ran into a field before the men got out of the car. . . The Bastards shot at me. They chased me and kept shooting. I had no where to hide so I laid down in the grass. When they got close, I killed two of them and wounded the officer. . . I panicked and shot all of my bullets, but the damn officer kept coming, so I knocked him down with my suitcase and pounced on him. We struggled. He tried to stab me, but I got his knife away from him. The next thing I knew he was digging his fingers in my eyes. I couldn't push him away and he wouldn't let go. It hurt so bad I pounded his chest. Then, he went limp. I couldn't see, but

I could feel his blood on my hands. I stabbed him in the chest and didn't even know it." Chip paused. I could see wetness dampening the bandages over his eyes. "Dan?"

"Yes," I said softly.

"I've never killed anyone before," Chip confessed. Then, he held his hands up. "I killed him with these. With my own hands." Chip made fists and pounded the bed. "I'm a murderer."

"No, you're not, Chip." I put my hand on his trembling shoulder. "You had to kill them."

Chip pulled away from me. "I can still feel his blood on my hands. It won't come off."

"You'll get over it," I said nonchalantly. "Now where did you hide the information?"

"Why?" Chip asked as he laid back on the bed.

"I need to retrieve it before I can get us out of here," I replied.

"I can't go back. Just leave me here," Chip cried.

"I can't. She'll give us away."

"No, she won't."

"I'll give you a few minutes to say goodbye, then we're leaving."

"Just leave us alone," Chip yelled.

I stared at Chip, and then at Veronica. Her face was devoid of emotion. I felt nothing for her. To me she was no longer human.

"You're going to kill her, aren't you?"

"I have to."

"You can't. I love her," Chip cried.

"Chip this is no time for one of your weekly romances. We have a job to do, and if I have to kill her so we can accomplish it, I will." I looked at Veronica. "Besides, you haven't seen what she looks like."

"I don't have to. I saw all the other women and they meant nothing to me. Since, I've lost my sight, I can finally see with my heart. It can look deeper into a person's soul than my eyes ever could. Don't you understand? I love her. She loves me. If you kill her, then you'll be killing me. I'll never forgive you. Ever."

"I don't expect you to," I said coldheartedly.

"Damn you. You still have Sarah. I'll have no one. Could you really live the rest of your life knowing you murdered the only woman I've ever loved?"

I sat at the foot of the bed and lowered my head. Tears came to my eyes and dampened my cheeks. I looked at Veronica, and then at Chip. "She's divorcing me. . . She's found another man and they're to be married next spring."

Chip moved his right hand along the bed sheet until he found my knee. "I'm sorry to hear that, Dan. Thought you two'd be married forever."

"So did I. Now, I don't have anyone to go home to. There's nothing left for me in Boston. This war. . . This mission is all I've got left."

"You've got me and my family. You've got Veronica too. . . And there's your family in Ireland? You've always wanted to meet them. They probably want to meet you too."

"Maybe they do. Maybe they don't. I'm still my father's son."

"No, you're not. The man's a jerk and you know it. All you needed was to become a man, and now you have. You are your own person now. One of the strongest people I've ever known. Don't you know you've been my hero for years. You've always had your life together, and I wanted that. But I've always been the goof off. The class clown. The playboy. I was a mess until now. My life's been too easy."

"But you've always been the most popular. The most likeable person I've ever known."

"Ah, popularity is superficial," Chip gleamed. "True friendship and love are what really matter. A person isn't complete unless they have both. I know you do. You always have. I'm the one who didn't. I never knew what love is until now."

"You've always been a good friend though," I stated.

"No. . . I haven't. I was selfish until I lost my sight. The only person I cared about was me. I used everyone. . . Including you. The only reason I was nice to people was to see what I could get from them. My father knew this. That's why he was glad I joined the OSS. He knew what I was getting into. He knew I'd learn the hard way what compassion was. I knew nothing of it until I came here. Germany's full of evil people right now. They pray for war and murder the Jews, and I didn't care. I was as evil as they are. After that Nazi gouged out my eyes, all I could think about was my life being over. I wanted to kill myself, but I couldn't bring myself to do it. . . I'm a coward, Dan."

"No, you're not," I stated.

"I stumbled through the countryside. Veronica found me when I was near death. She gave me another chance at life. Through her, I've learned what love is. Through her, I can finally see what a fool I'd been. I love her, Dan. You can't kill her," Chip pled.

"She'll talk?"

"No she won't. She's a good woman."

"Even if she doesn't report us to the Gestapo, she'll never hold up under their pressure if they suspect she helped us. I've no choice. I have to kill her."

"No, you don't," Chip snapped. "We'll take her with us."

I jumped off the bed. "You're out of your God damn mind. It's already too dangerous for the both of us. She'll only slow us down."

"But she knows the territory. She knows the best route into Belgium. We have to bring her with us, or I'm not going."

Veronica stared at us. She knew we were talking about her. She knew I had every intention of killing her. Somehow, I believe she understood why. Yet, she remained docile. I expected her to fight for her life, but all she did was stare at us with tears in her eyes.

I quietly removed the HiStandard pistol from my waist band and the silencer from my coat pocket. Chip was still trying to convince me to take her with us as I threaded the silencer onto the end of the barrel. Veronica lowered her head. Tears dripped from her eyes onto the cold floor.

The five steps I took toward her were the hardest steps I've ever taken. Each one felt as if I carried the weight of the world on my shoulders. My hand was steady as I pressed the cold silencer lightly against the top of her head. She didn't move. She didn't make a sound.

My eyes were dry. My index finger rubbed the trigger. My heart beat slow and steady. Emotion left my body as all thought fled my mind. Veronica was my enemy. Guilty solely because she was a citizen of Nazi Germany. A woman living under the tyranny of evil. Yet, she was a woman still capable of love. A sacrament I lost when Sarah ripped it from my heart.

Slowly, I pulled the pistol away from her head and let my hand fall to my side. Veronica looked up at me with tears falling from her eyes. "Go to him," I said softly. A smile creased her face as she wearily stood and went to Chip's side. "We're bringing her with us," I announced.

"Thank you, Dan," Chip sighed. "We'll always be grateful."

"Now where did you hide the information London wants?"

In German, Chip said that he hid the information on top of a truss under a shallow bridge at the southeast corner of Stolberg. Veronica offered to sketch a street map for me. Reluctantly, I gave in. Praying she wasn't leading me into a trap. That night, under the cover of darkness, I slipped out of the house. Veronica followed me outside. "Please be careful," she said. "Gustav told me what you're going to get is very important. He said the Nazis would use it to kill millions. You must not let them get it. This war must end."

I looked at her for a moment. "Take care of my friend," I said, and then left her standing by the front door.

The trek to Stolberg took much longer than I anticipated. There were many small farmsteads to bypass. The town of Eschweiler was directly in my path, so I bypassed it too. It wasn't until five in the morning when I finally arrived at the edge of Stolberg. The sun was rising fast. I didn't have any place to hide, so I stepped softly and entered the town. Not a single creature stirred in the quiet streets. Only a few birds sung in the trees.

The street map Veronica sketched was unbelievably accurate. I had committed it to memory and steered well clear of the local police station. The Police and Gestapo never slept. If they did, I wasn't about to wake them with my presence.

The bridge was exactly where Veronica placed it on the map. It was constructed exactly the way Chip said it was. I darted under the bridge, found the three rolls of microfilm, a camera and a one-time cipher pad wrapped tightly in a piece of cloth. Then, I scrambled from underneath the bridge. Luckily, the whole process took less than a minute.

Stolberg was waking from its slumber by the time I crossed the bridge headed toward Zweifall. The road meandered through the German countryside. Every step I took was filled with apprehension. I feared a Gestapo staff car would come barreling around a bend and catch me unprepared. Knowing the information I carried was vital to the Nazi war machine, they surely would've shot me from having it in my possession. '*At least I have my pistol,*' I thought, attempting to reassure my conscience that I would survive the ordeal.

About a quarter kilometer down the road, I heard the moaning of an engine coming from the south. I ran down a small embankment on the left side of the road and hid in the bushes. Moments later four Opel trucks loaded down with infantry sped by. None of the soldiers looked over the age of eighteen.

When the trucks were well out of sight, I turned east and traveled through farmer's pastures, plowed fields, and groves of trees until the sun went down. Then, I bypassed the town of Schevenhurte and turned toward the town of Langerwehe, thinking of the days when I could hail a taxi and be home in five minutes.

Travel was much slower at night. The moon was out but offered little light. The North Star was barely visible through thin patches of clouds, yet, I didn't believe it led to salvation.

Although, I had been awake for over forty-eight hours, walking most of the time, I wasn't tired. The urge to stop and rest never entered my mind. The temperature hovered near freezing, yet, I was sweating like a captain of a small boat on a rough sea.

When I reached Veronica's house, the sun glowed below the eastern horizon. I hid the film, camera and one-time pad under some moss at the base of the stone wall. Then, I entered the house and collapsed at the foot of the bed below Chip and Veronica's feet. There I remained until late afternoon when the aroma of fried chicken roused me from sleep.

"You awake, Dan?" Chip asked from the chair in the corner of the room.

"Yes, and please don't call me Dan until we get back to England. My cover is, Benoit Parlett. . . Truthfully, I don't feel like Dan Harrington anymore. I haven't for a very long time."

"Why?" Chip asked.

"I don't know." I stood and groaned. My legs were unbelievably sore from all the walking I did in the last two days. I stretched my back, which didn't help my legs in the slightest. "I keep having this dream. I'm standing at the altar about to get married to Sarah, but the woman standing next to me isn't Sarah and I don't know who she is."

"You've never seen her before?"

"No."

"How long have you been having this dream?" Chip inquired.

"Since, I arrived in France. It comes and goes, but it's so vivid that I actually feel like I'm getting married to her."

"Is she beautiful?" Chip asked, completely in character with the boy I grew up with.

"Yes. Very beautiful," I replied as I looked around the room. "Where's Veronica?"

"Making dinner. Surprised you didn't wake up when we slaughtered the chickens. Poor things let out the most blood curdling scream when she picked them up by the neck. Glad I couldn't see it. Too gruesome."

"You haven't been exposed to the realities of war, have you?"

"No. I've never been close to the fighting," Chip replied. "My assignment sent me to Berlin. My cover was so good, I fooled everyone. The stupid Nazis even hired me to work on their rocketry program. That's what's on the film. Did you get it?"

"Yeah," I replied. Then, silence swept over the room.

After a while, Chip lowered his head. "How can I go on living when I know I've murdered those men?"

"First of all, you didn't murder them," I snapped. "If they'd of captured you, they'd of tortured you for days before standing you in front of a firing squad. So, you did the right thing when you pulled the trigger. Don't let your conscience fool you into believing different."

"I'll try not to. . . Sorry for getting you involved."

"I volunteered."

"If I hadn't asked you to join us, you'd still be happily married to Sarah."

I looked at my feet. "She wasn't right for me. She's cut from the same cloth as my father and his friends. I would've seen that eventually. The war just made me see it sooner."

"Opens the eyes," Chip said softly.

"I don't know who I am anymore. I feel lost and I don't care what happens to me," I confessed.

"Aren't you afraid of dying?"

"Oh, I think every sane human being is afraid of dying to one degree or another."

"So you're afraid then?"

"I don't know. Can I still be sane after all I've been through?" I asked to no one except myself.

"I think so."

"I know I don't cower from death. I've danced with him so many times I know I can defeat him. If he wants me, he knows he's got a fight on his hands."

"I'm scared," Chip confessed.

Veronica entered the room. She gave Chip a kiss on the cheek and a glass of water. With fear filled eyes she asked if I would like a glass. I replied that I did, and then she left the room.

"What do you intend to do with her once we get out of Germany?" I asked.

"What do you mean? I'm going to marry her," Chip replied, surprised I didn't know the answer already.

"She'll be put in prison until the war's over."

"Then, I'll wait for her. No matter how long it takes."

That night, we assembled outside the front door of Veronica's farm house. I had already gathered the film from its hiding place. My suitcase was loaded down with food and equipment. My pistol and Chip's Luger were tucked in my waistband. Veronica kissed her cat for the last time, and then we set off for the Belgium border. Our only wish was to make it safely back to England as rain fell from the sky.

24

*T*he weather was frightful. By the time we came abreast of the dead elderly couples farmhouse, we were soaked and frozen to the bone. Veronica suggested we stop to wait out the weather. For a moment, I entertained the idea. Then, I remembered what lurked inside and told her the couple who lived there were dead. Veronica stared at me. Her eyes blamed me for their deaths, but I didn't care as we pressed on.

The wind whipped into a frenzy, pushing the rain sideways. There was no way to defend against the onslaught. I covered my upper body with a grey wool blanket, leaving a small hole around my eyes to see through, cutting my field of vision down to twenty degrees in all directions. Yet, I was better off than Chip and Veronica. They were each covered with a wool blanket, but Veronica, helping Chip walk, could barely see through the small opening around her eyes. On countless occasions they tripped over fallen trees, small bushes, and invisible depressions in the soft earth, slowing our progress to a crawl.

Everyone of us would have rather stayed in Veronica's cozy home to wait out the war, but the information I carried was vital to the allied cause, so we pushed on. With the German line of defense somewhere in front of us, our only consolation was knowing an alert sentry also had his visibility reduced in the foul weather. Therefore, it was far safer for us to travel under the adverse conditions, than the somewhat dry, silent countryside I traveled through in France.

The climb up the gentle valley slope was the hardest part of our journey that night. The soggy earth turned to mud with every footstep. I can't remember how many times I slipped and fell to my knees. I only know profanity came easier to my lips the higher we climbed. Once, when I fell down a deep depression, Chip laughed and remarked that I was a long way from my father.

"Are you trying to make me feel better?" I groveled as I clawed my way back up to him. Chip didn't respond. Shortly after, he slipped and pulled

Veronica down with him. They slid down the hill until a bush stopped their descent. I didn't laugh.

It took us over six hours to accomplish what I could have done in one. When morning came, we had traveled only two kilometers. Thankfully, the rain stopped with the rising sun.

When you're deep in enemy territory, your only concern is to escape undetected. I preferred to keep going after sunrise, but Chip was a wanted man. Every Nazi, military officer, and ordinary civilian was looking for him. So we hid in a small grove of trees to wait until dark.

The warmth of the sun never reached us, so I gave Chip the three dry shirts, two pairs of socks, and underwear from my suitcase to help him stay warm. He in turn tried to get Veronica and I to wear some of the dry items, but we refused and spent the remainder of the morning shivering ourselves to sleep.

By noon a gentle breeze filtered through the trees and dried some of the moisture from our blankets and clothes. Veronica thanked God for his kindness. I didn't know if I believed in him anymore. When the rain returned in mid-afternoon, I wondered how I could.

"I hear Florida's nice this time of year," Chip said through chattering teeth. "Think I'll buy a small house in Miami when I get back."

"I'd like to see the keys," I stated.

"Oh, yeah, the keys. Maybe I'll buy a house in Key Largo. Veronica and I'll stand in the warm surf and get married. We'll have the reception right on the beach. Barbecue ribs and beer. Make it a real beach party."

"They have hurricanes down there."

"Don't ruin my dream. Anything's better than this," Chip groaned.

I looked at his face. It was pale white. Hypothermia was setting in. "Gustav, I'm taking you back to Veronica's house."

"No, you're not," Chip snapped. "We've already come this far."

"But you don't look too good."

"I'm fine."

"I know where we can go," Veronica interrupted.

I looked at her for a moment. "Where?"

"My sisters house."

"That's out of the question. The only Nazis I want to meet are dead ones," I stated flatly.

"Where does she live?" Chip asked.

"Lichenbusen," Veronica replied, and then turned to me. "Benoit, not everyone in Germany is a Nazi. Some of us hate them as much as you do, but they're in power, and we have to do what they say."

"No, you don't," I snarled.

"We want the war to end just as much as you do," Veronica stated.

"If that were true, your soldiers would throw down their arms and surrender."

"The Nazis are strong. There are too many who still believe in Hitler. There's not enough of us to resist, so we are forced to follow them." Veronica looked at Chip, and then back to me. "I know you hate me. I don't blame you, but you must trust me for Gustav's sake. We have to get him to my sister's house."

"Why don't we take him back to yours?" I asked, piercing her with my eyes. "What're you trying to hide?"

"Nothing," Veronica pled. "We can't go back to my home. There's no more food there." Veronica wiped a tear from her eye, and then added, "I've lost everything."

At that moment, I knew I made a mistake in sparing her life. I knew I should have shot her. Chip would have forgiven me after his emotional wounds healed. He would find another lover, as he always did. Like the rest of us who walk this earth, he would go on living with the emotional scars we all carry to our graves.

I grunted as I stood. "How do I know we can trust your sister?"

Veronica looked at me. "Because she's my sister."

"Not good enough," I said as I pulled the HiStandard pistol from my waistband and pointed it at her head. "You're leading us into a trap."

"What?" Chip cried. His hands flailed in the air until he found my outstretched arm. In a flash, he felt the pistol and managed to pry my fingers from the pistol grip. Then, he yanked the pistol downward to free it from my hand. As he did, my index finger caught the trigger. The weapon fired. Veronica screamed.

"Bastard," Chip yelled as he let the pistol drop to the ground. Then, he turned and embraced Veronica while I quickly kicked the pistol out of his reach. "Damn you," Chip cried as Veronica choked for air.

I pushed Chip aside. He crumpled to the ground, engulfed in tears. My only thought was to find where the bullet entered Veronica's body to stop the bleeding. One moment, I wanted her dead. The next, I was frantically trying to save her life.

I ripped the blanket off her, and then removed her coat. There were two small holes visible on the left side of her sweater just below the rib cage, but there wasn't any blood. Veronica looked at me, and then down to her side while Chip sobbed profanities.

After pulling Veronica's sweater away from where the bullet entered, I sat back on my heels. Veronica stared at her bare torso, and then at me. Her jaw dropped. Then, she fainted.

"It missed. I missed her," I exclaimed rapidly. "She's okay."

"What?" Chip sobbed.

"I missed her."

If Chip still had his sight, I knew he'd be staring at me with bewildered eyes. All he could do in his present condition was drop his jaw and look in the direction of my voice. Then, he searched the ground until he found Veronica's body. "She's not moving."

"She fainted. Don't worry, she's not dead," I said as I moved his hand to where the bullet had passed through her coat, and then to the part of her body where the bullet missed her. Chip didn't say anything. He only cradled her in his arms until she regained consciousness.

That night the rain returned as we resumed our journey. Like the night before, our progress was slow, but we managed to make it to a small farm just north of Walheim. The stone house was demolished. At first I thought a bomb destroyed it, but a weathered sign in the front yard told me different. In the dim dawning light, the faded words said, "*Forbidden. Do not enter. Infested with disease.*" At the bottom of the sign was a yellow six pointed star.

Veronica pointed to a small barn still standing behind the demolished house. "We can stay in there."

"It says this place is infested," I remarked.

"Oh, dear," Chip sighed as Veronica led him toward the barn.

"Come! We'll be safe," Veronica said over her shoulder.

After staring at the sign for a moment, I followed them into the barn. They were sitting on a pile of damp straw that had turned black from mildew. The roof had three holes about two inches in diameter. Water gushed through them and landed in shallow puddles before draining into larger puddles of mud. At the back of the barn water trickled down the inside wall and disappeared through a crack in the foundation. In other places, water dripped from the roof through invisible holes. One hole dripped a single drop every twenty-seven seconds. Something I found out later through boredom as I timed the drips to help pass the day while Veronica and Chip slept. Hours later hunger pains woke them. I hadn't slept a wink.

"What time is it?" Chip yawned.

"A little after two," I replied. "We'll leave in a few hours."

"We can't. Gustav needs more rest," Veronica pled.

"This place is infested," I stated.

"No, it's not," Veronica said.

"It said so on the sign," I growled.

"Jews," Chip somberly replied.

"What?" I asked.

"Jews lived here," Veronica said slowly. "The sign was put there by the Nazis to keep people out. They tell us the Jews are filled with disease. They warn us we'll get the disease if we come in contact with them. They say we'll die. . . They're liars."

"The sign doesn't look very old," I observed. I knew from my time in France that when the Nazis came they immediately began relocating the Jews to concentration camps located in the east. What I didn't know was that Hitler and his henchmen waited until late in the war to remove the last remaining Jewish families from Germany, believing they would remove any suspicion of their crimes from the general population. In truth, most of the general population wished all of the Jews were removed a lot sooner, for they hated the Jews as much as Hitler and his henchmen did.

"The sign's not very old. Only about six months," Veronica stated flatly. "They should've left when they had a chance. Now they rot in a camp."

"Murdered. . . They're murdered there," Chip said slowly.

Veronica and I stared at Chip with disbelief written on our faces.

"Murdered?" Veronica asked.

"Yes," Chip replied.

"How do you know?" I asked.

"Because I've seen it with my own eyes," Chip sighed. "A year ago. Just after I joined the Nazi party, Colonel Lindhof took me to Auschwitz and showed me what Hitler calls the final solution. It was sickening. Indescribable. Men, women. Living skeletons staring at me through the barbed wire. Their eyes. . . Hopeless. Waiting for their turn to die. . . The lucky ones are murdered on arrival. Gassed in the showers. Then, burned to ash."

"That can't be? The Nazis told us the Jews were relocated to Poland to work in factories," Veronica said.

"The ones not murdered on arrival are worked to death. . . Exterminated," Chip replied softly.

For awhile, we sat in silence, listening to the rain fall on the metal roof, contemplating what Chip said. It just didn't seem possible the Nazis could murder a whole race of people. They were cold blooded, but the logistics of murdering millions of Jews wasn't fathomable. '*How could they cover up their crimes?*' I wondered. '*Allied intelligence had to know.*'

"We believed in Hitler," Veronica said slowly. "We believed in what he stood for. In the beginning, we all believed his ideology. In the master race. We were proud to be Aryan. We hated the Jews. I hated the Jews, but I learned hate comes from hate." Tears fell down her cheeks. "We'll never be forgiven."

Before we arrived at the farmstead, I was starving. But after hearing the fate of the Jews, I couldn't eat. I felt dirty. Back in Boston, long before I joined the OSS, the local newspapers seldom reported on the fate of the Jews. When they did, all that was written was the Jews were being relocated to ghettos. That Hitler wanted a Jew free state. After joining the OSS, I was told the Jews were put in concentration camps and only those who resisted were murdered. Occasionally, I heard rumors of entire Jewish communities murdered by the SS, but I took those rumors with a grain of salt. A mass hysteria propagated by Jewish refugees from Nazi occupied Europe. Never in my mind did I imagine Hitler's plan was to rid the entire world of the Jewish populace. Now, I knew it was true. Chip never lied to me in the past, and I had no reason to doubt him now.

The barn remained as solemn as a funeral drum for the rest of the day. None of us slept, nor did we talk. Every twenty-seven seconds, when the water dripped from the ceiling and landed on the dark straw, I imagined another Jewish life extinguished from the earth. To this day, every time I hear water dripping, I'm reminded of that day in the barn. I'm reminded of the fate of the Jews. My hatred for the Nazis returns.

When night came, Chip was in no condition to travel. We all huddled together on the damp straw. Our combined body heat barely kept us from freezing in the icebox called a barn.

All of our food, what little was left, was cold. Veronica chided herself for not bringing a small pan, but the Belgium border was less than twenty kilometers from her house. None of us thought we would have time to cook. Especially when a campfire could be spotted miles away. However, in the confines of the barn, a small fire wouldn't be visible from outside. Our only concern was the smell of smoke emanating from the wood planked walls.

We took our chance anyway, hoping the rain would dissipate the smell. I removed the throwing knife from the lining in the suitcase and dug a small, one foot hole in the middle of the barn. Veronica placed some of the rotting straw in the hole. Then, Chip gave me a box of damp matches, though our hopes of a warming fire slowly ebbed as match after match failed to light. Then, as the eleventh match moved along the striker, our hope momentarily rose as its red tip sparked into flame. When it quickly died we groaned. It wasn't until the sixteenth match that I had a flame strong enough to light the straw. I fanned the fire into a three inch mass of light. Veronica set more straw on top and put a tin of processed meat in the fiery hole. Then, we hovered around the fire and stretched our blankets behind our backs to maximize the heat.

In less than a half hour, we used up a quarter of the straw in the barn. The room was filled with smoke. At least the small fire warmed our souls and helped strike some of the moisture from our clothes and blankets. Yet, at the rate the fire was eating the straw, we needed something more substantial to burn. So, I left the confines of the barn and ran to the destroyed house. I sifted through the ruins and found two charred pieces of wood, each of them less than a foot long. Five minutes later, I was back in the barn, shivering from the ice cold rain. "Why didn't the Nazis destroy the barn?" I asked as I fished the tin of meat out of the fire.

"Who cares," Chip replied.

After we ate the hot meat from the tin can and some of the cold fried chicken, we sat around the fire until half of the straw in the barn was consumed and the charred wood reduced to ash. No one spoke as the flame extinguished. Darkness enveloped us. The rest of the night and part of the next morning the three of us lay close together. I didn't feel the need to stand guard against intruders and quickly fell asleep. For some reason, I felt safer in the barn than I ever did in France. Probably because no one would suspect two American spies and a German woman were hiding in a barn once owned by Jews. Looking back, I thank God my intuition was right. One of my greatest fears was to be captured by the Nazis. I knew that after they tortured me for weeks, maybe months, they would stand me in front of a firing squad.

Around ten in the morning, Veronica woke me from my recurring dream. She put her finger to my lips to keep me quiet. Then, she slowly rolled away from Chip and went to the far side of the room. I followed, leaving Chip sleeping on the straw. "Hear something?" I whispered.

"No, it's Gustav. I need to change his bandage before his wound gets infected in this stinking place. We've got to get him to my sister," Veronica replied softly, and then tears slowly began falling from her eyes. "He'll die if we don't."

I looked at Chip's sleeping form, and then back to Veronica. "Don't we have any more cloth?"

"No. Only our dirty clothes." Veronica's tears fell more heavily. "I can't lose him."

I thought about our chances of making it safely to Veronica's sisters house. In the daylight, Chip's bandaged head would attract attention. After dark, the Gestapo or local police force would arrest us for violating curfew. "It's too risky," I finally said. "Even if your sister doesn't turn us in, the Gestapo will catch us." I put my hand on Veronica's shoulder. "Sorry, but we'll have to make due with what we've got."

"But we must go. My sister will help," Veronica pled.

"We'll get caught."

Veronica looked away and lowered her head. "Gustav can't die," she said, and then looked at me. "You go."

"That's absurd. I don't know your sister and I surely don't trust her," I stated. Then, we argued quietly for a couple of minutes. My gut told me that if I entered Lichenbusen alone, something terrible would happen. That the journey would be the beginning of the end of our lives. Then, I glanced at Chip, still sound asleep on the bed of straw. I realized his friendship meant more to me than winning the war, completing the mission, or my life. After that, my decision came easily. Chip was still asleep when I slipped out of the barn.

25

I stood in the pouring rain outside the barn and removed a dead-drop canister, two pen-guns, the small lock pick kit, and the pair of gloves with the pistol attached before stowing the HiStandard and Luger pistols in the suitcase and hiding the suitcase underneath the rubble of the demolished house. Then, I took one last look at the barn before walking lightly to the road that would take me to Lichenbusen.

The rain soaked my clothes. The wind slapped my face as I walked along. When I was well out of sight of the barn, I stuffed the three rolls of microfilm, camera, and the cipher pad into the dead-drop canister and stomped it into the ground by a fence post before resuming my journey.

I passed a few houses along the way. Smoke billowed from their chimneys, but the occupants remained hidden behind locked doors. The only signs of life was a small flock of sheep and two dairy cows grazing in the pastures, oblivious to the war of man.

About five hundred meters from the edge of Lichenbusen, the hum of engines approached from the east, the faint rumble of artillery from the west. '*Are the allies breaking through,*' I wondered as I turned to face the approaching convoy. Panther and Tiger tanks, half tracks, armored cars, and Krupp trucks carrying infantry crept past. Some of the German soldiers looked too old to fight, others too young. All of them looked proud. "Go to your deaths," I said under my breath while I smiled and waved as they passed by.

German citizens, young and old, lined the streets to cheer their army. I joined in their praise to keep the attention off myself. No one noticed I was there as I walked the first block. When I turned right onto a side street, two small boys rushed past to join the roaring crowd, and I gladly left the pathetic scene behind.

At the end of the street, I turned left and walked another block and a half until I found the address Veronica gave me. Once again, her directions were exact. My trust for her grew stronger. '*Not all Germans are evil,*' I thought as I knocked on the front door of a turn-of-the-century two story white stone house. A young, blond haired boy dressed in a Hitler Youth uniform answered the door. He couldn't have been a day over twelve-years-old. "Who are you?" He demanded.

"I'm Benoit Parlett," I answered. "A friend of Veronica Hoffmann."

"What do you want?"

"I've come to speak with Franka Hinkle. Do I have the right address?"

"Why do you want to speak to her?"

"Amon, who's at the door?" A woman's voice asked from inside the house.

"A stranger," the boy replied.

Moments later a woman appeared in the doorway. She was frail for a woman in her mid-thirties. The rimless glasses she wore turned her brown eyes a shade darker and matched the color of her hair. Her navy blue pleated skirt and white blouse were partially covered with a white apron. "Can I help you, sir?" She asked as she stood behind the boy.

"I'm looking for Franka Hinkle."

"I'm Franka. What do you want?"

"I've come on an errand for Veronica Hoffmann. She's your sister, right?" I asked while watching the boy's reaction out of the corner of my eye.

"Where are you from?" The boy demanded.

"Amon, don't be rude," Franka said cautiously to her son, and then turned to me. "Yes, sir, she's my sister."

"I have some news for you then. Is there somewhere we can talk in private?" I asked.

"Oh dear, is she all right?" Franka asked.

"Yes, ma'am."

Amon pushed past me onto the front porch steps. "What's going on?" He asked.

I turned to the boy and smiled. "Our glorious Wehrmacht are driving through town."

"Come mother. We must join them," Amon ordered while pulling on Franka's arm.

"No, you go, Amon. I must speak to this fellow," Franka said, and then welcomed me into the house. Amon put on his hat and coat, leered at me for a moment, and then left to join the rest of the townsfolk. Franka watched him turn the corner before she shut the front door. Then, she led me down the hall and into the parlor. I sat in an easy chair similar to the one I had in Boston.

"I know my sister's not well," Franka said as she sat in a wooden chair that creaked under her weight. "She wouldn't of sent you if she was."

"No, she's quite well. I'm only here on her behalf because she's packing for Berlin and wanted to know if she could borrow the chiffon tablecloth that belonged to your mother," I said.

Franka laughed as she rose from her chair and walked toward the open doorway. I felt betrayed and pulled a pen-gun from my breast pocket. I was about to depress the firing mechanism when she called for Amon. I expected him to run into the room with a pack of blood thirsty Gestapo on his tail.

Franka called Amon's name a few more times until she was satisfied he hadn't snuck back into the house. I quickly stuffed the pen gun back in my coat pocket before she turned around.

"I don't trust that boy," Franka said as she returned to her seat. "Hitler has turned our youth into monsters. They follow his tenets with blind determination. Reporting their own mothers and fathers to the Gestapo." Franka paused and cocked her ear to the doorway for a moment, and then continued. "My son. My own son reported our neighbors to the Gestapo for having a Russian flag. Their son sent it to them as a souvenir while he was fighting in Stalingrad. After he was killed, my son had his parents killed by the Gestapo. He's a murderer and I don't know what to do. Neither would his father if he were still alive." Franka turned her head to wipe a tear from her eye. Then, she looked me straight in the eye. "The chiffon tablecloth you speak of no longer exists. Veronica and I ruined it when we were young girls. So, mister Parlett, tell me who you really are."

"I've already told you. A friend of Veronica's," I replied as I filled with rage, believing Veronica had set me up. I finally understood how Francois felt when he killed Yves, and I knew I could do the same to her.

"Mister Parlett. You may be who you say you are. You mentioned the tablecloth, so I know you're a confidant of my sister. What I don't understand is why she never mentioned you in her letters," Franka said coldly.

"I don't know either," I lied.

"I'm not accusing you of anything. There's too much of that going around these days. I just want to know why she sent you, and I want the truth," Franka demanded.

I sighed deeply to stall for time. Then, just as I was about to open my mouth, an idea struck me like a hurricane. No training course in the world would have suggested what I was about to do. In fact, my instructors stressed over and over how an agents cover is his lifeline. That if his cover is blown, then the mission is blown. Valuable information would be lost, and in most cases so would the agents life. Yet, in my present circumstance, I chose to ignore my instructors warnings, though, only slightly. After all, I held two trump cards.

I got up and went to the door and looked down the hallway. Franka calmly watched as I went. She was more fearful of her son than me, a complete stranger whose only ties to her was through her sister. Even then she wasn't too sure I was her sister's friend or foe. I put my hands in my coat pockets. My right hand found the pen-gun and gripped it lightly. "I'm Benoit Parlett," I began. "A Dutch national and a member of the resistance."

Franka's eyes opened wide, and yet, she showed no signs of fear. "What are you doing in Germany, and why is my sister involved with you?" She calmly asked.

"An American pilot was shot down and landed near her house," I lied. "I was sent to get him out."

"Veronica's helping you?"

"Yes."

"Why?"

My body turned cold. I realized Chip had what I lost, and I was bitterly jealous. "Your sister's in love with him," I replied.

"Oh," Franka said in a state of shock. Then, a smile creased her face. "I'm glad she's in love. I prayed she'd find a reason to live. This man, the pilot, is he a good man?"

"Yes. From what I know of him."

"Good. I'm glad for them, but it was wrong for you to come here. My son will report you," Franka coldly stated.

A sardonic smile spread across my face. "Your son doesn't know who I am, and you're not going to tell him."

"I'm not afraid of you."

"I know, but you're afraid of your son."

Franka's eyes cut through me. "What do you intend to do? If you kill me, my son will have all of Germany looking for you."

I chuckled and stared Franka eye to eye. "Oh, I'm not going to kill you. The pilot is injured and you're going to give me clean bandages and food. If you tell your son about us, when we're caught, I'll tell the Nazis you freely helped us. Since, Veronica's your sister, the bastards will believe me. You'll have signed your death warrant. Hand delivered to your son who'll be your executioner."

Franka lowered her eyes to the floor. Her chest heaved. She knew I meant what I said. She knew her only hope for survival was to keep our conversation locked away in the dark recess of her mind. When she finally looked at me, a shade of anger painted across her face. "I'll help only because you're helping my sister. You're an evil man like my son. This war has bled both your hearts."

Her words cut through my soul. At that moment, at that time in my life, her words were more painful than anything I was ever told, and ever would. For what she said was the truth. I realized at that moment, that when I lost Sarah's love, I'd forsaken my heart. I'd replaced my virtue with hate. I was truly as evil as my enemy.

Franka was more than helpful. She filled a black muslin bag with two clean white pillow cases to be used as bandages. A loaf of bread, three tins of sardines, a chunk of Limburger cheese, two navy blue sweaters, two pairs of wool socks, a candle, two boxes of matches, a bar of chocolate and a small, metal cup to heat water was thrown in the bag. Then, she gave me a pack of cigarettes. When I told her none of us smoked, she said they were good to barter with. I reluctantly took the pack of cigarettes and put them in my coat pocket.

The muslin bag wasn't waterproof, so, I removed my coat and hung the bag over my shoulder, and then put my coat back on. Then, I prodded Franka to the front door, though, she didn't need much coaxing. The faster I was out of her life, the better it was for the both of us.

Franka cracked the front door and peeked outside. I could still hear the German army moving through town and wondered how many men Hitler was sending to their deaths. At the time, I didn't know the entire German army on the western front was preparing for Operation Wacht Am Rhein. A battle that would go down in history as, 'The Battle of the Bulge.' How I wished I had a working radio to warn London. Although, the foul weather grounded the allied air corps, at least the ground forces would've had time to prepare.

Once Franka was satisfied the street was empty, she shut the door and turned to me. "What do I tell my son? He'll want to know why you were here."

"Tell him I came to collect a few of Veronica's personal belongings. Tell him anything you want that'll keep him from asking questions, but never tell him the truth. Need I remind you that our lives depend on you keeping your mouth shut?"

"No," Franka spat. Hatred flashed from her eyes as she opened the front door. "I'm holding you personally responsible if anything happens to my sister."

"I know you will," I smiled, and then walked into the pouring rain. The door slammed shut behind me. I walked down the front steps and headed toward the cheering crowd. The only chance I had of getting out of the town was to leave by the same route I had entered. My only dilemma was not attracting attention, so once again, I joined the crowd in cheering their soldiers on to victory.

There were no more than two hundred civilians lining both sides of the street. Obviously, not everyone in town cared anymore. Countless defeats had weaned their fervor for Hitler and his Reich. Only the naive and misled still believed they had a chance.

As I walked along, blending with the crowd, I cheered and clapped as they did. None of them noticed or cared who I was. Across the street, a hundred feet to my right, Amon stood amongst a small group of children. The boys wore the uniform of the Hitler Youth. The girls waved small flags. All of them beamed with pride.

A baker brought out a box of freshly baked biscuits. A few people helped him throw the biscuits to the passing troops, and I joined them. The soldiers greedily fought for the rock hard biscuits like a pack of rabid dogs. In the melee, I managed to stuff a couple in my coat pocket before the box was empty. Then, I casually pushed my way through the crowd and stopped at the edge of town. When the end of the slow moving convoy came in view, I broke away at a leisurely pace and left the town behind me. All the while, I cheered until the last vehicle crept past.

As I walked the roar of the cheering crowd died away. The sound of the rain and mud lapping at my feet was all that remained. Tranquility returned to the German countryside. My heart rate slowed. I sighed. My body relaxed. Then, suddenly the hair on the back of my neck rose. The skin on my face tightened.

I turned around. The road behind me was desolate. The bushes and trees lining both sides of the road remained still. There were no signs of life. No indication I was being followed except for my hair standing on end and I knew I was being hunted.

I turned back around and picked up my pace. The only way someone could follow me without being detected was to walk in the fields hidden behind the bushes and trees. I just didn't know which side they were on, or how many of them were following me.

My mind raced. My eyes searched for a vantage point. I knew I'd have to fight and wished I'd brought my HiStandard pistol. More importantly, I knew I had to fight before I reached the barn where Veronica and Chip were hiding.

The road veered to the left fifty meters ahead of me. I put on the leather gloves with the single-shot pistol attached to the right glove and clipped the pen-guns to the outside of my breast pocket. Knowing the pen-guns were only accurate up to ten feet, I'd have to lure the hunters to my position.

Once I was satisfied my weapons were situated for optimal access, I opened a tin of sardines and ate the slimy contents. Then, I wiped the flimsy lid on my pant leg before folding it in half and stuffing the lid and can in my left coat pocket. After that, I took a cigarette from the pack Franka gave me and put one in my mouth. Then, I struck a match and lit the end, taking a deep breath as I did. Smoke filled my lungs. I coughed. My eyes watered. My head felt dizzy. I stopped walking for a few seconds until the effects wore off. Then, I continued down the road.

When I passed the bend in the road, the cigarette was halfway gone. It wouldn't last much longer, so I dashed down the left shoulder of the road and entered the bushes. I found a small clearing in the middle of the vegetation and kneeled down next to a large tree. Then, I took out my throwing knife and the empty sardine tin can from my pocket and rapped the knife on the can twice before I set the can at the base of the tree. After that, I set the bent lid on the edge of the can to act as a shield from the rain as I put what was left of the cigarette underneath it. Smoke drifted from beneath and filled the air with its acrid aroma as I hid behind the tree with a pen-gun in my right hand. Moments later, I heard faint footsteps stepping quietly toward my trap. I released the safety mechanism on the pen-gun. As I did, the footsteps stopped.

"What the hell?" A gruff voice said from the other side of the tree.

"It's a trap," another voice screamed.

I darted from behind the tree and fired the pen-gun into a surprised soldier who turned in my direction. The bullet entered his chest cavity. He dropped his rifle as he fell to the ground, gasping for breath as I punched the other soldier in the head. The pistol attached to the glove fired a bullet into the man's skull, killing him instantly. Then, a shot rang out from the direction of the pasture. The bullet came within inches of my head, snapping the air as it went by.

"Don't shoot! We've got him." I yelled. Immediately, two more pairs of footsteps crashed into the bushes. I barely had time to release the safety mechanism on the second pen-gun before a German officer appeared and managed to squeeze off two rounds before I fired. My bullet struck him in the abdomen. He dropped his pistol and staggered toward me. I knocked him down. Then, just as I was about to plunge the throwing knife into his chest, another figure screamed from the edge of the clearing. I turned and threw the knife. The figure let out a yelp as the officer kicked me off my feet. I landed on the soldier I had shot in the chest. He groaned under my weight. Meanwhile, the officer crawled toward his pistol as the figure I hit with the throwing knife staggered into the clearing. It was Amon. The hilt of the throwing knife protruded from between his hands which were wrapped around his neck. Bright red blood oozed between his fingers. Red bubbles frothed from his mouth. Shock cascaded over his face.

I turned my attention back to the officer. His outstretched hand was only inches from his pistol when I pounced on him and slammed his head into the ground. He tried to resist, but I kept slamming his head until he lost his strength. Then, I pulled the thumb knife from its hiding place in my lapel and cut his throat.

When I turned around, the soldier with the chest wound was dead. Amon was on his knees. Blood trickled through his fingers. Shock clung to his face as his young life slowly drained away. There was nothing I could do except watch as death gripped his body. In slow motion, Amon turned his head toward me. His eyes were vacant, but I knew he saw me. For he gave a faint smile before his body fell forward. A lump grew in my throat. The blood drained from my face as Amon's body landed in its final resting place. His eyes still fixed upon mine.

I hated Amon for dying. I cursed him for being a Nazi. "Why did you alert the soldiers?" I asked softly, wondering if I would have done the same if I were in his position. I knew I'd never know the answer. For I had grown up when the world was at peace.

I said a prayer for Amon's tarnished soul. I asked God to forgive his sins. For he was a boy unknowingly led down the path of evil. Then, I asked Amon to forgive me. The faint smile on his lifeless face told me that he never would.

26

*T*ime crept by after Amon died. The rain continued to fall. The wind grew fierce. Yet, I remained frozen with my eyes locked upon his face. To this day, the picture of Amon's dead body lies on the fringe of my memory. His vacant eyes pierce my soul. His faint smile laughs at me from the grave.

When darkness fell, I returned to the road. My footsteps fell lightly in the mud as I jogged away from Amon's open grave. Stopping only briefly to retrieve the dead drop canister, I continued jogging until my legs felt weak and my lungs cried for oxygen. By then, I was within two hundred meters of the barn. I slowed to a snail's pace. My ears pricked up. My eyes scanned the area. My mind played tricks on me. Every dark shadow seemed to conceal a German soldier laying in wait. Every bush, every swaying branch, every subtle sound over the wind seemed to mark my enemies movement. Fear took control of my emotions. Panic set in.

Once, I had retrieved my suitcase and had the HiStandard pistol in my hand, my fear ebbed, but only slightly as I crept up to the barn. The interior was silent. '*Did the Nazis find my friends,*' I wondered as I stood beside the door and carefully pulled on the handle. Its rusty hinges squeaked as the door slowly swung open from its own weight. Then, I waited.

Five minutes passed and not a single sound came from inside. Ten minutes passed as I crouched next to the open door. Twenty minutes came and went, and still no sound. Then, when I was about to enter the barn, soft footsteps approached from inside. A hand reached out. I grabbed it. Veronica screamed as I pulled her into my arms. "Quiet!" I whispered in her ear as I clamped my hand over her mouth. "It's me, Benoit." Then, I let my hand drop from her mouth and loosened my embrace.

Veronica spun around and slapped my face. "Damn you," she cried while tears streamed down her face. "Damn you, Benoit."

"Where's Gustav?"

"Inside. You frightened us."

"Sorry. I had to be sure it was clear before I entered. How is he?"

"Not well. Did you get the bandages?"

"Yes. Your sister gave me a couple of pillow cases to use."

"How is she?"

"Fine," I replied, and then entered the barn. "Chip?"

"Dan?" Chip asked.

"It's me, Chip," I said as Veronica followed me into the barn and closed the door.

"Jesus Christ, Dan. You scared us half to death," Chip hollered.

"Quiet," I ordered. Then, I pulled the candle out of the muslin bag and lit the wick. In the dim light Chip's face was pale white and I couldn't tell whether it was because of his condition, or fear. "Can you walk?"

"Of course, I can," Chip snapped. Veronica sat down beside him and held him tightly. Her fright was still evident on her face.

"Good," I replied. "We'll leave as soon as your bandages are changed." I threw Veronica the two pillow cases.

While Veronica changed Chip's bandages, I paced on the far side of the room. My own fears still wrecked havoc on my mind. I felt like I had lost my grip on reality. Then, I made the mistake of looking at Chip. Veronica had removed his bandages and was cleaning his eye sockets. His eye balls were still in his head, but they had shriveled into small black orbs. Each were the size of a dime.

My stomach churned. It felt like a grapefruit was stuck in my throat. I couldn't shake the anxiety from my body. I couldn't expel the vision from my mind. That's when I turned around and pulled the pack of cigarettes from my coat pocket. My hands twitched as I pulled a cigarette from the pack and lit it. I chocked the smoke into my lungs, and chocked it back out. Then, I repeated the process until the cigarette was a mere nub of burning ash. My anxiety subsided. My hands stopped shaking, yet the horror of Chip's shriveled eyes remained.

As soon as Chip's bandages were changed, we packed up and left the leaking barn. Once again, we wrapped our blankets tightly around our bodies as the rain fell upon us. Wanting to stay clear of Lichenbusen, I set a course due west. We bypassed a few houses and traversed many fields. Luckily, by day break we found a nice grove of trees to hide in until dark. The Holland border sat only three kilometers away. The German army stood between us.

Throughout the day the rain came and went. A welcome reprieve from the previous days, though the cold still remained, freezing us to the bone.

Veronica and Chip managed to sleep for a while. They laid together, peacefully, embraced with warmth and tenderness, and yet, I wondered how two sworn enemies could find love in the battleground known as Europe.

It would be noble for me to believe I stayed awake to protect them as they slept, but, I can't fool myself. The truth was, I was too worried to sleep. The German defensive line stood directly in our path to the relative safety of Holland. The unknown threat the German army posed in our flight to freedom was incalculable, so around noon, I crept to the tree line.

A few Opel trucks moved about. The German defenses were well camouflaged. I had to visually plot their positions by watching where the trucks stopped to off load supplies and more men. On a few occasions the trucks picked up men and drove them either north or south. My guess was that the men were being sent to areas the allied armies were attacking, but I didn't know for sure.

Again, my mind drifted to my father and his greedy empire. How much money he and his cronies were making off the blood of men. I wondered how Sarah was doing. Was her new man making her happy? Did she love him more than she ever loved me? I wondered about Jack and our Maquis friends. What had happened to them? Which ones were still alive? Were they warm and dry?

Despite the thoughts that kept me awake on that dreary day, one thought overshadowed them all. One thought overpowered my fatigue and kept me fearful of sleep. It was my recurring dream. Who was the woman standing next to me at the altar? The woman with the lovely smile? The woman who sometimes had tears in her eyes? The woman who reminded me of Aimee. I wondered if she was real, what her name was. More importantly, I wondered why she haunted me in my dreams.

When I returned to Chip and Veronica, they were eating part of the loaf of bread Franka gave us. Chip turned his head in my direction. Veronica smiled. "Can we make it?" Chip asked.

"Yes, but we'll have to be vary careful," I replied. "The Germans are only six hundred meters from the edge of the trees, but they're spread out. We'll be able to walk within four hundred meters of their positions. Then, we'll have to crawl the rest of the way. Hopefully the rain won't stop."

"What if we're spotted?" Chip asked.

"Then you and Veronica run as fast as you can while I lay down covering fire."

"There'll be no more killing," Veronica said.

"I won't have a choice," I said calmly.

"I don't care. There'll be no more killing," Veronica snapped. Then, she stood and walked away. I watched as she fell to her knees and covered herself with her blanket. Although, I couldn't hear her, I knew she was weeping.

"God damn you, Dan," Chip cried. "Why'd you have to say that? And why do you have to be so damned serious all the time?"

"What the hell are you talking about?" I grumbled. My blood instantly boiled. "I'm trying to get us out of here in one piece. Do I need to remind you where we are? Have you forgotten there's a war going on out here? Have you forgotten you're a wanted man? Jesus Christ, the Nazis are still our enemy and I'm not going down without a fight. So if I seem a little too serious, so be it. I am. You of all people should know the gravity of our situation. You're an OSS officer for Christ sake."

"I know it, and Veronica knows it too. We've just had enough of this war," Chip said.

"You've had enough? Where the hell were you when I was in France? I'll tell you. You were going to the opera and eating in fancy restaurants while I was trapped in a cellar watching a friend of mine die inches away from me. I was trapped with her dead body as the whole town above me crumbled into a God damned wasteland. So don't tell me you've had enough of this war. Yours is only beginning. I'm just trying to survive."

Chip lowered his head. I was ashamed for lashing out at him. Our friendship was too important, too mature to succumb to petty insults. In one capacity or another, we were both fighting the same war. We had a common enemy. We were just fighting him in our own way. "Forgive me, Chip. I shouldn't of gotten angry," I said.

"You just don't understand," Chip sighed.

"What's to understand?" I asked as Chip turned his head away. Minutes ticked by and he remained quiet. His silence cut deep into my heart. I felt as if I had driven a wedge between us. That, I had severed my last ties to Boston. Then, he turned his head to me.

"Sorry you've had a rough time," Chip said slowly.

"Sorry you have too," I replied.

"Veronica. . . She hurts as much as we do. Probably more," Chip whispered. "This war has taken her heart. Her soul was barely alive when I came into her life. She would've killed herself if I hadn't. From what she's told me, I know I would've. . . Where is she?"

"About twenty-five feet to your right. Shall I get her?"

"No," Chip said, and then paused for a moment. "In 1926, she married Hans Sanger. A year later she had a boy. Linfred. Complications in the pregnancy made it impossible for her to conceive again. . ."

"Don't you want children?" I interrupted.

"Yes, but I'm not worried. There'll be a lot of orphans after the war," Chip replied. "Anyway, in 1938, Veronica's husband was drafted into the army. He took part in operation Barbarossa, and died in Stalingrad. Around the time of his death, Linfred was forced into the Hitler Youth. Like his father, he didn't want to fight. Last January, Linfred was sent to Normandy. He died on the first day of the invasion. He was only seventeen. So, please understand why she wants the bloodshed to stop. This war has killed the two most important people in her life."

"We all want the bloodshed to stop, but there'll be more of it before the war ends. I guarantee that," I stated, and then excused myself from Chip's presence. As I walked away, Veronica returned to his side.

The rain intensified as the day grew into night. We ate most of our food, saving just enough for one more meal. I was confident that by morning we would be through the German defenses, safely across the river, and joined up with our allied forces. It seemed London was only a few days away. A hot shower, hot food, and a warm bed awaiting our arrival.

A little past six we left under the cover of night. Twenty minutes later, we were on our bellies crawling through the wet grass and mud. Our blankets were tied around our necks and draped over our bodies to hide our silhouettes and muffle the sound of our movement. The rain and heavy wind helped, but the terrain was our biggest asset.

I kept our travel to the lowest depressions in the open terrain. In some places the depressions reached five feet deep. In others we were barely below the plane. Twice we crawled over deep ruts from vehicle traffic in the soft ground. All the while the mud sucked at our bodies, doubling our body weight as it clung to our clothes, while the near freezing temperatures stiffened our joints and slowed our progress.

After awhile, time became irrelevant. My only thought was on our safety as our stealth was tested time and time again. On one occasion, a German corporal led two soldiers by us only fifteen feet away. Another was when we slithered by a bunker. The inside remained quiet, like a vacant tomb, but I knew a soldier was poised inside. He was the hunter. We were his prey.

A hundred meters later, I heard water lapping at the shore and breathed a sigh of relief. From the beginning, I knew we would have to cross the river, but, I hadn't thought of a definite plan. I guess, I secretly hoped to find a bridge, but when we came within fifty meters of the water, I knew we would have to swim.

The flat ground sloped downward to the waters edge. Grass a foot high covered the entire area. Not one bush, tree, or shrub grew on our side of the river. Thin fog clung on the horizon and shrouded the far shore.

"What do we do now?" Veronica whispered in my ear.

"Do you know how to swim?" I asked.

"Yes," Veronica gulped. "But the water's freezing. We'll never make it across."

"Oh, yes we will," Chip smiled. "We got by the soldiers and we can cross the river too. . . How far do we have to swim anyway?"

"I can't tell with the fog. Do you know Veronica?"

"No, but I'm sure it's very wide."

"Should be an easy swim," Chip beamed.

"I don't know. Something just doesn't seem right. Why would this particular stretch of river be left undefended? At the Normandy beaches there were all sorts of obstacles," I stated.

"But they don't know we're here, so it should be a snap," Chip gleamed.

"That's what worries me the most," I said. "When things are too easy, something always goes wrong."

"My dear, Dan Harrington. You've got to stop being such a pessimist. You don't hear Veronica and I complaining, do you?"

I looked at Chip and Veronica. He was smiling. She had a frown on her face, and I could see she was as concerned as I was. I would even say as frightened, but neither of us wanted to let Chip know we were afraid.

I surveyed the river once more. Then, it dawned on me. I rose to a low crouch.

"What are you doing?" Veronica asked.

"Looking for a sign. Wait here," I replied, and then crawled up river. I searched a hundred feet and found nothing. Then, I repeated the process down river and found nothing.

"What the hell are you doing?" Chip whispered when I returned to their side.

"Looking for a sign."

"A what?" Veronica asked.

I looked at her. "The Germans mark their mine fields with signs so their troops don't wander into the area. The signs are usually placed fifty feet apart, but I checked twice that distance in each direction and couldn't find one. . . I know we're looking at a mine field though."

"Poppycock," Chip said. "Come, Veronica. Help me to my feet."

"Let me clear a lane first," I pled quietly as Veronica reluctantly helped Chip to his feet. "Damn it, Chip. Don't be a fool."

"Don't worry, Dan. We're going to be all right," Chip said, nearly pulling Veronica off her feet as he took his first step toward the water. After they had gone five meters, I untied the blanket from around my neck and followed after them, trying to step in the same places they did.

With each step, my fear grew lighter. By the time Chip and Veronica made it to the waters edge, my fear completely subsided. I was only ten feet behind them and mentally preparing myself for the cold water when Chip turned and smiled. His pearl white teeth glowed in the dark. I smiled back as Chip turned back to the water and took his next step.

The ground crumpled. I was knocked flat on my back. The air was forced from my lungs. My ears rang. A fine, cold mist with particles of mud landed on my face. A sharp pain shot up my left leg. My right biceps throbbed. Blood trickled down my forehead. Tracers filled the sky above me, but I couldn't hear the machine gun firing over the ringing in my ears. Then, a bright flash lit up the sky, and then another. In my dazed state all I could do was lay on my back and watch the white illumination flares drift slowly toward the ground.

Then, my hearing returned. Artillery, machine gun, and rifle fire rang out from both sides of the river. Bullets danced around my limp body. They sounded like tiny bees passing by my head. Instinct took over. I swung my body around until my head faced the river and crawled with all the strength I could muster. When I reached the water line, I rolled into the icy river exactly where the mine exploded. There was no trace of my friends. Chip and Veronica vaporized in the blast.

The gentle current carried me into the middle of the river. My left leg was useless. At least the icy water eased the pain. With my right leg and left arm, I kicked and pulled with all my strength. My right hand weakly gripped the buoyant suitcase. The muslin bag filled with water and dangled like a weight. By the time, I reached the far bank, the current had taken me almost two kilometers downstream. My energy was spent. I only managed to crawl a few feet up the bank before I collapsed. Then, I heard a distant voice as I slipped unconscious.

27

A brilliant light shone down upon me when I opened my eyes. My body was numb. My ears were deaf. I couldn't turn my head. My mouth refused to open. '*Where am I?*' I wondered. Then, the face of a man, covered in white except for his eyes, drifted into view, blocking the bright light. He wore black glasses. Sea blue eyes shined behind them.

Gradually, the man's face faded. I found myself in an ocean of dark red roses. A warm breeze blew against my face. The sound of birds singing filled my ears. My body felt peaceful and light. I was floating on air, soaring high in the heavens above. Upward I went, heading for the stars, then blackness. Like a shade was pulled over my eyes.

Then, my body jittered. My eyes opened to the sight of dark green canvas. I heard the scream of artillery shells just before they exploded. The ground shook with death. "Hang in there, sir," an American voice with a southern twang said on my right. I turned my head and saw a young soldier with a red cross painted on his green, steel helmet. His olive drab uniform was dingy with dried blood on the sleeves and chest. A single stripe was on his sleeve. A musette bag with a red cross painted on the front hung across his chest.

"Where am I?" I asked very slowly. The effects of some type of drug made my voice sound distant. My brain felt like it was floating inside my skull.

"You're in Holland, sir. I'm private Clifton. Your personal escort to the coast. Got your ticket home."

"I don't have a home," I muttered.

"What, sir?" Private Clifton yelled over the din of the artillery.

"Never mind. . . What happened?"

"Well, sir, from what I understand you were found by the river. Had hypothermia and lost a lot of blood. Almost didn't make it, but Captain Holloway patched you up pretty good. He's the best doc we've got in the battalion, you know?" Private Clifton grinned.

"Where?" I slurred, and then passed out.

Hours later, when I regained consciousness, private Clifton and another soldier were carrying me on a stretcher across a wooden dock. I turned my head and saw a giant windmill. Its blades were stationary. I tasted the salty air on my lips and saw seagulls flying overhead. Cold rain pelted my face and I remember thinking the weather would never change until the war was over. To me, God wept from the death and destruction his children were inflicting on each other.

From a dock in Vissingen, Holland, a small Dutch fishing boat took me to a hospital ship. I was put in a room by myself. A guard was posted outside my door. From time to time, another guard escorted a doctor into my room.

I slept most of the trip back to Scotland and vaguely remember being carried down the ship's gangplank to a waiting ambulance before losing consciousness. The next thing I remember was waking up in a quiet room lying on a soft bed. My left knee was raised at a twenty degree angle. An IV-tube stuck out of my left forearm. A doctor was reading my chart. The man who sent me to Germany sat in a wood chair by my head. No one spoke until the doctor left the room.

"How do you feel, lieutenant Harrington?" The man asked.

"Weak," I replied.

"Don't worry. That's probably the morphine," a mousy fellow in his late forties with slicked black hair and a black suit said as he approached the foot of the bed.

"Where am I?" I asked.

"Scotland," the man seated in the chair said. "Let me start by thanking you for a job well done. . ."

"What happened?" I interrupted.

"According to the report, you were found on the bank of the *Our* river," the mousy fellow replied. "You've been treated for hypothermia, a small wound on your upper right arm and a wound to your left knee. There are a few scratches on your face, neck and chest, but nothing a small bandage won't fix."

"Once the report came across our desk, we requested your immediate evacuation. Army intelligence thought you were a German spy," the man seated in the chair added.

"Where's my suitcase?" I asked.

"Safely in our possession," the man in the chair answered. "We came to personally thank you for a job well done."

"And to conduct your debriefing. Are you feeling well enough to talk?" The mousy fellow asked.

"Yeah, I guess so," I replied, and then for the next hour I gave them every detail of my mission. Nothing was left out. Every sordid detail was repeated over and over again as they asked the same questions in slightly different ways. In the end, I was more angry than fatigued. I knew they were only doing their job, but I wanted them to leave. I wanted them out of my life forever. When an armed guard announced that a nurse needed to change my IV-bottle, I got my wish. The two men reluctantly left my room and I never saw either one of them again. It wasn't until years later when I saw a picture of Bill Donovan, the head of OSS, that I realized he was the man sitting in the chair that day. The man who sent me to Germany. The same man Chip worked for before the war. If it weren't for him, Chip would never have joined the OSS. Chip would still be alive. Subsequently, I would still be in Boston, married to Sarah and never followed my destiny. My life would never have changed.

Two days after Bill Donovan and the mousy fellow left my room, I was moved to the main ward of the hospital. The room was overcrowded with wounded soldiers. Some of them were recent arrivals from the bloody battlefields in Holland and Belgium. Some of them came from the battles at sea. There were men with missing arms, or legs. Some were missing both. Other men had bandages wrapped around their heads, or casts on their bodies. One man was bandaged from head to toe due to injuries sustained from a German flamethrower. He only lived a few days before he died. Some men moved around on crutches, or in wheelchairs. The rest of us were confined to our beds. Conversation was minimal. We all sustained our injuries fighting the same war, but the battles we fought within our minds were private.

Daily mail call was held sharply at nine in the morning. A young nurse brought a cart around and handed out the mail, bringing a smile or a weary stare from a disheartened soldier. I was the only one who never received a letter, and I believed I really didn't care.

Late in the afternoon of my first day in the main ward, a British major hobbled into the room with the aid of a cane. His left arm was amputated above the elbow and his sleeve was bobby-pinned to his chest. Over his right eye was a leather patch. A jagged scar ran down from his left eye to his upper lip, creating a small gap in his neatly trimmed moustache. I recognized him immediately. He was the same officer who berated me on the docks at Clyde-of-Firth when I arrived in the British Isles, and he hadn't changed. The air of false British superiority oozed from every pore on his body. I wanted to tell him to go to Hell as he stopped to read my chart, but my mouth wouldn't cooperate with my thoughts.

"Nurse," he yelled to a dainty young woman across the room. "Why is this man here? Civilians aren't allowed in the hospital."

"I don't know, sir," the nurse meekly replied as she walked toward him. My anger toward the man boiled beneath my skin.

"He has every right to be here," a British colonel said as he walked into the room. He was the head doctor, and I almost laughed as the major snapped to attention. "This man holds the rank of leftenant. They tell me he's a hero," the colonel continued when he stopped face to face with the major.

"Sorry, sir," the major said as he snapped a salute before quickly hobbling out of the room.

"Leftenant Harrington, I'm Colonel Bennett. I apologize for Major Tillman's behavior. He lost all of his men at Dunkirk and hasn't forgiven himself. Don't think he ever will," the colonel said, and then left.

"You really a hero?" A wounded man in the bed on my right asked.

I turned to look at him. "No. The only heroes I know are dead. I'm just a survivor," I replied. Then, I turned my head and closed my eyes. Two weeks later, a Distinguished Service Cross and a Purple Heart were pinned to my pillow.

Twenty-seven days after my arrival, therapy on my left knee began. Within a week, I was on my feet with the aid of crutches. Two weeks after that, I was walking with the aid of a cane. My knee never fully recovered though. Now, I walk with a slight limp. Most of the time I have to use a cane.

Physically, I was fortunate. Emotionally, I was a total mess. The fate of my friends wrecked havoc on my mind. The disappearance of Margot and Emile, not knowing what happened to Jack, kept me up most nights. Chip and Aimee's deaths gave me nightmares. Losing Sarah brought tears to my eyes and shredded my heart. As the days passed, I quickly fell deeper and deeper into the cold Hell I'd constructed in my soul. Then, in the early hours of February 26th, 1945, a young man, no more than fifteen-years-old, was brought to the hospital. His name was, Franz Heiler, a German soldier, critically wounded in the allied push toward Berlin. Both of his arms were amputated above his elbows. His left leg was amputated below the hip. The only reason he was brought to our hospital was because of Colonel Bennett's expertise, and it was nothing less than a miracle that he survived the trip.

Major Tillman roused me from bed shortly after Franz Heiler's arrival. I was still awake and didn't need any coaxing to get out of bed. "What is it, sir?" I asked as I donned my slippers and grabbed my cane.

"They brought us a wounded Kraut and you're the only one who speaks German," Major Tillman sneered as I followed him through the heavy doors separating the main ward from the rest of the hospital. Blood curdling screams filled the usually quiet hallway. Fear gripped my body. My feet felt heavy as I followed Major Tillman toward the operating room. The screaming grew louder with every step I took.

"I can't go in there," I stammered when we stopped at the operating room door.

"Bloody hell, you can't," Major Tillman growled as he pushed me through the doorway. A nurse quickly strapped a face mask over my mouth.

Franz lay on his back. His eyes were closed. His chest heaved as he let out a constant scream while he writhed in pain. Two nurses fought to hold him down as Colonel Bennett cut the dead flesh from his left leg stump.

"Help us," A nurse yelled. I stayed frozen by the door, fear holding me in place. Major Tillman came into the operating room and pushed me toward the table. Then, he dawned a face mask and helped us hold Franz down.

"Can't you give him anything?" I yelled over the screams.

"He's already had enough morphine," one of the nurses shouted.

"Any more and he'll die," the other nurse added.

At the time, I didn't know Franz was unconscious. Even under heavy sedation, he still felt the pain of the knife cutting away the gangrene that settled into what was left of his leg. "What the hell am I doing here?" I yelled to no one in particular.

"Talk to him," Colonel Bennett ordered.

"What?"

"Talk to him," Colonel Bennett repeated.

"He can't hear, sir," a nurse said.

"Yes, he can," Colonel Bennett calmly said to her, and then turned to me. "Talk to him, please."

Immediately, German words spewed from my mouth. It took me a while to realize I wasn't making any sense, so I calmed down and began telling him about Boston. I told him about the people I knew, and the places I'd been. I told him about my recurring dream, and my divorce. Before long, I was confessing my sins as if he was my priest and I was his parishioner. As Franz's screams began to ebb, my volume grew that by the time his screams were only a whimper, I was nearly shouting. Somehow, I believe he heard every word in his unconscious state.

Once Franz's operation was over, he was wheeled into the recovery room. Major Tillman and I stayed by his side. An armed guard was posted inside the room with us. None of us spoke as Franz slept off the effects of the morphine. I believe they were, as I was, in silent contemplation of the state of Franz's broken young body.

Late in the day, Franz woke up. Major Tillman and I were asleep in a set of chairs at the foot of his bed. I was immersed in my recurring dream. My bride was smiling. It had been a long time since I saw the light in her eyes. Somehow, I knew her message. That my life was changing for the better, but I didn't believe her.

"Major Tillman. Leftenant Harrington," the guard said, waking us from our dreams. In a low murmur, Franz asked for water.

"What's he saying?" Major Tillman asked. I interpreted, and then Major Tillman barked at the guard to fetch Colonel Bennett. A few minutes later, Colonel Bennett ran into the room with the guard hot on his heels.

"What's wrong?" Colonel Bennett asked as he leaned over Franz.

"He wants water, sir," Major Tillman sheepishly replied.

Colonel Bennett looked our way and lifted his eyebrows. "You got me out of bed to ask if he could have some water?"

"Yes, sir," Major Tillman quietly answered.

"Of course he can have a bloody glass of water. He doesn't have a stomach wound," Colonel Bennett growled, and then smartly left the room, calling for a nurse as the door swung closed.

The endearing attitude Major Tillman had for Franz was unfathomable and completely out of character. Not once had he ever shown a smidgen of friendliness to any of his allied comrades. Jokes about him flourished amongst the hospital population. Everyone secretly called him the, "Rock of Gibraltar," on account of his unwavering ice cold demeanor. I personally referred to him as, 'Robert' because he reminded me of my father. Though, I stopped calling him that name when one of the nurses informed me that, Robert was in fact his real name.

Colonel Bennett ordered me to stay with Franz until another interpreter arrived, or when he was well enough to rot in a prisoner of war camp.

From then on, I was with him through his follow up surgeries. I was with him when he was fed and when he was bathed. I was even billeted in his room.

Major Tillman also stayed with Franz when he wasn't off harassing the other patients or driving the hospital staff mad with his endless tirades on cleanliness and order. Most nights he sat at the foot of Franz's bed and was still there in the morning. I spent countless hours interpreting their conversations. Soon, I realized why Major Tillman showed interest in the boy. For Franz was a healer. His spared life broke down the walls that Major Tillman and I had built around our emotions. His good nature brought life back into our deadened souls. We were once again learning to be compassionate human beings capable of love.

When I tell people about the effect Franz had on Major Tillman and I, no one believes me. I don't expect them too. He was our angle, released from the clutches of evil to deliver our salvation.

What I know of Franz Heiler is very little. For he spent most of his time mending mine and Major Tillman's souls. What I do know is that he was born in 1929 on a small farm a few kilometers outside of Straubing, Germany. At the age of two his parents drowned while boating on the Danube. He was raised in an orphanage until the age of nine when the Nazis took him to Berlin to bolster their growing Hitler Youth population. He hated his new life and rebelled. Many times he ran away, but the Nazi war dogs always caught him and brought him back to their sanctuary of hate. The more they tried to force their propaganda down his throat and mold him into one of their own, the more resistant he grew.

After the allied invasion of France, the Nazis knew he would never be one of their own, so they forced him into the army. He wanted to run away, but knew any soldier who ran would be shot. So, reluctantly he stayed. Once his initial training was over, he was posted along the German/Belgium border. He fought in the Ardennes offensive until the night of February 23rd, 1945 when he crossed, *no man's land* in search of an American soldier to surrender to. Fifty feet from an American observation post, a German artillery shell landed at his feet. His wounds brought him into Major Tillman's and my life. Eventually, that artillery shell took him away from us. On April 21st, 1945, Franz Heiler died. It was his birthday. He was only sixteen.

The story of Franz Heiler's life may not sound very inspiring. If I knew only his story, I would agree, but words cannot describe the effect he had on me. For words cannot truly explain the healing of my soul.

On April 23rd, 1945 we laid him to rest under an old elm tree in a quiet cemetery. Colonel Bennett had a modest headstone made. We all said a prayer as we set it upon his grave. Everyday since then, Major Tillman visited the site until the 2nd of July, 1963 when he was laid beside Franz. Their souls are now as one.

To this day, I can still hear the words Franz said to Major Tillman and I the day before he died. With a gleam in his eyes, he forgave me for my sins, and asked Major Tillman to forgive his. Somehow he knew the horrors I'd done. Somehow he knew the horrors the Nazis inflicted on Major Tillman's men.

After Franz Heiler died, the hospital wasn't the same. It's depressing, cold feeling returned stronger than ever. Patients kept arriving, although, in smaller numbers and less frequent than before. Everyone knew the war was nearing its end. We just didn't know when.

Although, Franz spawned the friendship between Major Tillman and me, I wouldn't say we were very close. Our conversations were always congenial, and always short. Most of the time we sat by Franz's grave and let silence speak for us. We still had a lot of healing to do ourselves. A process that neither of us would ever fully complete.

On May 2nd, 1945, I was released from the hospital. My orders said to report to London, but a car wasn't sent for me, so I hitched a ride with a ambulance to the train station. After many delays, I finally arrived in the early hours of the 4th of May. A car whisked me away to the headquarters at London Station. I promptly got out of the car without saying anything to the driver and walked the few feet to the front door, pausing for a moment before I went inside.

Another set of orders were waiting for me in London. OSS headquarters in Washington D.C., requested my immediate return to the States, but I didn't want to go. There was nothing left for me in America, and Germany continued its fight. So, I requested to stay in England. Literally having to beg up the chain of command, but I finally got my wish. Later that day, I found myself back at Beaulieu instructing an abbreviated small arms course.

There were times when I thought about quitting, but I vowed to continue my duty until the war's end. I didn't have long to wait. On May 8th, I sat alone in the Officer's Mess when a young OSS lieutenant burst in and announced Germany's surrender. He was excited the war was over, but I could see the disappointment in his eyes. He missed his chance of glory, and I would have gladly given him mine, but the horrors of war aren't given freely. For they have to be earned in the depths of Hell. A hefty price has to be paid.

The day after Germany's defeat, I was assigned to a task force made up of German linguists. Our job was to interview German prisoners held captive in the United Kingdom and find out if any of them posed a threat to the occupational forces after their release. Over the next month and a half, I personally interviewed over two thousand prisoners. Out of them, I only found eight who were questionable. All eight were high ranking officers. Three of them ended up being charged with war crimes and sent to Nuremburg to stand trial. The other five were eventually released back to Germany.

The one thing, I noticed about the German prisoners was their physical appearance. The longer a prisoner was held in captivity, the more physically fit he was. The newer arrivals were undernourished and their uniforms hung loosely on their bodies. Still, there was one aspect they all had in common. Every one of them was glad to be going home. Their families were more important than victory or defeat.

Around the time the German prisoners were leaving the United Kingdom, the OSS headquarters in London was dismantling its main operations and returning to the States. Only a small contingent stayed behind. There were a few OSS agents still in the field, and a few more were dispatched to Germany to set up shop in the U.S. Embassy. I was asked to go with them, but I declined. On August 5th, a day before the atomic bomb was dropped on Hiroshima, I resigned from the OSS. My superiors shook my hand and gave me a pat on the back for a job well done before they set me free. With only seven hundred and eighty-two dollars in my pocket and one suitcase to my name, I headed for the port in Liverpool. The next morning, I left merry old England on a ferry boat that took me across the Irish sea.

28

*T*he land of my ancestors was a mystery. The magical isle, shrouded in green, home of the shamrock, the leprechaun, and the family I had never known. Would I be welcome? Would I find what I was searching for? Would the questions that ached from the day of my birth be answered, I wondered as the ferry pulled into Belfast, Ireland.

The dock was filled with mothers, wives, sons and daughters. The men who they waited for were men returning from Hell. Some had visible scars. Others had scars concealed beneath clothing. Some were physically unscathed, but I knew they had pain. We all did. A pain we would carry deep within our minds for the rest of our lives.

For those on the docks waiting, those waiting on docks all over the world, or comfortably in their homes, they would never know our pain. They could never comprehend what we'd gone through. What we had to do to survive. No matter how much, or how little we divulged, they would never know.

It is said that a picture is worth a thousand words, which may be true. I cannot say whether it is or isn't. What I do know is a picture can never convey the true emotions of its subject. A photograph, a painting, or a newsreel, can never tell the true story of war to those who spent their lives in peace. For they haven't spent time in Hell. Their demons are only a dream. Our demons are a nightmare. Our demons are real.

I couldn't smile, as those waiting on the docks smiled. I couldn't smile as my comrades smiled when they embraced the ones who loved them. I had no reason to smile. I had no one who loved me, nor a place I called home. I had nothing. When the Customs Agent smiled as he asked me why I came to Ireland, all I could say was to find the family I had never known.

"Do they live in Belfast?" The Customs Agent asked. I gave him the faded piece of paper my father gave to me. "Bally Clare," he said slowly. "Can't say I've heard of it. Sure you got the name right?"

"I think so," I replied.

The Customs Agent smiled again. "Well, good luck to you then," he said as he brought a freshly inked stamp down on my passport. I thanked him, and then walked toward the heart of Belfast.

For the next three days, I stayed in a Bed-n-Breakfast close to the Botanic Gardens. The search for the place of my father's birth was proving fruitless. Everyone I asked never heard of the town, nor did I find the town etched on a map. My hope was fading fast, although, I wasn't about to give up. Since the moment the ferry docked in Belfast, I felt I was where I was supposed to be.

During the afternoon of my fourth day in Ireland, with suitcase in hand, I walked toward the train depot. I planned to take a train to Dublin to continue my search, but my heart told me I was close to where I needed to go. My mind said different. Logic fought emotion. Emotion fought logic. The conflicting paths only brought despair. With my last vestiges of hope, I walked into the Crown Bar to drink away what little of me remained. At the end of the bar, with a jigger of whiskey and a pint of ale, I hid myself on a stool and melted into my surroundings. The only time I was noticed was when I ordered another drink, and even then, the barkeep paid little attention to me.

The conversations I overheard were of the usual sort. The economy, women, weather, and the local sports. Politics and religion were off limits. Only once did I hear anyone talk about the war, but it was only a fleeting comment between two men who toasted one another in honor of their fallen friends.

From the time I had entered the Crown Bar to the time the sun fell below the horizon, I had said less than twenty words. When a young soldier wearing a Royal army uniform came in and sat on a stool beside me, I said nothing. He wore a smug grin. His eyes beamed with pride. Arrogance, the type I'd seen so many times from those who wore the same uniform as he, oozed from his pores. I almost left the bar without saying a word when he asked how I was doing. It took me a moment to answer that I was fine.

"A Yank!" He exclaimed. Then, he turned to the rest of the men milling about with pints in their hands. "Hey lads, we've got a Yank in here," he yelled. Then, he turned back to me.

I kept my eyes pasted to my pint glass half filled with ale. "Leave me alone," I grumbled.

"What's wrong, Yank? Don't you like Irish company?" He asked, trying to chide me into a fight. I held my tongue and took another drink as the barkeep sauntered over and told the soldier to leave me alone. "Just trying to be friendly," the soldier smirked.

"He doesn't want to be bothered," the barkeep said, and then sauntered away.

The soldier remained quiet for a few minutes. Then, he turned to me again. "What's the cane for, Yank? Too lame to fight?" He snarled.

Again, I didn't answer. Tension steadily rose between us until I could feel its stifling effects. My heart beat faster with every passing second. My hands began to shake. The young soldier took notice and called me a coward, and I didn't care. His words meant nothing to me. I knew who I was. I knew what I had been through. What I had done. More importantly, I knew what I was capable of. The only person I feared was myself.

Slowly, I stood and picked up my suitcase. The young soldier jumped to his feet and blocked my escape. "Bloody coward," he yelled as he pushed me to the floor. The entire bar fell silent. Everyone stared in shock.

"Please leave me alone," I said as I rose to my feet. Then, when I bent over to pick up my suitcase and cane, the soldier pushed me to the floor again.

"Stay down you bloody coward," the soldier yelled.

"Leave him alone," the barkeep screamed.

"No," the soldier growled and made a fist. "Not until he leaves my country."

I rose to me feet. The soldier swung. I caught his arm and swung him around, pinning his arm behind his back. Then, I grabbed his head and slammed it on the counter top. "You came here looking for a fight. Well, now you found one," I growled in his ear. He struggled to get free, but I leaned into him and wrenched his arm higher. Rage flowed through my body. The evil in my soul shined forth.

"Let him go," someone yelled, and I paid no attention.

"I've killed more people than I care to remember. Some of my closest friends died before my eyes. I've lost everyone I've ever cared about, and I'm in no mood to compete with you," my voice thundered in the young soldier's ear. The men standing close by slowly backed away. "Why do you want to fight when so many have died?"

"My brother," the soldier stammered while tears flowed from his eyes. "He was killed by American artillery."

I released the soldier from my clutch and sat next to him. "Fighting me won't take the pain away."

"But it hurts," the soldier said as he wiped his tears on his sleeve.

"I know it does. Just don't let it tear you down," I said as the patrons in the bar resumed their conversations as if nothing had happened.

The soldier remained quiet with his eyes painted to the counter top. I ordered two pints of ale and set one in front of him. Lost in his own world, he barely noticed.

After a while, the soldier gradually came back to reality. "Can you forgive me?" He asked.

"I already have," I replied.

The young soldier and I talked for the next hour or so. During that time, I never learned his name. Nor did he learn mine. An introduction wasn't necessary. When two people share a common bond, it is the essence of that bond that breeds their communion. Titles mean nothing.

Later, when I finally got up to leave the Crown Bar, I realized that I had consumed more alcohol than I had in my entire life. Regrettably, there is very little I remember after exiting through the stained glass doors. What I do remember is trying to keep my balance while carrying my suitcase in my right hand and steadying myself with the cane in my left. I remember the policeman helping me into his patrol car. And I remember having a blinding headache when I woke up on a hardwood bench in the train station. How I got there, I can only guess.

After downing two aspirin I bought from a kiosk on the loading platform, I walked up to the ticket booth. My face must have been green because the female ticket agent asked if I was feeling all right. "Yes," I replied. "A ticket to Dublin, please. I'm visiting my family in Bally Clare."

"Bally Clare you say?" A man standing behind me asked.

I turned around and looked down at an elderly gentleman who couldn't have been an inch over four feet tall. "Yes, Bally Clare," I replied.

"Why go to Dublin when you can take a bus and be in Bally Clare in a half hour?" The elderly gentleman asked.

"I can?"

"You're a very daft young man, aren't you? Bally Clare's only twelve miles from the very spot you're standing."

My eyes lit up. "Really? Twelve miles?"

"Twelve Miles."

"And I could take a bus?" I clarified.

"That's what I said."

"But, I've already checked at the bus station and they've never heard of Bally Clare."

"Which Station?"

"What do you mean?" I asked.

The elderly gentleman laughed heartily and made my head pound. "Oh, lad, you're as lost as the people who live here, aren't you? There's two bus depots ran by two different companies in Belfast. Didn't anyone tell you?"

"No."

The elderly gentleman laughed harder. "My dear boy, go to the station on Oxford Street. A bus from there will take you to Bally Clare."

I nearly shook the man's hand off thanking him. In my excitement, I completely forgot about my pounding headache and queasy stomach that when I came upon a small diner, I walked inside. Fifteen minutes later, after three scrambled eggs and greasy sausage, I was ejecting my breakfast into a dirty toilet. My headache returned ten fold. My stomach tied in knots. Needless to say, I should have stayed in Belfast until I was able to travel. Any rational human being would have, but I felt compelled to continue my journey.

After buying a ticket at the bus depot, I spent another half hour hovering over a toilet before boarding a bus. The elderly bus driver lifted his eyebrows when he saw me. My fellow passengers kept their distance. I must have looked as bad as I felt. I knew I smelled of stale booze and cigarettes, but at least I had a smile on my face.

My smile lasted for two miles outside of Belfast. The bus driver didn't complain when I asked him to pull over to the side of the road. After relieving my stomach of its contents, I asked the bus driver for directions to Bally Clare. To his and my fellow passengers relief, I announced that I'd walk the rest of the way. In a cloud of dust, the bus left me standing on the side of the road in the tranquil Irish countryside.

A few cars and trucks passed by as I walked along. The drivers of every one of them heading toward Bally Clare stopped and asked if I wanted a ride, but I always declined. In my state, I needed to walk. They surely would have kicked me out of their vehicles fifty feet down the road anyway.

When I finally walked into Bally Clare, it was well past sundown. Not a single soul wandered the streets. All of the businesses were closed, except for the pubs. Even then, they didn't look very lively as I walked by their windows. The barkeeps looked bored. The patrons, all men, could be counted on one hand. The dead social atmosphere made it easy to understand why my father left his place of birth for Boston. I on the other hand, immediately fell in love with the place. After my years in the OSS, the laid back atmosphere was just what I was looking for.

On main street, in the heart of Bally Clare, I stopped in front of Finnigan's Inn. It was the only hotel in the town and looked deserted. If it weren't for a sign on the wall next to a rope hanging by the front door, I would have kept walking. For the sign read, "Ring For Service."

'*Ring what?*' I thought. There wasn't a button for a door bell. Nothing except the rope hanging by the front door. It went up to the second floor and disappeared into the wall.

"Strange," I said to myself as I pulled on the rope.

Nothing happened. I waited a minute before pulling on the rope again. Still nothing happened, so I pulled on it a few more times. Then, a light came on in a second story window. A moment later, the window opened and a haggard old man poked his head out. "Know what time it is, lad?" The old man hollered.

"No, sir," I replied.

"Bloody late, it is."

"I apologize, sir, but I've just arrived and need a room for the night."

The haggard old man grumbled, and then shut the window. I waited a few minutes wondering if he was going to let me in, or if I would have to sleep on the street. Then, the front door opened. The old man, dressed in white pajamas with red pin stripes, leather slippers, and a long stocking cap tilted slightly on his head, put his oil lamp up to my face. "Do I know you?"

"No, sir," I replied.

The old man examined my face in the dim light of the lamp. "You sure?"

"Yes, sir. This is my first time here."

The old man flipped a light switch, illuminating us from a bare light bulb above the door. A wry look contorted his face as he examined me closer. Then, he scanned the street behind me before looking me eye to eye. "I swear, I've seen you before, but I can't remember where," he mused to himself.

"Maybe you saw me in Belfast?"

"Nope. Haven't been there in years," he said quietly, almost as if I wasn't standing in front of him. "Belfast, you say?"

"Yes, sir. I've just arrived," I replied.

"How? The bus doesn't run this time of night."

"I walked."

The old man looked down at my cane and suitcase before looking me eye to eye again. "Seems a long way to walk this time of night." He stared at me for a moment, and then added, "Well, you coming in or not?"

I followed him inside. After checking in, he led me upstairs to an eight foot by eight foot room complete with a bed, chair, and small wardrobe. "It's the best we've got," the old man said before handing me a key and walking away. As he left, he muttered, "crazy American."

No words can explain the vivid dreams I had my first night in Bally Clare. All night I dreamed of Ireland's lush green fields. The woolly sheep dotting the landscape. The somber waves crashing into the Emerald Isle's shore. I dreamed of the war. The friends I made, and those I lost. I dreamed my recurring dream of the woman standing next to me at the altar. How she meant more to me than Sarah ever had. My last dream was of my father. How greed blinded his heart, leaving him in the Hell he created.

When I woke the next morning, for the first time in a very long time my body was completely refreshed, my mind at ease. I felt I had changed over night. That my life had new meaning. A new purpose I had to fulfill. The destiny set by fate since the moment of my birth.

After showering, I spit shined my black oxfords. Then, I dressed in the finest suit I owned, a black flannel Seville Row number with black pearl buttons. A smile never left my face as I carried my suitcase downstairs to a small breakfast nook by the front lobby. A young married couple were seated by the window. The husband read the weekly newspaper while his wife filled the room with endless chatter about everything and nothing. Once in a while her husband would nod or grunt while keeping his eyes glued to his paper. Since divorce wasn't legal in Ireland, I smiled wider, knowing they were in for a very long marriage.

A few minutes went by when an elderly woman carrying a breakfast tray backed into the room. When she turned and saw me, her face turned white. The breakfast tray fell from her hands. Ceramic plates and mugs shattered. Silverware clanged. Scrambled eggs, toast, and hot coffee splashed on her legs. The young wife stopped chattering. The husband stopped reading. The three of us looked at the elderly woman who stared at me for a moment before running back into the kitchen.

"What the devil is wrong with her?" The husband asked to no one in particular.

"Watch your tongue," his wife immediately replied while slapping his forearm. Then, she blushed as she asked me excuse her husbands foul mouth. I kindly replied that I'd heard worse, and then turned my attention back to the dropped breakfast tray. The wife resumed her chatter. Her husband resumed reading. I just sat there with a smile on my face.

The haggard old man entered from the kitchen and approached my table. "I apologize for the fright, sir, but my wife thought you were someone else," he quickly explained.

"Oh, who'd she think I was?"

"That's not important, sir," the old man said, and then apologized to the young couple for the commotion.

"Should I leave?" I asked.

"Oh, no, sir. I'll be your waiter now," the old man replied.

At that moment his wife crept into the room. As she cleaned the spilled contents of the breakfast tray off the floor, her eyes never left my face. Her gaze was uncomfortable to say the least, so I stood and picked up my cane and suitcase. "It's best I be on my way."

"Please, sir, have a seat," the old man begged.

"I've clearly upset your wife," I replied.

"No need to worry, sir. She'll be fine."

"No need to worry about me either. I'm not very hungry at the moment," I lied as I walked into the lobby. The old man checked me out of the hotel and handed me a receipt. I thanked him and walked to the front door. "Oh, by the way," I said as I turned around. "I'm looking for my family. Do you know if the Harrington's still live around here?"

"Jesus, Mary, and Joseph," the elderly woman screamed. The breakfast tray crashed to the floor. Then, came a thud. Once again the young wife's chatter stopped.

"Lord help me," The old man blushed, and then quickly walked away. I watched him disappear into the breakfast nook before I left the hotel.

It was only around seven in the morning, but the sleeping town I arrived in the night before was wide awake. School children dressed in identical uniforms hurried toward school. Women with multicolored scarves on their heads walked by with a grocery bag cradled in one arm and a small child in the other. Small groups of men stood on the sidewalk and smoked cigarettes while cars and trucks motored slowly down the cobblestone street past a newsstand announcing Japan's surrender. It seemed I was the only one who cared the whole world was finally at peace. Yet, even I didn't care to read the news as I sauntered down the road in search of food.

Men my fathers age eyed me suspiciously. As I walked toward them, they diverted their eyes to the ground. Then, whispered amongst themselves after I passed them by. The younger generations barely noticed I was there.

Those who did wished me a good morning, and I replied in kind while I continued walking down the street.

Toward the edge of town the smell of fresh bread and pastries filled my nostrils. The pleasant aroma drew me across the street. That's when I noticed the small group of people following me. Thoughts of a sheriff's posse in a cowboy film flashed in my mind as I quickened my pace and dashed into the bakery.

"Can I help ya?" A lovely young woman with black hair and lively eyes asked from behind the counter.

"Yes, ma'am. I'm starving," I said as I bent down to look in the display case. Trays filled with croissants, scones, donuts, meat pies, and bread rolls begged for my attention. My stomach growled in anticipation. Everything looked delicious and in my famished state I could have eaten it all.

"You famous or something?" The young woman asked.

"No. Why?"

"Well, you've drawn a crowd," the young woman replied while pointing outside.

I turned to look. The group who followed me stood across the street talking amongst themselves as their number steadily grew. Some of them crossed the street and pressed their noses against the bakery window. "Seems they find you interesting."

"I wonder why?" I said in a daze.

"Probably because you're American. God knows we don't get many of you in Bally Clare. Where you from by the way?" The young woman asked.

"Boston, but I won't be going back there."

"Oh. . . Why not?"

"Nothing there for me anymore." I held out my hand. "I'm, Dan by the way."

The young woman shook my hand. "Pleasure to meet you, Dan. I'm Sadie."

"Nice to meet you, Sadie. Do you know if the Harrington's live around here?"

"Of course they do," Sadie sang. "You must be family then?"

"That's what my father told me."

"Ah, bet they'll be happy to see you then."

"I don't know. I've never met them," I admitted.

"Ah, of course they will. So what can I get for you," Sadie smiled.

I ordered a meat pie, two strawberry scones and a cup of tea. The group of people still hovered outside, so I sat in the far corner of the room with my back to them. A moment later the bakery door opened. I turned and watched a middle-aged woman walk slowly toward the counter. She flashed a nervous smile in my direction. I smiled, and then turned my attention back to my breakfast. Then, Sadie laughed. "Oh, he's, Dan Harrington. From America. Come to find his Irish roots, he has," Sadie proudly announced.

The middle-aged woman quietly thanked Sadie, and then smiled at me before leaving the bakery. Outside, the crowd gathered around as she spoke rapidly. In a matter of moments, the crowd slowly dissolved. A few of its members smiled and waved. I waved back.

"Do they always get like this when Americans come here?" I asked.

"Nope. You're the first," Sadie replied.

"First American?"

"Nope. First time," Sadie smiled.

After I ate every last tidbit, every crumb and drinking the last drop of tea, I ordered two more scones for the road. Then, I asked Sadie if she knew where the Harrington's lived.

"Don't you know?" Sadie asked.

"No. My father only said I had family here."

"That's it?"

"Yeah."

"Well, you're father's an odd man, isn't he?"

"Among other things," I grumbled.

"Now isn't that funny, mister Harrington," Sadie laughed. "All he said was, Bally Clare."

"Yeah. I don't even know my grandmother's name."

"Well, I only know her by miss Harrington, but she doesn't come into town much any more. Nora does though."

"Who's that," I asked.

"Well, from the looks of ya, she's probably your aunt. You really don't know any of them, do ya?"

"No," I quietly confessed.

"Well, Nora lives with your grandmother. And you have another aunt who visits in the summer. That's all I can tell ya."

"What's her name?"

"Oh, we've never been formally introduced, but you'll know her when you meet her," Sadie laughed.

"How's that?"

"Oh, you'll know," Sadie said while raising her eyebrows. It was obvious Sadie was hiding something, so I dismissed the matter.

Sadie gave me directions to my grandmother's house. I thanked her. Then, I picked up my suitcase and the paper bag with the scones and left the bakery. Outside, an elderly gentleman said hello. Another man just stared. Across the street a woman waved while her young daughter stuck out her tongue. Then, as I walked toward the town square, more and more people said hello and wished me a good day. I replied in kind, realizing that after they learned who I was, they wanted to be my friend. Never before, nor since have I ever been treated with that kind of hospitality from people I'd never met.

29

O ver the centuries, much has been said about Ireland. Mythology and folklore passed from generation to generation weave intricate tales and fascinating histories of its lugubrious past. Poets praise its beauty and lament its sorrow. Songs are sung for its people, their beloved Saint Patrick, and those who died fighting for freedom. It is called the Enchanted Isle where Christianity and Paganism define its customs and beliefs. Where the Shamrock grows, and the Green and the Orange abide. The land of my ancestors, and now, the land I would call my home.

For the first time since I stepped foot on Irish soil, my eyes opened to the beauty of the land. Rich, green pastures and fields stretched across the valley. Sheep, cattle and dairy cows grazed in the ankle high grass. Birds soared though the sky and sung from the trees. Lilacs and wild berries grew along the side of the road. I believed I had finally found heaven as a warm breeze touched lightly upon my face. When I reached, Abhaile Bothar, I turned right as Sadie instructed and walked a quarter of a kilometer before I saw four cottages off in the distance. They were whitewashed and farther away than they appeared. The first cottage was on the left side of the road, so I dismissed it and carried on to the next two cottages sitting across from one another. The cottage on the right, as was the cottage on the left, had tiled roofs, so I kept my pace and continued walking down the road.

Halfway to the last cottage, I came upon an elderly man herding a flock of sheep across the road. When he saw me, his face turned white. When I announced that I was on my way home, he let out a short scream, and then tore through an open gate and across a field as fast as his tired old legs could run. His flock panicked and scattered to the four winds. I was blindsided by a large ewe who knocked me to the ground. The force of the impact jarred the suitcase from my hand and sent it skidding across the road until it struck another ewe and burst open. My clothes went everywhere. Pants, shirts, socks, everything in the suitcase was strewn in all directions and trampled by the frightened sheep, and I laughed. After my reception in Bally Clare and the elderly man's reaction to my words, I laughed and laughed until my belly ached. Then, I laughed some more.

If anyone saw me, they would've thought I was crazy, but I didn't care. After my participation in the horror of war, I needed to laugh. I needed to laugh as much as I needed oxygen in my lungs and food in my belly.

When my laughter eventually died, the flock gathered around and stared. If they could speak my language, I knew they would ask me what they were supposed to do. Due to the elderly man's flight they wanted me to be their shepherd, and I gladly accepted. With the aid of my cane, I rose to my feet. The sheep patiently waited for my orders. So, I raised my cane high above my head, and then swept it down slowly in a large arc toward the open gate. The sheep instantly followed in the direction my cane traveled and fought their way toward the opening. As they went, I imagined I was still in France tending Pierre's sheep. When I shut the gate, I wondered if I led them to their slaughter as a solitary tear fell from my eye.

After repacking my clothes into the suitcase, I took one last look at the flock before resuming my journey down the road. The last cottage was over eight hundred feet away, but even at that distance, I could see that its roof wasn't thatched as Sadie said it should be. For a moment, I thought I was lost. My hope faltered until I realized I had followed Sadie's directions exactly as she told them to me. So, I scanned the rolling hills and through the trees for another cottage close by, but I only saw the four. Since, I didn't want to walk back to Bally Clare to ask for directions, I walked toward the last cottage to ask the inhabitants if they knew where my family lived.

The cottage stood two hundred feet from the road. A three foot high rock wall lined the driveway. The lawn from the cottage to the road was neatly manicured. Apple and pear trees grew along its edge. On the right side of the cottage was a rose garden with colors spanning the entire spectrum of the rainbow. A vegetable garden curved around the back. Behind it a grove of trees climbed a small hill before dropping out of sight. On the left side of the cottage a chicken coup sat with its gate wide open. A couple of chickens and a rooster strutted close by while a lazy Basset Hound laid under a tree and watched them out of one eye.

The cottage itself was one story with a brown tiled roof and whitewashed walls with red trim. The front door was painted red, as were the shutters on the two front windows, one on each side of the door. A chimney poked from the right side of the roof with smoke drifting from its flume.

The Basset Hound barely turned his head when I knocked on the front door. A few moments later an elderly woman in a navy blue dress opened the door. She stared at me for only a second before fainting, knocking a picture off the wall as she landed on the floor.

"Mother?" A woman's voice called from an adjoining room when the picture frame broke into pieces.

"Help," I cried as I dashed to the elderly woman's side.

In a flash, a middle-aged woman with black hair and oval spectacles kneeled by the elderly woman's head. "What happened?"

"She fainted," I replied while turning my head to look at the woman with the spectacles.

"Holy mother of Jesus. Get away from me," she screamed as she backed away. "Are you who I think you are?"

"No, ma'am. I'm, Dan Harrington from Boston, Massachusetts, and I'm looking for. . ."

"What did you say your name is?" She interrupted.

"Dan Harrington. My father said I have family around here, and. . ."

"Who's your father?" She demanded

"Robert Harrington. Why?"

The woman clamped her mouth shut. Her eyes filled with rage. "Robert Harrington is my brother, and she's his mother," the woman said slowly through clenched teeth as she pointed to the elderly woman passed out on the floor.

At that moment there was a lot I wanted to say, but the words failed to find my lips. My quest finally came to its end. The family my father hid from me was finally found and all I could do was stare at my grandmother passed out at my feet.

"Help me get her inside," my aunt said.

I nodded and cradled my grandmother in my arms. My aunt followed close behind as I carried her into her bedroom. Somehow, I knew exactly where it was, but in the small three bedroom cottage, it wouldn't be hard for anyone to figure out. For in most houses the master bedroom is usually located in the back.

When I laid my grandmother on her bed, she moaned. "Wait in the hall," my aunt ordered. "I don't want her to see you and faint again."

I looked at my aunt, and then to my grandmother. When she moaned again, I hobbled out of the room as fast as I could, barely making it into the hallway when I heard my grandmother confess, "I saw him, Nora."

"No, mother. You saw your grandson," my aunt Nora replied.

"I saw your brother, I tell you," my grandmother said.

"Mother, you saw Dan. . . Robert's son."

"Robert? My Robert?"

"Yes mother. His son. . . Your grandson, Dan is who you saw. It wasn't John," my aunt Nora replied softly.

"Where is he? Where's my grandson?" My grandmother groaned.

"He's in the hallway. Do you want to see him?"

"Of course, I do. He's my grandson," my grandmother said. Nora was about to say something else when I stepped into the room. My grandmother stared at me with a straight face for a moment before her lips parted into a smile. "My God, Nora. Would you look at that. He's the spitting image of his uncle. If only Rosalie were alive to see him, her soul would've been saved."

"Come now mother. We mustn't dwell on the past," Nora begged.

My grandmother looked at my aunt. "But we mustn't forget it either," she said, and then turned to me. "Do you know who Rosalie was?"

"No," I answered.

"That's easy to believe knowing your father," my grandmother lamented. "He's always been tight-lipped about his family, you know? At least since his father died. Never come to terms with it and blames me. Told me himself after Mary died."

"Why?" I asked.

"Oh, never mind. I've said enough already."

"I'd like to know."

"So would I," Nora said.

My grandmother looked at both of us, and then sighed. "Because my brother accidentally shot your grandfather during a fox hunt, that's why. Your father believes I had your grandfather murdered for his money, but he never had any. Oh, I loved that man more than anything in the world and would never do such a thing."

"Mother, you never told me that," Nora cried.

"I never wanted to. Didn't want to add to the ill feelings you already have toward, Robert. When he accused me after Mary died, I knew you'd hate him even more."

After hearing my mother's name, I asked, "My father said he stopped talking to you after my uncle John died. Not after my mother passed away."

My grandmother sighed. "Sorry, Dan. I love your father very much, but he's a liar," she said as she got off the bed and retrieved a small wooden box from the top drawer of her dresser. With frail fingers, she carefully opened the box and removed a wrinkled envelope. The postmark showed the faded date of November, 4th, 1927, exactly 27 days after my mother died.

Nora snatched the letter from my grandmother's hand and sat down on the bed. From where I stood, I clearly saw that it was written by my father's hand. The anger I held toward him returned fourfold and I had to leave the room. My grandmother followed me into the dining room and sat down next to me.

"Dan, don't hate your father," she said as she put her hand on my arm.

I quickly pulled my arm away. "He lied to me. Said my grandfather was killed by the British. Said he hated my uncle John because he joined the British army, and didn't want anything to do with his family because you allowed him to fight for the British."

My grandmother sighed. "Oh, he hated Johnny for joining the army. Ever since your father got involved with the Irish Republican Army, he hated anything and everything British. I think that's why he went to America."

"He left because he's a murderer," Nora growled as she marched into the room and threw my father's letter on the table.

"Nora, you don't know that," my grandmother said.

"Yes, I do," Nora snapped as she sat down across from me. Her eyes gleamed. "Somebody told your father that my fiancé was a Protestant and your father killed him. The damn coward shot him in the back only a mile from here. A week later, he forced Mary to go to America. She was afraid of him, you know. Terrified. But she was a Catholic, and as all Catholics do, she stuck by her husband. Poor woman."

"But my father's a Methodist," I stated.

"Like the Devil, he is," my grandmother snarled. "He was raised in the Church."

"Well, he's a Methodist now," I said.

"Robert doesn't know what he is," Nora said vehemently.

"Nora, stop," my grandmother begged.

"I will not!" Nora snapped. Then, she looked at me. "Six months to the day before she died, I got a letter from your mother. In it was a picture of you looking exactly like your uncle John when he was your age. Mary said your father saw the resemblance and despised you for it. She said your father intended to mold you into an exact replica of himself as a way to make up for his brother's treachery. Your mother feared you'd grow up to be as evil as he was and begged me to sneak you and her back to Ireland."

"Is this true?" My grandmother asked.

"As sure as God himself, it's true," Nora answered. "That's why Hattie went to America after Mary died. . . She was going to kidnap Dan and bring him back here."

"Who's Hattie?" I asked.

"She's your aunt Harriet, of course. Didn't your father tell you about her?" My grandmother asked.

"No, he never told me anything about any of you until a few years ago. I only knew you existed because mom told me before she died," I confessed. Then, I pulled the scrap piece of paper my father gave me and handed it to my grandmother. "This is all he gave me to find you. Since then, he's disowned me."

"Well, that's for the better. Don't need the likes of him in your life," Nora said.

"Nora, stop," my grandmother sighed.

"Well, it's true. Probably disowned Danny because he couldn't murder him like he murdered Mary," Nora sneered.

"What?" I cried.

"Hush Nora, we don't know what Hattie said is true," my grandmother ordered.

"Of course it's true. Hattie's never lied in her entire life."

"What about my mother?" I asked.

"I can't bear to listen, Nora. It'll be the death of me," my grandmother sighed, and then got up from the table and went into her bedroom. When she shut the door, I asked my aunt Nora to tell me how my mother died.

"She was poisoned," Nora said ever so softly.

"What?" I roared, and then stood up, knocking my chair over as I raised to my feet.

Nora remained calm. "It's true, Dan. When Hattie went to America after your mother's funeral, you were away at boarding school. Your father wouldn't tell her where you were, and he wouldn't show her where your mother was buried. He said Mary died of a heart attack and visiting her grave only added to his anguish. Since, Hattie knows your father well, she knew he was lying. Your mother was only thirty-three and Hattie rightfully assumed a heart attack wasn't the cause of death, so she checked with the State Examiner's Office. Found out Mary had arsenic in her body. . . Your father slowly poisoned her to death."

"That's not true," I screamed. Tears fell from my eyes, blinding my sight. "If it were, he'd be in prison."

"And he should be, but no charges were filed. There wasn't any proof."

"Then how do you know he poisoned her?" I demanded. I knew my mother's health was failing the last few years of her life, but I couldn't believe my father murdered her. He loved her.

"If you don't believe me, then I'll show you," Nora said, and then left the room. A few minutes later she came back with a weathered envelope in her hand. "Sorry, but I know your father," she said as she handed the envelope to me.

I tore the letter from the envelope and paced around the room. At the top in bold black letters was written: State Board of Medical Examination, Boston, Massachusetts. Below that the letter was stamped: Death Certificate. My mother's full name, age, date, and time and place of death were further down the page. Near the bottom was a short paragraph detailing the cause of death. Tears streamed down my face as I read how my mother had died from a heart attack due to a buildup of arsenic in her body. The letter fell from my hands as I read the source of the arsenic possibly came from rat poison, and I knew that was impossible. For we never had a rodent problem in my house.

"I need some air," I choked.

"I understand," Nora smiled as I walked out of the kitchen. When I got outside, I thought it was strange that within minutes of meeting my Irish relatives, I was told that my father murdered my mother. Then again, they knew my father better than I did. In addition, if he truly murdered Nora's husband, she had every right to hate him. Exposing his crimes to his only son was her retribution.

30

*T*here are details in all our lives we long to forget. Thoughts, memories, desires that plague our minds. Driving a wedge between what we hold sacred and profane. Creating a struggle between insanity and the sane. The severity of our afflictions bind our souls, pulling us deeper and deeper into the abyss we create. On the day I learned of my mother's murder, I grew numb. My emotions dulled. My spirit descended. My life lost its meaning. Then, the demons came. They brought me hate. Hatred like I'd never felt before. Rage grew inside. As the day passed, I cursed God. I cursed Satan. I cursed myself. My father would feel my wrath. He would die by my hand. Then, it happened, as it happens to all who are tempted by the minions of Hell. A hand reached down from Heaven and forgave my thoughts, forgave my words. I felt what most people refuse to feel, for I felt grace. Still the anger remained, yet, I was no longer intent on murder. I wanted justice. My father may be a powerful man, but I vowed to expose his weakness for all to see. To watch his peers topple him from the pedestal they set him upon.

I got to my feet from where I hid in the rose garden and walked back to my grandmother's cottage, finding my suitcase where I'd left it.

"Nice to see you're back," my aunt Nora said from the hallway.

"I'm not staying," I stated.

"Why not?" My grandmother asked from the kitchen doorway. "This is your home if you'll have us?"

"I appreciate it, but I have to return to Boston."

"Don't hate your father," my grandmother begged.

"I already do, and that'll never change," I growled, which brought a smile to Nora's face.

"You can't change the past," my grandmother said.

"I know, but he walks free while my mother lies in a grave, and I'll never rest until he's brought to justice."

Nora was about to speak when the front door opened. In walked a short, middle-aged woman with blond hair and rosy cheeks. She wore a white dress with red roses and a black velvet waist coat. A black beret sat lightly atop her head, and when she saw me, a smile spread across her face. "Oh, Johnny, you're home," she said as she walked up to me, threw her arms around my neck, and kissed me on the cheek. "I knew you'd come back."

"Hattie, that's your nephew, Dan. . . Robert's son," my grandmother said.

My aunt Hattie grasped my shoulders while keeping her eyes locked upon mine. "No, he's not mother. It's Johnny. He's finally come home."

I was too stunned to move. From the moment, I saw my aunt Hattie, the anger I had for my father vanished. The pain I had from my mother's death subsided. The love I still had for Sarah became a memory. Somehow, I knew Hattie would define my life and guide me in the direction of my fate.

"Hattie, listen to mother. That's Dan, your nephew," Nora said.

Hattie kept me in her embrace and looked at Nora. "Don't you know your own brother when you see him?" She asked, and then looked at me. "Tell them, Johnny. Tell them who you are."

"Actually, I'm Dan, your nephew," I replied.

"Oh, don't be daft. I know my brother when I see him," Hattie said, and then kissed me on the cheek again before looking around the room. "Where's Rosalie?"

"Who?" I asked.

"Rosalie. Your lovely wife," Hattie smiled.

"Hattie. . . Rosalie died years ago, and so did John," my grandmother stammered. "They're never coming back."

"But look mother. Look at Johnny. He said he'd come back, and here he is," Hattie purred.

I finally understood what Sadie meant when she said I'd know my aunt when I met her. For my aunt Hattie was off her rocker and I freed myself from her embrace.

"Where you going, Johnny?" Hattie asked.

"As far away from you as possible, if he knows what's good for him," Nora replied.

"He's going back to Boston," My grandmother stated.

"Oh, but your home is here. . . You still have to find Rosalie," Hattie said.

"Well, if you want me to stay, tell me why you think I'm uncle John," I said while winking at my grandmother out of the corner of my eye.

Between Destiny and Fate

"Of course Johnny. Of course," Hattie said, and then she grabbed me by the hand and led me to a picture hanging in the dining room. "Oh, just look at you." Hattie pointed at a family portrait taken long before I was born and I couldn't even tell who my father was in the picture.

"Enough, Hattie," my grandmother ordered as she and Nora entered and sat at the table. "Oh, Danny, I apologize for your aunt. She's a wee bit daft, you see?"

"A wee bit?" Nora laughed. "She's completely lost her marbles, she has. Probably drives her students bleedin' mad."

"Watch your language, Nora," my grandmother snapped.

I sat at the table and looked at Nora, and then to Hattie. "You're a teacher?"

"Oh, yes, Johnny," Hattie smiled as she sat beside me.

"She's also a writer," my grandmother beamed.

"Really?" I asked.

"Oh, yes. She's quite accomplished, although, her stories are a little strange for my likes. Always uses mice as characters," Nora droned.

Hattie put her hand on my arm. "My stories are for the children you and Rosalie will have."

"Please, aunt Hattie, I'm not uncle John," I said as I pulled my arm away. "I'm Dan Harrington. My father is, Robert Harrington, your brother. My mother is Mary Harrington. We all lived in Boston where I was born. So please understand, I'm not your brother."

"Yes, you are," Hattie cried as tears welled up in her eyes. Then, she ran from the room.

"Oh, dear," my grandmother said as she stood. "She can be difficult sometimes."

When my grandmother left the room, I apologized to aunt Nora for upsetting Hattie. "Oh, don't apologize. She'll get over it as she always does," Nora replied. "John was always her favorite. Because you look like him, she wants to believe you are him. She was only thirteen when he left, you know? Told her he'd be back and she's been waiting ever since."

"What happened to him?" I asked.

Nora cocked her head to the side. "He died in the, 'Great war.' Didn't anyone tell you?"

"Yeah, but how?"

Nora looked down at the table. "Oh, it really doesn't matter. . . He was awarded the Victoria Cross, you know? Actually, twice. The last one was for heroism in the battle of Langemarck." Nora fell silent to wipe tears from her eyes. When she resumed, her voice shook. "Mother was presented with the second medal. . . John died in the battle. Everyone's missed him ever since. Especially Hattie. She's never gotten over his death."

"What did the citation say?" I asked.

"The what?"

"It said he's a hero," my grandmother said as she entered the room.

"Where's Hattie?" Nora asked.

"In the living room," my grandmother replied as she sat down at the table. Then, she put her hand on my shoulder and looked me eye to eye. "Dan, your uncle John died on the 27th of August, 1917. The same day you were born."

My jaw dropped. Everything in the room, except for my grandmother's face, seemed to disappear. I tried to imagine how she looked when my uncle died. How she felt when she learned I was born on the same day.

"Hattie believes you're my reincarnated son," my grandmother said, snapping me back to reality. Nora began to laugh, and then quickly fell silent under my grandmother's glare. "The idea's preposterous to me too, but I promised Hattie that I'd ask a question for her."

"What's the question?" I asked.

"Come now, mother, Hattie's completely mad. We're Catholics for Christ sake," Nora groveled.

"Watch your language," my grandmother ordered. "I want to put this nonsense to rest once and for all."

"So do I," Nora said.

My grandmother turned to me. "Hattie wants to know if you've heard of, Periwinkle Rose?"

"Of course I have," I replied, causing the blood to drain from my grandmother's face. "Periwinkle Rose is the title of a poem I wrote while I attended Harvard. It was published in the Boston Globe and a few other papers. Why?"

"Oh, never mind. She probably read it in the paper then," my grandmother said as the color of her face gradually returned to normal. Then, Nora let out a slight chuckle. Stating once again that her sister was completely out of her mind, and I felt sorry for my aunt Hattie. Crazy or not, I didn't like the way aunt Nora treated her and excused myself from the room.

Hattie was sitting in a rocking chair in the living room. I watched her rock back and forth for a moment before entering the room. Her eyes lit up when she saw me, and I blushed. There was something about the way she looked at me that made me feel secure. Like she understood the meaning of life and had unlocked the secrets of the universe. In a way, I felt she was my angel, my protector, my sage. "I'm sorry, aunt Hattie," I said as I kneeled beside the rocking chair and embraced her in my arms.

"So you believe me now, Johnny?" Hattie grinned.

"Actually, no, but you can call me Johnny if you like."

"What about, Periwinkle Rose?"

I pulled away slightly. "You mean the poem I wrote at university?"

Hattie cocked her head. "Where?" She asked, and then giggled. "No, silly. The poem you wrote for Rosalie. The one you showed me before you left for the army. Don't you remember?"

I was about to reiterate that I wasn't uncle John, but realized it would break her heart, so I simply replied, "No."

"You really don't remember who you are, do you?" Hattie asked.

"Well, no," I confessed, playing along with her delusion.

Hattie ran her fingers through my hair. "Then, I'll help you remember. You must remember. Then, you can bring Rosalie home. You both have been gone far too long."

It was late in the evening when Nora called everyone to dinner. As we ate, we talked about our lives. We shared many laughs and a few sorrows. I learned that I had another aunt, Hattie's twin sister Rose, who died at the age of nine. My grandmother said aunt Rose was the complete opposite of Hattie and aunt Nora agreed.

Every time my grandmother told a funny story about my aunt Hattie, Nora was quick to point out her eccentricities. Hattie let the comments roll off her shoulders and laughed with the rest of us. To this day, I'm still awed by my aunt's ability to find the best in everything. She was the most gentle and caring person I've ever known. She taught me so much about the joys of living and how to find peace with my past, that I'm eternally grateful.

When Nora asked me to tell my life story, I reluctantly agreed, although, I didn't say much about my childhood. Nor did I say anything about my father. I did confess my divorce, which shocked my grandmother and aunt Nora's Catholic beliefs. Hattie only smiled. Then, I talked about the war, although, I didn't tell them much. I only spoke of the friends I made, and those I lost. My grandmother said that I should write to Chip's parents and tell them he was in love when he died, but all I could think about was,

'Don't worry, Dan. We're going to be all right.' The last words Chip said to me.

"You should find your friend, Jack," Nora said.

"You should visit your friends in France," Hattie insisted.

"I will when my heart has mended," I said.

"Visiting your friends will mend your heart," my grandmother stated.

"Finding Aimee's daughter will mend your soul," Hattie added with a wink.

Then, it was Nora's turn. She had three grown children. The oldest, Peter, was a fisherman living in Norway. When I met him a few years later, I learned he fought with the Norwegian resistance during the war. We spent many nights sharing our stories over a bottle of whisky. He was the only person in my family that I could openly talk to about the horrors of the war.

Nora's second born, Ian, was a professor of antiquities at Oxford University. He had many stories of exotic adventures and exciting treasure hunts to tell. My favorite was when a rhinoceros ran into his camp after sundown and stomped out his campfire. I can easily picture him hiding in the tree as the rhinoceros demolished his campsite.

The youngest of Nora's children was Helen who owned a flower shop in the Notting Hill section of London. Everyone called her, "The Wild Irish Rose," on account she could drink anyone under the table. Having learned respect for alcohol in the Crown Bar, I wasn't about to test her reputation.

A little past eight, our dinner party broke up for the night. "I better get back to Bally Clare before it gets too late," I said as I stood and stretched my back.

"Why?" My grandmother asked.

"You're welcome to stay in Hattie's old room, you know?" Nora said.

"Mother, why doesn't he stay in his own cottage?" Hattie asked.

"My cottage? I don't have one," I replied.

"Of course you do, Johnny. It's just over the hill. Don't you remember?" Hattie smiled.

"Ah, there she goes again. Good night everyone," Nora sighed. Then, she kissed me on the cheek and left the room.

I looked at my grandmother, and then to Hattie. They both waited for me to choose where I would stay for the night, and I didn't want to upset either of them. So, I turned to my grandmother. "I believe I should go home tonight," I said, and then winked. My grandmother smiled, realizing

I was playing along with Hattie's delusion.

"Grand! That's grand Johnny," Hattie nearly shouted.

Then, I turned to Hattie. "You'll have to show me where my house is though. I can't remember where I left it."

"Oh, Johnny, you're so funny," Hattie purred.

A few minutes later, I gave my grandmother a good night hug outside the cottage door. "If she drives you batty, we have room for you here," she whispered in my ear, and I quietly thanked her for the invitation.

Hattie led me along the edge of the vegetable garden and through a grove of trees behind the cottage. We hiked over a small hill and down into a gently sloping valley. I heard water running and the bleating of sheep. Then, I saw it. A hundred feet into the valley the trees gave way to rolling green fields. A small whitewashed two story stone cottage with a thatched roof sat next to a gently flowing stream. A small flock of sheep were gathered along the bank and stared at us in the bright moonlight. It was the same flock of sheep I herded into the field earlier in the day. The old sheepherder I frightened was Timothy Buttons who was hired by my grandmother to look after the livestock. He always believed I was my uncle's ghost, but eventually, he found the courage to talk with me.

"Who's car?" I asked, referring to the red Bentley convertible parked in the driveway.

"Do you like my auto?" Hattie asked.

"That's your car?" I stammered.

"Well, of course it is. People seem to think I'm rich because I drive it. Don't know why. I barely have a little over five hundred thousand pounds in the bank," Hattie humbly stated. It truly didn't occur to her that she was wealthy, and that's what I liked about her. Money didn't define her personality.

Hattie walked to the front door of the cottage. "I kept it just the way Rosalie left it."

"I'd like you to tell me about her sometime," I said as Hattie opened the door.

She stopped and stared at me. "I can't believe you don't remember your wife, Johnny," she said, and then entered the cottage. I lingered outside for a moment as strange emotions flowed over me. When they passed, I followed her inside.

The lights came on as Hattie proudly announced she had the cottage wired for electricity. She also had a toilet installed and asked if I was upset with the renovations. I replied I wasn't as Hattie ushered me into the living room to a photograph in an etched silver frame hanging on the wall. I stood, mesmerized, lost in thought as I stared at the woman's face staring back at me. Hattie was rambling, but I didn't hear a word she said until she gently nudged my arm.

"Does she look familiar?" Hattie asked.

"Huh?" I replied in a daze.

"Do you recognize her?"

I stared at Hattie for a moment. "Yes," I slowly answered, "I've seen her in my dreams."

31

*T*he woman in my dreams standing next to me at the altar was the same woman in the picture hanging in my late uncle John's cottage. She was his wife, my aunt Rosalie. *'Why is she in my dreams? Am I the reincarnation of my uncle John?'* I wondered. For a moment, I almost believed that I was. That is until I asked Hattie if my mother and father had a picture of Rosalie.

"Of course. Everyone does," Hattie beamed. "Your father was your best man and your mother was a bridesmaid."

Words cannot describe how relieved I felt. For me to believe for one second that I was the reincarnation of my late uncle John was completely absurd. Moreover, for Hattie, a devout Catholic who attended mass three times a week and read the Holy Bible everyday, it was just complete insanity for her to believe in reincarnation. How could someone of the Christian faith believe such nonsense, I wondered. Although, I must admit, the idea that a soul could be reborn into another human body was quite intriguing.

For the next hour after arriving at the cottage, I stared at my aunt Rosalie's picture. An act I'd find myself doing from time to time. Part of me believed I really knew her. From my vivid dreams, I believed that I actually stood next to her at the altar. That part of me was afflicted, as Hattie was, with insanity.

The other part of me knew it was impossible. For what we believe, what we feel, is only an interpretation of facts based on our own perceptions. Feelings, emotions, beliefs are only constructs of how we see the world around us, where as, facts cannot be denied. She was simply a construct of my imagination based on a picture my mother or father showed me. It was the only plausible explanation of why I knew what Rosalie looked like.

Hattie showed me to my late aunt and uncle's bedroom. As I entered, I was drawn to a picture of a young man in a Royal army uniform. He stood next to Rosalie, and I must admit, he looked exactly like I did when I was his age. When I was still in Boston. When Sarah was still in my life.

"Do you remember when that was taken? I was just before you went off to war," Hattie said softly. I was about to reiterate that I wasn't my uncle John, but refrained. It was late and I didn't want to send her into another bout of sorrow. For my own selfish reasons, I let her have her fantasy.

It rained steadily for the next four days. I spent my time conversing with my grandmother and two aunts, walking through the soggy Irish countryside, and sleeping. The direction my life would take was a mystery. The path I would choose was unknown. Hattie kept insisting that I find Rosalie. Nora kept asserting how insane Hattie was. My grandmother complained about the weather.

Then, during the afternoon of the fifth day, the sun broke through the overcast sky. I announced that I was going into Bally Clare to find work. To my grandmother and two aunts, it meant I would be staying in Ireland. To me, it was a reprieve. I needed a change. A purpose that would set my mind free and fill my soul.

"You can drive my car, if you like?" Hattie offered.

"No thanks. I can't drive," I confessed.

"Then, I'll teach you," Hattie said.

"What?" Nora raised her eyebrows. "You never offered to teach me."

My grandmother smiled. "Oh, stop complaining. Hattie offered years ago, but you said she was mad behind the wheel."

"Nora, I'll teach you and Johnny if you like?" Hattie said. I quickly accepted the offer. Nora was more reluctant, but after deliberating with herself for fifteen minutes, she also accepted. Then, for the next two weeks, Hattie gave Nora and I driving lessons. I quickly surmised Nora was wrong about Hattie. For she was an excellent driver. I, on the other hand, was the mad driver behind the wheel. Once on the way to Larne, I nearly ran an approaching bus off the road. Another time, I zoomed off the road and through a herd of cattle without hitting the brakes. Luckily, I didn't hit any of the animals, but the episode sent Nora one step closer to her grave. The cattle rancher wasn't too pleased either, or so it seemed as I couldn't understand what he was yelling at the speed I roared past him. Hattie just smiled.

Nora was a different story. She was my exact opposite. In our two weeks of driving lessons, she never hit twenty-miles-an-hour. Nor did she ever take her hands off the steering wheel. The few times she got the car into second gear, Hattie had to maneuver the stick shift while I sat in the back seat waiting impatiently for my turn.

The one thing I can say about Nora's driving was that we were always guaranteed to reach our destination in one piece, albeit many hours later. Hattie, on the other hand, always looked on the bright side of life. She sat patiently in the front passenger seat and commented how we all had time to smell the roses.

To my dismay, the first time my grandmother came with us on our daily jaunt into the Irish countryside, I wasn't allowed behind the wheel. Nora drove the entire way. After that, I vowed to get better. Which I did, however, I still wasn't allowed to drive when my grandmother was in the car.

Two days before Hattie left for, Saint Mary's Holy Resurrection, I was sitting on the couch staring at the picture of my aunt Rosalie when Hattie quietly entered the room and sat beside me. "Tell me about her?" I asked softly.

Hattie gazed at me for a moment. "You really don't remember her, do you?"

"No."

"Oh, well, if you don't, you don't." Hattie sighed deeply. "She was a nanny. From France. A lovely girl. Lit up the room, she did. Could turn any man's head, though she only had eyes for you. I still remember the first day she came to Bally Clare. . ."

"How did they meet? Uncle John and her?" I interrupted.

Hattie looked at the picture, and then to me. "At the summer social, of course. You got married the next year. . . She was seventeen and full of love. You both were. . . Such a tragedy. . .Such a tragedy to lose you both." Hattie sighed.

I remained quiet, knowing Hattie had more to say. Tears filled her eyes. Her heart wept for the loss she carried since childhood. A strain she kept secret all these years until now.

"On August 17th, 1918, mother, Rosalie, and I were on holiday. I woke early in the morning. Before sunrise. Rosalie was standing in the middle of the room wearing her wedding gown. She smiled at me, and then left. I wanted to follow her, but I didn't want to wake mother." Hattie paused to wipe the tears from her eyes. "I just lay under the covers waiting for her to return. Wondering where she'd gone." Hattie lowered her head. "When mother woke, we looked for her. No one in town had seen her, so we walked along the shore to where Rosalie planted a red rose bush in your memory. Tied to one of its branches was a dark red ribbon." Hattie pulled an envelope from her purse and handed it to me. "She left it for you."

I opened the envelope. Inside was a dark red silk ribbon, nothing else. "What happened to her?"

"At first no one really knew. Mother thought she went back to France. Nora thought she went to England or America to start a new life. But I knew. The dark red ribbon told me. Rosalie walked into the sea to join you in Heaven. Everyone laughed at me. Except mother. She didn't believe me either, but she didn't laugh. Everyone thought I was crazy. Batty Hattie, they called me. But I knew. I've always known."

I held up the ribbon. "Because of this?"

"You don't think I'm crazy do you, Johnny?" Hattie asked.

I bit down hard on my tongue to keep from laughing in her face as I stood and went to the picture of Rosalie. Her lovely eyes stared back at me. Her pleasant face calmed my urge to laugh. From behind the glass, trapped inside a frame, the picture of my late aunt brought me peace. I draped the ribbon over the picture, and then sat down next to Hattie. "Did they ever find her body?"

"No," Hattie replied.

"Then, she probably just left as everyone thought she did."

"No, she didn't. God took her."

I couldn't bite my tongue any longer and let out a quick laugh. "God took her?"

"Yes."

"Without her body, how can you possibly believe she's even dead? Where's the proof?"

"God told me," Hattie replied.

I laughed harder and went back to the picture of Rosalie. This time it didn't have any effect on me. I couldn't stop laughing. After all I've been through in my life. All the pain, all the joy, nothing compared to how I felt at that moment. Over and over, the words, 'Batty Hattie,' raced through my mind as my dear aunt sat quietly on the couch. She had more to say and waited, as she had waited many times in her life, for the laughter to die. When it did, she continued with her story as if she hadn't been interrupted at all.

"A year to the day after Rosalie vanished, a young couple walking along the shore saw a woman dressed in a white wedding gown kneeling by the rose bush Rosalie planted. They watched as the woman stood, turned, and walked toward the sea. Then, she vanished. After that, more people claimed to see Rosalie's ghost. Newspapers ran stories. People flocked to see her ghost. Some did. Most didn't. The Church sent a priest to bless the rose bush and perform an exorcism, but nothing changed. People continued to see her until the day her ghost walked into the sea. After that, no one saw her again. No one knows why, except me." I turned and looked at my aunt. A faint smile cracked the edges of her mouth. "Rosalie's ghost vanished the day she was reborn. That's why I live in Larne. I'm waiting for her return. Now that you've come home, you must find her. Go to France and bring her back home."

I didn't reply at first. The meaning of her words were lost on me. What she was asking was completely absurd. Her fantasy had to be stopped once and for all. "I'm not my uncle John," I said. Then, I took the picture of Rosalie and threw it on the couch. "She's not my wife. I was married to Sarah Witherspoon. We're divorced. My father is Robert Harrington. My mother was Mary Harrington. I grew up in Boston and became a lawyer."

I began pacing back and forth. My frustration grew rapidly. My head ached. "I left Boston to fight the damn war. I lost my wife. I lost my father. I've lost some of the best friends I've ever had. . . I've witnessed horror. I know the evil that resides in the human race. By my own hand, I've dealt that evil upon others. My crippled leg is my reward. My vacant heart is my reminder. I've destroyed my soul."

I stopped by the window. Tears welled up inside, yet my eyes remained dry. All the pain, all the sorrow I've ever experienced up to that day came crashing down on me. Its weight was stifling.

Slowly, I turned to Hattie and softly said, "A young boy, forced into Hitler's army, was brought to the hospital I was in. He was my enemy, but I wasn't his. He didn't know the meaning of hate. Only forgiveness. Through him, I began to feel again. My heart began to heal. My soul began to mend."

I paused as I turned back to the window. "When he died, part of me died with him. What was left of me was reborn. The friendship we shared gave me the strength to live. To go on with my life, and that's exactly what I intend to do." I turned back to Hattie. "I'm Dan Harrington. Your nephew. I'm not my uncle John. Rosalie was never reborn. They died a long time ago and they're never coming back."

Tears streamed down my aunt Hattie's rosy cheeks. She stood slowly, wiped her eyes, and then walked to the doorway. For a moment, she stood with her back to me. Then, she slowly turned around. "You're my brother, John. You've come back home to find Rosalie. You can't forsake your destiny. You must find her to be whole again. Remember, 'Periwinkle Rose.' When you find it, you'll find Rosalie. Then, you'll remember and bring her home."

"God damn it," I growled. "Periwinkle Rose is a poem I wrote in 1937. It was published in the Boston Globe. How you got a copy is unbeknownst to me, but it really doesn't matter because you think it was written by uncle John. It wasn't. Uncle John is dead. Aunt Rosalie is dead. They're both dead. Dead, dead, dead. So get out of your fantasy world, Hattie and come back to reality."

Tears continued to roll down my aunts cheeks. She didn't say a word. She didn't have to. I knew I'd gone too far. My tirade pierced a hole in her heart, and at that moment, I knew I couldn't heal the damage I inflicted.

At length, Hattie wiped her tears on her sleeve, and then left the room. The front door opened, and then closed softly. I remained standing by the window, staring into the vacant room. Too petrified to look outside long after Hattie had gone. Later that night, I wept until I fell asleep. In the morning the sorrow remained.

Weeks passed, and then months. Christmas came and went, and still no Hattie. I spent my days herding my grandmother's flock of sheep. I spent my nights writing my life story. All the while, I yearned for my lovely aunts return.

In early January of 1946, I wrote a letter to Chip's father and expressed my sympathies. I wrote about Veronica, and the love she and Chip shared. I also asked his forgiveness in their deaths. Three weeks later, Senator Taylor replied. He granted me the forgiveness I needed. From then on, he and I stayed in contact until his death thirteen years later. Over that time, he became my surrogate father and helped expose my father's crimes. Everyone rejoiced when my father was sentenced to life behind bars. No one shed a tear when he committed suicide.

I also wrote to Jack's parents. All I had was their last name and Holly Beach, Louisiana, the small town where Jack grew up. Forty-six days later a letter arrived in the mail. There wasn't a return address on the envelope, but the postmark identified it as coming from New Orleans. Inside was a handwritten letter, and this is what it said.

Hello Dan,

Glad to hear you made it. How is Ireland treating you? Very well, I hope.

As you can tell, I'm alive. Sorry to hear about your leg. Someday, you'll be able to run as fast as you did when the Boche shot at us. Hard to believe it's been two years since we dropped into France. Seems like it was only yesterday, but I feel much older these days.

Do you know what happened to our friends? A little while after you left for Saint Lo, my group had to split up. Simon and Jocelyn were with me when we got caught between the Germans and our forces about thirty kilometers outside of Paris. Simon was wounded by artillery. Jocelyn and I tried to pull him to safety when another shell landed near by. Jocelyn and Simon didn't survive. Everyday, I'm reminded of them when I look down at my wheelchair and realize how lucky I am to be alive. A small piece of shrapnel imbedded itself in my lower spine and paralyzed me from the waist down. The doctor says there is a small chance he can remove it and I'll be able to walk again, however, there is a chance I won't live through the surgery. So, I've decided to live with my disability.

No need to worry about me though. I've got no regrets. The job we did in France was vital to winning the war, and I'm proud to have served my country. Freedom is always worth fighting for.

I hope I haven't upset you with this letter. It wasn't my intention. The only regret I have is that you won't be able to be my best man. Remember Mabel? The girl I took to the high school prom? The one I said was the ugliest girl in school? Well, we're getting married five days from now. I wish you could be here for the wedding. You're my best friend and the man I would follow to the ends of the earth. Take good care of yourself.

Your good friend,

Jack

P.S. Do you know what happened to our friends? I would like to visit you all someday. We're all family.

I read Jack's letter a few more times until I had to put it down. My eyes filled with tears from every emotion known to mankind. That afternoon, I wept for Simon and Jocelyn. I wept for Jack's disability and shed tears of joy for the love he found. He was my closest friend and remained my closest friend for the rest of our lives.

By nightfall, my body was weak. My mind was exhausted. I went to bed without eating. The next morning hunger pains woke me from a restless sleep. All night long my Maquis friends came to visit in my dreams. They came because I didn't know their fate. They came because they didn't know mine. That morning, I decided to return to France and find out what happened to them.

32

*I*n life, there is a reason behind everything we do. Every action we take, every word we speak, has a specific goal we want to achieve. Whether it is to feed and clothe ourselves, or to tell a loved one our feelings, our motivation is an edification from our souls.

Most of the time we know the reason behind what we do. Sometimes we do not, only to realize our motivation afterward. Once in a while we do something in which we never learn the motivation, for the true reason lies shrouded deep within our subconscious. The latter was the case the morning the taxi dropped me off in the town square of Bally Clare. Earlier that morning I had called my grandmother to tell her I was leaving for a few weeks. Then, I called my aunt Hattie, but she didn't answer her telephone. Since the day I reproached her belief that I was my uncle John, she refused to answer my phone calls. The letters I sent were returned unopened. I missed her very much, but I had chided myself everyday since the last time I saw her that I needed to get away. My intention was to catch a bus for Belfast, take a ferry to Liverpool, and then a steamer to France, but when the bus heading to Larne arrived first, I boarded that bus instead and paid my fare. It was fate, guided by Hattie's invisible hand, that led me to her coastal town.

When I arrived in Larne, I asked a man in a black suit and Bowler hat the directions to Saint Mary's Holy Resurrection, the school where Hattie taught. He looked me up and down before answering. Ten minutes later I realized why when an ill-tempered nun demanded to know why I dared to enter the sacred school for girls.

"I've come to visit my aunt Harriet Harrington," I meekly replied.

"We do not allow visitors during study hours. Come back between the hours of three-thirty and five," the nun sneered.

"Could you tell her I'm here? It's very important that I speak with her," I pled.

The nun squinted her eyes. "I told you, come back between the hours of three-thirty and five. Now off you go."

'*No wonder my aunt's mad as a hatter*,' I thought as I walked away from Saint Mary's. For the next hour, I wandered the streets until I found myself at the edge of the sea. The time was 10:47 in the morning. Over four hours to wait until I could step foot on the sacred ground of Hattie's school, so I turned west and walked along the gentle surf.

About a half mile down the beach, I saw it. Standing two hundred feet in front of me, where the short, yellowish-green grass and peat moss met the sand and rocks, was a solitary rose bush. Its dark red flowers subtly waltzed under the overcast sky, summoning my presence as I made my way toward it.

An old fisherman stood in the surf close to where the rose bush grew. His fishing pole was bent toward the sea, straining under the pull of a fish at the end of its line. Their battle was a classic fight for survival. A theme I knew all too well. The man fought to live. The fish fought to get free. Their struggle continued as I knelt down in front of the rose bush. Which of them was the victor, was not my concern. All of my battles were over, or so I thought.

From the moment, I kneeled by the rose bush, time stood still. There was something magnetic. Something enchanting about the way the lovely plant swayed in the light breeze. At the time, I thought it was from a manifestation created in the subconscious of my mind. That after many nights of staring at my aunt Rosalie's picture, the way she stood next to me in my dreams, that there was a kindred bond between us. That the lovely bush was an extension of her being and somehow our lives were entwined. At length, I realized it was my desire to learn the truth behind her fate. I thought if I could prove what really happened to her, then I could prove to my aunt once and for all, that I wasn't my uncle John. Only then would Hattie finally allow the memories of her beloved brother and sister in-law to rest in peace.

"Strange isn't it?" A deep, male voice asked from behind me.

I stood and turned around. The old fisherman stood five feet behind me. He was a tall fellow with blue eyes and a crooked smile. Grey hair poked from under a black knit cap and partially revealed a purple scar on his forehead. Two small tears in his black wool sweater revealed a dingy white shirt underneath. His brown trousers were frayed at the bottom. His feet were bare.

"What's strange?" I asked.

"Why the rose of course," the fisherman replied. "It's awfully strange such a delicate plant could grow in the salty air all these years. When the northern winds fall upon these shores, she holds on. Never once losing a petal. . . Planted by the hands of a ghost, she was."

"I was told my aunt planted this rose bush," I proudly stated.

The fisherman's eyes opened wide. "Aye, she did. Planted the rose, and then walked into the sea."

"How do you know that?"

"I saw her with me very eyes, I tell you," the fisherman answered, and then he pointed to a spot on the beach. "It is there she entered Neptune's lair."

Rage gripped my body. I walked forward until the fisherman and I stood face to face. At that moment, I wanted to unleash my fury. Strike him to the ground, but the fear in his eyes, his pale white face kept me restrained. "Why didn't you stop her?" I screamed.

"Couldn't," was all the frightened old fisherman could say.

"Why the hell not?" I demanded.

The fisherman's mouth quivered. "She was already dead."

Rage kept its grip on my body. "What do you mean, she was dead?" I thundered. The fisherman stood frozen in fear as I turned my back to him and walked to the other side of the rose bush. Wetness dampened the edges of my eyes. The rage I had for the man turned against me. My anger gnawed at my soul, and then the weight of a hand rested upon my shoulder. I spun around to confront the man for touching me, but he was still on the other side of the rose bush. Nearly seven feet separated us, and yet, the weight of the hand on my shoulder remained. Gradually, my rage subsided.

"Tell me what you saw! What did she look like?" I demanded.

The color slowly returned to the fisherman's face. A faint smile cracked the edges of his mouth. "She was the prettiest young lass I've ever seen. Hair black as coal. Tied back with a ribbon the color of her rose. When she walked, she floated on air. Her white dress ruffled in the breeze. Her face, forlorn. Sad as she walked into the sea. Then, she smiled, as she always did when the water laps at her feet. . . For five seasons, I watched her. Every time, she kneels by her rose before crossing the rock and sand. The last time, she spoke to me." The old fisherman fell silent and stared at me.

"What did she say?" I asked slowly.

"She said it was time to live," the fisherman somberly replied.

Laughter burst from my lungs. "Nice story. I almost believed you, but you're as loony as my aunt."

"She told Hattie the very same words," the fisherman stated, bringing my laughter to a halt.

"How do you know I was referring to Hattie?"

"Who else would I be referring to?" The fisherman asked. "Hattie sees what I see. She knows what I know. We're cut from the same cloth, she and I."

"Got that right. You're both nuts," I laughed.

The fisherman sighed. "It's not we who are mad. It's you, John who needs to look inside for the truth."

"Did Hattie put you up to this?" I growled.

"She did not. What I speak of is the truth. The woman who you seek is waiting for you across the sea," the fisherman said while pointing his right index finger to the east. Then, he pointed his left hand, fingers outstretched and palm up, toward the rose bush. "She's the same woman who planted the rose."

"I've had enough of this. I came out here to kill some time. To be alone. Then, you show up with one of Hattie's delusions and try to convince me it's the truth."

"I know who you are, sir. Hattie knows who you be. The woman you seek is waitin' across the sea."

"Leave me alone," I yelled. Then, I turned my back to the fisherman.

"As you wish, John," the fisherman replied.

A minute went by, maybe two. Actually, I'm not quite certain exactly how much time went by, but I know it wasn't more than two minutes when the weight of the hand left my shoulder. At that moment, the hair on the back of my neck rose and I quickly spun around. The old fisherman was gone. His fishing pole and tackle box had vanished from where he left them by the surf. I scanned every inch of soil, every blade of grass and granule of sand while I slowly turned in a circle. For a half mile in all directions there was no sign of life. "Impossible, there's no place to hide," I said under my breath. Then, I looked down and noticed the only footprints in the wind swept sand leading up to the rose bush, were those of my own.

I panicked and snatched my suitcase from where it sat by the rose bush. My legs felt heavy. I strained under their weight as I hobbled through the short grass toward Larne. The point of my cane dug into the soft earth, slowing my gait, bringing new blisters to my calloused left hand. My suitcase battered my right knee. My lungs begged for oxygen. Then, as I ran down a sandy incline, I tripped and fell on the dry sand. My suitcase struck a rock and burst open. My cane broke in half, and I laughed. After being the hunter and the hunted, the misguided son, the blind husband and lost soul, I thought I was mad. That, I was as crazy as my aunt Hattie.

My laughter continued as I stood and brushed the sand from my clothes. I laughed while I repacked my suitcase and threw my broken cane into the sea. Then, I looked in the direction of the rose bush. Its leaves fluttered in the breeze, waving goodbye. I waved, and then hobbled back to Larne.

When I arrived, I bought a new cane, and then went straight to Saint Mary's Holy Resurrection. For the next few hours, I paced the sidewalk in front of the school. Then, at three-thirty exactly, the front doors of the school opened. Out poured young girls of all ages dressed in blue cardigans, white blouses, and blue and white checkered skirts. They swamped the sidewalk and chattered as they rushed past. I had to stand against the wrought iron fence to stay out of their way.

In less than five minutes the sidewalk was empty. The young girls were out of sight. I began walking toward the front doors of the school. Halfway there, Hattie emerged from the building. As usual she looked out of place, wearing a red, white, and black checkered jumper over a white blouse, and a purple waist coat over the entire ensemble. Propped on her head was a black velvet hat with silk flowers sewn above the brim. '*Only Hattie can get away with wearing something like that,*' I thought as I said hello.

"Ah, I knew you'd come today," Hattie said with a pleasant smile.

"So you got my message?"

Hattie cocked her head. "What message?"

"The message I left at the front desk."

"Oh, they didn't tell me you were here."

I was about to call her a liar, but decided against it as she grasped my left hand and led me to her small office on the second floor. The first thing I noticed upon entering was her books. Built into the north and east walls were bookcases which ran the entire length of the walls and were over stuffed with books on practically every known subject. On the floor in front of the bookcases were five cardboard boxes overflowing with books and a stack of books sat on her desk. Behind her desk was a large arched window and on its window sill were even more books. "I like to read," Hattie commented as she offered me a chair overflowing with another stack of books.

"No kidding," I said as I removed the books from the chair and sat down.

"Did you see it?" Hattie asked.

"See what?" I asked as I scanned the book titles all around me.

"Rosalie's lovely rose bush."

My eyes darted from the books to Hattie. I stared at her for a moment before I answered, "Yes, but something strange happened."

"So now you know."

"Know what?"

"Who you really are."

"What? . . . No aunt Hattie, I didn't come here to have this conversation again."

"Well, if that's the way you want to be," Hattie interrupted, and then she lowered her eyes to the desktop.

"Aunt Hattie, I didn't come here to argue. I came to apologize. I want to know if we can be friends again. Can we?" Hattie kept her eyes glued to the desktop and remained quiet. "Please look at me. Say something," I begged.

My aunt sat frozen like a statue. No words came to her mouth. Her eyes didn't blink. If it weren't for the shallow rising and falling of her chest, I would've believed she was dead.

After a few moments, I slowly stood and walked to the door. My hand rested on the doorknob. I paused hoping she would ask me to stay. That she would say we were still friends. That she was still my loving aunt, but she remained quiet, so I turned the doorknob and opened the door. Then, I looked at her. "I wanted to tell you about a strange old man I talked to earlier. I wanted to tell you that I'm leaving for France."

Hattie slowly turned to me. "Are you going to find Rosalie?"

"No. I'm going to visit my friends," I replied, and watched Hattie lower her eyes back to her desk. Again she fell silent, and I knew it was time for me to leave. "Goodbye, aunt Hattie," I said softly.

I managed to take one step into the hallway when Hattie asked, "This man. . .Where did you meet him?"

"By Rosalie's rose bush," I slowly replied.

"Come inside and shut the door," Hattie ordered as she stood. I shut the door and sat back down in the chair while she pilfered through one of the cardboard boxes on the floor. "Ah ha, here it is," she exclaimed, and then handed me a book on shipwrecks. "You know most people think I'm daft? They call me, Hopeless Harriet, the two leafed Shamrock, or plain old fool. My personal favorite is, Batty Hattie." My aunt leaned closer. "Even you think I'm crazy, don't you?" I didn't answer. "Well, it really doesn't matter, does it? I know what I know, and I see what I see. You say you talked to a man by Rosalie's rose bush? Did he tell you who he was?"

"No, but he said he's your friend," I replied.

"Did he have a scar on his forehead?"

"Yes."

"Was he fishing in the sea?"

"Yeah. . . Why?"

Hattie walked back to her desk and sat down. "Then you've met him. He's been my friend since I was a wee girl. And I tell you, as sure as God himself, he hasn't aged one bit since the first day I met him."

I stared a Hattie with my mouth wide open.

"Don't stare at me like that. See for yourself. Turn to page ninety-seven."

I thumbed though the book until I found the page. It was the beginning of a new chapter. The heading read, 'Errol Folwick,' which was a fishing boat that sunk on the 26th of March, 1878 during a violent storm in the Irish sea. But what really got my attention was the picture of, Basil McClure, the fishing vessel's captain. He was the same man who I talked to at Rosalie's rose bush, and according to the story in the book, he was fifty-seven when the Errol Folwick sank.

"This can't be," I said very slowly.

"Well, it tis'. The man you talked with today has been dead for over sixty years. A ghost, the poor soul," Hattie said dryly. Then, for the next hour she explained everything she knew about the Errol Folwick and its final voyage. She said that in 1929, she interviewed, Payton Hawthorne, a crewman of the Folwick. He related to Hattie how Basil McClure was swept off the boat's deck and drowned only ten feet from the side of the boat. A few minutes later, the Folwick broke in half. As the boat sank, Hawthorne latched onto a floating timber from the mast and hung on for dear life while the sea tried to pull him under. A couple of days later, he was found unconsciousness on the beach, the sole survivor of the doomed vessel.

"Are you sure the captain drowned?" I asked.

"Yes, I'm quite sure. I've read all the stories, newspaper clippings, and listened to many tales of the Errol Folwick in search for the truth. The captain, the man you talked to, drowned with the rest of his crew. Twenty-seven men in all. Payton Hawthorne was the only survivor. Check for yourself if you don't believe me."

"It's hard not to. I mean if I hadn't seen him and his picture, I'd think you were playing a trick on me. But, I saw him. I talked to him, so I have no choice, but to believe you."

"Then you must know you're my brother, John," Hattie said quickly.

I closed the book and set it on Hattie's desk. "I wouldn't go as far as believing that."

"But you must. Find Rosalie. Bring her home. You both belong here."

I walked over to the arched window and stared at the overcast sky. My mind raced. I searched for something to say to convince her once and for all that I wasn't the reincarnation of my uncle, but I couldn't find the words. I couldn't hurt her as I did months earlier and send her crying from the room. I loved my aunt and valued our friendship. So, in the end, I just asked, "What if I can't find her?"

"Find Periwinkle Rose and you'll find Rosalie," Hattie beamed.

I turned around and smiled. "Would you walk me to the bus stop?"

Hattie's eyes opened wide with a smile as she jumped to her feet. "It'll be faster in my car."

33

*I*nstead of dropping me off at the bus station, Hattie drove me to Belfast. Her enthusiasm should have been a warning, but frankly, I didn't care. Getting out of Ireland was my only concern and I barely noticed she drove worse than I ever had. After terrifying a flock of sheep, three other drivers, a bicyclist, and running two stop signs, we arrived at Belfast harbor. "Bring Rosalie home," was the last thing she said before I walked into the terminal. Fifteen minutes later, I was on the last ferry of the day. When the ferry docked in Portsmouth, England, night had fallen so I checked into a cheap hotel. All night I laid on a rickety bed staring at the ceiling. Thoughts flooded my mind. Emotions welled up inside. Apprehension filled my veins.

The next morning a steamer took me across the English Channel and docked in Cherbourg. The moment my feet touched French soil, my heart felt lighter. Excitement rushed through me. I felt that I had finally returned home. That night, I rented a room in a small hotel overlooking the port; although, I still couldn't sleep and spent most of the night drinking coffee in various cafes and talking to people as I wandered the streets. Because of my fluency, most people never suspected I was an American. The few people I told refused to believe me until I showed them my passport. Even then, some thought my passport was fake.

The next day, I went to the train station and bought a ticket to Vire. Shortly after, I stared out the window as the French countryside rolled by. After many stops and a forty-five minute delay in Granville, I arrived at my destination. From there I hitched a ride with a farmer and bounced around in the back of his truck until he stopped at the southern edge of Vassy. "Good luck, monsieur," the farmer said as he drove away. I waved, and then breathed deeply before I took my first step into town.

The difference between night and day cannot possibly describe how Vassy felt. As I walked down the street, I expected to see German soldiers marching by, or have a German officer ask to see my identification papers.

Instead, I saw children playing in the street while their mothers watched them through open windows. Small groups of men huddled together to share the latest joke, or talk politics. Long gone were the days when people feared to venture outside of their homes. When apprehension and hatred filled their faces.

When I reached the small store where Emile printed his newspaper, the front door was locked. The windows were covered in grime. I used my sleeve to wipe away a small section of filth so I could see inside. The room was empty. Dust covered the floor a quarter of an inch thick, and I could see small footprints where mice had scurried across the floor. Deep sorrow struck my heart. Tears filled my eyes. I wiped them on my sleeve, and then continued walking down the street.

At the northern edge of Vassy, my feet carried me down the familiar dirt road as the sun fell below the horizon. By the time I reached Margot's grandparents farm house, the sun had set. I stood on the road and looked at the pleasant home of my friends. The curtains were open. A soft light poured from the windows. Smoke bellowed from the chimney. From where I stood, I saw Annette washing dishes. Claire stood by her side with a towel in her hand. Jean sat in his favorite chair beside the fire. Pierre's chair was empty. For a brief moment, I prayed Margot would walk into the room. Deep down I knew she wouldn't, and I hoped my friends wouldn't blame me for her death. I sighed, and then slowly walked to the front door.

I raised my hand to knock, but it refused to fall. A few minutes went by and my hand remained poised in the air until I finally dropped it to my side and lowered my head. All that was left of my courage drained from my body as tears filled my eyes. I couldn't bring myself to face my friends and tell them their daughter was dead. She had to be. '*They never came back to the apartment,*' I wept as I thought about the last time I saw Margot and Emile. Then, the front door opened, and I looked up to see Claire standing in the doorway.

"Marcel," she cried and tackled me in her arms. A metal bowl dropped to the kitchen floor. Then, Annette and Jean appeared in the doorway.

"My, God, you're alive," Annette shouted as she wrapped her arms around my shoulders and kissed my cheeks.

Jean put his hand on my shoulder. "It's truly a miracle," he said, and then he kissed my cheeks.

"A blessing from God," Claire added as she pulled me into the house.

"How'd you survive?" Annette asked. "Margot said there was too much destruction in Saint Lo for anyone to survive."

"Margot said?" I stammered. "She's alive?"

"Of course she is, Marcel," Claire smiled.

"Thank God," I cried. "And Emile?"

"He's alive too," Annette replied.

"Thank God. When they didn't come back, Aimee and I thought they were captured. Thought they were murdered."

"The Boche are not strong enough to kill my daughter," Jean proudly stated.

"She and Emile returned to his apartment, but you and Aimee weren't there. So they thought you came back here. When you never showed up, we believed you were dead," Annette said.

"We're so happy you're alive," Claire purred, and then she hugged me once more.

"Where's Aimee now?" Jean asked.

I lowered my head and wiped more tears from my eyes. The room fell silent. "She didn't make it," I said, and then raised my head. "She passed away a few hours before the town was liberated."

"Oh dear, Marcel. I'm so sorry," Annette said softly.

"I think about her every day. I've lost. . .We've lost some good friends. All we have left is their memory," I said solemnly.

"For us the war will never end," Jean nodded.

"We have the freedom they fought for," Claire beamed.

"How true, Claire. How true," Jean said, and then we sat at the table. Annette produced a bottle of wine, and so our night began. For the next half hour, I told them about my family in Ireland. Then, a car pulled into the driveway. "They're home," Claire announced as she ran outside.

"They'll be happy to see you," Annette said.

"Who?" I asked as the front door opened. I stood and turned around just in time to catch Margot in my arms. She kissed my cheeks, and I embraced her tightly.

"All right, old boy, enough of that. Don't think you can come back from the grave and steal my wife," Colin joked from the doorway. Margot and I loosened our embrace and laughed.

"You're married?" I asked as I shook Colin's hand.

"Damn right, we are," Colin smiled.

"Well congratulations, but I believe Margot got the poor end of the deal," I said in jest, bringing laughter to the room.

We talked for a few more minutes, then Colin telephoned Gerard and

Emile. Twenty minutes later, Emile arrived. He brought with him five bottles of Bordeaux and his newly wedded wife, Brigette. Her long, beautiful hair was cut short. After Vassy was liberated, she was ostracized for being a Nazi sympathizer. Attempts were made on her life, and Emile spent more time fighting his fellow countrymen seeking revenge than the retreating German army. Luckily, British Intelligence got wind of Brigette's plight and informed the masses that she was an allied spy. Over night, she became a celebrity. General Charles De Gaulle personally awarder her the Croix De Guerre for bravery.

A few minutes after Brigette and Emile arrived, Gerard and Yvette pulled into the driveway. They had a passenger with them. A baby boy named, Stephan, in honor of Jack. "We're going to name our next child, Marcel," Yvette announced, and I blushed.

"What if it's a girl?" Jean asked lightheartedly.

"Then we'll keep trying," Gerard winked.

That night, we celebrated our reunion. We laughed. We cried. We said prayers for our fallen friends and made toasts in their honor. I found out that Pierre had a stroke a few days after Germany surrendered. He died peacefully after hearing of Hitler's suicide. Francois was still alive, but he was only a shell of his former self. Margot, who visited him often, said he was locked in a sanitarium outside of Paris. Over the years, I visited him a few times, but he never responded to my presence. The doctors said it was Catatonic Schizophrenia. I knew it was the war. Yves' treachery scarred him for life.

Until my arrival in Vassy, the fates of Aimee, Jack, Simon, and Jocelyn were unknown to the rest of my friends. Everyone was glad Jack was alive. We toasted them all. Glasses of red wine, symbolizing the blood of our fallen friends, were placed in a circle on the table. Aimee's glass was placed in the center. Simon's was placed beside hers. Pierre's was put on his favorite chair by the fireplace. Claire read Psalm 124 from the Bible. Then, Emile recited his poem of remembrance, followed by a moment of silence. After that, we raised our glasses and toasted the end of the war.

Our party carried on into the wee hours of morning. I fell asleep in Pierre's chair by the fire. Hours later, I woke from Claire's soft kiss on my cheek. I gave her a hug and told her I was glad to be home. "I'm glad you're home too," Claire smiled.

Annette and Margot cooked a grand breakfast for all of us. Afterward, we gathered in the courtyard to enjoy the morning. I was soon lost in my own thoughts. No one seemed to notice, except Margot. She gave a faint smile and nodded her head. All I did was stare back at her. Wondering if she knew what was on my mind. She did. For she got everyone's attention and announced I was leaving for Saint Lo. How she knew, I don't know.

"Saint Lo? Why?" Claire asked.

"I have to. For Aimee," I replied.

"Do you need a ride?" Yvette asked.

"I'll take the train."

"Then, I'll drive you to the station," Emile announced.

"No, I'll take him," Colin insisted, and then an argument erupted between the two men. In the commotion, Gerard offered me a ride.

"After the way you drove the German truck, I'd rather walk," I teased.

"Gerard's a good driver," Yvette smiled.

I looked at her, and then to Gerard. "Your wife has a lot of faith in you," I said, bringing laughter to Gerard's lungs.

"He's a better driver than those two babies," Margot smiled while pointing to Colin and Emile, so I agreed and got into Gerard's car. Brigette, Margot, Yvette and her baby, Stephan got in the back seat. Claire sat between Gerard and I.

"I'll be back in a few days," I said to Jean and Annette. Then, we all waved as Gerard started his car. We were halfway out of the driveway before Emile and Colin realized we were leaving. The astonished look on their faces brought laughter all around, and even more laughter as we watched them race to their cars. Then, when we were only three hundred feet down the road, Colin and Emile raced past, leaving us in a cloud of dust.

"They'll kill each other with their childish games," Margot said.

"They remind me of my brothers," Brigette laughed.

"They are brothers," I smiled.

"We're just one big happy family," Claire chimed, and she was right.

When we finally pulled up to the train station in Vire, Colin and Emile were sitting on a park bench singing a bad rendition of, 'De L'autre Cote De La Rue.' They had already finished of a bottle of wine and were working on draining another.

Margot went with me to the ticket counter while everyone else waited for us on the loading platform. The duet was now a choir and the elderly ticket clerk muttered something about murdering a sparrow. Margot apologized to the gentleman and grabbed the ticket from his hand. Then, completely out of character, she embraced my arm and began singing as she led me to the loading dock to join the choir. A few other passengers sang along with us. Most kept their distance.

When the train finally pulled into the station, we said our farewells. Hugs and kisses were passed around. Another bottle of wine was uncorked. The singing continued as Margot pulled me aside.

"Aimee once told me that she wanted you to meet her daughter. She said she wanted to know for sure," Margot said as quietly as she could over our singing friends.

"Sure about what?" I asked.

"I don't know. She never said. After we found out you were married, she dismissed the idea."

"Why?" I asked more to myself than to Margot. Thoughts of Aimee's last days flooded over me. How she led me to her café. The sound of the rifle as she was shot. The long, hopeless hours I spent trying to give comfort as she lay dying on the cold, cellar floor. Only to die in my arms as her home was liberated in the rubble filled streets above. I looked at Margot. "Before Aimee died, she asked if I remembered her cafe."

"Do you?" Margot asked.

"No. I'd never been there before she took me there."

"Are you going there now?"

"I plan on it," I replied.

"Good. Violette, has reopened the cafe."

"Violette?"

"Aimee's daughter," Margot clarified.

"How will I know who she is?"

Margot smiled. "Oh you'll know." Then, she gave me a kiss on the cheek.

I boarded the train and waved to my friends before I sat in a seat by the window. Brigette, Margot, and Yvette waved as the train pulled out of the station while the baby Stephan slept in Yvette's arms. Claire blew me kisses. Gerard just smiled while Colin and Emile, arms slung over each other's shoulders, sang.

"Friends of yours?" A staunch elderly woman asked me from across the aisle.

"They're my family," I happily replied.

"Hmmm. They don't look anything like you."

The train ride to Saint Lo is vacant from my memory. The entire journey, I gazed out the window, lost in thought, oblivious to the other passengers.

Oblivious to the scenery passing by. I was a million miles away. Thinking how surreal my life had been. Wondering if everything I had done up to that day was just a dream. A manifestation conjured from the fabric of my being. Was the pain in my heart, the sorrow in my soul, evidence of my past? The events in my life, the deeds I'd done, the people I'd encountered. Did they make me who I am? Was my being, in essence, a patchwork quilt? Sewn together by the invisible thread of destiny?

When the train arrived in Saint Lo, the conductor announced my final destination a few times before I heard him. A lump grew in my throat. My knees shook. My suitcase felt heavy in my hand as I stepped off the train onto the busy platform and walked into the station. A dull ache arose in my crippled leg. My heart beat heavy in my chest. '*Why am I afraid,*' I wondered, knowing I had every right to be, and yet, there was no reason to be at all.

Suddenly, I stopped. A man bumped into me from behind and cursed under his breath as he walked by. Then, twenty feet from the exit doors, I sat down on a bench. My hands shook as I put a cigarette in my mouth. The box of matches fell from my hand and scattered matches at my feet. My eyes locked on the haphazard design they made. It wasn't until a dustpan came into view that my senses returned.

"Are you all right, monsieur?" A middle-aged custodian asked as she swept the matches into the dustpan.

I looked at her. "Yes," I slowly replied and put the unlit cigarette back in my pocket.

"Are you arriving or leaving, monsieur?"

"I'm not sure," I said as I got to my feet and grabbed my suitcase. "Which way is the church?"

"Which one, monsieur?"

"The one at the edge of town."

"Do you mean the Notre Dame?"

"I guess so. Is it still standing?" I asked.

"Oh, yes, monsieur. Do you have business there?"

"Yes," I replied faintly. "How do I get there?"

The custodian quickly gave me directions, but I forgot them just as quickly, and left the station without saying thanks. Once outside in the fresh air, I felt relief and ambled down the ancient streets where new patches of cobblestone bandaged the wounds of the past. New buildings sprung up here and there, flanked by mounds of destruction. Trucks rolled slowly through the town carting away the past while builders framed the future.

Children played in the vacant lots while their mothers hung laundry to dry. Street merchants peddled their wares from carts littering the sidewalks as people sauntered by. No one was in a hurry. No one needed to be. For the French know the future arrives with every new day.

At the corner of Rue Franklin and Rue Porte Dijeau, I came to a halt. New apartments lined both sides of Franklin street. All that remained from when I was there almost two years ago, were my memories.

From where I stood, I finally knew where I was, and where I needed to go. My pace quickened as I headed to my destination. The church spire grew larger on the horizon as I drew near. Then, I saw it. Saint Lo's church of Notre Dame was almost as Aimee and I left it. Scaffolding lined its walls. The roof was patched. New stained glass filled its portals, but I would always remember it as I saw it that fateful night almost two years ago.

Inside the church, lacquered black walnut pews glistened row after row on the black and white checkered marble floor. Soft light poured through the stained glass windows, illuminating the white and gold pulpit sitting majestically at the far end of the room. Icons and statuettes lined the nave. Seven candles burned in front of the altar. Behind the altar a stone crucifix hung on the wall. Red streaks covered the body of Jesus.

Growing up Methodist, I was unaccustomed to Catholic ritual and dunked my hands into the holy water basin. I thought it odd there wasn't a towel to dry my hands so I used my pant leg instead. Then, I left my suitcase by the holy water basin and walked down the center aisle toward the pulpit. My leather soled shoes echoed off the marble floor as I went to the seven candles and blew one out. From there I walked behind the altar and kneeled below the crucifix. The red paint of the stigmata looked real, and I shuddered. '*A horrible way to die*,' I thought as I closed my eyes.

The last time I prayed in a church was when Aimee and I recited the *Rosary*. That afternoon, I couldn't think of anything to say. The furthest I got was, "Dear Jesus." Then my mind went blank. Minutes passed as time stood still. It felt like an eternity, and yet, the words crying from my soul failed to weep from my lips. Tears filled my eyes.

"You are not of the Catholic faith, are you my son?" A man's voice asked softly from behind.

I wiped the tears from my eyes, and then slowly stood and turned around. The parish priest rested his gentle eyes upon mine. His thinning grey hair and soft skin gave me his age. Black rimmed spectacles decorated his face. His hands were clasped and held in front down by his waist. "No, monsieur, I'm not," I replied.

"You are a man of Christ, are you not?"

"I don't know anymore, father," I confessed.

"Why is that, my son?"

"How can I?" I mumbled as I looked down at my feet while anger grew inside. Then, I stared into the priest's eyes and raised my voice. "How can I believe in a God that allows his creation to destroy itself? To allow pain and suffering? Starvation? Murder? If God is the embodiment of love, then why did he create evil? Is he not the creator of all?"

"My son, what you speak of is true, but God didn't create evil."

"He allows it to exist."

"That is true."

"Well, if he's so powerful, then why?" I nearly shouted.

"He has given us freewill, my son. Through it we find grace."

"Grace? If God created all, he created Hitler. He allowed Hitler's evil to exist. He allowed the murder of millions. Sorry father, I no longer believe in grace. Excuse me," I said, and then walked by the priest. He said nothing until I was twenty feet down the aisle.

"My son, God has forgiven you for the murder you committed within these walls."

Tears filled my eyes. I wiped them with the back of my hand and turned around. The priest was gone, so I walked back to my suitcase and picked it up. Then, I took one last look at the room before exiting the church. Outside, a young priest was tending the roses lining the walkway. He looked up and smiled. "Can I help you, my son?"

"Sorry, father. I've already talked to the other priest," I replied.

The young priest furrowed his brow. "What priest?"

"The one inside."

"That's strange," the priest said as he laid the pruning clippers on the ground. "I'm the only priest in the parish," he stated as he walked past me into the church.

Shivers ran down my spine as I walked away. My feet carried me closer to the sole reason I'd returned to Saint Lo, to fulfill the dying wish of my friend and meet her daughter.

When I got to the corner across from the, 'White Rose Cafe,' my feet wouldn't take me any further. So, I leaned against the brick wall and pulled a cigarette from my coat pocket. No one paid any attention to me as they rushed past. Nor did I notice them. For my thoughts drifted to the middle of the street where Aimee was shot, to the stairs leading to the cellar where she died, to the soft light now glowing from the windows above.

A pile of cigarette butts grew at my feet as the day fell toward night. I added another one to the pile as a young couple, arm in arm, exited the café. Then, I lingered a moment before taking a deep breath and crossing the street.

A small bell hanging above the door jingled as I entered Aimee's café. "Sorry, we're closed," A lovely voice sang from the kitchen. I gazed at the vacant tables and chairs, and then turned to leave. A poem in a picture frame hanging by the door rooted me in place. I couldn't believe my eyes.

"Monsieur, I'm closed," Aimee's daughter said as she walked into the room, but I couldn't move. My feet refused to flee. For the words of the poem were words I knew all too well. Words I would never forget. For they were written by my hand. At the bottom, I read the name of the author as Aimee's daughter stepped behind me. "My mother gave me that. It was written for me before I was born."

My suitcase fell from my hand as I read, 'John Harrington, 1914.' I turned and stared into the eyes of a familiar face. "My God," I cried.

"John?" She asked as a smile crossed her face. I swept her into my arms as joy fell from our eyes. I finally understood what my aunt Hattie knew all along. I was my late uncle John. The woman in my arms, Aimee's daughter, Violette, was my late wife, Rosalie.

AFTERWORD

I wanted to end my story as I had, but my editor said it wasn't complete. So, I'll be brief.

In May of 1947, Jack went under the knife. A year later he was on his feet. Unlike me, he didn't need a cane. Mabel bore them a child, a baby boy they named Simon. For his birthday, Violette and I bought the boy a toy train.

Every year since my return to France, on the 25th of August, my family and friends meet at the farmhouse in Vassy. We salute our fallen friends. A new wine glass is added to the circle for those who join them. The same Psalm is recited. A new poem is read. We laugh. We cry. We sing and rejoice for our freedom.

After my grandmother passed away, my aunt Hattie and aunt Nora joined our celebration. When it came time for them to leave, aunt Nora stayed a few more weeks. For she found a true friend in Jean. To this day, no one knows why they never married. Some believe is was out of respect for Nora's dead spouse. Others believe it was because of the Church. Truthfully, I don't want to guess.

As for Violette and I, she knew who she was since birth. As you know, it took me much longer. We remarried in 1948 under the elm tree where Aimee lay. Jack stood by my side. Aunt Hattie was a bridesmaid.

So, for those of you who don't believe in destiny and fate, well, there's really nothing I can say. For you won't believe when I tell you that our souls are eternal. That after we die, we'll all return someday. I only hope when I return there will be no more war, no more hate.

PERIWINKLE ROSE

Little flower soft and true
Small petals spread anew
Fresh springtime fills the air
Little flower your heart laid bare

Spread far and open wide
In green gardens you reside
Light breeze from heavens glade
Periwinkle Rose gently laid

Through winter snows
Through springtime rain
Through the summer you remain

In the twilight my dawning days
In green gardens I shall lay
Next to you for ever more
Periwinkle Rose Mon Belle Fleur

Entre Destinèe et Destin

Malgré tout, je n'a pas de regret

Also by Brian Bitton

A Few Days for a Lifetime

Left for dead, Brendan summons the will to carry his tired, broken body from the forest. In the pouring rain, he arrives in the town of Sumpter, Oregon where he meets Anna whom offers him food and shelter. As the days pass, their friendship grows, blossoming into love. But will their love flourish when each of them carry painful memories of a broken past? Or flounder, giving strength to the hands of despair? Only by confronting the demons locked within their souls can they give their love a chance. But will they?

ISBN: 978-0-9824036-0-0   199 pages. $ 14.95 U.S.D.

To order please use the order form at the back of this book, or online at: **www.myballyclarebooks.com**

Between Destiny and Fate

Order Form

Name:_____

Address:_____

City:_____ State:_____ Zip:_____

Phone:(_____)_____ Email:_____

TITLE	Qty.	Book Price (see list below)	Total
Between Destiny and Fate			
A Few Days for a Lifetime			

TOTAL for book(s)		
Shipping 1st book		3.00
Additional books add $1.50 (S&H) per book		
TOTAL (Books + S&H)		

Mail check or money order to: MyBallyClare Music and Books
                                P.O. Box 83974
                                Portland, Oregon 97283

DISCOUNT SCHEDULE		
Quantity	Between Destiny and Fate	A Few Days for a Lifetime
1 to 4	$ 17.00	$ 14.95
5 to 9	$ 15.30	$ 13.45
10 to 19	$ 13.60	$ 11.95
20 to 29	$ 11.90	$ 10.45
30 to 40	$ 10.20	$ 8.97

Special rates for book clubs and book stores available

All orders promptly filled within 5 business days.
Please allow 4 to 6 weeks for delivery

Postage and handling rates subject to change. Please check online at:
www.myballyclarebooks.com